CW01083541

TO LOVE
AND SERVE

Mary Flood

Published by Mary Flood in 2024

ISBN 979-8-89496-618-2

Book Cover Design and Formatting by Jason Conway/The Daydream Academy, Stroud, Gloucestershire.

To inspirational friends we carry in our hearts until time runs out

INTRODUCTION

During lockdown, I read a plethora of Irish novels: Sally Rooney, Anne Enright, Marian Keyes, Anne Griffin, Neil Tobin, and more. The singular factor that compelled me to write my novel was the complete antithesis in women's behaviour portrayed in the books, to that over recent decades. Liberalism, freedom of expression and sexuality are powerful forces in the lives of modern women, who seem to have cast off the clout of both Church and men.

How far has Ireland veered from the country I grew up in? Unrecognisable in attitudes to morality and 'sin'. Women are free to choose as they please.

All characters in this book are fictional but represent an amalgam of women from my youth. Therefore, writing the novel has proved cathartic.

In addition, I wanted to expose two-facedness within an ostensible 'holy Ireland'.

Mary Flood

Autumn 2024

CHAPTER 1

*A*ugust 1961

Their eyes met and held across a swarm of twisting bodies on the dance floor. Silver balls dangled from the ceiling over bobbing heads, and lights dazzled - red, green, and yellow flashing colour and excitement around the ballroom. Ten blue-suited musicians were strumming guitars on the bandstand, blowing trumpets, and belting out Ricky Nelson's *'Hello, Mary Lou'*. Voices rose in unison. It was Saturday night, and the Astor dancehall was swinging.

Alone and aloof, lean body propped against a pillar, the man surveyed the crowd, his arrogant expression showing he would choose whomever he wanted. His long nose, full lips, and dark eyes reminded Della of Eros, not that she liked Greek studies much. Averting her gaze, she shook her head in refusal towards Tom Killeen - been around the back with him once. A sloppy kisser. She'd had enough after ten minutes. Drawn again towards the dark-haired one, she nudged her sister, Eve. "Who is that fellow standing by the pillar near the mineral bar?"

"Don't know. Bet he'll go for a tall blonde," Eve replied, stepping onto the floor with Dermot Hoare. Like a speck of fire, her red dress and diminutive form disappeared into the morass of flailing arms and pulsating bodies. Underfoot, the floorboards creaked and groaned. Perfume and sweat wafted and mingled in the intensity of sound and smell. No one cared; the night, yet young, offered the promise of love. However, if you were not invited outside by midnight, you had no choice but to struggle towards a waiting car on the roadside, your toes bleeding, stilettoes prodding - alone and loveless.

Della let her eyes find him again, and as if summoned by her desire, he crossed the space between them and smiled. "Would you like a drink?"

Not a dance, a drink.

"Yes, I'd love one, but not alcohol." Silly remark. Halls did not sell alcohol. "I'm Della O'Reilly."

"Ed Egan. Nor I, maybe a soft drink?" His smile drew a yes from Della, and, mounting the steps, they found chairs at the back of the hall. On the bandstand, the music rose. Talking was difficult. Up close, he looked even better; deep blue eyes, compelling and searching hers. He waited for a lull and smiled a soft smile. As they talked under muted lights, Della felt herself falling further under the spell of his gentle tone and effortless expression. Here was a man comfortable with himself, aware of his looks, his attractiveness. A voice whispered in her brain: I will be a nun in two months; my path, vocation, and calling to a life of self-denial already planned. Della O'Reilly must resist temptation of the worldly kind. But with every syllable from Ed's lips, her resolve melted under the power of his allure.

Ed worked in Edinburgh during winter but was home for the summer to help his ageing father save hay and harvest crops. "You don't look like a farmer," she told him. "And I can't picture you in greasy jeans fixing a mower."

"Work is one thing, pleasure another." With a smile softening the sarcasm, he went on. "I plan to stay in Scotland for a couple of years before settling down. Shall we stay in touch?"

"Sorry, but I'm to join the convent in October." Oh Lord, why had she said that? He did not reply and would get up to leave. Instead, he asked her onto the floor. At first, she was afraid of appearing clumsy, but as his arm twirled hers, they jived and twisted in matching rhythm, weaving a pattern through the crowd towards the bandstand. In all her nineteen years, nothing had been this magical.

Ed drew Della close as they danced to the sound of Bill Haley's Rock Around the Clock and Jim Reeves's seductive, Put your sweet lips a Little Closer to the Phone. Her heart seemed to beat in sync with his, the scent of woody aftershave blending into her cheap violet and lemon perfume.

They fitted quickly into each other's style, and when the band played the National Anthem, Ed whispered, "I'll walk you to the car."

On nights like this, love beckoned from the riverside, overgrown meadows, behind marquees, and wherever 'love goes'. Girls in clingy dresses, men in open-neck shirts and tight jeans had only one desire - to find love. Hot blood roused in harmony with Nature's fruitfulness throughout a fiery August. In O'Reilly's fields, ripened corn bowed its head across the golden countryside, and purpling branches dripped luscious blackberries along the hedgerows. It was the harvest season when lovers loved, and, according to Bridie O'Reilly, a rash of births in May and June the following year brought bountiful rewards for the clergy conducting hastily arranged marriages. Fruits of sin, Della's mother said.

Ed held her hand as they walked from the hot ballroom toward the street. Ranged along the narrow walkway, couples snuggled into recesses, fulfilling passions aroused on the dance floor. Ed did not attempt to draw her towards a vacant space, but she would not have minded if he had. At the waiting car, he leaned forward and kissed her lightly. "Can I see you next week? Perhaps I'll change your mind?" Just that. Could he? Did she want to? She had promised the Mother Superior to become a Sister of the teaching Order.

"I oughtn't. Well, alright." Della watched him stride across the Square under the dim streetlight, get into a white Corsair, and, with a last wave, zoom out of town. Pauline, a neighbour, and Sive Hearn, their cousin, moved across the back seat of O'Reilly's car to make room for Della. Eve tutted annoyance in the front beside Matt Regan, their patient and trustworthy family friend, ready to drive all three home in the old Vauxhall. Della's father trusted the man with his car and daughters.

"Come on, tell. A good kisser?" Pauline demanded as Della lay back against the leather. Postmortems, they called it when someone got lucky. Della's fingers touched the cheek his lips had kissed. She struggled to sound normal and unshaken, but something had changed and subsumed her in its enormity, more potent than anything experienced with Ben, her last boyfriend. She could not share the feeling but had to see him again. Having someone take her out during the time left would be nice.

"I liked him, but he described the rickety 'Paddy' ferry crossing the Irish Sea from Glasgow to Dublin and passengers vomiting over the rails. I felt sick," Della said. "Not romantic. But he looks divine."

"So, no more of him? A shame, he's some dancer."

"Well, maybe..." She must appear nonchalant but not fickle nor wonder aloud why this gorgeous man had come along when she was preparing to leave all worldly things behind.

When Ben Mullins asked her out during a carnival dance two years back, she immediately liked his lopsided smile, Elvis sideburns and dance moves. If you could jive to Jailhouse Rock to the end, you were a hit. But at seventeen, naïve and trusting, it was enough for Ben to kiss her goodnight, no more. Ed had qualities the girls talked about in the dorm when lights went out—good-looking, a superb dancer, and owned a car, a distinct advantage. Now, despite her holy promise, something profound was stirring in Della. Oh God, direct me. Her lips moved in a silent plea.

Time raced. Ed came twice a week and took her dancing to great bands in Ruskey, Longford, driving as far as Moate whenever the Clipper Carlton, his favourite band, played. By the end of three weeks, the thought of leaving him was transmuting into a personal doomsday. It was as if she were stealing time from a set future - and banishing a present which would never come. She tingled at his touch; his kisses burned her lips, and his eyes filled her with disturbing sensations. Within her soul, Della prayed for strength, the adage, 'spirit willing, flesh weak', a constant thorn.

He confided in her more with each encounter. There were tensions between him and his father.

"The 'old man' complains to my mother about my late morning start. He hasn't the guts to say it himself. It's summer - my reward for saving during the winter months." His confessional tone fell comfortably on Della's ears, as did his husky voice, attractive smile, languorous attitude, and the fact that he never wanted to say goodnight.

"Well, farmers must save hay, Ed. My dad is out early with the men in the fields. Never know when the weather might change, he says. Hay and crops lead to a good harvest, and money in the bank."

"My, you're sensible, Della. So, stay home, marry me, and we'll make money together." His half-laugh came out both light and serious. Serious? Marry?? It was as if she were surfing a tidal wave towards something exciting but also precarious. Be strong, she told her inner self as the hours drifted towards dawn - basking in his closeness and lingering kisses that made her heart somersault in their insistence. Other sensations bubbled inside that she did not understand, except that the entire world could crumble for all she cared. But instinct told her they were on the verge of that big word - SIN. No, she cried. Ed, you must go. He pulled away.

"Della, see what's happening to us."

"Yes, but I can't be with you. Please go."

A flicker of annoyance crossed his face. "See you in a few days, Della. We'll talk again."

As the noise of his engine faded into the breaking light, Della lay down to ponder. Could she go ahead now? And was there enough reason to shut herself away from life and LOVE? Yes. Love. Of God? Of man?

As August melted into September, the 'holy call' faded. 'Mammy, what am I to do?" she cried one morning. It was eleven o'clock, her mother scraping carrots at the sink, Della sipping tea languorously by the range. Sunlight streamed through the window onto the shiny black range, onto the wooden 'hot-press' by the door and all the familiar things Della would never see again if she left home.

"You go into that convent as planned, Della. That man is not good for you." Bridie O'Reilly's tone held an ominous note. But what about love?

Three weeks to rid herself of earthly, hot-blooded inclinations. Before Ed, her plan to enter a convent was immutable. Now, it seemed ludicrous. But she had promised the Mother Superior she was holy enough to be a nun, and it was all arranged; the clothes bought: plain cotton vests, long-legged knickers, acres of serge for her new habit. Gosh, habit. The word loomed large in her psyche. No, she must not renege on her agreement. It was not honourable.

But in the dying hours in the car one Saturday night, as their bodies fused, the urge for capitulation almost took Della and Ed to a point beyond which no convent mattered. Ed whispered the magic 'L' word, and Della's heart lurched in her chest. "But I'm to become a nun, Ed."

"Say you don't feel the same, Della, that you can leave it like this."

"Yes, I do, but my feelings are not the issue. It's the commitment."

"Never mind that. It's not too late, but perhaps you should see it through and rid yourself of this honourable thing. Remember, I'll be waiting, and you *will* return to me one day." The sudden sharp edge in his tone did not disguise Ed's pain. Lighting a cigarette, he sucked in the nicotine to dull the hurt. For a time, they sat in silence, only an odd corncrake breaking the stillness of the night. Overhead, the wind rustled through the elms. Della stole a glance towards the driver's seat. Surely it was not a tear wetting Ed's sculptured cheek - the man whose aloofness had drawn her to him six weeks ago? Why, oh, why was he making it so difficult?

As if to cover his 'moment', Ed revved the engine, pulled out of 'their' gateway, and drove the short distance to O'Reilly's. At the door, he said, "Goodnight, Della, see you on Wednesday." A brief kiss and he was gone, the harsh sound of wheels on the shingle a blatant symbol of the anger he'd striven to suppress.

In the kitchen, Eve was making tea. "I think I'm in love with Ed," Della said, pouring milk into a cup her sister passed across the table. It was always the same. Before bed, their mother left out scones and tea things for her two girls and whoever might come in for a late snack.

"Then why leave him? It's not too late. It's daft entering a convent, the way you carry on. You were in love with Ben before Ed came along."

Eve's voice held a weary note, but her exasperation was irritating. Della had to make her sister see that her relationship with Ed was on a different plane from the young in-love-for-the-first time with Ben. "I was only seventeen when we started dating, and I planned to become a journalist. Anyway, Ed is better-looking."

Eve, as always sensible, sighed. "Sometimes, I find your in-love phases tiresome, and we argue about it." The more pragmatic of the two girls, her brusque tone edged on Della's nerves. "You'll be content in the Convent, Della, as will Dad and Mam. They worry about your giddiness." In other words, life would be peaceful in the house when she left.

"Ed tries to dissuade me. He'll stay at home and give up the job in Edinburgh. I told him I'd set my sights on a higher calling and that nothing would impede my decision to follow Christ."

"You said those words, Della? Talk about the moral high ground."

"Once you've put your hand to the plough, you cannot look back."

"Rubbish. You're not in the cloisters yet."

"Philosophical, teachers dubbed me - dissecting essays on Chesterton, Mills, and Yeats. How I loved those English lessons."

"Philosophical, maybe, but you're a ditherer. And you're dithering now. I can see how you might change your mind about being a nun. You're dreamy and not focused any longer."

True, the decision had been hers, despite the urgings of holy people. Like rain on stone, a continual drip of pious nudges, displays of black babies, and promises of a hundredfold reward had worked. Every year, they drew girls into the Order to a life of dedication. As a nun, Della could go to Africa and convert heathens. Christ said, *Go forth, teach all nations, baptising them in the name of the Lord.* Besides, a 'Religious' in the family brought honour to loved ones. And wasn't Ireland an excellent cradle for priests and nuns?

Her brain buzzed. Was she about to make a mistake - renounce her pledge, break free, and marry her handsome, clever, gorgeous Irishman?

Ed came on Wednesday, at seven o'clock. "Let's drive out to the lakes. It's nice this time of year."

"Fine", she said, "it'll make a change from hot, sweaty halls." Every moment together counted now that time was not hers to store up. She took in his appearance. Ed could not be more attractive, his face and arms tanned and smooth in a short-sleeved white shirt. But his body language gave off a serious mood, and he did not speak on the way.

He took the slipway off the Sligo road towards the main lake, Lough Key, five miles outside the town. On the water, moored boats rose and fell in harmony. This spot amid the sloping hills drew families in the summer to eat picnics and dip their feet into the calm waters along the banks - the best inland. The nearest seaside resort, Strandhill, forty miles away, people deemed wild and dangerous.

Della's eyes scanned the darkened hills encircling the navy-blue lake. Behind the scrubby weeds and wild grasses, she saw couples close together in vehicles, some in the back seats. It was still light - the evening sun was low on the horizon. Why hadn't he brought her here before? Perhaps it was too far out and a double journey back to her house before getting home to Carrick.

The moon dipped into gentle waters as the day died, and courting couples aroused passions around the lake. A warning voice whispered, be strong; Ed's nearness was a powerful force - persuasive, handsome, irresistible, and a torment to resist. But instead of moving over beside her, he said, "We ought to talk." Gosh, he was serious.

"Apart from you, I've only ever wanted to marry one other girl, but she got herself engaged to an engineer in Boyle. Better prospects than me, I expect."

"Ed, please do not put more regret on me. I've got to see this out. And truthfully, if I weren't going to be a nun, I'd be off somewhere and not settling down yet. Dublin with the girls perhaps, but not into country life at nineteen. And although you say you love me, you'll return to Scotland soon, so we could not plan a future, even if I were to rescind my promise right now." Like a wounded animal, his look brought a pang of remorse.

Silence. She waited. No outburst. Instead, he moved across, drew her close, kissed her tenderly and whispered. "Every hour with you is precious."

Over the hill, a golden orb peeped through wispy clouds, shining light into darkened cars around the love lake. An hour drifted by. Cars moved off. She said they should go.

"Dance on Saturday, then? We must enjoy what's left of our time together." That she had hurt him, Della did not doubt.

Saturday. Ed brought Della to the bandstand and introduced her to Don, the lead singer, who smiled down from
the stage. "This the latest one, Ed?" The latest one? How
many had there been before her? Had he wanted her to
know how others saw him? Della quelled the questions that
bubbled inside. What right had she to care? Did it matter?
So what if he'd had many girls before her? He'd said she was
different and wanted to settle down with her. Striving for
indifference, Della did not feel indifferent.

Wrapped in his arms during the slow dances, it was as
if he was squeezing the breath from her body. Only two
lifetimes behind convent walls would appease the Lord's
anger for her sinfulness.

Later, at two-thirty a.m. in O'Reilly's, they ate chicken
sandwiches her mother had left covered in a tea cloth. Ed
took out a Player and offered one to Della. "No, they're too
strong," she hesitated. "I prefer Silk Cut."

Cigarette smoke rose and swirled over the tea things as
Ed pulled deeply on the cigarette, screening the lips that
had kissed her tenderly in the car. His mug of tea sat cold
and untouched on the shiny patterned oilcloth. The only
sound in the kitchen was the ticking of the large clock on
the wall. Della wondered if this was how a doomed lifer felt
on Death Row. "I'll write to you," he whispered, getting up
from the chair.

"Don't. They won't allow me to reply. And it would only
make our separation harder to bear."

"Right then, this is it," he said, an arm clinched around
her waist, the other lifting her face for a last kiss. "I think
I'll always love you." Love.

"Go then. Have a good life," Della gasped.

"I'll be waiting. No 'call' as you put it, no urge, desire to be saintly or whatever you like to describe it can change what we have."

As the sound of the engine faded into the distance, she sobbed into the pink pillow.

Soft curtains rustled in a puff of wind on the windows, her mother's handiwork offering safety against the world beyond. In the night's stillness, Della heard a barn owl's soft 'twit twoo' calls from the boundary wall. Tomorrow night, she would sleep in a postulant's cell with bars for curtains.

On October 1, Della turned her back on love as the convent door closed behind her.

CHAPTER 2

J im and Bridie O'Reilly lingered on the doorstep of the
Presentation Convent, Sligo. Goodbyes like this should
leave an everlasting sign, an indelible print on something.
Della's father clasped her hand. "I hope you won't regret
this, Della. I've said all I can to stop you from becoming a
nun." The quivering tone made her want to run back to the
old Vauxhall parked by the side of the Convent and return
to the outside world - and Ed. Why did parting have to
hurt so much? Her father's desire for his oldest daughter to
study journalism - himself a part-time columnist for a local
newspaper - was no more.

In the visitors' parlour, Mother Superior, presiding over
tea served in dainty china cups with sandwiches and pretty cakes, smiled gratitude to parents for 'giving up' their
offspring to follow Christ. But on whose shoulders lay the
actual sacrifice?

"Hush, Jim," her mother interrupted. "Della, we're proud
of your choice, and you'll be safe here; no more late nights

or lying in bed all day after dances. We didn't know what might happen. That Ed was leading you astray." Bridie O'Reilly's lips thinned in disapproval of the one who had almost changed the direction of her daughter's life plans. "Thanks, Mam." Della laughed. "Is that the only reason you're glad for me?" But the very utterance of *that* name stirred emotions she must now stifle. With Ed, she could have had fun, dances, closeness, and the rest. "Well, I gave him up for a vocation. So go home and don't worry."

As Mother bolted the big oak door, Della turned to Kate and Maura, both girls sobbing into white handkerchiefs doled by a smiley Sister Agatha. What was a pretty woman with dancing eyes doing as a nun? Holy women rarely smiled. Silly. She was going to be one.

In a sudden urge for solidarity, they locked hands. Around the room were seven others of various heights and build - a mix of ordinary nineteen-year-olds drawn together by a heavenly voice. Ten new postulants would henceforth embrace austerity in pursuit of final vows in the Presentation Order on the northwest coast of Ireland.

Della took stock of the group; most, she figured, were the nun type, quiet and studious. She could see it in their eyes, their calm demeanour. Unlike herself, often dubbed shallow by the nuns in her convent boarding school, they would adapt without a qualm. She, however, had to prove everyone wrong, including herself. After all, she had insisted on going ahead with her promise to the Reverend Mother despite seductive temptations of the flesh, the sheer delight of rock and roll music and wide swirly dresses. Greater than the sound of music, of whispered love in her ears, of passion and resistance, one insistent voice had endured. And Della would make restitution for her sins in austere environs within high walls.

"Cast him from your mind, Della," Mother Superior observed when Della bared her worries. "The devil uses many ploys. Do not quench the voice of God."

Mother Benedict, the Mistress of Novices, facial expression devoid of the previous pleasantness to parents, gestured Della to sit down, her command breaking through the sniffles.

"Girls, Sisters as you will soon become, today marks the start of dedicated service to Jesus. First, however, there is evening prayer in the chapel. Then, after tea at six, you will go to your cells upstairs, wash in the basin on the washstand and then get to bed. You cannot speak again until seven a.m. We call it the Greater Silence. I will come to your corridor in the morning, ring a bell, and take you to the chapel myself. From thence, you will rise when the bell rings at six-thirty." The face relaxed into a half-smile.

"Mary," Della whispered to a tawny-haired girl, "Is this real? Bed at seven o'clock? Wash in a basin? I was out dancing with Ed Egan a week ago and went to bed at seven a.m." She stopped, hearing her laugh plop like a stone on a pond - the one in O'Reilly's bog.

"Ed Egan? He lives by me near Carrick," the other girl said. "He only went for the glamorous ones."

Della blushed. Glamorous? Her? She'd been in the line-up of the annual carnival beauty competitions more often than winning, but yes, glamorous fitted. Others said so, but that was all behind her now. The black dress and cape she had donned an hour ago would shock them back in Fairyland if she appeared among the dancers. She could picture Della O'Reilly minus the mascara and stilettoes. Take a check, she thought. From this moment, no music will blare from bandstands; the only sound that of women's voices chanting Holy Office three times a day in the chapel or the bell summoning the inmates - gosh, not inmates - to prayer and duties. Inmates, a prison? Well...

Why? Why? And why? No mystery why she, Della O'Reilly, had taken an enormous step and entered the Presentation Order in Sligo. Tired of being considered light, frivolous, and easily tempted, she had pledged to join the Order and take vows of poverty, chastity, and obedience in four years. Miles away from dance halls and passionate backseat encounters, she would train to be a teacher, a nurse, or a missionary. The Lord would direct her path.

Della remembered how her pals laughed in disbelief.

"You won't last a month," Mena whispered during dinner in the Refectory. "You like boys, dressing up and dancing. Not long since you got caught coming in late."

Yes. As twilight fell one Sunday evening, Della, creeping through a side entrance of the Convent, walked straight into a black-robed figure by the tennis courts. Shock, horror. She mumbled an excuse about a cousin home from England. Unnoticed by the Sisters at the tail end of the serpentine stream, Ben Mullins pulled his car close to the line of girls on the Sunday walk, opened the door and let Della slip into the back seat to lie low until they got to a layby for a quick smooching session.

The nun's response came sharp and severe. "Do not speak, Della O'Reilly," Sister Rosarii ordered, marching the miscreant into the Study hall where she made Della stand, shamed before sixty navy uniformed girls smirking from their desks. Worse still, the pious head of the Community threatened her with expulsion. Della pleaded and vowed to chasten her wickedness if they did not tell her parents. They had to, came the reply. It was her punishment. She must face the consequences of her sins.

"I'm not the light-head Mother Mercy says I am," she cried in the dorm later. "I'll join the Order. That'll show them."

"Good on ye, Della. Go with the others and be a nun. Show them there's more to you than a silly light-head," Maree whispered from the next cubicle.

"Rona's going, Mary Mac and Margaret, but they're holy," Eileen said, pulling aside the curtain on the left, dark hair rippling in waves around her pretty face. "You say you want to prove your depth, Della, but it's not right for you."

Two different perspectives. So what was right? The flicker of doubt clung like an extra skin. In Study, she cried a tear over *Macbeth*, her love of Shakespeare doing little to assuage the pain or dull the voices within. Ahead, twenty rows of girls sat, heads bent, eyes fixed on homework. Della tugged strands of golden hair across her face and vowed to show them she was good enough to do something worthwhile for God and the world.

"You'll wear long, horrible, black serge skirts and white stiffened coifs that bite into your face," Maura, 'Mol,' Gallagher prodded from behind Della. Hidden by a mass of navy bodies in the room, they could whisper at will without drawing attention from the black-clad person on the podium.

"I quite like the habit," Della mumbled. "It sets nuns apart."

"You're mad," Maree said. "Big shapeless clothes that hide your body. "But you love boarding. Most of us hate it."

Yes, she liked the regulated school day: lessons, mealtimes, and study periods. Striding along country roads in navy uniform on daily walks made her proud of the Order: their dedicated teaching, preparing students to be doctors, teachers, scientists, and perhaps homemakers.

Despite their assertions, the others did not hate boarding but basked in the knowledge their parents could afford the fees and that they were privileged students.

"You're not the nun-type, Della," Mol tried again. The dark-haired girl hoped Della would share college accommodation in the city come autumn.

"The type? Is there a type?"

"The other nine are sensible, top in maths and science. They're not like you, mad about boys and dancing."

"You mean more grounded than me, Mol? That I'm not holy enough?"

Not saying that. You are just not the 'holy' type."

She knew what her friend meant. With her pals back home, Anna and Mary, two brown-eyed beauties, Della would spend hours before the mirror applying mascara, a camouflage for her fair lashes and sandy eyebrows. Then, in cotton dresses billowing over slim bodies, all three would set off for a night of excitement. Yes, they loved life and fun.

"It's a free choice, not a jail sentence," she said, ducking their jibes but not their honesty.

But when her actual nature broke free during Recreation, Della hooped and hollered in sheer abandon to Maree Carley's fingers rippling across the keyboard. The sound of Bill Haley, Cliff Richard and Elvis's *Wise men say only fools rush in, but I can't help falling in love with you* rose in harmony to the rafters of the Performance Hall each night. In love with love, they hungered for romantic bliss. Later, after lights out, excited and hyped-up, they would share boyfriends' names within the dimness of curtained cubicles, and pretend.

At first, eager to adapt and conform, Della immersed herself in the new routine except for the early bedtime. But, like her idol, Elvis Presley, back in the real world, who slept by day and played by night, her body rejected a command to sleep. With the onset of vespers each evening at seven, gnawing anxiety wormed inside her in proleptic dread of long wakeful hours until dawn broke. Hours dragged on in deliberate precision, each successive night sucking strength from Della's light body. In Mother's lectures during the day, she struggled to concentrate.

The routine never changed: Breakfast and refectory duties followed daily Mass, then two hours of instruction on the Holy Rules and the triple vows of poverty, chastity, and obedience. After lunch, it was Apologetics, theology, Church history, a nun's etiquette, and decorum. She should not raise her eyes unnecessarily nor initiate a conversation with a superior unless bidden. Novices must not run in corridors or be late to prayer, *never* stare, but assume a holy demeanour. They could not go outside to a dentist or doctor unless accompanied by a professed Sister.

In the silence of her mind, Della heard her father's warning as if he were close. Her headstrong personality would never adapt to a life of self-denial in such a severe environment. But she was no longer Della but Sister Elise, an adaptation in hand. It mattered little which persona lived in her body, as neither could quell the inward rebellion raging within. Should she succumb and accept that suffering was part of the vocation? Or give up and go to find Ed again? The latter urge faded with each successive 'holy' day.

November rain pelted the stone battlements like bullets from a Sten gun. On the country's northwest coast, winds blew at a dangerous rate during the winter months, skies were perennially grey, and the mighty Atlantic lashed the coastline northwards to County Donegal. Each morning, dipping her hands into the water basin on her washstand, Della's skin chilled, her weak circulation a legacy from a childhood bout of scarlet fever.

Two months into her soul's transition towards compliance, Mother beckoned Della to the Novitiate office after breakfast.

"Sister, I have a letter for you here. As my duty, I've opened and read it. A young man, Ed, wrote to you from Scotland. You knew him well on the outside. I must say that this cannot happen again. You will not respond, and if other letters arrive from him, I will not pass them on."

Della felt her face blanch, her heart up its rhythm. Ed had written. How he must miss her. Love her. Shoving it into her deep black pocket, she retreated to her desk and opened the envelope with trembling hands. A single page in a neat, slanted style fell out.

Dear Della,

It's been a month since we parted, and as you can see from the address, I'm back in Edinburgh. It's cold here, and we're working outside. I wish we could be together, going to dances and planning for the future. Let me know if you intend to stay inside if you can write. You must realise by now if it's the right place for you. I hope not.

All my love.

Ed.

One month and this had to happen. Emotions almost squashed surfaced again, pressing into Della's temples, engulfing her whole body. Go back and marry him, an inner voice said. But no, she had promised to become a Bride of Christ and follow her vocation, her calling. Della rose from her seat, tore up the paper, and dropped it into the wastebasket. The Mistress of Novices watched from the door, a half-smile flickering across her starched features.

Another month passed. Gradually, a spiritual metamorphosis took hold. Della saw it in her peers, their downcast eyes, quiet gait, and speech. If the chapel bell rang during the day, everyone hurried demurely to Mass. She counted seventeen Masses one Sunday. Priests were duty-bound to say daily Mass, and convents welcomed them. "It's a privilege to attend," Mother explained. "When the priest offers Mass for a soul in purgatory, its suffering is suspended."

But when the bell for Lauds clanged at six-thirty each morning, unholy thoughts engulfed Della, struggling to get into the coarse habit and fit the headband and lace veil on her long hair. She fumbled with fasteners and adjusted black stockings within ten minutes to present herself in the corridor. If only there were mirrors in the cells. She had seen none in the building. During the daily walk at five p.m., Della asked a senior novice why there were no mirrors. "Mirrors encourage vanity," came the response. "We practise self-denial."

"But I can't see how I look and don't want to get into trouble."

"Concentrate then. Get up on the call. It's a discipline. You won't have a problem when your hair comes off," But Della loved her long golden hair. And Ed had loved it, too. She stifled the name but could not dull the image of perfect aquiline features in her head. Daring to remember was a betrayal - she, a traitor to her new family. But she had until next summer to push her tresses into place under the little black net veil. Amusedly, she compared it to Marie Antoinette's headdress on the gallows. The Queen had lost her head, and Della would lose her hair. Not quite an equaliser.

But when her hair straggled across her eyes going into the chapel one morning, a tug on her sleeve alerted Della to Mother's omnipresence. "Sister, you will reveal your untidiness in the Prostration on Tuesday."

Tears stung. Della drew a white linen handkerchief from the deep pocket and wiped her eyes. The postulants had yet only witnessed one powerful ritual and evocation of guilt. The 'faults' confessed would seem ridiculous on the outside. *I tripped, forgot to say morning prayer in the cell, lapsed during meditation in the chapel, and did not polish my shoes.* Trivia, but now she would also have to join the miscreants on the floor - and endure humiliation.

On Saturday morning, the room filled with Senior White veils, first-year white veils and postulants sitting in rows around the large novitiate. At the top table, Mother started with a prayer asking the Lord to forgive his children for their faults. Then, each 'sinner' came out and lay prostrate, face downwards in the centre of the room. The scene reminded Della of a Roman amphitheatre, where gladiators fought to the death before an audience.

"I was late coming up from school yesterday as I stayed back to speak to a child," one sister confessed. Seniors attended lessons in the convent school to prepare for teacher training later.

"I rushed to the chapel without lacing my shoes and tripped on the steps" from another. It went on. Della nudged Sister Mary on the right. Her co, their new title, shook her head. They would have to wait until the daily walk to share thoughts.

"Sister Della, you must not speak. Come forth and prostrate."

Della moved into the middle area, bent her knees, stretched her arms out, and lay flat on the floor. Nothing ever endured in boarding could match this moment's degradation. She waited for her penance, and when it came, an hour extra washing dishes in the pantry, relief consumed her inert body. This was nothing like going to Confession after a late night with Ed and sterilising your sins to a priest behind a grill. *He* couldn't see your face. Here, fifty eyes watched.

Della moved back to her seat and saw the grin on Rhona's face. How well the co's knew her. The voice spoke again. "Sit straight, Sisters. No slumping."

At once, backs straightened, pairs of hands folded on laps.

"Postulants, heed and learn. As befits nuns, you will become ladies in every aspect. Hold your knife in the palm of your hand, not like a pencil, sip your soup, tip the plate away from you, cut your food into small pieces, and place your hands on your lap while chewing it. If you do all that, you will find a foothold on the stairway to sainthood."

Della put up her hand. "Saints, Mother? Don't think I'll be one until I get to heaven." As soon as the words came out, she could bite her tongue.

"True, Sister, but you will strive towards it. As humans, we are flawed, but our goal on this earth is the perfect image of Christ."

Afterwards, along with four other postulants, Della washed dishes in a cavernous sink and passed them to Margaret to dry. Rhona then placed the pile on the shelves, ranging around the walls. They would change roles each day. But the dishes were slippery; Della let two fall. A lay nun (one who lacked formal education and worked in the kitchen and gardens) said, "Breakages cost money, Della. Tell this in the next Prostrations."

Surely not again. None of the co's were committing faults like hers. But she could not argue. Maybe as one advanced in the holy life, inward calm would take hold and cleanse the mind of sinful longings. When Ed's face impinged, Della uttered the Holy name, "Jesus, help me," until gradually, the image came less often. In addition, wise words spewing from Mother's mouth on cue helped to brain-feed her soul traveller:

> *As they go through the bit-*
> *ter valley, they make it a*
> *place of springs,*
> *the autumn rain covers it*
> *with blessings.*

Della bowed towards Sisters on the corridor, learned not to pass older nuns without a respectful head inclination, and to stand aside when a senior member walked by. A nun must own decorum until fully immersed in its tenets.

CHAPTER 3

N ine months later. All ten postulants were preparing to take the white veil in a ceremony at three o'clock on the afternoon of July 1, 1962. It was the second step on their journey to becoming fully-avowed nuns in the Order. No longer would Della be herself, but Sister Elise, after St Elizabeth, Our Lady, Mary's cousin. Parents and relatives could view the ceremony from the side chapel.

A sense of finality enwrapped her like a body bag. Della O'Reilly was on course to become a Bride of Christ! A shiver shimmied down her body as a senior nun placed a towel on her shoulders, the cold steel of the scissors sending fear rippling through her veins.

"Sister, before I cut off your hair, think hard. Are you ready for the ultimate act to separate you from girl to nun?"

"Yes, Sister." Bowing her head, Della felt the steel bite through her tresses as the cutting began - down the sides, across the back. As the mound of gold on the lino grew higher, it felt like an arrow piercing her heart, losing her beautiful hair so great. She wanted to gather it up and hide it in a drawer. The older nun stopped. "It's difficult, Della. But in a few hours, Mother will place the white veil on your head to symbolise purity and a visible sign you belong to Christ."

Della cast a look at the pile. It was more than hair, but the last symbol of her other self. A tear welled.

"The tight coif will fit better over a bald head." A bald head. Della almost shouted stop. Then it was over. All gone. "I look like a gooseberry," she pined, seeing her face in the mirror provided for the occasion.

The ceremony in the Convent chapel lasted two hours. Like angels' voices, the choir's chanting rose in adoration, filling every crevice of the town in the valley below. Before the main altar, Della lay flat on the red carpet amid the ten co's in the centre aisle. The bishop's voice prayed in a sonorous and pious tone.

"You came down from heaven; you gave them ordinances, just and certain laws, good statutes and commandments. Follow Me."

The Lord had spoken, or rather the bishop, whose sermon, effusive in dignity and encouragement, entered his listeners' ears like a heavenly voice. The Order now had ten new saints. Saints! Sister Elise let the significance sink in. Did she have the nuts and bolts of sainthood? And had she quenched all earthly desires? Only time would work that out.

Afterwards, in the parlour, parents smiled with pride in clusters around the long dining table as trays of sandwiches and cakes passed among the throngs of white veils and visitors.

"My," her mother said, "Della, you're a proper nun now. Calm and poised. What a transformation. I'm proud of you, girl. Or should I say, Sister?"

"It did not happen overnight, Mam."

"You've done it, Della," her father said. "I thought they'd never bend your wild spirit to a life of obedience. Never. What a change. That Mother Bonaventure sure did a good job. But are you happy? You're skinny."

"Yes, Dad. It's what I came to do - to live my life in the service of God."

October 1965. Sister Elise was not sleeping. Waves of fatigue swept over her body each day as she struggled to control the nausea that thrashed about in her stomach. After Mother's lecture one afternoon, she asked her superior for help. The response came in measured sentences. "Sister, calm your mind before rest. Your brain is not a marketplace. Calm, Sister, calm. You must not dwell on outside influences." Surely the nun was not referring to that letter again? It had cropped up in tutorials over the past two years, Della insisting her previous life was just that: previous. She was intent on becoming a good nun.

The holy one's eyes stared into Sister Elise's. Words flitted into her awareness - sin, moral degradation, penance. Forget the frivolous life, the ballrooms and gilded images.

Mortify yourself at your sinfulness. The vanities of life will not get you salvation.

"Yes, Mother.

During the monthly Prostrations, she confessed to more breakages in the scullery, not separating the brown eggs correctly from the white ones in eighty nuns' egg cups or putting milk into glasses instead of water for some older Sisters. She could not offer an excuse that her hands trembled, her stomach lurched, and her sleep was patchy. One did not make excuses.

Worse still, her guilty pleasure when strains of songs wafted into her wakefulness during the Greater Silence. Bobby Vee's *The Night Has a Thousand Eyes* and Gene Pitney's *If I Didn't Have a Dime* repeatedly came, internal intrusions assaulting her soul. But no one would hear about them.

Then, one morning at seven a.m., a row of black and white veiled heads clustered like bees on a honey jar around the notice board outside the chapel. Sister Elise heard gasps of shock along the corridor. What could be so awful as to jolt holy nuns out of strict observance? And what so powerful to jeopardise sanctity early in the morning? Della strained to read the pinned sheet.

The President of the United States has been assassinated in Dallas, Texas. May the Lord rest his soul in peace.

The beloved 'Irish' president of America was dead. He'd visited County Wexford last year, where adoring not-so-close relatives paid homage to him and his beautiful wife, Jackie. Proud of a Catholic Irish President, one of the

American nuns had brought in a paper detailing Kennedy's reception in Wexford and Dublin.

This morning, however, the convent bowed its head in sorrow - death, resonating along the hallowed halls in union with a grieving world. But no one spoke aloud.

Months passed. Sister Elise sought with all her will to quiet her busy mind and to ground herself in virtues. But no longer coeval with her body, it fought to succumb. Mother lectured on the dangers of reneging on the Lord's call. One could lose one's vocation and, worst of all, one's soul. Della shrank in desperation. Soul. That word broke another piece of her away, letting fear rush through the crack.

With the elusive sleep pattern, Sister Elise's spirit weakened. Ahead lay the ceremony. In Mother's words, she must place her hand firmly on the plough and not look back, a cowardly act. If lousy health was the cross where she must hang with Christ, her Saviour, it was her burden.

When Sister Maura began acting oddly, Della wanted to reach out to her co. She liked the girl from Elphin, the youngest of the group, who seemed the right nun type. Maura stopped going to the rails to receive the Body of Christ during Morning Mass. Scruples, they called it, when someone felt unworthy. How could it be so when Della used to confess far greater sins in her former life? Nuns' sins were mere angel dust. She must try to help her sister, perhaps share worries. But they couldn't exchange troubles under the rule of silence.

After kitchen duty the following day, Della saw Maura on her knees polishing the steps at the end of the corridor as if her life depended on it, repetitively waxing one spot.

'Maura, are you alright?' The white veil lifted, and the glasses fogged over. Tears slipped down onto the starched coif.

"No, I can't go on much longer. I feel sick all the time."

"Me too. Mother says it's anxiety that we're not pure enough to be professed nuns. That we'll settle down after the ceremony."

As if called, the dark-swathed figure of their Mistress swept through the door from the chapel and stood arms crossed before her novices. It seemed to Della as if she hovered in the air they breathed, in every creaking floorboard, forever vigilant, watching.

"To my office at once, Sisters."

What happened next would remain in Della's mind for as long as she lived.

"Sister Maura, why are not you receiving the Lord? And Sister Elise, why were you talking in the corridor? I'm not sure either of you is fit to become holy Sisters."

What could they say? That Della was trying to help her co, who was in dire need of support, and that she, Mother, was not giving it? Conversely, Della might confess that both were falling into an abyss of separate demons.

Instead, she muttered. "Sister needs to talk to you, Mother." But the expression on their Superior's face quenched further comment.

"Sister Elise, move on to your duty. I'll speak to you later." Wooden-like, Della headed toward the novitiate and fluffed a film of dust along the polished wood. Were they never to feel anything other than guilt? Were they not meant to serve in joy?

One Sunday, Della's parents paid an unexpected visit on their way to visit relatives in County Donegal. Other nuns, too, had family in the parlour. Della saw Sister Patrick glance in her direction. In stolen moments, the nun, her confidante, worried for her, whispering encouragement when she saw Della's body wilt under strain.

"Della," her mother's voice sounded anxious. "You look awful. What's wrong? Have you talked to Mother?" Blunt as ever, Bridie would not stop until she unearthed the problem.

"Yes, they tell me to pray for guidance and not make a fuss."

"Well, I will," Bridie O'Reilly's determination rose like a gale-force wind.

"No, Mammy, no."

"Enough, Della. You're a ghost of the girl we left here three and a half years ago."

"It's Spiritual Year when doubts attack our minds, but Mother says we can overcome them with prayer, and root out our faults before taking vows. One Sister, Maura Kenny, from Elphin, has depression. She may not last." Della could have added that another, Sister Ann, had stopped going to Holy Communion, that her outbursts sometimes erupted during lectures, and that she spent hours in the medical room when her nerves galloped out of control.

"That's it," Daddy said. "Bridie, stay with Della. I'll ask Mother for a quick word in her office." He strode towards the top of the table where the older nun conversed with Sister Rhona's parents. Della felt a weight lifting at once, his firm approach a reminder of loving advice on her past behaviour. She'd resented it then, but now valued his concern. At the end of the table, she saw Mother's face change from smiley to stern and somehow agitated.

After a few minutes of tense conversation, her father returned, colour heightened, a sign heralding seriousness. "We're going now, Della, but you will be fine. Mother has agreed to let you see a doctor."

Bridie stood up, anxious and fretful. "I hope you were nice to the nun, Jim."

"I showed respect but laid down conditions to her. You must get treatment at once, Della."

They bade goodbye on the doorstep, assurance uppermost. Della saw how much they cared and that her family's opinion still counted despite belonging to an Order wherein Superiors ruled. After all, she was not yet a fully-fledged nun. Mother approached and offered a hand to both parents. Della saw the anxiousness on the older nun's face and something akin to that on her mother's, numbness in the face of unravelling change.

The following day, after Refectory duty, Mother called Della. "Sister Elise, you are precious to us, and we want you to serve our Order in good health. So, I've made an appointment in the Bon Secours Hospital in Glasnevin, where you will see a specialist. Tell him about your nausea and sleeplessness." The Superior's expression, with her usual seriousness, this time held a tinge of anxiety.

Dublin, the word spelt hope, but downtown Sligo to a local medic or one who came in when Sisters were too ill to go out would have been a start.

As the days wore on, a premonition of impending change took hold of her waking hours and ever so slightly eased the belly-wrenching nausea and inertia. Instead, worming in her guts came a powerful sense of exhilaration. Were the years of abnegation and self-denial over, or was she to adapt still further to life as Sister Elise?

Inward somersaults increased as Della drew a small bag from her wardrobe. There were few possessions to pack; a second clean veil, long-legged warm knickers, and black stockings. She folded an ankle-length nightie and a white cotton bra into neat rolls, thinned after four years of wear and wash. Finally, with toothpaste and toiletries on the top, she was ready. As she entered the taxi outside the front door, Della, Sister Elise, looked again at the long three-storey building, her home for nearly four years. Hope, a saying said, springs eternal in the human heart. But gradually, something else had crept into her being.

On the journey, Sister Damien, a professed nun, was pleasant and hopeful that the hospital would resolve the difficulties. Her words filtered through to Della as prophetic, though the nun did not realise the implications.

As the fields flashed by, Della wondered if she'd recognise anyone in Boyle when the train drew into the station. A waft of diesel smoke saturated the air in the carriage as a few passengers got off, others on. She strained to see someone, anyone. No one. Well, it had been a while...

On the outskirts of the city, Della's excitement mounted. She made out the famous Nelson's pillar in the distance and, farther off, the Dublin mountains. Memories surfaced of dances, the Irrawaddies, and a student vet. He must be qualified now.

In the city, they took a taxi to Glasnevin. The Bon Secours, one of Ireland's finest, was a private clinic where religious and well-off people came for diagnosis and treatment.

Sister Damian bade goodbye inside the building and handed Della over to an admittance officer. A swathe of new doubt gathered in her stomach as they proceeded through the sterile, polished, white corridors. What if the doctors found something awful to finish her off? Like TB. No. It had been wiped out by vaccination a decade earlier. Don't overthink, urged her brain.

A nurse in white and blue cotton conducted her to a pristine, clean, four-bed ward. In one, a smiling nun from Cork introduced herself as Sister Stella. She was waiting for a tonsil operation. Della reckoned the Sister was a few years older than herself, with the proper demeanour of a professed nun. She spoke hoarsely about wanting to return to her convent.

"Why Dublin?" Della asked. Surely Cork had its hospitals?

"Well, it's where nuns get priority treatment," came the reply. Consoling but also worrying.

Tea came, delicious lamb chops and mashed potatoes. This place was more like a hotel.

In the morning, the tests began. Fear gripped her as a doctor slid a camera down her throat. "It's nothing," he explained. "No need for an anaesthetic."

It was painful, but over in a minute. Stomach x-rays followed, and worst of all, a camera up her backside. Della had never felt so embarrassed. No one, not anyone, had ever looked there before. He told her to relax, but the humiliation could not be worse. No man had ever touched that part of her, and now this pleasant, smiley person, albeit in a white mask, pushed something into her end, tilted upwards for better access! She wanted to die on the spot and never see his face again. After all this time untouched by another, she was now little more than a piece of meat. Offer it up, she whispered inwardly. It's for your good.

Days passed, more tests, no tablets except for relaxant drinks, until one morning, Mr O'Connor came to her bed, pulled up a chair and started his diagnosis. "Introspection and continual fault-finding in yourself have induced a nervous state affecting your physical health. Your condition is called psychosomatic. My advice is to leave the enclosed life and save yourself. Neither pills nor medicine will cure you."

His words, blunt but honest, impacted like a boxer's fist on Della.

"How can I? They'll stop me, say I'll lose my soul if I leave the cloister."

"You'll lose your mind if you don't. Here's some money. I realise nuns don't have any. Ring your family and tell them to meet you back in Sligo on your return."

Kind man. He appeared to know how tenacious and persuasive nuns were, how they might, on her return, stress the merits of suffering for her eternal soul. He saw her pain, her plight, and also that a life of self-denial had pushed her into an unsafe condition. Forever reminded of her faults, Sister Elise was in a broken, spiritless state, like the old tractor abandoned in O'Reilly's lower yard. But now, a kind doctor had shone a light from where the wind blew free.

Through the hospital window, the moon gleamed gold as night fell over the city.

The following day, she found a public phone in the corridor, lifted the receiver, and dialled O'Reilly's home number with a trembling hand.

"Can you come to the convent on Friday and take me home, Dad? Please don't be ashamed of me. I tried."

A gasp, a moment of silence, then a rush of words from her caring father made everything better. "Ashamed. Not at all, Della. You looked so pale at Easter we worried." No recriminations.

It was evening when the train pulled into Sligo. In utter default of the rules, Della walked alone to the high granite building on the hill, a wave of defiance urging her not to care. Slipping in the side entrance of the granite boundary wall, she went straight to see Mother and did not falter in her delivery.

"I didn't want this to happen, Mother, but there is no choice if I am to get better. The Consultant in Dublin said I must leave the Convent to become healthy again."

"Oh, my dear Sister, your health *will* improve. Stay here with your holy family. Don't rush into a decision now. Jesus welcomes us with open arms, and He loves all sinners. I'd like to see the doctor's report before you can leave here."

Sinners? So she was a sinner for deserting the holy life? Fear of sin had driven her here in the first place, and now it was drawing her out again.

Della delved deep. "My parents are coming tomorrow. I must go for my sanity and well-being."

"You could take time to heal, then go to the American missions, a place of sunshine and wellbeing." The nun's voice, unusual in its softness, did not disguise the insistence. After all, her role as Mistress of Novices demanded leadership and guidance. But from across the miles, Della heard another voice, that of the kind doctor in Dublin.

"No," she answered. "Release alone will cure me."

High on a ridge over Sligo town, the Presentation convent nestled amid a profusion of autumnal golds, reds and browns. Around extensive grounds, mighty oaks and beeches creaked and moaned in the north wind. Lonely leaves fluttered downward to settle in disarray across the manicured lawns and neat paths between shrubs and flowerbeds. Soon, a soulless November would claw icy fingers across the landscape, the days would die, and rusty hues mutate into purgatorial greys. Winter was about to grip the house wherein women strove for holiness or pined to escape.

Della, Sister Elise, whispered a silent 'goodnight' to anyone who cared from her cell midway along the corridor. The single hard mattress, stiff and penitential, pressed hard against her spine. Here, not the softness of her bed back in Leam and the pink room. Shades of doubt ebbed and flowed through her brain, the idea of parting from co-novices filling her with apprehension. No longer would stone walls or cloistered walks guard her against those dreaded enemies of the soul: the flesh, the world, and that mighty master of evil himself - *the devil.*

At the end of the corridor, a stately grandfather clock struck one a.m. on its persistent march, tick-tock, tick-tock, towards dawn. Consumed with anguish, she would count the hours until the bell summoned the nuns to chant the Holy office at six-thirty. Relentless the sound in the night; tick-tock TICK TOCK, up to the strike, hour by hour, every sixty minutes. The thing, the fear, the anxiety, the scruples, had fixed a grip so powerful on Della she could not escape its power.

No ambient noise would break the silence in the Novitiate wing of the granite building where ten young women lay sleeping. From the muffled sound of distant traffic, Della imagined a voice calling *to jump, jump down to the street below, and hail a car. Get away from here.* But, within this high battlemented building, none would dare break the sacred Greater silence. Nor would they venture to the toilet, their bodies young and unheeding of the physical weakness age would bring. Young, yes, and wiser than that which they had rejected.

Distorted images clawed into Della's soul, dragging her from each attempted descent into unconsciousness. Her body, no longer hers to command, seemed to float to a barren place beyond the city to stand outside an old ruin, a hostile, dark, empty, derelict building. Desperate to find the others, a cold sweat broke on her skin. She had to find a way out or hear that Voice again amidst the tiredness and pain.

Strained and drawn in the brightness of day, it stayed inside her, quenching the birdsong on the gothic windowsill. Hers now to confront the truth. No longer could Sister Elise pursue a spiritual life of self-denial, abnegation, soul-searching, fault-finding, and ultimate sainthood. Only four years before, Della O'Reilly had come to the Motherhouse in answer to a call she could not stifle. Now, it was suffocating her.

CHAPTER 4

Della sat and waited on a high-backed parlour chair amid a spread of cold white marble. Her thoughts came and flew - back straight, hands on lap, head up in keeping with a nun's etiquette.

'Will I stand out, and people laugh at me?' Her eyes travelled down along the box-style jacket suit worn that October day. Ridiculous? Old-fashioned? She smoothed the green skirt, a little tight, but she would only wear it on the sixty-mile journey home. On visits, her mother looked smart, dressed to meet nuns in a nice coat and hat. Her father, a charming man, could converse with nuns or laity alike. But Della had seen the sadness in his eyes each time they shared goodbyes at the arched door of the convent. He would be glad she was coming out. What about her sister? Might Eve want her back?

What music was popular? Eve mentioned a group called the Beatles on a visit. However, her sister did not like their tinny sound; few jived anymore, just rhythmic shaking opposite partners on the floor.

During the Greater Silence, strains of songs had sometimes wafted into her semi-consciousness. Bobby Vee's *The Night has a Thousand Eyes*, Gene Pitney's *If I Didn't Have a Dime,* and her favourite, Elvis Presley's *Return to Sender* - appropriate. Wasn't the Order now returning her to the sender from whence she had come? She stalled her racing thoughts. Being free would be a start.

Poised on the cusp of a new phase, she had no plan. A face quivered before her mind's eye. She let it stay, not expelling the image that no lecture or prayer could banish over four years of self-denial. It was that of a tall man with a husky voice that had intruded at night when sleep was elusive. At once, she realised why she had never settled in the cloisters.

"I'll find Ed, and I'll marry him." She would make it happen like Scarlett O'Hara in 'Gone with the Wind'. Had she not once imagined herself as another Scarlett, loud and forceful, but now more like Melanie, the gentle one who listened and followed?

The clock struck eleven a.m., no longer a threat but bringing the moment of departure closer.

Waiting was tedious. Would they come? Had Dad's old car broken down on the Curlews? She tried to imagine the outside world from a place where no radio played, and no words were uttered except for holy women chanting in the Daily Office.

The doorbell rang. Della turned the knob. On the doorstep stood her parents. They looked anxious, unsure, and diminutive in matching camel hair coats. Was it 1961 again? Were they clones of themselves?

"Let's go, Della," Dad said. "Have you said goodbye to your nun friends? You always talked about them with affection."

"I wasn't allowed to, Dad. Mother said it might affect their stability." She did not add that Maura, Sister Patrick, had left only a week ago, before daybreak. When they missed her in the chapel and at breakfast, Mother explained that Sister had gone away for treatment. But they knew she would never be back. As for the early hour, she'd heard, on daily walks, during recreation, of Sisters leaving at dawn, before light. The reason for covert departures had something to do with shame. Abandoning a vocation was a disgrace and best executed without emotion or tearful goodbyes.

"Home, Della, to sleep in your bed and get up when you feel like it." Mammy's voice broke the reverie.

Della, head relaxed on the back seat, no need to sit upright now, said, "But I can't sleep, Mam."

"Tonight, you'll have a glass of milk and one of my scones. We'll pray for a miracle." Miracle. Wasn't Della leaving behind the miracle-making place?

Silence fell. The Curlews loomed high on the right as the old car sped onwards and down towards Boyle and the flatter central plain of Ireland. In the front seat, Bridie O'Reilly sighed. "So we will not have a nun in the family, Della?" Oh God, how her mother stated facts. Her daughter was bringing dishonour to their door.

But I *will* be happy again. And the sinister shadows will fade into nothingness, no more to haunt my dreams. Somewhere out there is a dark-haired man with blue eyes. He said he would wait.

Home. Della ran along the passage to her old room, opened the door, and soaked in the sweet, comforting glow of the pink wallpaper. Frilly pink curtains at the window, soft pink carpet underfoot, pastel pink bedspread and pillows. A pink world, in stark contrast to the sparse white and grey cell she had left behind. Here, dark images would never again occupy her tortured brain, nor irrational fears intrude; unworthy, unworthy, unworthy.

She shoved the green suit into the wardrobe's darkest corner and placed the kitten heel shoes on a rack beside the bed, her few possessions into the chest of drawers. On the dressing table, a statue of the Virgin Mary smiled in her direction, comforting, protecting. She might have reneged on her promise to God, but it didn't mean He would eliminate her from His care.

How often had she yearned for this room over the past four years but not expected to see it again? Nuns never got home except for a family funeral.

Back in the kitchen, Eve was in from the fields. Her hug gave off the warmth Della needed - the world complete. If the family wanted her, nothing else mattered.

They sat down to dinner, the smell of boiled bacon floating around the kitchen. On the wall, the same picture of

Christ on the cross; in the corner, the two-tier electric oven, and, through the window, a view Della had longed for over four years - the glittering blue waters of the mighty Shannon. Conversation floated around everyday concerns - the farm, lambing season, and seeding of crops, with no real seriousness. Mammy seemed eager to veer the conversation away from the convent. Della said the food was lovely.

"Cabbage and bacon should not be boiled too long," Bridie said.

"I was used to it like blotting paper, divided into eighty portions and flavourless." There was a brief laugh, then silence. Bridie got up and busied herself at the sink, passing on local gossip. One was getting married, and another was going to work in Dublin. Jimmy, up the road, was building a new house. This and that. Skirting the obvious. Yes, she was home.

"I'll go to bed if you don't mind," Della said, drying the dishes. It was only nine o'clock, but the day had begun at six a.m.

Sleep did not come at once. Instead, odd sounds from the wood behind the house pinged through the curtains. Crows scuffled amid wide branches. Starlings fluttered on the weeping willow, and robins hopped along the thorny hedge by the boundary wall. Welcome, familiar sounds. She drifted off.

The following day, Della woke at six-thirty, jumped out of bed, pulled on her skirt and top, and opened the door onto the long corridor leading to the kitchen. All quiet. No bell would summon her to the Daily Office in the chapel, nor would she struggle to shut her mouth. A leisured feeling coursed through her body, no hurry. She went back and lay on the bed.

An hour later, Della found her mother cooking eggs and bacon and slicing homemade brown soda bread in the kitchen.

"Eve's out on the land. Busy day ahead. You might like to wander along the path to the old quarry and maybe watch the boats in the harbour. And you don't have to come to Mass with us on Sunday if you'd rather not face people." Several suggestions at once. Which to process first? It had to be the Sunday Mass one. Face people. Were they ashamed of her? Was Mam hinting?

"I'll go." Everybody attended Church on Sunday, mid-week, during Lent and Holy Days. Inside, they shared prayers, gossip outside. It was the place to meet the parish locals, the nice ones, and the critics.

"Just checking. You haven't been well, so I thought you might like to stay in for a bit. Get your strength back."

The now mattered; her future uncertain. Today was Saturday, the following Sunday. Why wait?

Eleven a.m. Sunday morning. Father Beirne smiled a welcome on the top step of the Church entrance.

"Time will ease the pain, Della. Come and see me if you need to talk." She had not expected the word pain. Shame, perhaps, but not pain.

Dad led the way to their pew right at the front of the church. A family tradition, he'd insisted, keeping the long wooden high-backed seat as a 'matter of pride'. Della saw familiar faces; some aged, others plumper, a girl from her National school who'd had a baby recently. Didn't Betty look matronly, and she only twenty-two? But, God, what did settling down do for one? To the left were the same families in the same pews: the Fallons; hadn't the boy gone off to Kiltegan to be a missionary priest? She saw the Diffleys, Mullallys, and Gatelys in another row. A noteworthy congregation, they'd sent girls and boys off to seminaries and convents over the years. Maybe she shouldn't have come to Mass.

During the Holy Sacrifice, the priest talked about compassion, comparing Jesus's treatment of the woman at the well with that of the Government minister who'd just announced the opening of another orphanage in Galway. After fifteen minutes, rustling beads around the building signalled he should finish. How different from the sacred enactment of the Eucharist in the convent with communal singing rising sweetness to the throne of God.

After Mass, the congregation poured out onto the car park. Della, walking close to her mother, sensed many eyes x-raying her. Loud murmurs reached her ears: 'Didn't last long', 'no job, a burden'. She shrunk closer to Eve. A few women shook her hand on the steps and whispered, "Welcome home". Others hovered on the fringe of the congregation, casting glances in her direction. 'I'm a freak, an object of pity. Get to the car. Get away'. She dropped her head and thought about the effect on her family.

Mrs Fallon from Tullaghan village rushed over. "My Andy will pray for you. Nearly a priest now in his final year in Kiltegan."

Her Andy. Her pride. This mother personified it; her mother did not. In her pushy manner, the way she drew her shoulders back, Annie Fallon exuded it. Della's heart thumped inside her ribcage as if the woman had stabbed it. In comparison, Nora Lally's kindness melted like honey over Della. "One day at a time," she whispered, leaning close. A friend of Bridie's - they'd come to the parish the same year,1940 - Nora oozed sincerity.

Eve tapped her on the shoulder. "Home, Della. Dad needs to get back. Someone's coming to see him."

"There weren't many girls my age in the church. I expect they've left home, graduated, emigrated, or married. But here's me, with no job, purpose, or proper sense of direction."

Mam spoke from the front seat. "Right now, recuperate, get back your health. Then, in a month, you'll have a better frame of mind to plan."

"Della, no one is making you do anything right now," Dad said. His words had an immediate effect.

Della breathed out. So what if people gossip? She was free, albeit a burden the family had not expected to bear. A teaching degree had lain ahead in the convent and the promised Californian missions.

Where could she now turn for advice? Not the nuns in school; she had let them down. Her parents, well, they had ideas. Take a course and find a secure job. The truth was that right now, Della O'Reilly belonged to that unwashed, unwanted, work-shy lot who hung around street corners, fags lolling, askew, from dribbling mouths. *Oh, God, stop yourself.* Quashing the terrible images, she sat down and ate breakfast, to her mother's delight.

Days broke and receded, and soon, the first euphoria waned and mutated into a mixture of emotions. Doubt rose, fear gripped, tears flowed, and negativity spread its tentacles, encumbering her battle for clarity.

"Eve, can you get this prescription from the chemist, please? The doctor in Dublin said to take them until I became stronger."

"Sure, but why don't you come along? Let's go shopping and get a dress for the dance on Saturday night. Pauline, Sive and I are going."

"Oh, I'm not sure. People will stare."

"It's bound to be awkward at first, but you'll feel better when you face them and meet old friends." Her sister's insistence was more than Della could counter.

"Yes, if you think so, but making decisions is difficult. In the novitiate, we followed the rules."

"Yes, and that was how it should be, but you're twenty-two and an adult. I remember how stubborn you once were and how difficult it was to put you off when you wanted something. Della, it's a vast change for us all seeing you like this."

"Not having a daily structure feels odd. I need things to do." Something to pass the time and shift emphasis from her anxiety and nebulous state. Walks along the lakeside and up lofty hills on their land were soul-soaring activities, but Della needed a goal. After four years of concentrated effort to attain perfection within an enclosed life, she must utilise those skills in ordinary life.

"Mammy will give you plenty to do. We rarely dust the furniture in the drawing and dining rooms unless someone is coming to visit. Lots to do. Keep positive."

Over the following week, Della cleaned surfaces, polished ornate cabinets, and chaise longues. She pulled weeds, grounding and peaceful but non-directional chores. Each morning, she slipped calmers down her throat, those little pills the nun nurse had given her to quell anxiety spurts. But Bridie, rooting for the wash on Monday, found them in the drawer.

"Stop taking those drugs and overcome the bad feelings yourself, or you'll never be strong. Where's that self-willed girl now? The one who insisted on joining an Order to please a Reverend Mother, who thought her light-headed."

Della blanched. Not once had she expected her mother to lash out thus. But Bridie O'Reilly didn't stop.

"And read the papers. You might see a course you like." The last sentence, if intended to be a softener, came too late to stem the tears that slid down Della's face. How could her mother be so harsh?

"Yes, Mam. Don't tell Dad." No doubt her mother was right, but the nerve endings in her stomach would not settle on command, nor would her fragility melt on cue. As for the stubborn girl, she had drowned in a sea of suppliance and conformity. And wasn't a breakdown a mental illness that caused the body to ail with no apparent physical condition? Della explained how the doctor in Dublin had instructed her to continue with the medication until she was well enough to make decisions. And yes, Della had suffered an illness of the mind rather than the body. Bridie's face softened into a weak smile.

"One day at a time, Della." Her mother's attempt to dilute the previous invective hung in the air. She had not meant to hurt her daughter, Della knew, but had. She also knew her mother had not found life easy, starting married life at forty against family opposition. But now Della needed help, let it be from a little bottle or a smile.

On Thursday, an insert for a two-month secretarial course at the tech in Boyle leapt out of the Boyle Herald. She rang the number. The secretary offered a place to start next month, bringing a glimmer of hope.

Saturday night came. The green dress Eve bought for Della fitted perfectly. Her skin, devoid of the spots that had dogged her teen years, seemed to glow with a luminescence that made her look no older than in 1961. "That's because you didn't wear make-up, Della," Eve said. "Your skin is fresh." Another positive.

Eve drove the car to town and parked it on a side street close to the dancehall. As they rounded the corner on foot, Della gasped. Ahead stretched a queue several hundred yards long towards the entrance. "I can't do this," she said. "I want to go home."

"No darn way," Eve insisted, "You have to face people."

Inside, they found seats by the wall as the Miami Showband tuned up on stage. Pauline shouted over the brass, "Great to be here early to see Dickie Rock." Who was Dickie Rock? The tall, thin, smiley star at the microphone was undoubtedly not an Elvis type. But then, who would ever come close to her beloved icon?

"Not the usual pop star type, but his voice compensates for physical appeal," Eve explained.

Della did not know any of the songs. '*From the candy store on the Corner to the chapel on the hill,* the golden voice trilled, drawing a horde of girls to the bandstand.

"Gosh, they love him."

"Great voice," Sive answered. "He's the number one favourite in Ireland."

Couples formed on the floor. Della felt a hand touch her elbow. It was Martin Gately asking her to dance. She knew him from their National School days as a friendly lad from a big family. Hot sweat prickled her skin. Could she? Yes, she smiled; after all, they'd played hide and seek once upon a time.

It was a slow waltz, *Just for old times' sake*. Was she happy? Martin asked. "Never thought you should have gone, anyway."

"Well, I had to see it out. But it wasn't for me in the end."

He smiled. Martin's lot - set like the concrete around his hilltop home - was to remain on the farm, marry and raise a family. His siblings, however, would choose careers. Better still, if one or two became priests or nuns, solid, respectable life choices. That's how it was with large families.

"Thanks, Martin," she managed as he led her back to the girls.

"Maybe we'll have another later," he smiled.

"He always liked you," Eve laughed. "Could do worse, you know."

"I'm not settling down with anyone for years. Need a career first."

Then, a man came from the back of the hall and asked her to dance. Della remembered the face vaguely as one of Ed's friends from Carrick, John Tarpey. The band struck up *I'll hide my teardrops*, Dickie's voice hit the highest rafter in the hall.

"It's good to see you out again, Della. You know Ed Egan is coming home in a couple of months."

Despite the loud beat of the band, the one in Della's chest pounded so hard she was sure John could hear it. "Really. Hasn't he settled down yet?"

"Not him, a wild one. He loves the girls, and they chase him."

"Oh well, I'll be in Dublin by then. Just doing a short commercial course and hoping to get into the Civil Service."

She'd appeared unmoved by the information and hadn't let her turmoil show. Ed was coming home. Something stirred and grew inside her. A feeling suppressed for four years. Not a word to the others, she vowed, dulling thumping innards.

Two weeks later, her mother came in from the yard where she'd been chatting to Pat, the postman. Like all wives doing daily chores, she liked to hear the news and gossip he shared from house to house.

"Della, there's a letter for you with an English postmark. One of your friends over there? Mary Lally, perhaps." The curiosity in her mother's voice found an echo in Della. Mary, too, had entered an English convent. So it must be from her.

But the handwriting was familiar. When had she seen it before? That letter in Sligo? No, it couldn't be.

She should have left the kitchen to read it, but with both waiting and watching, there was no choice but to take out the neatly folded paper and read.

Bride St, Glasgow

My dear Della,

What a shock when John wrote saying he met you at a dance. I couldn't believe it and thought you were staying for good when you didn't come out earlier.

I often passed through Sligo but could not get the courage to call and see you. I wrote three letters in the first year but knew there was no point when you didn't reply. John said you look as glamorous as ever. So that's good, considering where you were.

If it's alright with you, I'd like to call as soon as I get settled in at home. Can we start again and be more than friends? It's what I've dreamed of.

All my love,

Ed.

Della's hand shook. She felt the colour drain from her face. Eve gasped. Her mother, busy at the sink, turned around. "Surely, Della, you'll give yourself time to get well and find a job before doing anything rash. Ed will wind you around his finger, and you won't know where to turn." The intensity in her mother's tone filled the kitchen.

CHAPTER 5

"You're weak and still dependent on pills to steady your nerves. You cry at little things. And if you stumble headlong into a wrong choice again, you'll never return to health. Don't say I didn't warn you."

"I'll see Ed, of course. He was lovely, and it was hard to leave him. Also, having someone to go out with will be good."

"But if he settles here, you won't want to work in the city, where you could study, take a night course."

Eve butted in, "Della, you're not the strong-willed girl he knew in 1961, the one who did what she liked. Instead, you're quieter, more subdued. Ed has a powerful personality and knows he is attractive. I've seen him at dances during the summer months. Never with the same girl, though."

"That's good, but he still loves me, it seems."

"On your head, be it." Eve's exasperated tone and the inference in her statement were disturbing. But she'd see him, and they could not dim her excitement.

Surprisingly, her father did not dwell on Ed coming. "You're going soon," his sole comment at tea.

Eve went off to a Young Farmers' quiz with her friends on Saturday night. Della declined; she'd rather watch TV and the Late Show again with Good old Gay Byrne, the nation's favourite presenter—normal life.

"All ages love him," Dad said. "Brings on controversial guests, though." The hint of disapproval in her father's voice made Della perk up. Her father was critical of anything of a risqué nature when morals were in question.

"Some of that stuff isn't suitable for a Christian audience. Gay Byrne has no right inviting Miceál MacLiammóir to the show. Talking to queers on public television is not acceptable."

"What do you mean, Dad? Queers? He's an actor. We went to the Gaiety to see him play Macbeth before Leaving Cert."

"Never mind. What you don't know won't trouble you."

It kept niggling. Della asked her mother to explain. Bridie laughed. "Some don't want to marry, only like their own sex."

"Really? We had to read books on how to avoid 'particular friendships' in the convent. They told us not to walk with the same one every day. I never got it."

"You're not safe to let loose in the world, Della O'Reilly."

"Mam, I have to learn about such things."

"Hush, Della," her father interrupted. "Listen to the News, starting now. You need to understand what's happening in Northern Ireland. It's worrying. There are violent outbreaks between the UVF and the IRA. If you don't understand what that means, it's the Ulster Volunteer Force and Irish Republican Army."

"It won't affect us in the twenty-six counties?"

"After the 1922 Treaty, Ireland established the Free State, but the six counties in Ulster remained in the UK. Republicans want an all-Ireland State. We're one small island."

"I learned it in school. So the Republicans are upping the fight for civil and religious rights?"

"Yes, in recent elections, they came second to the Unionists. It's worrying. Blood will flow. I'm sure of it." Surely not. Over nine hundred years of submission, Irish blood had indeed flowed across the land in a fight for independence from the invader. But the invincible spirit of a nation never flagged, and, again, it seemed as if one tiny part remained dogged in resistance to change.

"Awful, but I care little. What does the North have to do with my job chances? It won't be in the North, where Protestants discriminate against Catholics." Not that she did not care about it, but the North, right now, was on a very distant trajectory of her life, her dreams and her needs.

"We're a small population, including Ulster."

"Back in Sligo, one nun, Margaret from Derry, used to tell us about hearing gunshots at night over the bogs of Donegal. IRA terrorists, waging their war against the UK, sought shelter in the wilds after attacks on Unionist outposts."

"Ulster will always cast a long shadow over the South, and its troubles will worsen."

"I'm ashamed and ignorant," Della said. "Awful things happened, and I knew nothing about them. We didn't hear about the Vietnam War until two Sisters returned from the

Missions one summer. But I could quote the Papal Encyclical by heart."

April blew in, breezy. With each new day on the course, Della's expertise in shorthand and typewriting improved as her fingers tapped the keys to the sound of William Tell in the background - valuable skills to set her on the road to employment. Shorthand was complex, but the other ten girls on the course said it didn't matter. Dictaphones were the thing in offices nowadays, and soon, computers would take over. Still, typing was vital for an office job.

And Ed would come soon.

One day, the phone rang. Studying shorthand symbols in her bedroom, Della heard the sound and ran along the corridor; must be another IFA call for her father. An unfamiliar voice on the other end said, "Ed, here, Della. I got home last night. I can't wait to see you."

There are moments in time one never forgets. And this was one of them. She let the drumbeat settle in her chest. "Yes, yes. How come you're not married?" What a silly question. Why ring if he were? A soft laugh wafted over the airwaves, conjuring a rush of memories of nights.

"Of what you knew of me, did you think I would? Always thought you'd come out of that nunnery." Again, a laugh and a note of longing. "Can I call over?" Over? From Carrick to Leam, the far side of Boyle, maybe twenty miles.

A mixture of nervousness and excitement mingled. What might she expect? Four years was a long time. Did he lose his hair or have an accident in the ironworks? There had to be a reason. He must be all of twenty-six now.

"Yes, come tomorrow night."

"I can't believe this is real, Della." And the line clicked dead.

Forget the course, the shorthand manual. Nothing else mattered except how she looked. The next day, she laboured, conditioning golden hair longer in 1961, but would it matter? Encasing her legs in sheer nylon, Della flattened a black skirt tight on her hips.

"Gosh, to think you were still wearing long-legged knickers and droopy white bras a few months ago," Eve laughed.

"It's not funny. Ed's home from Scotland, where girls are smart and glamorous. I can't seem frumpy."

Not just frumpy but naïve and out of touch with everything. The thought of his nearness brought on a quiver of excitement, not a shiver, but a quiver. The mirror said she looked good. Never mind where he'd been or with whom. A new dawn was breaking, golden.

At eight o'clock, the white car pulled into the yard. Despite her shaky pins, Della walked outside and tried to assume an air of normalcy. He was not to see how nervous she felt. Ed got out of the car and stood before her, tall and angular, hair flopping over his forehead, eyes bluer than blue, long, slim frame inclined towards her.

"Hi, Della. Good to see you again," he said in that husky voice that had intruded at night when sleep was elusive. He was the reason she had never settled in the cloisters. In 1961, she fell in love with him, and despite her attempts to shut out the world and its attractions, she had never stopped wanting Ed. Here lay her destiny, her search for a future over, its entirety fixed firmly in the person of this man, this god who stood before her in tight hipsters, black polo neck, and beige cardigan. Over one eye, a shock of brown hair was, she guessed, sprayed into a neat flick.

But, gosh, he is vain, an inner voice whispered. And gorgeous. I must not let him lead me into sin. I want love, not lust.

"I left Scotland because my father can't manage the land. Not that I intend to farm full-time. No, just a small herd. I'll get into machinery, buying and selling as I did abroad."

She did not care, nor did it matter what he would do. He was home. She was here, not two months since leaving the other life.

"Can we date again?" his words, lilting and soft, came out as musical.

"So, you're not involved with anyone?"

"I've had girlfriends, but nothing serious. And it's more than a coincidence we're both back for good?" His smile, winning and mysterious, said: leave it. Now was not the time to probe, nor did she want to. After all, he had rung her. But if he were used to dating others, would she, backward in worldly matters, be enough for this suave, slim man before her? A surge of incompleteness welled inside, like the gnawing, gut-wrenching sickness of that final year.

She did not say that it wasn't a coincidence, but fate, or in her case, God's will. A half-smile showed he would agree. Over two hours, Ed asked questions about the convent but told her little about himself. Della said it was too painful, and she wanted to move on. He understood.

"Did you get the letter I wrote after you entered? You didn't answer."

"Only one, early in the first month. Mother told us to eliminate all worldly distractions from our minds and to concentrate on becoming holy. No, I got nothing after that, Ed. I'm sorry I didn't reply, but I couldn't."

When Ed stood up to leave, a word floated into her consciousness when he bent down to kiss her goodbye. SIN. Sin, sin, sin. A mixture of pleasure and guilt took over. W*ould* she ever be free of the latter? His straightforward manner and ease seemed genuine, and for Della, enough that he cared and respected her. The anguish and insecurity of the previous months would soon melt away. Love, as the song said, conquered everything,

On Saturday, they could go to a dance in Boyle, he suggested, then waved goodbye and drove off down the avenue. Della turned, adjusted her hair, and composed her emotions. Inside, three sets of eyes bored into hers. She said, "Things are looking up."

"Seems a nice enough, fella," her father replied. "Just go easy for a while." But the inference could not deflect from Della's joy nor undo the fact that love had re-entered her life. And she would not let go of it ever again.

"He seems more mature, Della. Yeah, I liked his manner." Gosh, approval from her mother. Maybe they would not now pressure her into a job in the city.

On Saturday, Eve suggested a trip to Boyle, ten miles from their townland in Leam. Set on an incline to the Curlew mountains, the quaint town was famous for its association with the King family estate nearby. But history was not

Della's focus right now. Instead, she needed decent clothes to go out with a handsome man.

When her father pressed notes into her hand, she gratefully accepted the money despite the tinge of shame engendered. Most offspring her age earned a living, but Della needed trousers, skirts, and nice bright sweaters. She would pay him back one day. "No, you won't," he said.

Della stood on the hill over the main street and took in the familiar shops, narrow streets, and the historic King House, founded by Sir Henry King in the 1700s, a constant reminder of the nine-hundred-year occupation of foreign forces in Ireland. She wondered if there was a town or village that did not reflect English Occupation.

She strained along the streets for a glimpse of familiar faces. None, but comforting still to see the same names over shopfronts and friendly staff behind counters. "Eve, I can look at clothes again without feeling guilty or diverting my eyes from worldly images."

"Worldly images? Is that what they call it in the cloisters? How could shops sell clothes if nobody looked at them? But you never went beyond the convent walls?"

"Only twice, to the dentist, and was shocked when I saw myself in the window, enveloped in a big black habit sweeping the pavement. I didn't recognise myself."

No need to cringe now, however. Slim and medium height, the years behind convent walls had not left Della looking plain or dreary. No weight gain, a little blusher on high cheekbones and a puff of powder were enough to mask those annoying freckles and, not least, her awkwardness.

"Buy some makeup. You can't manage with the few bits I lent you," Eve said. With sheep to sell at the market, her sister's income was ample to spend on clothes and a good time. But Della's aptitudes lay only in prayer and religious knowledge.

"Della," a voice called from under Boles' canopy, a renowned drapery in the town centre for old and young alike.

A tall girl with light brown hair stood smiling in their direction. "I don't know her," Della muttered to Eve.

"I think it's one of the McMahons from our schooldays, Laura, older than you by a few years."

Yes, there were three McMahon sisters in the school between '58 and '61 - Laura, a senior when Della was a junior, was a pretty girl with unusual green eyes. She had left Ireland for a nursing career in London and must now be twenty-seven. If you did not get into university after Leaving Certificate, nursing, the bank, and teaching were popular choices for a life career. Of course, one could be a nun, as she had, or for a boy to enter a seminary and train for the priesthood, but they heard a special calling.

"Della, I remember you in Joan's class, and when I heard that you joined the Motherhouse, it was not a surprise. You seemed holy."

Eve cut in, "Laura, are you sure you mean the right one? Della would talk for Ireland and was in constant trouble for it." In an instant, all three relaxed.

"Time for a coffee, girls? Come to The Royal," Laura suggested.

"I've got loads to do in town. Della, chat with Laura. Maybe she knows Ed and the other lads in Carrick." Eve turned towards the bank entrance.

"Ed Egan. Yes, I know him. I've just got engaged to Joe Linehan from near Ed in Cortober. We met in pub sessions there. My, he is handsome. No shortage of girls chasing him."

As heat seeped into Della's cheeks, Laura stopped. "Della, how do you know him?"

"We met in 1961 and went out briefly before I left home. We're supposed to be going out." Supposed - a careful reference to cover possible hitches.

They ordered coffee and scones in the hotel lounge; the kind Irish restaurants present on little doilies and trellis-shaped plates. Laura paid, and they sat at a table at the back of the room. It was two p.m. Three couples were drinking tea, old folk out for an afternoon in the hotel for a treat. Outside, horns blared, dissipating the sparse traffic in town. The Carrick bus pulled in, and passengers piled off.

The coffee came, drawing Laura's gaze away from the strangers. Buttering scones and spreading jam with little pearl-handled knives, Della laughed. "Gosh, aren't they posh in Boyle? I never tasted coffee in the convent, but my dad likes it. It reminds him of Boston."

"Coffee is the mainstay of medics. Keeps them awake on night duty."

An hour passed, during which they talked about London, Laura's sisters, and her mother's poor condition. Della had little to offer but curiosity. Desperate for information, she blurted, "Laura, how much do you know about Ed Egan?"

"A bit. Della, be careful. You have returned to a changed world from the one you left four years ago. And Ed is, let's say he's a man of the times."

The times; freer, less inhibited than four years ago? Laura's hint, though subtle, was unsettling.

"Thanks, Laura. My parents, too, are wary. I suffered a breakdown in Sligo and still have anxiety issues. Sometimes, I take Valium and get teary at the slightest hint of conflict. But I've no intention of getting tied down yet. Tell me how you met Joe." Best get on to the more neutral ground.

Laura's face lit up. "I came home on holiday two summers ago. My mother complained of a 'bad leg', y'know how they say it. A bad leg with an abscess, it was. She let me change the bandages and wanted me to sit with her all day. The others were out working, so I looked after her because I was a nurse. Then, one day, Mam fell asleep, and I escaped for an hour. Do you know the fair green in the middle of the town? I sat on a bench, the sun on my face, smelling the honeysuckle in the corner of the park, and just watched."

"It's pretty in the summer but drab in the winter with those grey-slated houses around the square. Carry on, Laura."

"Locals passed and said hello. Others nodded, recognising me but not bothering. The sound of water flowing through the town, the sun's rays reflected on the surface, and the birds singing made the place attractive. Better than I ever remembered it. Then I spotted two lovers hiding from sight under the oak trees; she was on her back, and he was half-leaning over her. I saw how the light flashed golden specks onto her hair, her shiny and soft skin. It hit me I hadn't yet found love in my mid-twenties. I was jealous.

Then I heard music wafting from a bar on the Square and followed the sound. The place was murky, but I recognised the bartender, Jim Jordan. He knew me at once, said it was good to see me, and asked if I'd married. I said no, been busy nursing. Then he said something that kindled a spark in me. 'You were always one for the music, Laura. Played the fiddle, didn't you? And the piano. Come along to the session tonight. Joe Linehan from Carrick is singing. Has a great voice."

Laura's voice lightened. "Della, my life changed that night. Joe's lilting voice won my heart with *Waltzing Matilda*, *The Fields of Athenry*, *The Minstrel Boy,* and more. I clapped so loud it drew his attention to me. He came across and asked Joan for an introduction."

"What next, Laura?"

"I fell for his broad smile and silver tongue, and we went out a few times. Then, after a week, I returned to Whipps Cross, the job I loved, and handed in my notice. I've been working in the hospital here ever since."

"Laura, that's so romantic. If I eventually settle down with Ed, we'll be friends. I'm glad we met today," Della said.

Had she uttered the words, 'settle down'? On the way back to the car park, she pondered over Laura's revelations about Ed. It was disconcerting to hear he was 'wild'. But he'd told her there were many girls, and he'd not lived as a celibate for four years. She had.

Eve asked, "What did Laura tell you about Ed?"

"Nothing much. She does not know him very well." No reason to pass on the negativity to Eve with her razor-sharp mind. But she could not rid herself of the lingering doubts.

At home, dinner was ready, cabbage and bacon, her favourite and Bridie's best. Green cabbage, pink bacon.

"I should be married," she tried "... and cooking dinners."

"Married? You've lost four years and are, of course, older than girls just out of secondary. But that is how it is. Accept it." Her mother's reprimand held an insistence untypical of Bridie's serene nature. "That Laura must have put ideas in your head."

"Take your time, girl. Marriage is life-binding; the convent was not." Her father's eyes narrowed, the norm when he disapproved of something.

"Yes, Dad."

"There's enough land here for the two of you, and we could build another home if you want to be a farmer like your sister."

"Dad!" How could he suggest she'd muck out animals, chase sheep across boundaries, walk the hundreds of acres looking for a beast in a drain? Heavens no. Her dream of further study was a cherished goal she would not sacrifice for anyone. Land might be treasure, Mother Earth her roots, but not the hardship that went with it.

"I'd like a post in Galway, a bustling city of light, sea, sun, nightlife – and a university. Yes, Galway, if Dublin doesn't come up."

"Better prospects in Dublin," Mam said. Gosh, how she persisted.

When Ed pulled up on the drive on Friday night, her heart missed a beat, seeing the admiration in his eyes as she emerged from the house and sat in the passenger seat. Eve had sewed together a white linen dress that fitted her slender form in all the right places. "Wish I had your skills, Eve, but I hate sewing," she'd uttered in gratitude.

"You've other talents in biblical and church studies. You'll never lose that. And soon, you'll have a certificate in office skills."

Ed looked gorgeous in a white cardigan and tight blue pants, and Della could barely keep her eyes off him or the women who came close in the dancehall. Tall, slim, and broad-shouldered, he was a magnet for the tiny, big, plain or pretty ones on the floor. She said he should not encourage them.

He laughed. "Used to it, but I'm with you." Then, pulling Della close, he kissed her cheek, and in an instant, her fears flitted away like the dust on the tinsel above them.

Della watched the other couples over Ed's shoulder, their heated faces, eyes glistening in desire, mouths nuzzling necks in anticipation. Stimulated by the slow music beats, bodies grew closer, barely moving from a chosen space around the bandstand in a trance-like rhythm, as the band stimulated passion. Jim Reeves's "*Put your sweet lips a little closer to the phone*" brought dancers to a near standstill, and as Della sang "*He'll have to go.*" Ed whispered, *but he won't, not now or ever.*

Della's mind whirled. With most couples, what started on the floor might lead to the inevitable fumbling, denying, refusing, or capitulation in cars way into the night.

And her soul, scoured of sinful passions by pious thoughts and teaching, would again arm itself to battle temptation. Laura's words whispered from afar. Della pulled away and looked beyond him, saw the shameless smirks from pushy ones who smiled directly at Ed. Any of them would give him what he wanted.

"What's wrong, Della?"

"I'm not sure I can do this, Ed. Trust you." As soon as she had said the words, Della wished she hadn't. His expression stiffened, and he walked ahead of her to the side of the hall. "Need the loo."

Della stood and watched him go to the Gents before entering the Ladies, where a mirrored image scowled back, a face clouded with uncertainty and doubt. Her insecurities, albeit from a different impetus, did not differ from those in her religious life, where she'd harboured worries about worthiness. But Ed was with *her*. She drew her long hair into shape, smiled at someone from the town and walked out into the hot ballroom again. She would not be jealous.

At once, her resolution plummeted. Ed was talking to a dark-haired, painted-doll type blue eyeshadow, red lipstick, and long eyelashes. Yes, a painted doll. Their body language suggested more than mere acquaintance or friendship. It showed in the girl's pouting and smirking. Della stood back and watched from behind a pillar. God, he had been with her; she knew it at once. Della moved forward; the doll slunk into the crowd.

CHAPTER 6

"Another of your past conquests, Ed?" Drat it. He could not avoid the obvious or take her for a fool. But twirling her around the dance floor, he said. "Nothing to tell. Let's say I've gone out with a few."

But his interaction with the other girl had killed the night, and it took every ounce of self-control to still an inner warning voice. They might lure him away from her; she, Della O'Reilly, out of touch; unworldly, unused to ... anything. The intense exchange she had witnessed cut deep.

Three tunes segued into the next without a break as the band played on. Couples stayed together, singles said, 'Thank you', and walked away. The touch of Ed's arm around her waist gradually eased the earlier worries, and the bad feelings melted into nothingness. A few former school friends came over and hugged Della, then returned to their seats to sit out dances and watch.

"No change in four years," Della said. "It's wrong that women can't dance unless they're asked onto the floor by a man."

"It's the man's right to choose," Ed said. "Why wonder at it?"

"It's cruel. Some girls sit by the side all night. I've just come back from an all-women establishment. While we obeyed rules, we learned to use our brains, aiming to teach, nurse, and work in communities for the betterment of others. But in our modern world, men rule as they always did."

"You talk nonsense sometimes, Della." However, the dichotomy in their views and values was unsettling. Only the previous week, Gay Byrne had interviewed a group of women on the 'Late, Late' who had founded a women's movement in the city, Nuala O'Faolain and Mary Kenny, the leaders. If she were to work in Dublin, Della could join them, and later on, if Ed proved to be a dictatorial husband, she could counteract his control based on strong opinions and a liberated outlook. Her goal, Dublin, must, she realised, become a reality. Tonight proved how little she knew of the man who purported to want her but could not give up his ways for any one girl.

A face Della remembered that of Josh Sweeney, a sallow-skinned brown-eyed boy came alongside. Nodding towards Ed, he said, "Hi Della, good to see you're looking well, considering where you've been."

Della blushed; she had nurtured a secret crush on the O'Reilly solicitor's son like most of her year group in the boarding school. Ed nodded when Della introduced them, but his hand, encompassing hers, squeezed so tight it hurt. "Nice to meet you. Bye."

In that brief encounter, she realised someone else liked her, perhaps a potential boyfriend if she were not with Ed. Knowing there were other possibilities felt good. The next dance was a slow waltz. Ed pulled back, his gaze on her face, and saw her smile towards Josh. He tensed and crushed her fingers again. "You're with me, remember?"

"What about that one I saw you with when I went to the loo? Tell me nothing was going on."

A covert, masked expression crossed his face. "Went out with her last year, just catching up. I can't avoid talking to them, but we two are together. So don't mess with me."

"I want to sit down and watch the dancing." She meant everyone on the floor and him; where he looked, at whom. Again, fears gnawed into her innards. Rather than making her feel wanted, his possessiveness was becoming stifling.

Eve came across the floor and sat down with Pat, her on-off boyfriend. The two men nodded. Eve whispered, "Are you alright?"

"Fine, just taking time out." Her sister had seen the encounter.

"I saw the pointing finger, the glowering looks, the tight lips, your sad face. Della, you'll lie on a thorny bed if you stay with him."

"Why's that?"

"You were arguing, and he shook his finger at you."

"I stopped to chat with Josh Sweeney on the way around the floor and smiled at John Mullally. Ed told me off. But I saw him speaking to that Lynch girl from The Batteries."

"He's dominating you. How shallow is that, Della? Seems you can't break free from control or work things out for yourself."

"Go easy, will you? I'm just getting used to him, and he to me. But I'd like to live a bit before getting too serious. Ed came after me."

"So well he can, tagging you along while having fun behind your back. I'm right. You shouldn't commit to him. Break it off, Della, before you're in too deep." Eve's inference that Ed was untrustworthy and a womaniser ushered in new misery. Was the euphoria of meeting him again to be a mere fairytale and nothing more than fire and ash?

They'd brought Eve and Pauline to the dance, but both girls had other plans for getting home. Pauline went out with Andy Connor, a local boy. Eve would go home with Pat Flannery. She liked her independence, and if it didn't suit him, she'd cool their relationship. So tonight, Della was glad for more time alone with Ed, willing him to dispel her doubts and tell her she was the only one that mattered.

Dotted along the road between Boyle and Carrick, no gateway was vacant. Della saw old Cortinas, Fords, and Mini-Minors. How little had changed in four years? The car, it seemed, was still the only place to fulfil the longing ignited on the dancefloor: darkness and fogged-up windows, a perfect cover for courting couples. Hadn't she resisted it herself? But back in 1961, her armoury - determination and conviction - were the bulwarks that had veered her along a chosen path. Now, dithery and unsure, her resistance might not withstand powerful persuasion.

Back in the convent, she'd agonised about staining her eternal soul with infringements of the rules and sins of the flesh, mere angel dust now in the light of present forces. Yesterday, Della visited Pauline looking for information about intimate things. The other girls didn't need prompting.

"It's a devil of a fight when Alan gets worked up. There's nothing I can do to stop him. I try to say no, but he doesn't care." Loose-tongued, or maybe conscience-pricked, the girl would not hold back.

"What do you mean, can't stop? If Ed carried on like that, I'd jump out of the car."

"Alan says it's lovemaking, that it's alright. So I tell him it's a sin. But when he persists, the 'no' vanishes, along with my guilt. Della, it takes over my body."

"And your conscience, by the sound of it. Not for me. Ed doesn't expect me to do bad things."

"Bad! It's love, and I can't let him down. But, sure, it's the same in every car. And that quarry near Cortober is a great place. Lots of us go there."

"And watch each other?"

"In the dark, no. Anyway, everyone is doing the same. Love explodes into passion in the back seats, and we forget sin and guilt. Last Saturday night was glorious. We parked at the back wall of the quarry. Only the sound of the odd corncrake broke the silence. That and the rocking of the car." Love explodes into passion." Where did the girl, a country sort, find the words? Not from books. More likely sitting under a cow's belly, pulling teats for milk.

"We park in the gateway near Coyles' barn, but it's only kissing, though Ed gets het up. You're all hypocrites going to Mass and receiving Holy Communion on Sundays."

"You might criticise, Della, but I love Alan. Why would I resist? Don't resist. His kisses make my heart flutter and my head swoon. Right and wrong merge when I'm in the back seat of that car. Sure, I'm on a march to the altar."

Did Pauline hear herself? Understand the inference? The altar and serious sin?

"But afterwards, you feel guilt? Shame? I could never do it. The thought of breaking a cup is enough. You're committing a mortal sin, Pauline."

"Well, if I am, there are plenty more like me."

"Get confession. Ask God to forgive you."

"Della, there's a long line outside the confessional box on Friday nights." Pauline's laugh sounded hollow, like a knell calling her soul to hell.

"But it's a farce, doing the same thing again. To receive absolution in confession, one must have the purpose of amendment, never to do it again."

"Arrgh, Della, you're full of religion, just out of the nunnery. Yes, but I can go to the altar on Sundays, and no one knows the difference. Alan does not hear or care when I say no, and when he lifts his shirt and my dress, I give in, too weak to deny him."

"How do you avoid getting pregnant?"

Pauline laughed. "Della, you're innocent for sure. There's a fancy term for it. I believe it's Latin. Look it up in the dictionary. I can't explain." In Della's ear, Pauline whispered a word Della vowed to retain.

That was yesterday. Now, Ed's voice broke through her thoughts. "Been in the fields all day mowing meadows, saving hay, and counting cattle. I'm not cut out for farming," he confided, which was comforting and normal, away from bloodsucking girls.

"Same going on at home. Dad was tired tonight. A farmer can't take breaks."

"Well, there'll soon be less of it now that I've planned the business. Modern machinery is the way forward; people want more than the rusty old tractor, a two-pronged fork, and the little paintbrush. Ireland is on the cusp of change, and I aim to be part of it." Was he trying to impress her?

"But I need cash. My savings have evaporated on a new car, updating the tools at home, etc. So, I might try for a bank loan. I should be a sound investment for any bank manager, with a farm of land behind me and business taking off."

She didn't care what he did; his black leather jacket, white shirt, tight trousers, and shiny, white Corsair impressive adornments enough for anyone. "Talk to my dad. He knows about banks and security."

"Plenty of that for now." He moved over in the front seat, so close she could feel his breath on her cheek. Della's heart fluttered, expecting his touch, but she drew away.

"Tell me more about that girl I saw talking to you. It seemed like a serious conversation to me."

Ed slid his hand off her arm and returned to the driver's seat. "I told you already. We used to go out."

"When? Last year when you were home? Did she want to start up again?"

"Maybe, but it's over. I'll drive you home. I'm not up for an argument at this hour of the night, Della. You suspect everyone because your exile from the real world has left you with a warped mind."

"How dare you. It's all one-sided with what you want and when to see me. Don't bother."

He drove the last mile in silence. At the house, Della got out and slammed the door. Ed turned the car in a whirl of shingle and disappeared down the avenue in the moonlight.

A flood of regret engulfed her. Should she have questioned him and destroyed their time together? But the expression on the other girl's face had sewn seeds of doubt in Della's mind. There *was* something, a knowingness.

In the kitchen, Eve was drinking cocoa at the table.

"He has a wandering eye. I saw him smile and wink at several when you were dancing. Better off without him. Set your sights on Dublin." But her sister's words did little to quench Della's feelings for the man whose presence had shadowed her existence over four torturous years. "No tea," she said.

In bed, sleep did not come. Regret piled on regret. Why had she not accepted Ed's explanation but allowed personal demons to prevail? She drew the cover over her head and prayed. The little pink pill would soon work.

"Your eyes are puffy, and your face pale," Bridie said at breakfast six hours later. Della, hunched over the table in a dressing gown, sat sipping tea and pushing scrambled eggs around the plate. "Have you been crying? What now? It's barely three months since you came home. So please listen to us when we ask you to take things slowly. Tell Ed you won't see him for a month, and if he cares enough, he'll return."

"What do you mean, Mam?" Della said. "I love him and can't do that. I'm going back to bed. I'm tired; I didn't get to sleep until four. It was a long night, a great dance, but we argued, as Eve probably told you. And he might not come back, you'll be glad to hear."

"For the best. You're too fragile for any of this."

Della recognised the sense in her mother's statement. Camouflage did not work with Bridie, nor argument, but now she needed sleep - oblivion. Della put the cup and saucer in the sink, left the kitchen, entered the sitting room, and pulled a dictionary from the shelf. C - coitus. There it was. Gosh, that's how they escaped, or maybe did not. And it would account for the shotgun weddings and the altar rush. One thing was sure. She, Della, was not prepared to take a risk.

In the corridor, her father's raised voice filtered from the kitchen. "Bridie, that girl isn't in a fit state to decide. She came out of the convent broken and depressed. She needs time to recover."

"I know all that, Jim. But yes, this thing with Ed is moving too fast."

"We must get her to Dublin soon."

"Agreed."

They were right. She should find an independent existence far away from everyone.

Three hours later, Della ran a bath, and as the soothing suds encompassed her aching frame, a plan formed. She would continue to see Ed but not let him rule her life. Others told her how attractive she looked with her long hair and slim body. A voice in her head urged her to look further afield, find someone new. Joe Ward, a local boy she liked, lived a mile up the road. A good looker, he had big brown eyes, and Della had always been a sucker for brown eyes.

One day, later in the week, she walked toward Jamestown, hoping to meet him. As if summoned by her need, Joe appeared on the roadside by his car and smiled. "Hello, how are you?" Della said fine, but she wanted to get out more. There was no mention of Ed; if Joe knew about him, he said nothing.

"Would you like to go to a dance in Longford? Twenty miles away, it's less than an hour's drive."

"Yes. Can you bring Eve and Pauline?"

"Fine, sure, we're all neighbours." His smile, gentle but attractive, had an immediate effect. A glow of satisfaction spread through her body. She was about to go on a regular date with an ordinary boy.

Back in the house, Eve lectured. "You *are* silly. But I'll go. Love the Royal showband."

"You keep telling me off, so I'm doing something about it."

"But not by cheating. Talk to Ed and say you'd like to see others. I bet he'll agree. Who'd have thought you were a nun?"

"No way. Ed would not allow it," Della retorted. "And he might not come back."

Of course, she did not want that, and tonight was just a frisson, a quiver off-piste, a bit of fun.

On the journey, all four chatted about local life, the priest's sermons on sin, the craic at the dances, and light-hearted banter. On arrival, they found the hall heaving with bodies. Della, a new man in tow, prepared to enjoy the night. Chancey, yes, but that gave an edge to the pleasure, to her newfound freedom. Of course, no one would tell Ed.

Joe led Della onto the floor and twirled her to the rhythm of Heartbreak Hotel. She liked his style. Della relaxed. He wasn't Ed, not as tall and dashing, but attractive and different. After three fast jives, they sat and drank orangeade in the mineral bar during a break and talked. By day, he worked in Sligo and travelled home each night; tiring, but the money was good.

They shared light conversation, danced, and sipped minerals for two hours. Then, midway through the night, Della looked up towards the balcony from where onlookers could watch the action below. She froze on the spot. A figure in a white sweater was leaning over the rail. It couldn't be Ed. It was - god-like within that mysterious aura that first drew her to him in 1961. His stance, leaning on the rails, showed him rapt in the music. He mightn't have seen her. Had he? She couldn't get caught; was guilty as hell.

At that moment, the night ended, not just for Della but also for Joe, Eve, and Pauline. "Let's get out of here," Della whispered. "I'm seeing Ed Egan. So sorry, Joe."

"I understand, Della. You're his girlfriend, and I'm happy to leave early. But are you sure you want him at all? You seem afraid."

"We argue a lot, mostly about his former women, but we've been together since he returned to Ireland. He says it's fate, but Ed is controlling, and I just wanted a night out with someone like you without suspicion or questions."

At once, a wave of guilt hit her. Here was this nice guy who liked her. Was Joe just a test case to assess her feelings for Ed?

Eve came across. "I said you'd get into trouble. It was a great night until now." Her words tumbling out in anger made Della ashamed.

"Don't think he saw me."

During the forty-minute drive home, Eve did not stop complaining; Della was stupid. "Shut up, Eve," Della said, mortified her sister was lecturing her like a ten-year-old in front of a man. "I'm sorry, Joe," she repeated.

"Don't worry, Della. Maybe I'll see you nearer home next time." What a lovely man. But she had not allowed herself to meet others once Ed came back. Misguided? Too many negatives were now confronting Della. And she did not know what to do. Without rules and her dulled obeisance, she felt lost.

Bridie lectured again. God, why did Eve have to report everything? Concern, she supposed. Here she was, upsetting the even tenor of their farming lives—the lambing, a cow calving, a new tractor to trial, all the normal events in rural Ireland at its best. Della was a miscreant of sorts, upsetting the natural order. Bridie's voice cut in. "There's an old saying, *'between two stools, you'll fall to the ground'*. I'm just trying to advise you."

"Only last week, you told me to take things easy with Ed. He's going out at night and not telling me."

"Have sense, that's all I'm saying. Try to find common ground."

"I'm not a basket case." If they kept inferring she was unstable, how would she be anything else?

"Eve, do you have to worry Mam like that?"

"Look, Della, we saw your state when you came home. Crying at the least thing, sensitive, unable to make choices. We have to watch over you."

Two weeks passed, and then Ed drove into the yard one Saturday. Inside, the girls were preparing to go to Longford to hear Larry Cunningham. Rather than let him face her mother's ire, Della ran out quickly and sat in the passenger seat. "Well. It's been a while."

No smile softened his expression. "If we're going to make it work. Della, there must be honesty between us. Agreed?"

A swathe of guilt washed over her. Yes, honesty was best. Despite going out with another boy, she did not want to finish with Ed. She waited for him to say he had seen her from the balcony. He didn't. She stuttered out the details. Only a slight glimmer of annoyance crossed his chiselled features.

"Well, I follow the bands. That's why I was there, Della. Not that I was with anyone else." No recrimination. She wished he would say more, even argue.

"Want to see a film instead tonight?"

"The girls are off dancing, but yes."

Here she was, soft as putty again. If *he* wanted, yes, *she* would.

They drove to the cinema in uncomfortable silence. Where had he been for two weeks? With whom had he spent his nights? Oh, let it go. She was guilty, too.

She liked it when he slid his hand along the back of her seat during the showing of Doctor Zhivago. As the twisted love story unfolded, she sniffled and accepted Ed's white handkerchief.

"He never saw his wife again," she whispered. Once more, kernels of need shimmied inside her. Why did the man always get away with infidelity? Well, Omar Sharif was another gorgeous man.

At the house later, Ed said, "OK for Saturday in Fairyland, Della?" Was he dangling her because she had been unfaithful, or didn't it matter? Again, Ed's inscrutable mask on his handsome features revealed nothing of his mind.

Later, he did not come in at the house but kissed her cheek softly. An ugly image of a smirking, coquettish, shiny-faced doll danced in Della's head again. He'd probably kissed and done whatever that type allowed during his two weeks' absence. He lived far enough away to do as he pleased. "You don't know what Ed does during the week," Eve had warned.

Duplicity and lies were already shaping their relationship. Six months ago, she had lived in a place where honesty and openness were vital. A voice came from the depth of memory, 'Beware of Satan's red fork, Sister. It probes deep.' Mother Bonaventure.

Ed seemed distant when he picked her up Sunday evening. As they jived to Johnny Flynn's music, she noticed the Lynch girl brushing close during dances. His smile towards her seemed to come from one side of his face, away from Della. During the next slow waltz, Ed swung her round with a three-step on corners, intent on his steps. Della floundered. He frowned.

"He's gone off me," she told Eve in the Ladies.

"Well, be cool. Assert yourself. Don't be a weed." A weed!

But in the car, Ed said he had to travel to Dublin the next day to see a machine. He drove past their usual gateway and said a brief goodbye at the house.

CHAPTER 7

E d did not phone. A week passed. She could not ditch the negativity, the persistent gloomy thoughts. It was as if she were a puppet he dangled on a string according to his whims. So, when Eve said they might go to the cinema the following weekend instead of dancing, Della cheered. Something different.

The Ritz cinema, perched on the bank of the River Shannon, drew hordes to its showings. With RTE, the sole TV channel, there was little variety for entertainment besides the black and white Zane Grey films. Della recalled her dad describing the growth of cinema in Boston: *Gone with the Wind, The Greatest Show on Earth*, plus Wild Westerns.

It was The Amorous Adventures of Moll Flanders tonight, starring Kim Novak. Della laughed along with the viewers in the high-ceilinged building beside the Shannon's lapping waters. How good to immerse oneself in something new. Soon, she relaxed in a bubble wherein neither arguments nor scrutiny pervaded her existence. She was ready to let him go. So be it. Her spirits rose. Tomorrow, she would plan.

On Friday midday, Ed rang and asked if he could call on Saturday. He had been busy and late getting home from work. Put it behind us, he said. Mingled feelings took hold of Della: delight, fear, and shades of anxiety at the thought of more arguments. "It was nothing, really, Ed. I just went to a dance with a neighbour and the girls."

"Don't go back on it again, Della. I've thought a lot and want us to continue."

A relief? What he'd done or with whom, she had to bury in a mire of obliviousness. She told the family. "All's fine. Back on again."

Eve stood up and pointed a finger. "Up, down, happy, sad. What is it with you, Della? I'm tired of your moods. You surely do not believe he was sitting in at night, a man like him who follows the bands all over the country? You are like a lovesick teenager. Cop on to yourself." The tone in her sister's voice stung. "Dad's right; break free. Go before you're in too deep."

"You're suggesting I'm stupid," Della said. Well, in a way, she had not lived out her teenage years as normal.

Dad cleared his throat. "I've been in touch with Olive Kenny in the city. She will let you live with her for a while if you accept that Civil Service job you applied for last week."

His statement fell like lead on her ears. "Gosh, Dad, that's a shock. It would help if you had told me first." Not that it made a difference. And he cared for her welfare.

"Just what you need, girl."

"Ed won't let me go."

"Then you're a fool." That her father should use a word untypical of his nature was hurtful.

"But Ed loves me."

"Della, the only thing you know about love is based on fairytales—face facts. Ed is domineering and controlling. He comes and goes at will. Show some character." Jim got up, grabbed the whitethorn stick from behind the dresser and set off to count the cattle. No comment came from her mother.

Ed seemed happy to see her when he came on Saturday. But doubt, an unseen presence, hung heavy in the car as they set off for Boyle in a stilted atmosphere. She ventured nervously. "Sive and Eileen, a girl from the course, and I are thinking of going to the city to work. Our families will give us enough money to rent a small flat until we're sorted. Dad wants me to live with a neighbour there instead."

"For feck's sake, shouldn't you have talked to me first? Aren't we a couple?" His swearing and sudden outburst both startled and frightened her.

"A couple? Talk? I haven't seen you for weeks. You come and go at will. I've written to offices, hospitals, hotels, and banks, but there's nothing here for me."

Daring to look at him, she saw the thunder in his expression. "Think of the good times. You can visit me and see my cousins in Skerries by the sea at weekends." The worst over, she waited.

"Dublin is over a hundred miles away. Petrol costs money."

"Our recent problems prove we need space apart. I'm unsure I can trust you, but I'd like some freedom. I've been home for seven months, and it's time to move on to the next goal: a career. Let me go, Ed. Please." The pleading note in her voice brought a sense of shame. Assert yourself, she mentalised.

But part of Ed's mystique lay in his ability to absorb things in silence, to wait, think, and then communicate. Right now, he did just that.

"It was you who went behind my back, remember? Be clear. You're going to work, nothing else, mind. It's not ideal, and I may not get up every weekend, but I'll try."

As she breathed relief, he said, "Would you like to visit my parents to see where I live before you go?"

His people? Why now, after the uncertainty of the previous weeks? To commit her to his people, his place, his anchor? But go with the flow, she thought—must not doubt everything. Her family did not see this side of his character. Just as she was steeling herself to leave, pick up the threads of city life, and distance herself from him, he did this. Either it was genuine love or to establish binding links, Della could not fathom. Ed's economic phraseology, once again, left her wondering and unsure.

"A bit soon, Ed. We're not engaged or anything."

"Don't you want it? Us? I love you, and you love me. Isn't that enough?"

"Well, I thought it was, but we've changed over the months. You're used to getting your way, and I'm not strong enough to disagree."

"That's what I like about you, Della. You don't argue, and you differ from others." A compliment! He admired her virtues. But others? What others? Faceless girls without names. Never mind, she was going to Dublin. And she *would* find herself. Partly pleased, partly anxious, she wondered if he just wanted a suppliant woman to marry into his family home. Oh, the very thought!

One evening, towards the end of August 1965, Ed picked up Della and headed east towards Carrick-on-Shannon. Again, she sensed a determination in him to achieve something, in this instance, to introduce her to his family. He appeared reticent to talk on the journey, a familiar characteristic when his mind was on serious matters. She noted the hooded expression, perhaps a sign of his reluctance to divulge activities since their last meeting. Frustrating, but had it not been that inscrutability his attraction from the start?

On the edge of the town, he veered right by Cortober towards Kilmore, the northern part of County Roscommon, sparse and alluvial. Here, smallholdings pickled the landscape, and little white-dash bungalows squatted in fields where cows and sheep apportioned themselves, tribal fashion, across the countryside. Mixed farming, Ed explained. But, to Della, it was bleak and uninviting. Surely, he did not live in such a backwater. Shades of melancholy gripped her, but she could not ask.

Ed rarely spoke about his parents, except that his mother was approachable and friendly, and his father was a taciturn type, entrenched in his ways, though a voracious reader. One sister, Lena, lived locally; another one, between Carrick-on-Shannon and Boyle, Mona taught English in Germany. Just a year older than Ed, Ann was nursing in New York. The eldest, Jo, had emigrated to Australia with her Kerry husband. Ed was the youngest, the spoilt only son, no doubt.

"They don't have a television, but we'd buy one later if you wanted. My father reads. My mother sews and makes quilts but isn't a good cook."

"Ed, it sounds like your father is set in his ways. Like you, stubborn." Her little laugh came out jittery and brittle.

"We don't get on. He judges me and asks how much I make on sales and outgoings."

"Sounds as if he cares." Any snippet of information, albeit dealt out sparingly, was important. A thought came. Would she become entangled in their disputes as Ed's wife if father and son argued? Stop, she told her whirring brain. It's a visit, no more. And what did Ed do at night? Sit at home? She thought not.

As the car turned off the main road, steep hills rose on the distant horizon, in contrast to the flat, marshy landscape behind them. Far down in the valley, an egg-shaped lake glistened in the evening sun, its gold and blue waters mingling into one brilliant phantasmagoria.

"It's stunning. I had no idea you lived in such a place."

"I don't. We're not there yet." Could he not lift her spirits a little?

As they descended from the higher terrain, the scene changed from picturesque to bare, with no further sight of the lake on the western edge. Instead, a dispersed scattering of tiny, slated houses with bolted-on outhouses flew by before Ed halted at the gate of a white two-storey building, in front of which mature shrubs dotted a green lawn.

"Not bad," Della muttered. "Except for those black trees so close to the house. They remind me of the high convent walls and dense plantation."

Ed's mother, Molly, opened the front door, a smile lighting up her withered, once-pretty face. Wisps of iron-grey hair fell about her features, remnants of a grown-out perm. Behind her, his father offered a hand in welcome. Shorter than his son, Della supposed the older man's back stooped from hard work and age. That he needed his son home was clear. Quenching her previous negativity, she smiled and shook their hands.

Inside, a hallway led to a big kitchen-cum-dining room with neat, shiny cupboards. It was modern and comfortable. Ed's mother made tea served with raisin bread and jam at a table by the window, then placed the kettle back on the range, ready for the last meal in true country fashion.

All the while, Pat Egan talked. He managed a tailoring business in Carrick for a cousin during his youth. But he, too, had to return to the farm when his father slowed down. As the older man animatedly described his achievements, Della noted Ed's silence, an added tension in the room.

"I'm proud of my time running the business. Had to do the books and the end-of-year accounts, oversee twenty tailors, and the work output." The blend of nostalgia and dignity in his voice indicated an intelligent recall of a previous life he was rightly proud of. So why did Ed not value his father more?

"See that plantation around the house? I sowed it forty years ago to fend off the wind blowing in from the bogs." Della looked again at the shadowy, green, dense trees encircling the building. Few specks of light penetrated the thick foliage. Only the birds perched on top could survey the countryside. Pat continued, "The thing is, they cast long shadows into the house in winter."

But it was not winter now, and the nearness of the giant trees was claustrophobic. Della felt a knot tighten in her stomach as if the shadows of the enormous trees were sucking her in.

The back door opened. A small woman with straggly white hair and deep-set eyes walked in. Around her ample frame hung a crossover apron down to her short legs. At the sight of Della, a smile lit the woman's face.

"You must be Della. I've heard all about you from our boy here. I'm Margie Malone. I live next door." Next door was the long, slated house a hundred yards away.

Our boy, Ed? Oh, my God. Not only in his mother's eyes but also in Margie's did the sun shine from Ed's backside. Della shook the gnarled hand as Margie moved to sit by Molly in front of the warm range. She must have known of Della's visit, and come for a look.

"What's the *besht* news ye have, Margie?" Molly's thick guttural sounds fell awkwardly on Della's ears. Oh God, were they all like that around here?

"Well, I was in the garden today and saw May Shannon goin' to town on the bike. Then, two hours later, she passed with a parcel on the carrier. What was in it, do ye think? Where did she get the money?"

"Well, I don't know," Molly said. "Surely the mother got a letter from Jimmy in England. He *must* have sent a few pounds." Together, they continued to obfuscate the language and ponder on one of the grand mysteries in the parish. A girl had brought home something from town. Why? Where had she got the money?

Della listened. *I'm going mad. This can't be real. These women live for gossip.* Their insularity would stifle and dull her spirit. Neighbours, bikes, and parcels. She wanted to shout aloud, 'For goodness' sake, listen to the news about the Vietnam protests in America, anything but local trivia'. These women depended on the radio for world news, but their pedestrianism was more notable than any world event. She wanted to run away from them, from this house.

After two hours of being pickled with questions she did not care to answer about her future, a job, and marriage, they said goodbye and headed back towards Leam and Reillys.

"Can't see me there, Ed. Rent a flat in town." He had to know her feelings. Better now than later. Later?

"It's my home and will be yours, too." His firm tone told her he would brook no argument and that underneath the facade of charm lay a steely determination she might never budge. The son moulded in the same grit as the older one would prescribe her life, too.

"Hold on, Ed. I'm not sure about any of it. But, for a start, what would I do all day?"

"Help with the housework, feed the calves, and milk the cows. My mother is getting feeble."

"I've never milked a cow in my life. So, what do you think I am?" Her stomach lurched. Did he expect her to be a servile, pliant little wifey home all day with older people?

"You grew up on a farm."

"But I did none of that stuff. My parents and the men did the work. I know nothing about animals except that they're smelly! In the convent, I was preparing to become a teacher."

No response. Della glanced sideways but could not determine his expression behind the sunglasses. Only the stiff mouth showed he would no longer discuss his home. She was a disappointment. He had wanted her to meet his parents and like them, but she did not want to live there or with them.

As for Margie, one thing puzzled her. "Is Margie married? Who is Peter?"

"Her brother, they live together. She leaves each night in time to open the gate for him on return from the pub."

"Drunk? Is she afraid of him?" The idea of the little woman holding a gate open for a car to pass through conjured up images, both primitive and harsh. Della's mother, Bridie, often helped after milking, standing at the yard gate as the stream of cows passed out onto the green slopes by the Shannon. They shared tasks with equal familiarity.

"Yes." No more, just that. Again, the shutters came down. But Margie must be another woman who had to do as her master said. A thought chilled. She must *never*, ever end up like them. Right now, she would ignore the tumult raging in her brain about an unpredictable future that might never materialise.

On arrival in Reillys, Ed said goodbye. It was late. "See you on Sunday," he said with a quick kiss. If he had doubts about them as a couple, he did not say. But the visit had not been to his liking. Or hers. Were they now drifting into an anaphasic state at opposite spindle ends? Of course, but she *was* going away.

Back inside, her mother listened to the account of the visit, a frown creasing her forehead. Bridie's disapproval filled the kitchen. "You know little about farming, Della, except for what you saw here as a child." Sipping her usual night-time cocoa, her mother nibbled on a Marietta biscuit, always a pack in the house for when the stomach rebelled.

"You played in the fields when we saved hay and sometimes helped after school. But Eve is the actual farmer, knows her stuff, and is deep into youth farm activities, public speaking competitions, gardening, and drama groups."

"I love him, and he wants me to stay here, but I will go to the city and see where life leads us afterwards."

With the sight of relief on her mother's face came Macbeth's prophetic words. *Tomorrow, and tomorrow and tomorrow ...*

CHAPTER 8

O n the last Sunday in August, Jim drove the girls to the city with bags of clothes, pillows, sheets, and food packed into his old Vauxhall. On sight of the dingy building on Harrington Street, his face reddened, true to character when he was upset. Della waited. It came.

"How can you live in a basement flat accessible from the street above? And what do any of you three know about the city? I must be mad letting you come."

Sive's sister, Máire, who worked in the city, had scoured the papers and found the low-rent basement flat. With enough money from the parents until they got jobs, the three would, hopefully, manage after that. Jim descended the stone steps and followed the girls inside. Three beds in one room, a tiny kitchenette and sink with rusty taps, a toilet, and a greening shower artifice completed the 'flat'.

"It's great, Dad, and enough until we earn decent money and move on." Had she not learned in the novitiate never to complain? Hardship, the holy ones had instilled, was character building. Fair enough, but their bare cells were hygienic and spotless; this was on the bottom of the heap.

"Great, my eye. I'll not sleep easy. How can I tell Sive's and Eileen's parents their daughters are in a dingy room yards below street level?

"Say nothing. It's an adventure." Would he ever leave?

"Another weight of worry, Della. You should have stayed in the convent."

Her father's comment stung like the bees back on the lawn at home; the pain soused with vinegar until it faded. But Jim's concern for all three showed his weariness after the long drive to the city and unloading bags. Later, when they settled, he would be at ease. He kissed Della goodbye and said, "Go to Mass on Sundays, and be good."

"Yes, Dad." She stood on the kerb and watched the old black car setting off towards Dolphins Barn and home. One who enjoyed company, he would find the hundred-mile journey tedious.

Inside, the girls were filling the chest of drawers and hanging clothes in the sole wardrobe. Then, a handle fell off the dressing table. Sive laughed, "San Quentin or what, girls?"

"It's basic," Eileen agreed. "What the heck? We're in Dublin. Exciting."

After a tea of ham and cheese sandwiches, they lay on the beds as the sky darkened outside. On the street above, feet rattled by on the footpath. "I wish the windows had bars," Sive said, "Your dad was right, Della. It's basic. Worse than boarding school without the fun."

"Listen," Della whispered. "There's something in the corner. Hear the noise. It's a ghost. These old city buildings have secrets where murders happened."

"Oh, shut up, Della, don't be so dramatic. Only water trickling from a tap." But it took a while to get to sleep, each coughing in response to the others.

After breakfast the following day, Sive went up the dimly lit back stairs to ask the landlady about the dripping water. She tapped on the door of the sitting room and prepared her question. A small, withered-faced woman opened the door. Sive told the girls afterwards she'd "seen a shrivelled old witch up top." Hesitantly, she asked about the noise.

"There's a fault in the system," Mrs O'Meara said. "And when someone runs a bath, the water drips from all the taps in the building."

"Thanks, Mam," Sive muttered, kicking herself for not knowing what else to say. Water, taps, problems. How could she know about such things?

"Don't care," Della said, back in the basement. "It's freedom and independence, and sorry to disappoint; no ghosts."

"We have just enough money to live on until the end of the month," Sive said, practical and grounded. You learned how to make food last when you grew up in a family of seven. "Let's buy the necessities for now."

In a small grocery shop on the street corner, they found a few essentials to add to the potatoes, brown bread, bacon, sausages, beans, and more that the three mothers had packed into brown paper bags. They would learn to cope.

The following evening, Sive's sister called on the way home from her sales job at Arnott's. "Get out and walk along the streets, sample city life," Máire suggested. "But avoid the Med student hops because *they know everything* and could trick a girl. The Ags and the Irrawaddies are popular too, and you can walk to the hall at the top of Harcourt Street, only ten minutes away."

Great. Avoid the Meds. Tosh. "But dances cost money, Máire. We must mind ours," Della said.

"Not much, about five shillings to get in."

"Right. Let's go. This is the first time I've felt truly free since leaving Sligo. We'll soon have jobs and money to spend on everything." Then, seeing the amused look on her cousin's face, she added. "Time to move on, Máire."

The older girl left, content that her sister was safe.

"And what about Ed? Will you keep him on a string?" Eileen queried.

"He's supposed to be coming up next weekend. Meanwhile, let's get to that student dance—no need to dwell on him now. We'll get Mass in the Carmelite Church in Clarendon Street on Sunday. Dad said it's the nearest."

Eileen shook her blonde curls. "Della, I don't get it. You preach to us yet want excitement. Right?"

Sive's huge violet eyes lit up with mischief, "Wait until Ed arrives, and she won't be so strict."

"Thankfully, he won't come every weekend."

"So why are you glad, Della? You seemed so happy when he came home from Scotland, and you two were together. What happened?"

"I went with someone else, and he found out and didn't return for weeks. And although he wants us to marry, he sees others. Honestly, we needed space to find ourselves again. I want to date other men, but he is obsessed with the idea we belong together. He even took me to meet his parents last week." There she'd voiced her worries aloud.

"Well, you're miles away from him now. Let's live!"

Over the next week, they walked the streets of Dublin, always ending their trudge in Grafton Street to watch employees tumbling out of offices into Bewley's for a quick coffee before boarding buses for the outskirts. Eileen said they would soon do likewise. Happy days ahead. As one, they yearned for a bustling life in a big arena and for Della to be as far away from contemplation and 'peace' as possible.

On the corner of the Green, Sive spotted an ad for a receptionist in a stationery shop. She went inside, filled out a form, and afterwards declared her first step to a new life.

"No Civil Service for me," she boasted. "Drab and dull, my aunt said, and she was there for forty years." But Eileen and Della had applied to the Civil Service as planned. They would hear within a week, as jobs were plentiful. Boring or not, it would lead to better things.

"Don't care," Eileen said. "We need work and a constant wage. The soles of my shoes have worn thin. Can't afford new ones."

"Don't get depressed," Sive offered. "We'll look back at this time as an experience. And we're getting to know the city."

Ed was coming at the weekend. He'd rung Della on the number she'd given of a phone box on the street. He needed a place to sleep. Della ventured upstairs; the landlady had one room on the top storey of the house. Up close in the daylight, Della peered at the woman. What a sight - the skin around the woman's mouth and cheeks, ingrained with brown and ugly nicotine stains.

"Yes, it's away from you girls in the basement. No hanky-panky business, mind." The face creased into a wistful expression.

From a polite distance, Della said the room was fine.

Ed's expected arrival became an anti-climax. As one, all three cleaned and polished the few bits of furniture and bleached the grimy, rusty toilet bowl. He mustn't see it as anything other than pleasant.

Six o'clock, then seven came. At eight, Della was despondent. Sive said, "He's not coming, Della. Let's go to the Irrawaddies."

"I daren't. You two go ahead."

The doorbell rang. Della ran and opened it. Ed, on the doorstep, stood tall and slim under the streetlight. Della threw her arms around him.

"Gosh, Della, slow down," he said, grinning. "I had to sell a machine before I left, plus the traffic was heavy on the way here."

His apparent pride in the work and his down-to-earth attitude surprised her. She had expected a more effusive greeting, perhaps a passionate kiss even. But she respected his attitude. Earning a living was paramount, and the added expense of travelling was a nuisance. However, she wanted excitement, and his reference to mundane things lowered the mood. After tea and a sandwich, she said, "Let's go to the club, Ed, and dance."

"We'll all go," Eileen shook her blonde curls in Ed's face. "It's cheap for students, you see." Della mouthed 'shut up' in her direction.

The lights were low in the hall, and students in baggy pants and trainers already cramming available floor space. Ed pulled Della into his arms and led her towards the bandstand. At once, the magic wove its spell. Rocking and rolling, waltzing to dreamy slow dances, they floated around the floor until, at one o'clock, he said, "Let's go back to the flat."

Eileen and Sive would follow later.

Della climbed the stairs to the spare room with Ed. But she would not sleep in it. Her bed was in the basement. His look said otherwise. "I'll change your mind. Come here."

Soon, pent-up passion made her skin burn, cold from the walk back along the street. Outside, the streetlight threw a modicum of brightness into the sparse room. Della pulled away. Was not this precisely what she wanted to avoid? Sin, him overpowering her.

"What is it, Della? You seem different? The night is ours."

"Ed, I want to be me, not the girl who lets you decide."

"I see." The flat tone, heavy in hurt, made her twinge; after all, he'd travelled a long journey to love her.

"Alright, but no silly stuff." He calmed, went quiet, and for a while, he held her close, his kisses light and tender. Nice, she thought. No pressure. After an hour, Della pecked him on the lips and said she'd come up for him in the morning. As she left the room, he whispered, "Something's not right, Della".

Back in the basement, the other two were settling down to sleep. Sive put her head over the cover and said, "What, not staying with Ed?"

"No. It's wrong."

"Wrong! With that god upstairs, who cares?" Their laughter cut deep, though both knew how conscience ate into her being. They were right, but sin was a sin. Outside on the street, the traffic thinned. A tap dripped into the sink in the gloom, the sound dragging her back to *that clock on a convent corridor; tick-tock.*

Sive whispered, "What if Ed doesn't want you any more? Will you mind? You're pushing him away."

"Yes, but no, I don't know." Indecision, uncertainty. She was never sure of him, of them, except that nothing must mar her experience in Dublin.

Della made toast and tea at eight the following morning and served it on the table to Ed in the middle of the bed-sit where the two girls lay sleeping.

"Bit primitive, Della. I hope you get a better place soon."

She saw the room afresh through his eyes: towels on the shower floor, toilet door ajar, and knickers hanging on the rails to dry. She blushed, letting her eyes roam around the kitchen, a hutch in the corner, standing room for one.

"Yes, but it'll do until we earn a decent wage." But if Ed thought the flat a dump, it was.

At Mass in Clarendon Street, Sive, Eileen and Della went to the altar to receive Holy Communion. Ed stayed in the pew. An immediate surge of suspicion sparked inside Della, but she would not ask him about his life at home. Nor would she behave in subservience but instead suggest they be free to do as both wished. From the moment of their reunion, the relationship had been intense. Now, they were at a point to assess it from a different perspective. She'd talk to him before he left.

But, an hour later, sitting at lunch in a café off St. Stephen's Green, Della faltered. Were she to speak her mind entirely, the atmosphere would plummet and destroy their calm. It was early September, leaves turning gold, and streets busy with Sunday window shoppers, glorious Dublin at its best.

"My dad was born here, his father a hotel manager from Wexford. He loves Dublin, as I do. Would you consider living here, Ed?" Holy smokes, that came out unplanned. Drawing his eyes away from the busy street, Ed appeared shocked.

"Not possible, with the farm and the old pair. My business is up and going well." His reference to the parents at once summoned unsavoury images of trees, bogs, and remoteness. A world away from the throbbing city. Della let the silence ride, and over the hour, they sat observing the busyness of the street. Time drifted. Not once did he refer to his night-time activities. "I've got to get home, Della. I'll come again in two weeks."

"Great, Ed, I'll look forward to it." Would she?

Packing his overnight bag in the top room, he ventured. "Della, if you want me to return, you could be more welcoming. I think there's stuff you're not telling me."

"Exactly, Ed, same for you. But so what? Let us be free to do as we please while apart. It'll make us either want to be together or not. See it as a testing time. I haven't queried your movements back home. Neither have I asked for a separation."

She stopped as his expression froze into an icy glare. Better not construe a confrontation that might lead to an immediate break-up. If she were to do as she pleased here, it seemed only fair he did likewise. But she had said it.

The thought was liberating. A hundred miles away, Ed would not know about her conduct.

"You're changing, and I don't like it, Della. First, you wouldn't spend the night with me, and now you want more freedom. You know how I feel about us. We're destined for each other. So, bye. We'll talk next time."

She watched the car speed off towards the West, to his other life. Had she ruined it for them, and did it matter? Turmoil, always turmoil. Never clarity. Destined or not, time would either increase or decrease the ruffles.

Sive got the job in the stationery place on the Green: *McCabe for all typewriters and office stationery models*. A prime location, she could walk across the park to Grafton Street during lunch breaks, browse the shops, and wish.

On Monday, Eileen started work in the Department of Agriculture on Harcourt Street, a short distance from Harrington Street and the flat. Della took a bus to Social Welfare on Store Street by the quays, the soles of her shoes now too thin to pound the pavement. She could not buy a new pair until money came in. End of the month, roll along.

At eight-forty-five, a wave of shyness gripped her. Naïve and inexperienced, she paused outside the tall glass building overlooking the River Liffey. Not nine months since her exit from the enclosure, she was going to work with strangers. Thoughts tumbled through her head like clothes in a drier. Would she be able to do it? Would they accept her? Fears gnawed into the innards of her stomach.

At Reception, an officer checked her name and said he would take her to Records Five, where she would start work. From within the glass bubble soaring upwards, the street below appeared to bustle and busy itself, placing little elves on corners at red lights, crossing over and back in ceaseless motion. Farther on, men were hauling fishing nets from the smaller boats on the quays while big tankers sat in the oily waters, waiting to unload cargo. As the box zoomed upwards towards the sky, trepidation gripped her; a country girl marooned in a glass box over the city.

An official led her along corridors, then stopped at a section where a thin, tall woman named Sheila, explained the process. Each form she completed would entitle an applicant to special benefits. In the Section, six people smiled a welcome. A mix of features swam into focus—fat, thin, big eyes, small nose and more. Della smiled and read the forms.

Throughout the morning, gossip rose and fell, and women shared tittle-tattle about boyfriends or, most times, a lack of them. Sunday walks in the Dublin mountains made up a good weekend. Mere trivia. Yes, trivia.

More snippets floated. Mediocre details of life, love, and losses. Of an age when life's possibilities were slipping past, the women epitomised what Della had always heard of the Civil Service - dull, dreary and unimaginative. Would she, too, melt into that blob of humanity, forever lost in a parallel sphere of form-filling and longing? Cáit, a pale mouse-blonde, asked her to join the Legion of Mary. This Church group visited and supported needy families.

"Later, when I'm used to the city," she replied. "I'm hoping to attend night classes."

At the eleven o'clock break, the entire floor trooped out towards the lifts, wherein they zoomed upwards to the top floor canteen for food and drinks.

"Gosh, what a relief from the tedium," she commented to Millie, a friendly girl from County Clare. Perhaps not a good start. Over twenty minutes, the group consumed an assortment of cream buns and chocolate, regardless of weight, which they laughingly blamed on a sedentary job. Della tried a hot dog, and although she had never eaten sausages in a roll, she fell into an instant addiction.

"Do you intend to stay in this job, Millie?" she asked the older girl.

"No, but it's a wage, and I want my home. Been living with my parents since I was born." She must be twenty-eight, had dark hair, wore square glasses, and was chatty and helpful.

Della reckoned that a quiet life in a little red-brick terraced house would make either happiness or a lonely decline for most of them. And the men would stagnate in departments until they retired with a substantial government pension. But no. She would *not* stay in the Civil Service but soon apply for a uni course.

She found a telephone box near O'Connell Street at six o'clock and rang home. "Dad, just two floors above ours is the Minister for Social Welfare's office." He would like that.

Jim sounded pleased with the seat of power association. "You might see him one day, Della. The Civil Service offers decent pensions and promotion opportunities. Yes, sign up for a night course. Dublin is the place. Stay there." What he meant was to be ambitious and ditch the Ed factor.

It was on a Wednesday night she met Neil. During a hiatus in the dance sequence, she noticed a young man in a dark suit looking over. Della felt attractive in a figure-hugging grey dress, hair loose over her shoulders and eyes darkened with velvety mascara. She smiled. He smiled back, then came across. The man seemed 'nice' with dark eyes, strong cheekbones, and tendrils of black hair falling over a high, intelligent forehead. No superlatives came to mind. Just nice. A good word, but not how she'd refer to Ed.

When he asked her to dance, she nodded. Though less flashy than Ed on the floor, his rhythm was easy to follow. Della relaxed.

"Like a drink?" he asked. "Get to know each other?"

His voice was easy on the ear, drawing her further into his personality. Over the next hour, they sat in the corner, unpicking details of her breakdown, subsequent re-emergence into a changed world, boredom in the Civil Service, and her commitment to Ed. No adverse comment fell from his lips, thinner than Ed's but nice, happy lips. Just one year older than herself, Neil was a final-year veterinary student from Donegal. Later, she would tell the girls about his attentiveness and genuine concern as she stumbled over the bad bits of her past. That he had aroused new emotions, she kept to herself.

Afterwards, they walked, hand in hand, along Harcourt Street towards the flat. He did not ask to come in, but if he might call the following Wednesday. She said, yes, please. He brushed a light kiss on her cheek. No pressure, no touching, and no remorse. Disloyal to Ed? Probably.

In bed, sleep was elusive. The thought of harbouring a secret burned her cheeks and causing her heart overstep its beats. For now, she would keep Neil in the inner regions of her soul and see how things panned out. Almost like a bank deposit – safe.

The following day, Eileen and Sive expressed delight. "Good on ye, girl. Move on. But you're too trusting, Della. He might not have been safe." Sive cared.

"You'll have a man at the weekends and another during the week. Well done, Della. Nothing like an ex-nun for a bit of fun." Their squeals hit the ceiling, Sive's index finger shaking in imitation of Ed laying down rules. Then, as one, they collapsed on the bed. Life was looking good.

CHAPTER 9

At the Irrawaddies the following week, a girl tapped Della on the shoulder. From amid the crowd, her face, familiar from school, smiled in recognition. Della quickly drew back from Neil, fluffed a wavering 'hello' and stepped onto the side.

Ann Conlon said she was in the capital for a wedding but returning to Boyle in the morning. "You're going out with Ed Egan from Cortober. I've seen you at the dances back home." Heavy in suspicion, the pointed, deliberate comment brought a rush of embarrassment. Della stalled. How might she answer?

"Yeah, Ed comes up twice a month but is busy. I've got to know people at the dances here. Nice crowd." Hoping she'd pulled it off. Della asked what Ann was doing - working in a bank, a friendly crowd, pleasant enough. *Oh, go away*, Della fumed inwardly.

Drawing Neil to the seats at the back of the hall, she unloaded her dilemma, which he absorbed with equanimity.

"You can decide whether you want us to be close, Della. We have similar values, and you need something beyond the ordinary. Let life take us where it will. A year to my degree, time to live and learn."

What a lovely thing to say. And how different personalities could be? Ed, the confident one, dominated decisions, but Neil was the type that *sensed* feelings. The freedom he generated suggested Della needed to discover herself on a fresh path in life. But she loved Ed. Love? Or obsession? Here in the city, she could assess her feelings without pressure, removed from the intensity of their relationship.

"Just enjoy it while you can. Ed can't keep tabs on you, so you don't have to drop him," Eileen advised. But in Della's head, a voice whispered, *a lie is always sinful.*

When she opened the door on Friday evening, Della knew he knew. No smile or even a kiss. Hard temper lines on his face made her shudder. Eileen said, "Sive, fancy a fag?" Then, like the little mice running around the floorboards at night, they fled for a cigarette.

"I bumped into Ann Conlon last night in the Abbey, or rather she bumped into me. She told me she met you at a dance with a man. So what do you take me for, Della, a pushover? Cheating in Dublin while I come to see you as often as possible. I don't need this or you."

Scrounging for an excuse, she stuttered. "Don't lecture me. I was only dancing with someone. You're out too, seeing others, I suspect."

"So, we finish it. That what you want?" Now the accuser, Ed Egan, the perennial charmer, would brook no argument. *Oh God, no.* Ed, the handsome man few could match, was about to flip out of her life. Why had she not thought it all through? Had his image not carried her on wings of hope when darkness enveloped her mind? Now, he was about to ditch her. *I hate myself; I'm a ditherer. What can I do?* A momentary prayer flitted upwards to the heavens. *Guide me?*

"Well, no, yes, not sure." *Finish? Yes? No? Could she bear it if Ed ditched her? It was too much of a risk to take.*

"Ann deliberately came to me and was shocked by your conduct, Della."

"She should mind her business. The same crowd goes to the student dances every week."

"I'll have to think about it, about us."

Two days eked out in a whirl of rows, barely resolved, even when they were close or rather lukewarm. Ed's anger, emitted in temper bursts hung like a cloud over everything they did. Shopping in Grafton Street for trousers evoked an argument. He wanted a tight black one, but Della said it was too tight. They drank coffee in Bewley's. He watched where she looked and at whom. It was as if she were lying on the floor again during Prostrations, confessing faults. But, instead of a severe nun administering punishment, a sharp-faced man sat in judgment.

Sunday midday, he loaded his bag, still grim and cold. "If you want us to continue, leave this city and get a transfer nearer home."

"There's no Civil Service in Boyle or Carrick, and I've only just got used to being here."

"Try Sligo or even Galway; only an hour's drive for me, but find one, or we're finished. And I'm almost certain there's a Labour Exchange in Carrick."

"But I like Dublin and plan to study here." Her attempt at resistance came through quick breaths. Mother Bonaventure, transmuted into Ed's body, was dictating again. It was not a broken plate this time, just broken trust. Her comment made him stop the tirade, but she might as well have slapped his face.

"Plans? And I'm not part of them? Thought we had a future together."

Have courage, she told herself. "This is the first time I've settled since my breakdown, and it's not fair you insisting I leave the city."

"Well, don't go dancing or seeing others. I'm warning you." He hopped into the car and zoomed off without a glance or a wave.

Della cried all evening, Ed's demand a sword through her heart. To forsake the city she loved would mean letting go of the opportunity to study journalism. And she would lose Neil. His face floated before her in complete contrast to Ed's. Kind, caring and gentle.

Sive urged, "You fit in here. We have fun. Let him go."

Eileen added, "Why do you care, Della? You're happy and light-hearted, even in this dump."

Della sobbed. "I can't. I love Ed. And he said that during those four years, while I was away, he thought about me and wrote letters. The nuns let me have one, but no more."

Sive burst out. "Love, my eye. If you loved him, Neil would not attract you. You're an idiot. He'll rule your life. Ed is cruel, Della, and doesn't care what you want. Neil is a nicer, better guy."

"I like Neil, but not in the same way."

"For Chrissakes, Della, the same way? You haven't got that far with him yet. Your attraction to Ed blinds your judgment."

"I'll return to my parents and ask for their advice."

Her father was waiting on the platform at Boyle's station on Friday night. Soon, they were sitting down to a rich Irish stew dinner. And as the smell of onions and brown meat wafted around the kitchen, they chatted about Dublin, Jim's birthplace - always special to him. Della told them about the dances, the young vet she liked, and that Ed had found out about him. Listening intently to Della, her father's face reddened, then paled.

"Della, I tried to stop you from entering the convent and was glad when you left. I worried about your quick commitment to Ed, and now you're giving in to his demands. You're vulnerable and hasty. Do you want an overlord, someone to decide for you?"

"No, Dad," she whispered, tears welling.

Bridie passed a hanky. "Della, I'll pray you make the right decision." No recriminations, just love. Eve puffed disgust and something about backbone while rattling the dishes in the sink.

Ed came the following night and appeared happy she was back in his kingdom. No expression of rebuke passed his lips. Instead, he seemed eager to express love, to hold her. During the dance, he murmured, "It'll be like this when we're married. Let's spend Sunday together before you get the train." He'd uttered *it* again. Married, or in Della's mind, a word connoting enclosure and prison walls. But once again, his magnetism enveloped her in its mesh. Born out of self-assuredness, Ed wielded power to which she readily assented. Away from Dublin, she was again the malleable, compliant girl he wanted. An internal voice whispered O*h, my God, you'll be on Valium again.*

On Sunday evening, he took her to the train. "Be sensible, Della. Please think of us. See you in two weeks."

Over the two days, she had resisted asking where he went or with whom. An unspoken agreement hung between them, gossamer thin - they belonged to each other. Her life without Ed, a reincarnated god in Eileen's imagery, was unimaginable. Less than a year ago, she entered a changing world without an idea of a future. Then, he came along and painted a magical picture of everlasting love. But the choice of rural domesticity or a thriving metropolis brought a fresh flush of anxiety. The quiet respect Neil showed her, deep and supportive, had come when most needed, but Ed, a hot-blooded man, aroused feelings dormant for over four years. His constant insistence was a force too powerful to resist. Ambition alone stood in the way. Hers.

On Monday, the workload was heavy. Not until coffee break did Della pluck up the courage to ask her colleagues for advice. Of the six, just two had men; others yearned. "Don't let him go, Della. Get a transfer," one said. A single girl in her thirties, she longed for children before her life cycle waned. "Only you can decide, Della, but a shame you'd leave so soon," another added.

At dinner, Sive and Eileen tried. "It's a terrible mistake, Della," her cousin insisted. "You'll miss the shops, the parks, the dances, us."

The word 'us' hit hardest. "But I can't let Ed down. I've promised, and it would be wrong to rescind." No matter how she chose, pain was inevitable. If she left the city, precious newfound freedom and the opportunity to study further would dissipate. But losing a loved one might cast her into an unbearable abyss if she did not.

Sive despaired. "You felt obliged to enter the convent, and now you're obliged again. Your dad said to slow down, stay, and study."

"Might get on a course in Galway."

"You won't," Eileen said. "You'll marry him and live out your days with an enormous family and nothing but hardship." One of seven, she vowed never to enslave herself to bottles, nappies, and constant washing.

"I can't save money here, can I?" A flimsy excuse but all she could muster. Both girls shook their heads.

Della did not attend the Wednesday night dance. Neil asked after her. Sive deterred him. Della had the flu. Flu? Well, something or other. The following week, no better. He came to the flat. Della told him the truth and cringed at the genuine concern on his face.

"I'm so sorry, Neil, but I can't break my promise to Ed. He depends on me."

"From what Sive told me, Della, he owns you, not depends on you."

The wetness on her face drew a look of the kind Ed never showed, a mixture of sincerity and emotion; unique qualities in young men. But there was no choice. She offered a weak goodbye, closed the door, and went to bed. A young man pushed a slip of paper onto the mat; *Neil Conry: 14 Rathgar Road, Dublin.*

Eileen said, "That boy was nice, Della." The words floated undisputed in the room, and she could not pretend they were wrong.

In a pocket of her case under the bed was a box of pills, untouched since they came to Dublin. Della shook four from the packet and swallowed them with a gulp of water, enough to blot out faces: Ed's, Neil's, and Mother Benedict's, the latter disapproving and vexed. Within minutes, she felt herself wafting into a dream wherein angels dipped low and lifted her from a house in the trees to somewhere bright, a citadel of love.

"Della, wake up, wake up." A voice thrust into the dream: It was Sive, crying, hysterical. Eileen's hand bit into her shoulder - hard, insistent; her face, white and fearful, floating over and back. "The doctor's here. Wake up."

A grey-haired man was bending over her face, pulling at her eyelids. Next, he stuck a metal spoon thingy in her mouth and tut-tutted, "Silly girl, no more Valium for you." Then, accepting two pounds from Sive, he left.

Eileen was distraught. "Della, we've been out of our minds with worry. You're the first to get up every morning, put on the kettle, and call us for cereal. Thank God I woke before eight. You were facing the wall in your bed. I shook you, but you didn't respond. I roared at Sive. We panicked and thought the worst. I ran to the house four doors away, with the brass plate showing Dr M. McKenzie on it. Luckily, it was near." Eileen stopped for breath.

Sive took over. "Some doctor. That grotty little man carried a small dirty bag down the steps to the flat, made you swallow salty water, and left again. No concern, no bedside manner. He looked around the bedsit with disgust. God knows what he thought of us."

Through a muggy haze, Della muttered, "Let me sleep."

Right, they said, but no more funny stuff. Funny?

She stayed in bed for a day. Then, on Saturday, all three went to confession together. Della told the priest her story that she had sinned and nearly died. Go back to your people, he said. Safer. From what? Sive said afterwards the old priest must miss his country roots and dislike the city and its noise.

No one else knew what had happened in the flat and never would. It was over. Della took stock. Ed dominated her life journey, and she must not let him go. As much as her head told her to stay in the city, an indissoluble truth existed. She loved him. Neil and their brief interlude had offered something bright and prosperous. Still, none could foresee what might lie ahead - mere hypothesis.

Ed's delight at her decision manifested in visual and tactile signs during Christmas. Through smiles and whispered love murmurings, he strove to reignite the passion and near adoration she had felt for him in 1961. As the week passed in family visits, pubs and dancing, the inward pinging doubts slowly drifted into nebulae. Was it from above or fate? The plan now fitted neatly into the jigsaw. Hadn't she learned from Mother in the convent that an internal voice would guide her if she prayed? Of course, there would be sadness at letting go of aspirations and ambitions but didn't love matter most.

"You've done the right thing for both of us, Della. And to be truthful, if you hadn't, we were over. I'd doubted you loved me, what with your excuses and flitting around Dublin with the girls. So now we can plan for the wedding next summer."

"No, Ed. I've done as you asked, and I can do a course if I get to Galway. Why marry so soon?" Here he was again, shaping her like putty to his will.

"Why not? No reason to wait. Best to have children in our twenties and live life to the full afterwards." Children? His light but determined tone sounded a hollow chord in Della's ears.

"I've few qualifications, except for office skills and religious studies, and always wanted something more. One day, I may get a proper job."

"Job? You'll be married with children, enough for any woman." Intelligent reasoning or control? An inner voice said, *do not answer*. He is orchestrating your every step. Stall him.

Chapter 10

On January 6th, Della applied for a transfer through the Floor Supervisor, a simple signature on a document, its implications more significant than the act. However, processing the request could take a while; few left the city for a job in the provinces, usually in reverse order. Della let the information filter slowly, the reprieve akin to that of a condemned man on death row in an American high-security prison.

When Ed came on the second weekend in January, he wanted to get to the sales. Parking near Grafton Street, they walked to Switzers, where he bought himself a sweater, two shirts, cuff links, and a top for Della, though she said he needn't. Post-Christmas sales were genuine, he said, handing over a lump of cash. "And we're celebrating, Della. You're coming home." Home, Dublin, Galway, or away from what she wanted to be home? Conundrums - she a vacillator, according to Sive.

The vanity of the man, Eileen commented later. Cuff links. He's so full of himself. Della tried a defence; he looked fabulous in the blue designer cashmere.

On Saturday, they went to Skerries to visit Aunty Peggy and Uncle Phil McCabe, Jim's cousin and husband. She and Eve had always called them that, comfortable terms ensuring lasting loyalty and friendship. Jim and Peggy shared roots in Wexford. Again, as in the glorious summer holidays, she smelt the salty air blowing across the harbour and saw trawlers unloading fish. Young and free back then, Della had loved Skerries.

During tea in the high-ceilinged dining room, Aunty Peggy asked Ed about his work and plans. He had acquired a bank loan to invest in his company. Della noticed how he floundered in the face of the older woman's piercing eyes. "I can't tell you my annual turnover, Mam. It's too soon."

Della blushed when his grammar faltered; them is, instead of they are, and so on. In this learned household, one had to hold one's own. Peggy drew her into the kitchen afterwards. Della noted the tall fridge against the wall she remembered from childhood visits. The O'Reillys used to spend a week in the family-run hotel in late August, the end of the season when most guests had gone.

"I have to say, Della, you're doing wrong leaving Dublin. You already possess a sound foundation for a suitable career with your ethics, religious education, and social studies. But I can see that Ed is a forceful personality, and you're pliant. Unfortunately, whenever you mentioned taking a course or liking the city, he veered you onto something else."

"Thanks, Aunty Peggy. Everyone says the same. But we're in love." Seeing the half-smile on her 'aunt's' face, she bit her lip. This woman was a straight talker.

"Too soon for changes. Patrick just graduated with a degree in history and English. Going for a top job in the Civil Service. As for love, it changes, often flees."

A top job, an intelligent young man. He'd get it. They had shared similar propensities. But she, Della, would relegate to *the fields of Athenry*, in County Galway, while he would likely work in Brussels or a job where diplomatic skills and political knowledge counted. She loved the song about Athenry, but it was only a tiny place. Wasn't anybody on her side? The girls, her family, and now Aunty Peggy advised against leaving Dublin except for the few stagey women in the Section.

On the journey back into the city, Ed asked, "What did Peggy say to you in private?"

"That I ought to stay in Dublin, and it's too soon to think of marriage, considering how short a time since I left the convent."

"None of her business."

But Aunty Peggy cared.

When the transfer to Galway came through, Della breathed relief, much better than the small office in Carrick-on-Shannon, near Ed's home. But on life's tapestry, this thread hung loose and limp.

Sadness engulfed all three in the flat as the day approached. Tears trickled, the enormity of her actions bearing down like an avalanche. Sive and Eileen had just found a flat in Rathmines and would move out at the end of the month. "Always room for you, Della, if you can't hack it down there. I liked Galway when I boarded in Taylor's Hill School, but we rarely got out, so I know little about the nightlife there." Her cousin's words brought a semblance of hope.

"I love you both. Have fun, meet someone and settle down here. I'll visit."

Outside, they placed her possessions, little more than on arrival months back, in the taxi, and waved goodbye; their smiles no camouflage, her tears real. Once more, Della O'Reilly was on a path to an uncertain destination. And she would never see Neil again. Now, like two great noblewomen, Marie Antoinette and Anne Boleyn - though not of their ilk - she would prepare to meet her 'gallows'. Wasn't there always a parallel in history or the lives of the saints or someone great? It made her seem almost heroic.

Galway: a royal city of the tribes, Spanish Armada, horses, music, and culture. On March tenth, Della stepped off the train in Ceannt, the main city rail network centre. Named after Eamonn Ceannt, one of the executed leaders of the Easter Rising in 1916, it connoted the fiercely held values and traditions in the West of Ireland. But Della, languorous after a three-hour journey through stations and 'Céad Míle

Failte' signs, strained to see Ed in the car park. He looked pale and tired.

"Working hard, Ed?" she queried, accepting his kiss.

"That and late nights."

"Nights? You say that as I arrive in Galway. You ordered me to come."

"Only dancing. You know I follow the bands. Glad you're here now." Relieved and at ease, he appeared genuinely happy to see her. So well he might. "Let's get you to the digs and have dinner."

Dancing? With himself? Taking her bag, he put it in the boot and turned the car towards the city centre. Better not quiz him or start on a sour note. Doubt must now nebulise her heroism. Heroism? She smiled despite the seed of pessimism rooting in her guts.

The boarding house, off Eyre Square, was a long, white, cheerful building. Ed had booked a room for her the previous weekend. In the foyer, a dark-haired girl smiled admiringly at him. Della pushed forward. "I'm Della O'Reilly, just arrived from Dublin to work in the Welfare office here. This is Ed Egan, my boyfriend." Stating a claim to her territory somehow seemed important before this smiley female.

"Nice to meet you. I'm Roisin McCrann, a waitress at the Great Southern Hotel. I can get you cheap drinks."

Ed smiled, "We'll take you up on that when I'm over, won't we, Della? I've only recently taken to beer."

Drinking? Surely not. Or was it his attempt at disambiguation? And he a master of the art?

"But you'll hardly go out during the week. What about work and all?" Ed said, worry edging into his tone.

As Roisin opened her mouth, Della rushed to agree. "Of course not." The boss had spoken. Words from a psalm came to mind. *Am I trying to win the approval of human beings or God? Am I trying to please people?*

From a window table of a harbour restaurant, they watched sailboats and cabin cruisers ruffling powerful waves. It was late winter, and the weather unusually temperate on the Atlantic coast. Della got out of the car and walked forward to get a closer look at tiny jellyfish cresting high waves and slithering onto the beach's soft brown sand. Here, air and sea eddied, stirred, and whispered in the space between land and eternity beyond the city's confines.

"Della, you'll be content here," Ed said. "And it's only for a while."

She wanted to yell, 'I was happy in Dublin'. Instead, she murmured, "It's lovely."

"And we can plan now."

"If you mean marriage, Ed, give me time to settle into the job first. I want space to find myself in a new environment. Maybe next year." Perhaps he would not impose further changes if he saw her sincerity. Looking straight into his face, she willed her stalling mechanism to work.

Instead, he insisted. "We found each other again, and it was right. We *will* be happy together and have kids."

"Just give me time to overcome the turmoil of the past few years, Ed. Do you understand?"

"Not really. It's history. I have things in my past, but I don't feel the need to dwell on them."

"And I'm the one making a sacrifice?"

"A sacrifice? Is that what you call the move?" Yes, it was a sacrifice of place and person. She would never, ever forget *his* blue eyes and gentle smile. Instead, she shook her head in obedient agreement.

Ed's forehead creased into a frown, but instead of arguing, he smiled. "Look over there, across the bay, at the Cliffs of Moher. Seems like they're rising out of the sea. It's called the Burren, Della. We'll drive down there one Sunday." His words had an unexpected effect, an immediate dispersal of her despondency. Ed was trying, really trying, and it was a fresh start. She *would* be positive.

As the last rays of golden light danced on Galway Bay, staining the sky above the hills of Co. Clare, they turned towards the car. "Ed, no more arguments, please."

"You're here now, and I won't worry as much." His arm, encirclingd her waist, felt secure. Then, one last slow kiss. "Must get back. We'll have longer next time."

Ed hopped into his Corsair and sped out of town towards that quiet country place he called home. Maybe he'd move to Galway.

In the lounge, Roisin introduced her to four girls, and for a couple of hours, they sat together and exchanged life details. Amazement spread as Della unfolded most of her life story. The night drew in.

"In six years, Della, you've created a huge life tapestry," said Mary, a Council official. She seemed a friendly, sincere girl with a pretty face that exuded maturity within a cameo of thick black hair. Della needed people like Sive and Eileen who understood her.

The next day, in the Labour Exchange, she met another Civil Servants group: three girls, two men, and a supervisor, Mr Gilman. At first sight, she did not like her new boss, as his beady eyes burrowed into hers from behind thick lenses. She figured that Sean, Gerry, Maura, and Chrissie were in their mid to late twenties. Over the next few hours, they showed her where everything lived: the filing system, stationery boxes, and more. Uncomplicated. She would no longer be a minor cog in *that* machine as in Records Five, Floor Five of a glass building on Store Street.

Within a week, Della felt a new calm envelop her, exploring fashionable shops, walking along the fantastic seafront, exploring a city steeped in atmosphere. The friendly faces in the post office, Church, and bars brought well-being. After all, it was THE welcoming city of the West. But the most significant compensation for bustling Dublin was the beach, and when she lingered on its yellow sands after work in the evening, her qualms about Ed, her memories of Neil, frittered away on the wind. She almost heard them taking off in the seagulls' squawks as they dived to sift titbits along the shore. According to the Book of Genesis, water prevailed over the earth from the beginning, covering all the high mountains. And now, six billion years later, it still masked life's unwanted stuff. John Masefield's haunting lines came:

> *I must go down to the sea*
> *again for the call of the*

running tide,
It is a wild call and a clear
call that may not be denied.

Yes, the sea brought its brand of wisdom.

Weeks passed, and soon Easter arrived. Della took the six o'clock train to Boyle on Holy Thursday. Across the country, offices closed for the most solemn period on the Church Calendar.

At home, Ed arrived at nine, after the ceremonies. Would she come to The Royal to meet other couples on Sunday night?

"We're just in from the Holy Week ceremonies. You?"

Yes, Ed said he attended with his father and mother. Everyone went. He meant Easter Sunday night.

"And you'll go to confession, Ed dear," she laughed. "Tell your sins. It's obligatory once a year, you know, between Ash Wednesday and Trinity Sunday."

"I go more often than that," he laughed. "What sins, Della? You're too smart for me." Smart, yes, but the battle to keep him at bay brought back the same old tension as the shadow of sin lingered in every kiss and touch. Were she to admit it inwardly, Della concluded such worries were a strong propellant towards marriage, after which there would be no sin. Just love. Sive once said, "You're in love with love, Della." Perhaps Sive was right. Della wanted the man and the love without the attendant actions. Possibly, her four years of inner cleansing and striving for perfection had left her constantly fearing the flesh. And had it not been her desire for pure love that had attracted Della to Neil? His memory she would forever cherish, not least his respect for her at a vulnerable time.

"I'll take you to see my parents first. Pick you up at about six o'clock on Sunday evening, Della. OK?" Calm and comfortable in his world, Ed seemed happy with life and her.

"Do we have to?" She had no desire to let them suck her into their lives yet. Nor did she want to see those high leylandii trees again.

"They'd like to get to know you better." Put that way, there was no choice.

On the journey toward Carrick on Sunday, Ed discussed his plans to expand the business. "Our future," he reiterated, in a cosy but determined manner, "is on track."

Let him plan, Della prayed - for the strength to sidestep premature capitulation.

On arrival, the dwelling appeared somewhat brighter than before, though the dark fronds falling randomly from the high trees appeared to weave spidery patterns on the white gable wall.

Inside, Molly did her best to make the visit pleasant. "I believe you know one of our neighbours, Della. Laura McMahon married Joe Linehan last year. She gave up her nursing in England to marry Joe. Charmed her, he did, with his singing. Joe performs in concerts and functions. She fell for it."

"I know. We had coffee together in Boyle once. Why did you say fell for it?"

As Molly hesitated, Himself piped up from behind a novel in the depths of an armchair. "A useless so-and-so if ever there was one. He's an only boy with three sisters, has a large farm and doesn't look after it. Joe likes to shoot and hunt with the German tourists but neglects the beasts and the crops. Not that he sows much."

Della drew in her breath. The portrayal uttered in a sour tone, oozed disapproval and sheer dislike. How similar Ed and his father, both trenchant in judgment and stance, the block from where the chip had fallen and all that. But Pat's reference to the Linehans sounded ironic to Della. Wasn't there a similarity in this family, an only boy with six sisters, and did his disapproval include *his* only son?

"She has to graft hard," Molly said. "Joe doesn't believe in spending on the home, but he likes to buy rounds in the pub, play the big man."

Here it was again, the parish-pump small-time gossipy snippets they thrived on. "Let's go, Ed. Time to meet your friends."

Della smiled goodbye and walked towards the white car. Laura Linehan might have a frail old woman to look after and a cussed husband whom she could not bend to her will, but there were two parents in this house. Defining cussed might, however, not extend to Molly, a hard-working mother who'd done her best for her family, though birthing them had reduced her spine to a supine state. Della shuddered. What if this was her lot at a time in the future?

Ed turned the car and pulled up sharply as Margie, stick in hand, shuffled into the middle of the road. Della guessed the brother in the field was urging cattle out of the haggard across the road. His voice, sharp and loud, rang out. "Go on, ye dumb animals, out, out." She glimpsed strong, weather-beaten, rough features.

"Is that Peter Malone?" she asked. "Is Margie afraid of him?"

"Only the usual." Infuriating. Margie waved. Ed waved back. They drove off. Again, Della fumed at the camouflage. How dare he subsume her in their ways? She did not share her thoughts. He might not like it.

In the hotel, a pleasant, warm interior greeted them. Della took stock of the soft furnishings and matching drapes on the window. A polished counter spanned the room's length, designed for sizeable crowds. At the bar, Ed bought her vodka and lemonade and a beer for himself, and they sat on two high stools. He smiled at acquaintances drifting in and introduced her to a few. Then the lounge door opened, and Laura came in with her husband. Of medium height and moderate looks, Joe Linehan's curly black hair and laughing eyes projected a man of substance but not her type. He ordered a pint of Guinness and a shandy for Laura.

"Hello, Laura. How nice to see you again! It's been a year." At once, both shared genuine pleasure.

"Della, this is a surprise. Let's find a seat." It was not just the surprise of meeting Laura again but her appearance that struck Della. The woman's dull exterior epitomised everything Della rejected, a drab brown coat, black jeans, and no makeup. Didn't Laura take the trouble to look attractive now that she had a husband? Or was there something else?

They chose a table in the corner, out of hearing of their men at the bar downing beer and Guinness. Ed seemed eager to keep up with Joe Linehan, a man he opted not to like.

"If you're around for Easter, Della, maybe we could do something together. Ed tells everyone you'll get married this year and returned from Dublin to be near him. Sounds encouraging, considering his free spirit." The reference, the hint, again.

"He wants us to get engaged at the end of the summer. If there's anything to tell me, Laura?" Her voice trailed off.

"Rumours go wild in rural areas. A brief spark soon flames into a fire." Which Laura would not fan. After a while, they relaxed into easy companionship, the other woman's gentle disposition a soothing foil for her worries.

"I've shilly-shallied, wanting Ed, wanting others, not strong enough to say no to him. I'm useless at standing up for myself."

"Well, you've had little practice. I did warn you Ed has a certain reputation. But he's in good form, and you seem happy together." Laura twisted the gold band on her finger and laughed nervously.

"And you, Laura? What's married life like?"

"Joe's set in his ways. The old-fashioned house needs new floors, a toilet, and a bathroom." Laura sighed a subtle but needy sound. Then, fiddling with her glass, she delved deep. "Necessities, Della, but he won't give in."

"I still remember when Dad put in ours. It was 1952, and I was nine. Horrible pots before that."

But it was still 1952 in Linehan's.

"He won't spend money on the house, and to be truthful, my back aches cleaning the rooms, stairs, and landing, scrubbing clothes without a washing machine. I try to argue with him, but his temper rises, so I leave it. But never mind, enough of that. Next Wednesday, Della, there's a talk on childcare, measles, mumps, and more in Boyle's Community Centre. Do you think Ed might drive us there? He can have a pint while we're inside, about two hours."

"I'll ask him." What a pleasant idea to do something with this woman. Like water eroding stone, her objections were fading towards settling in the area. She wondered why the men remained at the bar except to bring over rounds of alcohol for their womenfolk.

"Della, they're tribal Irish". Too right they were, but she would like to size up Joe Linehan more, this man of whom, so far, she'd heard little good.

As the night deepened, she made friends. Locals drifted in and out, some smiling in her direction. All the while, Ed beamed from the bar, preening in receipt of drunken compliments. "Always picked a good one, Ed," Della's ears alerted to Ned Dolan's drool. Always? Well, he hadn't lived a hermit's life before her return. Would she have wanted him were it so?

CHAPTER 11

E d agreed to drive them to the talk on Wednesday as arranged. "Good of you to get Della interested. It'll educate her." Della smiled politely, the idea of child immunisation a distant priority. But if everyone was glad, who was she to tip the cart?

At six o'clock, Ed hooted the horn outside Linehan's. The door opened, and Laura emerged, face blanketed in a warm scarf. A cold, sharp wind was blowing down the hill - the path from her front door slippery with a light dusting of frost. Sometimes, Easter could be chilly when the date of the Liturgical festival fell early in the calendar. In the house, a lone light shone from behind heavy curtains.

In the back seat, Laura sat back on the red leather and sighed a relieved sound.

"I'll have a pint in The Royal to while away the time. It's near the Square, and ye can join me afterwards in the bar."

"A pint puts a man in good humour, Ed," Laura said. "Joe likes his Guinness."

"Mind you drink little—it's a fair drive back to my house," Della warned. "I have to get to work tomorrow." She would return to Galway on the train the following morning.

"We know where to find you, Ed," Laura nodded.

The Community Centre was already filling up with young women eager for information on diseases that plagued ordinary people's lives throughout the country. Measles, mumps, chickenpox, and rubella were commonplace, lasted nine days, the effects longer, and, sometimes, for life. However, with the recent promise from the Health Minister of widespread immunisation, a new awareness of such illnesses was seeping slowly across the land, even into County Mayo's remote regions and mountainous Donegal. Children lay sick and 'donny' when a virus spread, often condemned to a life of deafness or ugly skin indentations.

"It's important to immunise babies early to prevent the disease. Modern medicine makes an enormous difference, but we Irish are often slow to change our ways," Laura said. "Let's hear what the Health officer says about signs to recognise and how to act."

Just as Laura and Della took their seats, a powerful voice addressed the audience from the front of the room. It belonged to Olive Keating.

"Northern Counties," Della whispered. The speaker's strident tone, physicality, full bosom, and bulky frame combined to augment her presence before the large group of women.

"Yeah, maybe Monaghan, not too far away, I reckon."

The bronze-haired woman launched into a speech. None should take for granted that children contracted measles, mumps, or whooping cough. They suffered, and many died because Ireland accepted diseases that ravaged the population.

A buzz of indignation filtered through the audience. Hands flapped. From the crowd, a voice shouted, "Sure, our fathers and mothers and generations before them had those diseases, Mam, and got over them."

Laura whispered, "Stupid, backward."

"Well then, it's time they didn't. Ireland must emerge from the darkness of ignorance and look after its wee children properly." The intonation of the voice, emphasising syllables, increased as Olive Keating strove to counter gullibility.

"For years, TB riddled families and decimated the population. With immunisation, the disease will no longer maim or kill off our children. Nor will polio invade the core of our society, leaving behind paralysed and broken homes."

A voice rang out. "God's sake, once you've had the measles, you're immune. Always been the case."

"But the virus leaves children in a poor state, that time can't heal. So prevention is the answer."

Pockets of dissent filtered around the room and died off. Laura whispered. "I hope they believe her."

"Always a few hardliners wanting to thwart progress. I like her, Laura. Let's talk to Olive afterwards," Della whispered. "Maybe ask her back to the Royal for a drink?"

Olive Keating came to the end of her talk, her face redder than the lipstick smeared over tulip lips, her ample cheeks shining with sweat. Despite their errant attitude, the audience clapped as one. Laura tugged Della over to the table.

"We're from Cortober, near Carrick. Thanks for your information, Olive. Della isn't married, but I have a little girl, Siobhán. I nursed in the UK and am glad you're teaching Irish women to understand diseases."

"Nice to meet you both." The lurch in pronunciation evoked a northern origin. "I got into this work because of my childhood. Measles left my brother deaf when he was a wee boy." Again, the 'wee' resonated in a northern twang.

"Would you join us in The Royal for a drink, Olive? Della's husband is waiting for us there. Not that we'll drink anything but a mineral."

Yes, Olive would. "Mark is there too, expecting me. I'll introduce you both."

Together, the three women walked the short distance towards the hotel, its lurid sign pale and bleak in the otherwise darkened street. They passed Gaynor's haberdashery displaying domestic accoutrements: brushes, washing powder, basins, rakes, tin cans, etc. Amid a farming community, the shop also offered simple everyday wear.

"Only one decent fashion shop in this town, Olive," Laura explained. "My mother-in-law comes here if there's a funeral, a wedding or if she needs something new."

"I prefer Dublin or Sligo, myself," Olive commented. Judging from the cut of the purple tweed coat, it came from Brown Thomas or one of the exclusive stores in the city.

"I buy little. And I make terry-towelling nappies. Saves money." As they crossed the narrow bridge to the hotel, Della mulled, I will *never* be like Laura.

Inside the hotel, the smell of whiskey enveloped them, and a pall of cigarette smoke wafting low over the customers' heads almost drove Della back outside. Stuffy and stale, it clung to her nostrils.

"I've never smoked, girls, but we are now. Passive smoking affects our lungs," Olive stated. Della wondered if anyone dared question her.

"I have an odd Silk Cut," Della replied. "Lighter than most, I believe. Only when I'm having a drink. It's a social thing."

"Me too. Smoking and black coffee, staple tools for nurses on night duty. But I can't afford them now. Gosh, it's only Monday night, and the bar is full. So much for a scarcity of money," Laura said. "Isn't it good to get out of the house? I've not had a chance in ages."

At the counter, Ed was not alone. A tall, brown-eyed, angular figure stood drinking beer with him. The two appeared deep in conversation. Della caught a phrase, 'Maybe next Saturday night,' from the man as they approached. Olive stiffened. "What's that about Saturday night? Remember we're going to the Abbey to the Health Board dinner dance?"

"We'll talk later. Who are your friends?"

"Meet Della, Ed's girl, and Laura Linehan, from Cortober near Ed."

A long, tanned hand held Della's, two hazel eyes burrowed into her soul, and a lean body tipped low in recognition. The man exuded magnetism. Stop yourself, she thought. Have sense. He's gorgeous in a distinct way from Ed, somewhat shorter now beside Mark. The grins exchanged between the two men showed mutual admiration, that they liked each other. Something had occurred. Ed's expression, lit-up features, and how he laughed at every word from Mark showed an indefinability. What was going on? Was Ed, the ultimate controller, being sucked into someone else's web?

"Pleased to meet you both. What are ye having?" Mark gestured towards the women with a polite tone and an inscrutable expression. As his eyes lingered over her form, Della felt uncomfortable. She was the only single woman present.

Sipping a lemonade, she watched the interaction, always an intriguing practice. Life in veritable silence taught one to understand expressions denoting anxiety, and back in Dublin, she'd used the same techniques when deciphering body language. Not that she was an expert, but it was fun. Now she picked up tension between the Keatings, Olive loudly proclaiming opinions, which Mark contradicted on cue. But Olive was not under subjugation, and Della liked her. Laura, too, it seemed.

"Della and Laura, the best thing we women can do for ourselves right now is to join political parties, the Feminist movement, or both. Agreed?"

Laura tittered weakly. "Can't imagine having time for anything like that, Olive. What about the kids and the farm? And Joe would not have it."

"See, that's exactly why you should, Laura."

"Let's get off," Della said. "It's eleven o'clock, too late for heavy arguments on women's rights." She did care, but the situation was not suitable for such topics. As Mark and Olive headed for a white Mercedes in the square, Ed, Laura, and Della got into the Sunbeam, Ed's latest passion. He loved his cars. Olive's voice came loud and shrill across the near-empty car park, "I heard you, roping another man into your net, someone else to roam the night spots with you."

"Now, now, don't jump to conclusions. I've only just met Ed. Seems a good guy with similar ambitions to myself." The doors closed, and the engine whirred up the hill and away. It had been an interesting, if somewhat disturbing, night.

Laura, talkative in the back seat, remarked that Olive was an energy powerhouse and an expert on medical care. Della said nothing, her mind veering in another direction. Ed and Mark. Olive might be a strong woman, but her concerns were palpable. Also, her suggestion, though far-fetched and daft, held a note of hope for women. Yeah. She'd join.

Ed's voice, slurred from beer, broke through the reverie. "That woman is the last type I'd pick for a wife."

"Because you couldn't control her?"

"Has it worked with those two? I was with Mark all evening, and he's not happy. If that's what being an outspoken woman has done for marriage, they're doomed."

Laura laughed a weak little laugh in the back. At the house, the lights were out. She said she'd go in quietly not to wake anyone. Why? Would she suffer the consequences of being out late? Better not ask.

"Don't know when we'll meet again, Della. Ed, bring her to the Royal soon and let me know beforehand."

He smiled in agreement. That Ed wanted her to make friends in his local pub boded well for their future, but she had enjoyed meeting the two women.

Della returned to Galway on the train the next day.

Midweek, the girls drifted into the Seapoint Hotel after the cinema. Roisin chose a long leather banquette in the middle of the lounge and ordered Babycham for Della, Mary, and herself. In the warm atmosphere, tongues loosened, chatting easily about the film, careers, and their hopes for the future. Roisin might do an evening course at the uni. Plenty on offer, but fees cost money. She did not earn enough to live and save. "No, it'll be a husband or the hotel for me, girls."

Like the women in Records Five, Roisin would forever labour under thwarted ambition. *Kick yourself into gear*, Della uttered to that person within, *or you'll be another one*.

At 11.30, she noticed a man drinking beer at the bar. The room seemed to zoom in on him.

"Who's he?" she asked.

"Dermot Dolan, his family owns the newsagents on the square."

"Gosh, he's nice."

"Not for you, girl. Don't be tempted."

"New friend, Roisin? Introduce me." It, he, the idol at the bar, wanted to meet her.

"This is Della O'Reilly, new at the Exchange."

Two big brown eyes smiled into hers, like Joe Ward's, the boy back home who'd taken her to the dance in Longford. Gosh, how she loved eyes that held you spellbound. A tingle spread through her body; this man was *handsom*e. A hand gestured acknowledgement. Once upon a time, Della used to say she'd marry someone with brown eyes before Ed came along.

Roisin whispered under the beat of the music, "Don't be a fool, Della. You're nearly engaged."

"Yes, Roisin, just flirting."

"If Ed were my boyfriend, I'd be happy," Mary said, her eyes flashing stop. But a tiny voice in Della's mind urged, oh hell, enjoy the moment. Her freedom span was fast escaping her grasp.

The vision in white jeans and a blue polo shirt said, "Can I buy you a drink?"

"Yes, yes," exclaimed Della, rubbing her sore arm courtesy of Roisin's pinch. Her friend, urging her into a sensible state, was becoming a nuisance. Music blared from the bandstand. *Take a chance, take a chance, take a chance on me.* Roisin said, "To the loo, now, Della."

Inside the white cloakroom-cum-toilets, Della rubbed the black, pinched spot. "It hurts." She did not yet know Roisin enough for the other girl to act as her minder.

"Have you no shame, Della?"

"Shame, sense, care. I've felt all of it, but soon, I will be bound for the rest of my life. No harm in a bit of fun."

"To the man you've chosen."

"Chose me. Yes, it was wonderful initially, but he's possessive and controlling. I'd never have left Dublin, only for he insisted. I love Ed and don't want to lose him, but he's miles away tonight."

Della gazed at her reflection, bright in the mirror, eyes shining with new excitement. Then, with a final flick of her ponytail, she turned and walked back to the bar, letting

Roisin make her way to the table where Mary sat, sipping a gin and tonic. A current of something indefinable shot through her body, like that experienced in Dublin when she had met Neil. This man, however, was a flatterer, a girl magnet. She saw it in his crooked, sexy smile. He reminded her of Elvis Presley, the most incredible heartthrob on the earth.

Dermot worked in the family business and possessed little ambition to do anything academic. She explained little other than that she had come from Dublin to work in Galway. Dermot was for the here and now. Within minutes, they planned to meet the following night.

"If he hadn't arrived on the scene, it would be someone else. It's plain as day, Della. You're dithering."

"Dithering maybe, but marriage is a commitment, and I've already walked away from one. So, I might settle down happy if I get it out of my system."

"Della, you're not ready for that," Mary offered.

"You get more excitement than us." In Roisin's flat tone, Della caught a hint of jealousy. "It's that long golden hair of yours. No man can resist it and your come-on eyes."

"Holy smokes, Roisin. I'm not a hussy!" In Dublin, Sive and Eileen had tried to stop her from leaving the city and, in hindsight, were right. They cared deeply and saw she needed freedom to fulfil her potential. But here, newfound friends considered her disloyal. Were women less ambitious in the country, wanting only a husband, children, and little else? Did no one long for adventure?

"Why is going out for a drink, chatting, and kissing wrong?" Hackles rising, she had to stop their objections and nip them in the early bud.

"Because it's cheating. You see five of us dying to meet the right fella, and you come along, nearly engaged, but with another in the wings," Roisin said,.

"If you knew Dermot Dolan as we do, you'd cop that he's just collecting scalps. He's done the rounds on us all," Helen added.

Done the rounds? What did that say about them? Easy or desperate?

"Do I care?" Della felt her cheeks burn. "Maybe I'm the one collecting scalps." Long disapproving sighs. She needed neither conflict nor castigation.

"Have you heard the saying, '*there's many a slip between the cup and the lip*'? Know what it means?" Roisin said.

She had.

Ed did not come at the weekend. Helping his father knock trees around the house, he said on the phone. Despite the older man's objections, he'd insisted on felling them on one side of the building. Pretending she would miss him, Della said, see you soon, and on the way home from work, called at the newsagents and told Dermot she was free until Monday. His face lit up, re-igniting an excitement not experienced since her first encounter with Neil at the Irrawaddies.

When he pulled up outside the digs at seven in a red sports car the following evening, she didn't bother to look at its make; it was a fast sports car. Enough. On the outskirts, he drove along the Dublin Road for ten miles to a small pub in Claregalway, a quaint, pretty, Irish-themed place with bodhrans, fiddles, and leprechauns in nooks around the interior. Della had never been in such a pub. Dermot explained it was a tourist magnet.

They ate rice and chicken and drank beer. Della hated beer, but it did not matter. After one, she felt light-headed and a little wild. When Ed's face impinged, a smidgin of guilt filtered through her haze, but not enough to ruin the experience of being out with someone else. Was she cheating? Yes, but it was fun, and she deserved it.

Two hours passed in light chat about Galway, his surfing and boating. One Sunday, Della might like to come along and sail around the coastline to Spiddal. It would be nice, but she went home a lot. With little else to share, she soaked up the company of the good-looking man beside her.

Later, outside the digs, Dermot leaned across and brushed his full lips against her mouth. She liked his lips, like marshmallows, and the touch of his hand on hers. Could you love more than one at the same time? Well, she was learning fast. But of course, this was not love, just attraction—no more.

"Come to the cinema on Wednesday," he said as Della hopped out of the car onto the pavement. Delighted, she replied. Dermot waved goodbye, turned his red machine, and disappeared.

It took a magnum of courage to hide her guilt when Ed came to take her home to Leam on Friday. He looked genuinely pleased when she walked out the door in narrow navy trousers and a white shirt blouse. No matter what else influenced her life in the week, it was important that Ed still fancied her. In his eyes lay the answer. He did.

On the drive along the winding road by Mount Bellew and Athleague, he wondered why she did not ask him about his whereabouts during the week or tell him what she did with her time. Oh, working as usual and walking on the seafront, she said. Dull, as you can imagine. Surely you do more than that: go out with the girls in the digs and drop into the bars on Eyre Square. Oh, none of that, she said, too tired after work. Gosh, would he ever stop?

Two hours later, when the house quietened, they kissed and cuddled in the sitting room. He seemed unwilling to leave. But the thought of her duplicity hung between them, making her pull back when his emotions intensified. Her inner voice prodded, *last year, I told my sins in confession every week and feared committing them, but now I'm a practised two-faced liar.*

After dinner on Saturday, helping to wash up in the kitchen, Della told Eve about her dalliance during the week. Her sister's reaction was both surprising and settling. "Good for you, might as well, considering you're on a march to the altar. Get the most out of Galway, the best place outside Dublin."

Approbation from her sister. Gosh, what a relief, one that helped ease the conscience bites.

On Sunday, Ed took her back to the city, and they ate dinner in a small restaurant on Eyre Square. He chose steak, she shellfish. After all, fish had to be good by the sea. Ed's continued contentment phase triggered remorse in Della as he drew her to himself in the car afterwards. God forgive me. I'm a two-faced ****. The last word she could not utter within her soul.

He would not see her for a few weeks; too much on, evening meetings, stocking up. Fine, come when you can, she said as they parted.

Inside, the girls were suspicious. What was he up to? It didn't seem right. Don't care, Della responded. Again, as in Dublin, she would languish in glorious freedom and let be what would be.

Chapter 12

Wednesday came. Della met Dermot outside the cinema, excited at the prospect of whatever the night offered. He chose a row near the back and rested a hand lightly on her cheek within minutes. It smelt of after-shave. She didn't know which one nor cared - less aromatic than Ed's but of pungent leaves. Nice.

Two hours later, they emerged from the building, holding hands, the night ahead theirs for whatever. Then Della saw a familiar figure on the street. It couldn't be. It was. Standing by the car as the crowd filed past, Ed did not spot her in the semi-darkness.

"Goodnight, Dermot," she whispered. "Sorry, I've got to fly." Ducking down a side alley, she ran to the digs. She had seen the frown, the - foraged for a description - and the vicious expression on Ed's face. She fixed her hair in the loo and powdered her face, flushed from her moments watching the film. *The Good, the Bad and the Ugly* wasn't her kind of thing. She'd missed parts of it.

In Reception, she picked up a magazine and pretended to read it. Seconds later, Ed walked in.

"Where were you, Della? I've been running around town looking for you? One girl said she thought you'd gone to the cinema, but I waited outside, and you did not come out." The thunderous expression on his face made her cringe, shame and fear fighting for dominance before his anger.

"Come on," he ordered. "Out."

Neither spoke during the drive to their usual space in front of the darkened County Council offices.

"What's going on, Della? Why weren't you at the digs?" His harsh tone forced her into a state of contriteness. Longford, Dublin, Galway. What was she becoming?

"Just slipped out to see Roisin at work. She gets bored." Shakily, she stuttered the lie.

"I saw her behind the desk, alone. You weren't there."

"Probably in the toilet." But after years of hearing 'a lie is always sinful', Della's face could not lie. He waited. Della caved in and cried.

"Talk," Ed said, self-righteous, strident. "Go on." Emotionless, devoid of either insult or disapproval, he waited.

"Someone who likes me took me to the cinema.. Unlike you, I've not had many boyfriends, boasting about your women in different countries. So, I went to the cinema with Dermot Dolan. He's a newsagent on Eyre Square. Harmless fun. Nothing serious."

There, she'd aired the secret and put it to bed. Now, they could move on. Ed jolted the car to a stop; she fell against the dash and saw his ghostly pallor under the streetlight. Then it came.

"You might have secrets to confess, but so do I. Think I was working nights when I did not come over? I was dancing, seeing others. How do you like that? After Dublin, I couldn't trust you, so I set you up and arrived tonight, knowing you weren't expecting me."

It was not just the word 'confess' that struck home. It alone intimated shame, but how things fell into place, the mystery of his absence, his recalcitrance. That Della had not minded mattered now. She could not lose the man she had fallen for before their love became tainted. Had she not set her sights on him when the door closed behind her in Sligo?

"Maybe I should abandon you. I can get the best of women. Still do."

"I wish you'd said that in Dublin, where I was happy and free. Ed, please calm down," she tried, each syllable incensing his anger. Yes, she had made a mistake, but here was someone who did not respect confessions, never made them, but wanted a woman without blemish. She should have lied.

Della shivered. The person beside her was transmuting into a stony-faced tyrant who demanded answers. As a cloak of self-pity enveloped her body, she went down onto that floor again, confessing faults.

"No point in this relationship. We're done. It's over. I'm going, and you won't see me again. To think we planned our wedding last week! Go back to Dublin."

Distraught and crushed like a worm underfoot, Della swallowed the salty tears that slid into her mouth. She felt ugly. Lines from a favourite poem nudged – *The Song of the Worms*:

We know what a boot looks like
when seen from underneath,
we know the philosophy of boots,
their metaphysic of kicks and ladders.
We are afraid of boots.

"Out. Go." Leaning across, he slammed the door behind her and drove off as if the devil were on his tail.

Della stood trembling on the pavement. Her eyes stung, her throat sore from racking sobs, and her body heaved in self-loathing. Shivering, she turned towards the river, its murky waters a sure escape. And quicker than waiting for pills to work. One step and the waters of the Corrib would take her away; out to sea, the sun would still shine from a cloudless sky tomorrow, and the Cliffs of Moher would smile across the bay.

Then, a voice from within the recesses of her soul spoke. Her angel guardian? *Don't. You're punished.* She stalled just a foot from the riverbank's edge and cried to heaven, 'God forgive me'. A Catholic believer in God's mercy, she had been ready to commit a dreadful crime that would besmirch her soul in the next life. Again, on the verge of disintegration, Della felt lost. Turning, she stumbled towards the light in a window on the street corner.

The girls were sitting at the open fire in the lounge. On sight of the tear-stained face, Roisin got a blanket from the room, wrapped it around Della in an armchair, and waited. She related the evening's events in spurts and that Ed had gone and would not return. She did not tell them about the lure of the water.

Mary started. "Della, you've let your heart rule your actions again."

"Yes, I cheated. I am a cheat." As one, they nodded, forming a circle around her, a court wherein she was the accused. Ed, albeit absent, was the accuser. Roisin said Della was foolish for 'messing around' when engaged to someone like Ed. "You're in an awful state, Della. Be honest and tell us what you want."

Encouraged by their concern, Della replied hesitantly, then picked up momentum in the face of their genuine anxiety. "It's as if the gates are closing on my freedom, as in 1961. Marriage is just another sentence; yes, I have doubts about commitment. Two years ago, I'd almost taken final vows. Is this so different? More vows, more obedience?" She blew her nose to stem the wet flow. They must understand and not judge her.

"The rite of marriage still includes the words 'to love, honour and obey', so you would be in another stranglehold. But with Ed gone now, you can do as you please," Mary Earley said. Della liked the tall girl more than the others for her sincerity and friendship. Tittle-tattle was grist to the mill in small towns. One needed real friends.

"Let's go for a drink tomorrow night," Roisin suggested. "We might think up a solution after a few gins."

"Yeah," they shouted as one. "A few gins. Drown your sorrows for a while. It's all too heavy. Off to bed."

Sleep did not come. Outside, the wind rose, and the sea lashed its might against the cliffs of Galway Bay, her present journey akin to one of the fishing trawlers caught in an

Atlantic storm. Still, a persistent voice hammered in her brain, '*Don't let Ed slip away.*'

Della imparted details of the debacle at work the next day, excluding the dark temptation that had almost taken hold. Instead of judging, her colleagues offered support, their concern a balm. Devoid of reprimand or accusation, their niceness washed over her, soothing the misery. Finally, at home time, she felt better.

At eight that evening, Della, Rosin, Mary, and others started drinking in the Seapoint Hotel. The night wore on. Gin poured down welcoming throats. Della liked the taste, though stronger than her usual Babycham. But after the third glass, her stomach heaved. She ran through the doors to the toilet, retched into the bowl, and fell sideways onto the tiled floor. Ceiling and walls closed in. Fluorescent lights zoomed close. Her 'blinder' to blot out problems now left her sick, pitiful, and utterly defeated.

"Get her home," Rosin said, half-dragging Della's body through the bar. Then, as the night air hit her face, Della puked on the pavement. Rosin sniffed disgust and hauled her up the steps of the digs, into the bedroom and onto the bed. She pulled a rug over Della and said, "Sleep it off."

"I've never drunk gin before. It's vile," she sputtered, pressing a cold flannel against her forehead. "I only wanted one, but it tasted nice and was easy to swallow."

"Gin is out for you, then. Better stick to Babycham."

"Spirits and I don't mix," Della said. "I'll never drink again."

"Oh, dear, you are pale," another one said. Prone to popping 'purple hearts' brought back from England on visits to her boyfriend, Rena had not entirely made the inner circle yet. "Gin can be a depressant, depending on one's state of mind."

"My God. How could you drink so much of it, Della? Worst drink for depression."

Despite the crying and vomiting, Della heard them discussing her 'terrible state'. "You must *not* ring or chase Ed. Have self-respect," Rosin warned. "And no more tears."

Within an hour of wanting to die, Della fell into a troubled quiescence. Like her heroine, Scarlett O'Hara, she vowed that tomorrow would be another day, and she would 'get him back'. She loved that film, the strength of character and the powerful spirit of the woman at the end. That's what she needed now. No more shilly-shallying. Determination. Her childhood friends, Nan Hall and Mary Lally, planned to marry soon. And she would not remain single. Fate alone had united her with Ed. And she had sacrificed a lot for him by coming to Galway as he'd wanted. It must not be in vain.

Three agonising days and nights passed with little food or sleep. Then, like a mist over Galway Bay, despair took hold of Della's spirit. He was not coming for her again.

Work ran late throughout the week, but it helped assuage the pain. Automaton-like, Della totted up optical and dental benefits. She issued support forms for impoverished families in the County while listening to unbidden advice from caring colleagues. Though miserable and again on an uncharted voyage to god knows where she smiled her thanks. Dermot called. No thanks, she said, too ill to go out.

Thursday came. The clock ticked ever so slowly. Della longed to get back to her room and sleep. The phone rang. It was Mary. "Ed's in town. I saw his car going towards the office just now. Act surprised when you see him." Oh heck. As the shock set in, Della tried to assemble her feelings. Running to the ladies, she dabbed on pink lipstick and a feather of blusher. The dark circles under the eyes she could not disguise. But it was night, and it did not matter. Had he come to finish for good? Or not? A trickle of hope filtered into her head. No, yes. Let him talk; only one way to find out. Face him, anger or no anger.

Despite trepidation and a useless attempt at calm, Della walked towards the white car parked by the kerb under a streetlight. There was no use pretending to pass by. She stopped by the driver's side but did not assume to get in uninvited.

"Sit in!" Ed said tersely, opening the passenger door from the driver's seat. His command came like a bolt. The lord and master had spoken. Striving to quiet her heart's uneven beats, she muttered, I didn't expect to see you." A whiff wafted across, seductive and alluring. He always used the same one. Only a few days ago, another smell had found her.

Turning the car, he drove past her digs along the main street to the Council office car park, spacious and empty at night. At the back wall, Ed turned on the overhead light. He looked drawn and tired. Good, she thought, he's suffered too.

"Well, you almost didn't, but from the first time I met you in 1961, I wanted you, and afterwards, when you came home, it seemed right for us to be together, but I won't tolerate your silliness or dithering. So let's bring the wedding forward to the summer. And no more skulking around when I'm not here. Understood?"

A whispering voice said, '*You're twenty-three, not a child. Stand up for yourself.*'

"No, Ed, I'll earn a salary for as long as possible. I never have time to settle. Not in Dublin, nor here." She saw his face stiffen.

"You didn't behave yourself there either. We need rules."

Behave herself? His dictatorial tone rasped in her ear. No, she would not succumb like a lamb to his bidding.

"Rules. Convent rules, your rules. I hate them. Rules crushed me."

"Odd, you told me you'd enjoyed boarding school, that they made you safe."

"Yeah, back then. Not so sure I'm safe now." Sive and Eileen's warning stirred: *Stand your ground.*

Ed's aloofness had been the catalyst that first attracted her to him years back. It depicted him in an almost surreal light, different from other men, and cast a spell on her then. Despite misgivings and nearly 'healing' herself' over the past few days of his influence, Della realised she was still submissive to it. But she would never determine his inner thoughts or the masked expression that rarely conceded emotion.

"Marriage should be a partnership, not one obeying the other," she tried.

"How else can it be? Isn't obedience part of marriage ceremonies?"

"Outdated idea, that men rule their wives who give up employment to stay home and rear children."

"It's worked for generations."

"If you watched the news or read the papers, you'd realise that women are challenging old-fashioned views, women's liberation and all that. Olive was right. We women should join movements that fight for rights."

"That Feminist lot! You are joking, Della. Surely, you're not one of them?"

"I want equality, not compliance."

"No more arguing if we're to make it work. I've come tonight to get us back on track because I love you and cannot imagine life without you. Come here."

Pulling her close, he kissed her passionately until her body became limp. Tired from lack of sleep, the comfort of his touch was enough to tip her into submission once again. She could never resist the sheer magnetism he exuded, more so now, having agonised at the prospect of a bleak future without him for three days. Their separation had proved effective. She still desired him. A feeling of calm enfolded her, comforting her tired body and fevered conscience. She *would* strive to avoid distractions and further misery from now on. It was a matter of self-discipline.

"Della, do you love me?" That sweet little word. How brilliant his ability to cast spells.

"Yes, but it's a bittersweet kind, Ed. Regardless of love, our relationship cannot abide in fear or guilt." The latter she could never shelve. Pauline's revelation about ' ..... interruptus', forever vivid in her mind, continued to imbue Della with an innate fear of sinning. No trace of it must exist to receive the Holy Sacrament at Mass. Conversely, she would not be another Pauline whose race to the altar six months previously had resulted in a son, Andy. So, marry, she must.

Agreed, he said, kissing her again. Time passed. The night sky lightened.

The Reillys sat down to roast beef served with Bridie's special gravy on Sunday. Della quietly recounted some events of the past fortnight but held back on the drunkenness and riverside debacle.

Jim's knife clattered onto the plate. "You fight and are jealous of each other. It's not exactly a foundation for marriage."

"I can't back out now. Ed forgave me and came looking for me."

"On your head, be it." Jim sighed. "Sad thing is, we're helpless to stop you."

"And from whom did she inherit the obdurate strain, Jim Reilly?" Bridie said, face red and hot after serving roast potatoes from the oven.

"Me. Condemned as accused, but Della should have the courage and the experience to avoid an enormous mistake again."

"Exactly, but it's not the courage she lacks. It's the sense to create a space in her life and not marry Ed for at least another year. Be careful, Della. I was in my late thirties when I married your father. Old enough to want a husband but still young enough to give birth to you two."

She saw the strain in her mother and knew she had upset the evenness of their lives. Eve spoke up. "Della, our parents are not young, and you're hurting them, ruining their peace. Don't marry Ed. Go back to the city and start again."

But it was too late to change course again.

Chapter 13

It was 1966, a year Della would remember for several reasons. England won the World Cup, which meant little to the Irish, Gaelic football being the national shrine of adoration. A newspaper strike was in full swing, restricting the circulation of information except for radio and TV news broadcasts. Not until the end of the summer did horrific details percolate through the population of terrible murders on the moors near Manchester. Nothing so evil had ever happened in either country. It marred daily life and was the subject of conversations after church, on the street, and in pubs. During Masses, priests offered prayers for the families and the discovery of one last body.

And in the valley near Leitrim village, someone murdered a local girl. Two weeks later, the Gárdai arrested a neighbour, an odd type. Jim said he'd never liked the loner who hung around the local pub after closing, but no one would have put him down as a woman-hater. Little information trickled into the locality except that he had 'done something' to the girl first. Her mother's wails rose above the church steeple at the funeral. Among the large crowd of sympathisers, Bridie heard whispered insinuations. Better not repeat such things, she said at home. *He* would go to prison for the rest of his life.

From the wildness of Donegal to the southern tips of the MacGillycuddy Reeks in Kerry, the horrors emerging brought the country to its knees. For Della, it was as if ugliness and evil were tarnishing her wedding preparation. However, her mother had a different opinion.

"A wedding is just what we need to lift our spirits," Bridie said. "No further objections from us, Della. You seem happier."

"Well, Ed is very persuasive. Since that break, we both realise we want to be together now."

On the first Monday in July, Della notified the staff officer, Mr Gilman, of notice to quit work. His reaction surprised her. "Women lose their independence when they marry. You'll become a chattel, producing babies and keeping house."

Della gasped. A touchy-feely type, he sometimes brushed close to her chair in the office, making her skin creep. At other times, she saw him by the adjoining door, listening to her colleagues recounting their night's antics. The two boys would arrive in the Council car park where Ed's car stood close to the wall, hooting the horn and hollering at the top of their voices. One night, Gerry shone the headlights onto the pair in the back of the car. Ed lowered the window and said, "Feck off, rascals." Their narration of the event, a mix of hyperbole and truth, plus suggestive comments, brought work to a halt in the office the next day. She would miss both.

Mr Gilman called Della into the office to check on a Benefits claim. He touched her hand and asked if she was alright, his slimy pat making her recoil in disgust, excuse herself and move back from the desk. "Ed wants children soon," burst from her mouth for no reason. No married man had ever made advances to her before.

"We'll miss you, Della. You're a ray of light in this place. It won't be the same after you leave. We need more girls like you."

Under her breath, Della muttered, '*I bet you do, but I won't miss you*'.

She would, however, miss Galway and the city she had grown to love. Giving up a bustling, urban lifestyle for a remote country village was a sacrifice, her second in a year, and this one was an irreversible life-changing action.

Before going to the office in the morning, she sometimes walked to the seafront to sit and mull over the sheer speed life had taken in eighteen months. The ceaseless murmuring of the waves was comforting. No matter what paths she or anyone else chose, those waters would continue to wash the shores of Galway Bay until the end of time. She had met Dermot for a final liaison and explained she was on the brink of marriage to Ed. He understood but said how sorry he was; they could have made memories together - memories, not marriage. Well, that was that.

On Monday morning at eight, Della sat and listened to the soughing of the wind blowing in from the sea, the smell and taste of salt cloying to her skin. It was early, few about, except for an odd dog walker. A red glow in the east showed that the sun would rise shortly, and in minutes, it did, bright shafts of sunlight piercing the clouds like rays of hope across the landscape.

The park near the seafront was pretty, with flowers and shrubs awakening to the warmth of the morning. The leaves, tree trunks, and damp benches sparkled with tiny drops of glittering water, soon to dry and yield to the heart of another summer's day.

Galway would soon awaken to wheels, boats, and the music blaring along its streets. Tiny green leprechauns would grin invitingly from beneath coloured awnings. They'd skip, dance, and sing to the sound of Celtic beats, bodhrans, and fiddles.

Yes. The city of the Armada, the chieftains, and the tribes would come to life like no other. The tinkers would drag their wares around Eyre Square and tell old ladies they were beautiful and young. Their eyes were diamonds. Some would nod and believe, but all would smile.

Her cheeks warmed, cold when she awoke in the digs. Unable to sleep, she had donned a warm coat and come here to sit and ponder.

'If it were done when tis done it were well it were done quickly' crept into her head. She loved Shakespeare's sayings; wise ones, silly ones, the stitch in time ones, easy to understand, follow, or reject.

As the sea caressed the rocks in the morning glory, pulling and pushing life's detritus in and out, Della sat and meditated. Tasting the salt in a puff of wind, she longed to escape on one of the fishing trawlers setting sail from the harbour. There, on the high seas, she could cast overboard the doubts and distractions of life.

Straining to hear a voice in the breeze, she heard whispering through the branches of a mighty tree, like a warning of broken promises, lies, and doubt, limbs of deadwood falling before its force. Wind dispersed the stench of oily fish, rotting carrion, and seaweed, smearing the flotsam and jetsam along the beach. It waved a creative wand upon the earth. If her heart were still and her thoughts peaceful, perhaps she would find her promised land, not here by the sea but far from its lapping waters and shifting sands.

The sun got warmer, gathering intensity as the clock on the top of Seapoint urged towards the busyness of a working day. Soon, she would leave this spot and its tranquillity. "I'm not afraid. I'll claim my treasure of love." An emerging coherence in the sea's roar; louder, shriller, almost commanding now, seemed harmonious, like the blending of orchestral sounds. Standing, Della headed back towards the city, the people, the laughter, and the future.

CHAPTER 14

E d took her to Carrick-on-Shannon on Sunday. Only a mile from his home, the scenic hamlet on the banks of Shannon River in County Leitrim drew large numbers of tourists from all over Europe. Della liked it immediately. "If we were to live in the town, Ed, think of the fun, the boats, the waterside in summer, the fishing," she tried.

Ed, puffing a cigarette between brown-stained fingers, frowned. "Don't mention it again. We have no choice." Then, as if to avoid further contentions, he continued. "Visitors, attracted by the banter and singsongs in the pubs after a day's fishing, fill the town in summer. See the German, Dutch, and French names, an international community on the cruisers' sides. I come here a lot."

"You never mentioned it before." She stemmed a quick stab of jealousy. How little her awareness of him other than the person he presented on dates. With a hint of pride, he went on. "That three-storey shop on the main street was

Egan's Tailors, belonged to my father's cousin, but they sold up and went to Dublin."

"The place where your father managed twenty tailors?"

"Yes. Della, we have a history in this town. Later, I'll buy a boat and sail on the Shannon when we have children."

"Holy smokes, you've planned it all, Ed Egan."

"Well, we can try," he said, kissing her lips. It never failed; how he controlled, ruled and got around her! "Anyway, best get you back to Galway. Soon, I won't have to face the dreary journey along that winding road through three counties. Tedious."

"You complained when it was Dublin, Ed."

"Petrol costs, Della. But it was worth it, and now you're here." When he said things like that, Della glowed in the knowledge he wanted her that much. But inside her head, turmoil still reigned, tossing and turning the 'what ifs' amid flashes of opportunities fading beyond reach. When Sive rang, Della filled in the details of the past month and its outcome.

"Della, I can't believe you're letting him rule you again after all you suffered and sacrificed for him last year. I can see that you're still pliable and soft to manage. Think seriously. What will it be like later on if he's so controlling now?"

"He wants it more than me, Sive. It's got to be alright." As the words left her mouth, Della's stomach heaved, partly in fear but also self-loathing.

Here she was, doing what Ed wanted, with no one to blame but herself. She could not let him go, nor did she possess the strength of character to choose another path. But if they loved each other, surely their union would be happy?

It had to be. In hindsight, she had entered the convent with firm purpose, but now there were doubts, niggling darts that came during the night. Again, she popped the Valium, a tested tactic that dulled those inner voices.

The day of her leaving drew close. She would miss the staff in the Exchange. Nine months had fled since she joined the intimate mix of personalities. She asked if they would come for a farewell drink in the pub on the last Friday evening. All agreed.

Surrounded by the girls in the digs, she stood to speak in the lounge of the Seapoint. "I've loved every day in the office and with you girls. You gave me advice and stability when I needed it." A tear ran down her cheek.

"You brought something different to our daily grind," Gerry said. "We'll miss the fun, solving your arguments with Ed and our lengthy discussions on religion." The latter, fruitful in the light of her knowledge, was a stimulus she could only hope to reignite someday in the face of someone else's curiosity.

Stepping forward, Rosin presented Della with a picture of Galway Bay and the Cliffs of Moher across the sea in County Clare. Dabbing her nose, Della said, "Thanks so much. I'll treasure it and promise to visit when I learn to drive."

The following Monday, Della and Eve took the train to Dublin to buy material for the bridal wear Eve would make. They made a list: dresses, trousers, underwear, nightdresses, and more. Eve said Henry Street was the best place, with various reasonably priced shops.

Della felt ashamed. With few savings, she again depended on the fistful of notes her father had pushed into her palm at the railway station. Within one year, he had brought her to Dublin, tolerated her move to the West, and abandonment of a career for a marriage he considered premature. Poor Dad. To copperfasten the damage, he had to fund a wedding with its attendant outlay. "I ought to be happy and excited, Eve, but it's wrong to put another burden on you all."

"Della, stop moaning and get into a better frame of mind. By tradition, parents pay for their daughters' weddings."

Her sister was right. She would make the best of it and trust God to see her through. But the thought she was losing something precious pervaded. Her independence, brief but wonderful in Dublin and Galway, was slipping away. Aloud, she said, "Why can't women have a career and marriage?" Olive Keating was right to promulgate women's equality, but it would take years for the status quo to change. After all, how many women sat in government? Two.

The city buzzed with traffic, noise, shoppers, and restaurants. A wave of nostalgia engulfed Della on sight of her bus stop at Clerys, where she used to get off every morning before walking down Store Street to the high glass building by the Liffey. The job she could blot out; Dublin, never.

In Arnott's, they chose guipure lace for the wedding dress and rose-pink shot silk for Sive and Eve, her bridesmaids. Again, Della listened to her sister's advice; this would crease, that material too flimsy, Eve's expertise a guiding influence on every purchase. After all, Della only knew how to sew vestments and mend altar cloths.

By four o'clock, her wad of notes had shrunk.

"Don't worry. You'll get money presents at the wedding," Eve said as they boarded the Sligo train for the return journey to Boyle. No matter how bleak life was, folks always found a few pounds to shove into a child's hand after the First Communion and Confirmation ceremonies. The same practice abided at weddings and was more welcome than an abundance of sheets, bedspreads, and coffee sets. Silly little shiny bronze sets gleamed from glass cases across the land, never on tables - few drank coffee at home.

"I'm exhausted after all that walking," Eve said, stretching back onto the plush seat in the carriage.

"You'll do it all again when your turn comes," Della laughed. A thought struck. Would she need to immerse herself in stitching clothes and other country crafts to prove her worth? Readiing novels would hardly constitute an asset amid pigs, sheep and hens.

At home, Bridie displayed her day's work. Pungent smells of cake ingredients soaked in brandy and aromatic spices wafted around the kitchen. She would uncover the bowl and pour liberal amounts of brandy into its rich depths as the days passed. "Help me make it, Della, and learn. There'll be three tiers, the smallest at the top, which you don't cut until the first christening."

"First christening? Holy smokes!"

"And watch me sew up the dresses," Eve said.

"No. I can't stand sewing because of the torture I suffered in school with Sister Juliana making me rip up and redo everything I made."

"Forget all that, Della. I'm a pioneer and don't drink," Bridie said, "but I love the smell of brandy. It has a powerful effect on the fruit." There is nothing like a good fruit cake to bring out pride in a woman."

"I drink brandy and Babycham, Mam," Eve said. "Don't need a reason or a cake."

"Shame on you, girl. That's too much alcohol in one glass."

Excitement, smells, lace, and silk filled the house. When Ed came, Eve reminded him to buy ties that would match the pink of the bridesmaids' dresses.

"Have you and your father been for a fitting of the morning suits?" she inquired, his duty as a man of chic and sartorial elegance.

"We're not wearing formal dress."

"But Della assumed you were. You planned it ages ago. Our family expect it," Eve gasped.

"She planned it, but my father won't wear that."

"And you tell me now," Della shouted. "Our relations and guests expect it. We'll appear common."

"When you said you'd get the men's clothes in Carrick, I'd assumed you meant wedding attire."

"Snooty, above yourself," he flared now. "A good suit is better than a hired one you don't own."

"I'm not above myself, but my family has standing in the community."

"But *my* father doesn't like a show, wouldn't be comfortable in a 'monkey suit'."

Against herself, Della conceded. Her brief encounters with the older man showed his disgust for fancy trappings. "OK, I am very disappointed, but you should have cleared it with me first."

"Thanks, Della. You understand?" His relief showed in the half-smile and relaxed lines around his mouth.

Then, two nights before the wedding day, Ed dropped another clanger into the mix. Old Pat Egan would not make a speech. This time, Della could not stem the rage. In a fury, she shouted. "How dare you Egans spoil another convention?" Her reflection in the mirror, arms akimbo, face suffused with anger, induced a tumult of disgust for him and his family. "Put out that stinking cigarette, Ed Egan. It's a bloody nuisance."

He quenched the Player on the hearth. "You lot don't half demand."

"Seems to me I'm making the biggest mistake to date."

"Don't then," he said and walked straight into Bridie in the doorway. She had heard their voices along the hallway and come, unbidden, into the room.

"Are you still going ahead with this wedding? You quarrel over every detail. Ed Egan, it's not too late until you put a ring on her finger. Call it off."

Her mother's distress, flaming cheeks, and wide eyes immediately stalled a potential volte-face. For a moment, Della feared for her mother's condition. Bridie had high blood pressure. Of calm nature, she did not deserve the conflict in her home.

"OK, whatever you want, Ed. There'll be plenty of speeches on our side." Her attempt at sarcasm immediately struck home, and the barb pierced his ego. Ed's lips tightened into a grim line. A silence fell. Then he looked from mother to daughter and smiled, that winning smile that made women wilt. "Sure, Mam, no bother."

"Yes, Mammy, it'll be all right," Della said.

Serious now, Bridie faced her future son-in-law. She had something important to say. "I haven't got the strength of character my daughter has, going into a marriage when everything is not right. When I was younger, girls wanted a decent husband, healthy children, and to be homemakers. Nowadays, failed marriages are common. There's poverty, broken homes, and heartbreak. Della is intelligent, but it seems a force beyond reason propels her into this union with you, Ed. Can you guarantee me you will not let her down? Within my heart, I have doubts, but I must quiet them for her sake. She is hurtling along a road towards God knows what because she wants to please you."

"Nothing to worry about, Mam," Ed replied, getting up. Then, saying goodnight, he left the house as Jim came in from the yard.

Bridie explained, "For a man who'd suffered the lash of my tongue, he did not lose control."

"But isn't that it, Bridie? He's the master of control. So what's happened now?"

"We'll tell you at dinner, but everything's about Ed and what he wants."

Eve agreed. "Let's eat in peace." The utterance of 'peace' spread over the family like a veil as they ate. Not cabbage and bacon, for once, but lamb chops and carrots. Jim listened silently as his womenfolk imparted the latest details.

"Right. At the end of the honeymoon, when you get back to that farm, your world will change. Ed will be at work, and you'll be in the house with two people you hardly know."

"I've been there twice already. Laura Linehan lives a mile from the Egans."

"And Ed will allow you to visit her?"

"Allow?"

"He decides everything, Della, and you go along with it. Just like you did here an hour ago."

She could not challenge her father and muttered that Ed was too good to lose despite his authoritarian nature. He drew admiration from girls and men alike. What more might a girl want? That he was selfish and vain was a fact, but they would settle down to a happy life after marriage. One of her favourite songs, '*Love Conquers All*', an aria from the musical 'The Maid of the Mountains', jingled in her head. Only love mattered. *Quell the niggling doubts*, she told herself. There's no turning back.

In Boyle next day, she met an old flame of Ed's, Agnes Brennan, her senior by a year in boarding school. They chatted about the wedding, life in Galway, this and that.

"I went out with Ed while you were away. Don't get me wrong, it finished a year before you came home, but he was self-centred and couldn't pass a mirror without looking at himself. Immaculate dress sense - everything a girl might want - except he lacked sensitivity to feelings and needs. He even boasted about all the girls he'd dropped. I couldn't marry someone who put himself first."

"I knew you'd seen him, Agnes. He liked you, and I'd wondered why it didn't work out."

"I told you the reason, and he mentioned you a lot, hoping you'd come back someday. That was enough for me. I finished it."

"Seems Ed's had his choice of girls, Agnes, but he says I'm different from others. Gullible, more like."

"He fell in love with you on that first meeting five years ago. But you and I go back to schooldays, and I had to warn you, Della."

The dresses were ready in time, and all three fitted perfectly. Sive came from Dublin to try on her bridesmaid's pink gown two days before the ceremony. Eve's, well, she had made it herself. Ed's cousins, David McNiff, and John Egan, would be best men. Della had met John, his Dublin cousin, a financier in the city. An affable, educated man, his role as master of ceremonies would include a speech and presenting the bridesmaids' presents.

"One last time, Della. Are you sure of this? Of him?" Bridie tried. Fixing the fasteners on her daughter's dress at the back, she had yet to change into her two-piece primrose suit, bought in Boles' to complement her brunette hair.

"Oh, Mam, I am. We argue about everything and probably always will, but it's good. Don't worry."

In the church, Ed's four sisters, two over from the States, joined the Irish two with aunts and uncles in one pew while chosen relations filled the rest on the groom's side.

The O'Reillys, having few cousins, had invited neighbours and friends along to boost numbers. McCabe's from Skerries and the McDonald's from Wexford complemented the bride's group, while Bridie's brothers, Pat and Francis, and cousins Hearne's and Conry's, made up the marriage party. Jack Conroy's brother, Monsignor Patrick, back from Rome, would perform the ceremony. Bridie said it was a matter of pride as she sent the invitations.

"Gosh," Della said, "I couldn't care less about that." In her long white dress, the reflection in the mirror brought back a very different tableau. Just two years ago, she had proclaimed allegiance to the Lord as a Bride of Christ in a convent chapel. Her mind now conjured up the row of white-veiled bodies, prostrate on the aisle before the altar, uttering solemn words. But she had reneged on that promise and was now about to declare obedience to a human lord. It had to be worth it.

CHAPTER 15

On the altar step, they knelt in the Church of Mary Immaculate, ready to become one in the eyes of the Lord and the world. Della could not hold back a ripple of pride as he stood beside her. Ed, the most handsome creature in a black Italian-style suit and white shirt, was to become her husband. And despite the horde of difficulties strewn along the way, her voice did not falter in enunciating vows to love, honour, and obey before God, the priest, and the wedding party.

Ed's responses, barely audible, came in a series of halting words, his green pallor and trembling hands evidence of his inner anguish. She squashed a compulsion to gloat. Even the mighty fell sometimes. He stammered, got her name wrong, and couldn't put the ring on her finger. Yet, all the while, she smiled serenely. Today was hers, theirs.

Finally, it was over, and they went outside for photographs amid fluttering confetti. Ed's brother-in-law opened the door of his car and helped her in. Spreading the guipure lace train on the back seat, Della waited for a kiss from her new husband. But he leaned forward to Tony at the wheel. "How did I look inside the rail?"

Had she heard right? The unbelievable crassness of the man, his words hit hard; they would forever remind her of his self-love, raw and explicit. A sickening knot of revulsion gathered in her stomach, and a shudder of discomfort pulsated through her body. Not an hour married, and he was talking about himself. Embarrassment and hurt shot through her being. Then, she heard the muffled, diplomatic response through a mist of tears, "You were both lovely." Ed sat back and smiled. It would be alright. God, I'm like a child first punished and later rewarded with sweets, she thought.

On arrival at the hotel, Ed got out and turned to help her with the lace train. Maybe he was nervous before. Together, they walked along the red carpet towards the old-world Abbey, once the home of the great O'Connor Dons, high Kings of Connaught. Ed, who liked to boast of his teetotal years in Scotland, accepted a large brandy from Anne Greany, the hotelier. Throughout his working years in Scotland, he had never touched spirits but worked and saved for his ultimate life in Ireland. Now, he was swallowing brandy. The odd beer did not bother her, but spirits, the potent stuff, did. "Ed, slow down, please?"

"Dread, Della. I dread making a speech." Teeth chattering, he downed the remains of the drink and handed it to a waiter bearing an assortment of hors d'oeuvres and petite filo pastry sweetmeats. Della filled a plate; breakfast had been a slice of toast and marmalade, then pushed a vol-au-vent towards him. He looked at the food and turned green.

"When you sit down, you'll be fine. Those photographs at the church took so long, and I'm starving. Did we need that many pictures?"

Proceeding towards the dining room amid applause, they sat in the chief seats at the top table, surrounded by family, as custom demanded. Everyone was smiling, Della noted, even Ed's father, who appeared happy and, she had to admit, smart in his black suit. So much for protocol - people mattered more.

"The room is swimming, Della. Whose house am I in?" He clutched her arm tight.

"You daft thing, you're in the hotel. We're married."

"Oh, is that it?" She brushed aside his silly expression. "Pull yourself together." Where was the suave poser now?

"Are you joking or plain drunk?"

"Just a bit tipsy, I think."

The meal was delicious, roast beef from the rich pastures of County Roscommon, with all the usual green and orange vegetables. Amid smiles and congratulations, Della smiled and relaxed. They were, for better or worse, man and wife, like the priest said. It had to be better; she'd forever buried the worst into one big hole.

Ed stood up to speak, face blanched, hand trembling. Della lifted the sheet of paper and held it upright as he stuttered through one brief paragraph. "I'd like to thank you all for sharing our happiness." He halted.

Della whispered, "And to the O'Reillys for welcoming me into their family."

He stalled again. Gone the vanity and self-assuredness as he floundered through the excruciating ordeal. Della whispered cues, and eventually, his torment drowned in an ocean of claps.

Next, it was Jim O'Reilly, to whom public speaking came easy. Widely recognised as an orator, he welcomed Ed and the Egan family, praised his lovely daughter and thanked everyone. Della laughed. "My, oh my."

"What's so funny?" Ed asked.

"No one wanted to tell the truth that we were rushing into marriage."

"We did, didn't we?"

"You say that now, but it's all your doing." She squeezed his hand and whispered, "But we'll show them, won't we?" A weak smile was all she would get from him.

At the end of the speeches, while Monsignor Patrick was praying Grace, Ed rushed away from the table. What now? The loo? He had sipped water during the meal and had not tasted the wine. 'Never drank it, won't start now'. Fifteen minutes passed, and still no Ed. Della smiled and stood for photographs in the lobby with anyone who asked. "Where on earth is he?" she mumbled to Eve.

"Sick, I've been sick. No more brandy for me - ever," Ed appeared at her side. Relief washed over Della. He had not run away. So why did the thought enter her head?

"That'll teach you. Never drink spirits again."

"Easy for you, sitting there in a white dress and smiling, but it was a nightmare for me."

"You got through it, Ed. Don't spoil our happy day."

Four hours later, amid effusive congratulations, they left the wedding group behind for a honeymoon in Kerry. Ed, sobered after dancing, cups of coffee, and wedding cake, seemed calm and at ease. He placed the two cases in the boot, sat in the driver's seat, turned the car away from the turreted historic building, and waved. The last face Della saw was her mother's. Bridie's expression bore a look Della had seen before, on one October day back in 1961, on the steps of a hilltop convent building.

The Gleneagle Hotel offered a welcome sight at the end of a winding avenue in Killarney town. Kerry was the country's southern tip, where dark summits loomed over the southwest coast, and the sea battered the coastline relentlessly. To this place came an eclectic mix of tourists, drawn by rugged topography and glittering lakes, mainly from America. Most hotels included nightly entertainment and top Irish cuisine, perfect magnets for newlyweds.

But the sky over Killarney was dark, with low clouds masking the mountain tips. Della shivered. "It's July. It ought to be warm."

"It's Kerry, Della. What do you expect?"

"Gloomy skies are a bad omen."

"You read too much into signs. I expect holy nuns dinned them into your head. Hear God's voice in the thunderstorm and his smile in the sunshine." Ed's laugh fell flat on her ears. Why be capricious? Oh well, the weather changed daily.

In Reception, Della signed the register, Della Egan, and an unexpected wave of nostalgia infused her being. She'd been proud of the O'Reilly name, glorious Celtic chieftains in long-lost centuries. Giving up one's maiden name seemed like yet another female sacrifice. Olive Keating's words resounded again. *Women must change to achieve change.*

She rushed to open the windows in the bedroom and survey the scene below. Beyond the tall trees encircling the lawn, the tips of snow-clad peaks loomed high in majestic kingship, possibly the reason folks dubbed Kerry 'the kingdom'. Within a circumference of expansive grounds, neat flower beds dotted the manicured lawn. Perfect.

"Unpack the cases first, Della. Can't have my shirts creased." His shirts, what about her dresses, carefully folded the day before by her mother? "Then let's try out the bed."

"I need a rest, smart-alec. It's been an endless day."

If time were at a premium, theirs was precious. They would explore beautiful valleys for two glorious weeks, dine in pleasant coastal restaurants, and love each other. But the bed looked inviting, with its pristine white sheets and matching eiderdown. For no reason, a silly shyness crept over Della. They had never slept together before now.

"Bath first, Ed. I feel grimy after a long day and the dancing."

"And Della, no more talk about sin. I won't wear it." His hint, though subtle, carried an intensity that suggested an immediate end to the moral struggles fought over the past fifteen months. "Have your bath. I'll shower."

Longer than usual, she lay suffused amid Eastern aromas and fluffy suds. He'd never seen her without make-up. Would he think her plain? She would have to apply fresh mascara to make the eyes look deeper.

Fifteen minutes later, she emerged in a soft white robe. Ed drew her onto the bed. She felt the warmth of his skin as his arm encircled her waist and his lips found hers. Potential protests finally vanished into the pall of cigarette smoke yellowing the ceiling above. He'd smoked in the room.

An hour later, they sat at a table for two in the large restaurant. "Glad to be here, Della? If I hadn't insisted, you would still be in Dublin, and we might never have married."

"Yes, everything will be perfect, Ed, except for those loud Americans talking about their roots." In the centre of the large dining room, a group of big, corpulent Yanks sat waving their hands and expounding to anyone who listened.

"In the bar, before you came down, I heard one say his forebears boarded a coffin ship after the famine and sailed for 'the land of hope and glory.' And he's here now backtracking his genealogy."

"Yanks always seem to think everyone is interested in them."

"They bring a lot of money into this country. So eat your dessert, and I'll have an Irish coffee. I've only ever had one before, but it tastes nice."

"No drink for you, Ed. I know little about alcohol, except that it's dangerous. You had brandy earlier today, and it made you sick. Now you want whiskey." Dark memories of a gin-infused night in Galway intruded. She shuddered. He would never hear about it. "Mustn't let spirits get a grip now. You've been almost teetotal. Stay that way."

But he had a beer, and she a sherry. Enough.

The following morning, as Ed shaved, Della sat on the balcony, red rose scents wafting across the ironwork. A puff of sea air floated in the breeze, and occasionally, the clouds parted to reveal a bright sun in the blueness. Below, leaves, trees, and shrubs sparkled in the morning glow, in perfect communion with her spirits. She looked at the gold band on her finger.

Today, they would tour the valleys of County Kerry and smell the scented heather on the hillsides. She'd read it all up: where to go, what to see, where to eat, perhaps Killorglin, where locals held a famous fair every year, and, farther on, Blarney Castle in County Cork. Visitors came from across the world to kiss the stone, which allegedly brought good luck.

Ed came onto the balcony. "Let's have breakfast and find out where the dog track is."

"Dog-track? It's our honeymoon! I want to see the Gap of Dunloe, the scenery, and eat oysters in beach restaurants."

"But it's famous, and it would be a shame not to go when we're here."

Anger swept through Della at the idea that they would watch dogs run on the first day of their honeymoon! At once, a voice within her subconscious, that of her mother or Roisin, came whispering. *'Do it. Please him first'*. She had pleased him last night and, in a haze of halcyon bliss, expected nothing to come between them again. But now, the haze was clearing fast in the light of what Ed wanted.

"OK, but you can't gamble the wedding money." The cash pressed into her hand at the wedding reception was safe in an inner pocket of her handbag, and it would pain her to part with it foolishly. His, they'd agreed, would go on petrol and expenses. But dog racing was beyond the pale, unlike horse racing, ever popular in Ireland.

"You never mentioned the dogs before, Ed. Another secret, I expect." She stopped as a frown formed on his brow. *Keep it peaceful*, an inner voice said.

"Never seemed important. I sometimes go to the dogs in Longford or Sligo. Something to do of an evening." Another gap in her knowledge of what he did. Her father's fears nudged; they did not yet know each other well enough to settle down.

At the track, eager gamblers lined the barriers as the names of favourite dogs blared loud and sharp over the crowd. Della stood back while Ed handed notes to a bookie on a stand, roaring favourites at the top of his voice.

"Holy Moses, hope that's not all I gave you, Ed."

"Never mind. Sure, I'll win it back. Six races to follow." His expression, twinkling in expectation, stirred unease in Della.

The 'off' shot resounded, releasing a pack of brown, black and grey dogs from kennels that whizzed past like streaks of lightning. Ed's dog did not win, nor did the next one. His features, like chiselled marble, conveyed little, but he refused to say how much he'd lost before demanding more cash.

"No, Ed. You lost," she said. "On every bloody dog you backed."

"No need to swear. Yeah, but only the money you gave me at the start."

"*Only* thirty pounds. That would do us several days on petrol and food. You lost thirty pounds gambling on nothing in one hour, ten dogs dashing by in seconds. You threw away a lump of our honeymoon money."

"I'll get it back next time. Maybe we could go to the horseraces here."

"Do you think I'm a naïve fool that I'd let this happen again? Do you know me at all?"

"It's the wedding money. Ours, not just yours."

"Seems I'd better mind it after your performance today." No response came except for his tightened white knuckles on the wheel as they drove away from the track. Silence weighed heavy like the clouds over MacGillycuddy's Reeks in the setting sun.

"I must admit I gambled on cards, horses, and dogs during those years in Scotland at a local racecourse, Musselburgh. We lads had a bet or two every week. I never drank alcohol but spent money instead on the horses. Not so much the dogs."

"I understand; horses are part of my heritage, too. It's in my blood, but thirty pounds is a lot of money to lose on one night."

"Della, help me give it up," Ed said. Good. Conscience at work, wedding vows newly imprinted on the hardened brain.

"How? It's up to you. Seeing how quickly money could melt from your fingers scared me back there, Ed. But I'm puzzled you never drank yet gambled. Surely the two go together?"

"Except for the dances and horses, nothing else could distract me. So, let's drop it now."

The following day, they set off early for the Ring of Kerry, a drive around circuitous bends on winding roads and steep inclines. Despite the fabulous scenery, neither spoke. Their first time away for an extended period ought to be light-hearted. Still, the conversation did not come easy after the dogs' debacle. She'd heard stories of awful honeymoon discoveries, missing toes or droopy bits. Once, Sive had regaled Della and Eileen with a tale about Maggy McDonnell, who'd seen an extra nipple on Billy's chest on their first night together. No such blemish on Ed, though. His faults were of a different kind.

At the foot of the cliffs, waves crashed and rolled, in and out, foam topping foam, dragging rubble back into the Atlantic, like Della's journey from a secluded convent to an unknown destination. She'd almost crashed in Galway before the wedding but clung to the safety of the shoreline and survived. When they got engaged, she accepted the solitaire diamond he bought 'with a fair lump of savings, Della', and despite her reservations, Ed wanted a life together. Now, unbidden images of girls who hung about him pushed inside her head. Their faces waved in the wind, smiling, laughing, and pointing. But that was in the past, and they would go home to a life of bliss and contentment. Now was the time to suggest she look for a job.

"If we had a second income, we could move out and build our own house."

"And lose my home there? No way. We'll have children soon, and it'll be useful having the old pair to let us get out."

"Why? I'm only twenty-three and could have children later." A sprinkling of rain dribbled down the window. He slowed down.

"There were six of us, so I want a big family. And anyway, you can't plan to have children or not, Della. It happens."

"Doesn't have to." Back in Galway, she'd get pills from Rena and put a family on hold. An attractive notion. Was it so wrong to want time for themselves?

"Not on, Della. Better now, when we're young." Another idea knocked on the head because Ed said so. There was no point in hinting she didn't want to lose her figure, to be fat and unattractive so soon, or to be weighed down by a crying baby and nappies.

They drove towards Kenmare and entered the famous Gap of Dunloe, the country's wildest and most beautiful scenery in the southwest of Ireland. Della did not like remote places, but this was special: a tapestry of colours, green ferns, mosses, and purple heather pickling the slopes. Skeleton trees wafted eastwards in the wind, away from the wild Atlantic wind. She wound down the window. The rain was petering out, the air warm, and the earth smelt fresh.

"Stop, Ed. Let me take some photos."

He posed for a picture on a grass verge on a mound of heather, then took one of her by the car.

"Let's stay here awhile," she said. "So peaceful."

"Too peaceful. Wouldn't want to break down here."

Bathetic, as always. No poetic streak going astray in Ed. In the car once more, they drove down the sloped road into a valley.

On impulse, she set about clearing the air of all secrets. Ed should know the truth about her brief flirtations in Galway. Not Dublin; Neil, she would never mention, his name select and his memory sacred. She started slowly. "Remember that guy, Dermot, you saw in Galway?"

"Sort of. Why?" No hint of annoyance.

"Well, I went out with him a few times before I went to the cinema that night. I want to clear up misunderstandings between us. You said we mustn't lie, and I didn't tell you the truth back then."

There, she'd uncovered the monster, and they could move on. She looked over and waited. Ed jolted the car to a sudden halt. "You bitch! How could you do that to me? I knew something was going on, and your excuses made little sense. I should abandon you. Something to tell, eh? Well, so do I."

"Ed, please calm down." Frightened by the grit in his voice and the sudden nastiness, a feeling of dread gripped Della. She would never forget what he said next. Nor would the pain ease at any time in the future. In harsh invective bursts, his confession spilt out as if in relief that he could do it without fear of rebuttal. As he continued to inflict details of dating an English girl who visited near his home, he was no longer human but like a fox unleashed, snarling and vicious.

"I've known her since childhood. Carol and her family came last month. I nearly went back with her. Look. See how gorgeous she is." Then, without pity, he pulled photographs from the glove box and pushed them into her hand. "Not bad, eh?"

A beautiful face smirked and pouted in different poses, modelling swimsuits, dresses, and more. Della's throat constricted in pain as she choked and fought for breath.

"Let down the window, please," she gasped. "I need air." This man sitting beside her was now admitting to something far worse than her minor 'fall'. And he had dared adopt a highhanded, moralistic attitude towards her little 'aside'. What a farce.

"You nearly went off with that woman while I pined in guilt. You make me sick."

Heart thumping in anger and disgust, she sobbed. "I can't compete with a model, a beauty queen from Essex, with long legs and a perfect body."

An inner voice whispered, *now is the time to turn and run. Do it, do it*. Where? Up the Kerry mountains? She flung open the door, got out, and walked downwards into the valley. He followed and called in a softer tone. "But it's over."

"Over? It bloody should be. We just got married."

Gone the guilt, the remorse, her past actions now a mere blot in the light of his confession. "Ed, you made me seem like a child caught truanting. I need to think."

"No, Della, we're a couple now. So, let go."

"Were you in love with the girl? How do I know you won't be tempted again?"

"Yes, I was. There you have it. But her family background wasn't good enough. Her mother grew up in a small cottage, got pregnant with Carol, and had to go to England years ago. My parents would never accept her."

"Oh, my God." Despite being smitten with her, he'd had to reject the girl. Dizzily, tormenting thoughts forced Della to cry, "Ed, we can't go on. You punished me for a brief flirtation with Dermot while you did God knows what with a blonde beauty."

The knife piercing her heart was akin to that which Caesar (always a parallel in Shakespeare) felt when he said, 'Et tu, Brute'. In disbelief, she faced the man beside her. "Seems there are rules for me, but none for you."

Another character, Angel in 'Tess of the d'Urbervilles', came to mind. When Hardy wrote in the Victorian era, society accepted that men had affairs, but a woman must be 'pure' for the man she married. Poor Tess had died for her sins. Well, she, Della, wouldn't go that far, but Ed's stance towards her 'sins' was ironic now in the light of his confession.

When he stopped and looked into her face, it seemed to Della that Ed enjoyed seeing her blanch before him.

"My mother and father were right," Della screamed. "This marriage is teetering on deceit. You think it's fine for a man to do what he likes, but it's a grievous fault if a woman cheats. We've married because neither would let the other go. I could have got better than you."

Ed squirmed, pride in his attractiveness a solid characteristic that sustained his self-belief. That Della should find a chink was unthinkable. A nasty atmosphere enveloped them. Her sin, liking someone else, amounted to treason, while his paled into irrelevance.

"We've both lied during the past few months," he rasped. "And you're right. It's different for men; they do it but always come back. You pretend to be holy, but you're a hypocrite. I thought you were different."

"You have the cheek to say that."

"What choice have you?" Ed shouted, jumped back into the car, and slammed the door. Was he going to leave her here, in the wild? Della pulled the door open and fell into the passenger seat. An ominous ghost-like mist had spread over the picturesque scene, dissipating any trace of former beauty. Soon, darkness would shroud the valleys. Gone the magic, gone the love.

Chapter 16

They did not speak during dinner or later at the dance in the hotel. Della dabbed the mascara running down her cheeks between attempts at swallowing the pink salmon on her plate. Half-way through the meal, she looked directly across the table, but the stony-faced man ignored her. She picked up the silver cutlery, forked bits of salmon into her mouth, and then pushed the plate away. Afterwards, he took her arm as they veered by other tables. After all, one must keep up an image. He ordered a beer at the bar in the ballroom and a sherry for Della. They sat at the back of the hall in a shadowy corner.

When he stood up, walked off, and asked a girl at the counter to dance, Della went to the toilet, dried her eyes, and applied more mascara. She would not take his treatment for another minute. They would dance to soft music and claw back some lost romance. But he was on the floor with another one - tall, blonde, and gorgeous like the English model in his pictures. He was wreaking vengeance.

Della turned away, went to the honeymoon suite, fell onto the marriage bed, and slept. Later, she did not know how long, she woke to the sound of a key in the door. Her head pounded from the effects of the sherry. She should have stuck to Babycham.

His voice broke through the pain. "Too soon to break up, don't you think?" Bending over her, he touched her hair. "No divorce." It had a heart.

Della felt her stomach churn with bile from the sherry overdose, consumed fast when the talk was at a premium.

"I still love you," he offered.

"Really? But love, the vows, mean nothing. How many do you love?"

"Sleep it off," he commanded and, getting into bed, turned away.

Della woke the following day with a head full of cotton wool. She needed aspirin. Ed's form was in the same position as last night. She tiptoed out, took the lift and asked at Reception. The pretty girl smiled a knowing smile as if to say; we see it all the time. Overindulgence.

Turning towards the main door, Della walked out into the shrubbery amid its trailing clematis and pink roses. *A thing of beauty is a joy forever* sprang to mind. Didn't Nature always offer a balm or provide a natural remedy? She walked back and forth between the sweet peas and the dahlias, pretty colours in a lovely place. Unlike her mind, no weeds cluttered the handcrafted beds or dotted the manicured lawn. She whispered a silent prayer to the heavens. *Direct, oh Lord, all my actions.*

In the dining room, Ed was already at the table eating porridge. The Gleneagle made porridge special, with honey and cream. The Americans loved it, wrote about it, and sang about it. Della tried a spoonful.

"Ed, where do we go from here? Deal with our jealousy and let go of the past?"

"I don't want a suffocating life, I warn you." His half-smile did little to soften the bluntness. Filling the teapot, he beckoned the waitress, who fluttered towards the table. Ed's attractiveness had that effect wherever they went, simpering things wafting around him when he sought attention. In his blue shirt and white jeans, he was anyone's fancy.

"We're in a one-sided union, and only what you want is important?"

"We'll see. Our marriage has begun with lies. Hard to forget."

"Lies, yours multiplied by God knows how many. Mine about one man." Neil, never. The thought of him made her cringe with shame. *I'm a fool, a silly fool.*

Della pulled a photo from her handbag and handed it to her new husband. "What does that show? The hotel photographer took it last night at the dance. Happy honeymooners! No. You look angry, me sad, and alienated."

Despite the pretty polka dot navy and white dress and backswept corn-coloured hair, her image reflected the anguish of the previous day. Della would never forget that episode in Killarney. Blemished by her silly confessions and his disclosures, their honeymoon was on the verge of collapse. Worst of all was Ed's harsh attitude, which frightened Della. Would he, could he, be a fit husband after all this? That she had to query it, albeit in silence, was worrying. She would advise Eve, "Don't tell a man all your secrets. What they don't know won't trouble them!" A cliché of sorts, but in her life, a truism.

"No dramatics, Della. Let's go see the sights and do what we came for."

"But are we right for each other? I kept secrets from you because I longed for other encounters. There's a gap in my life that I can't now fill because I'm married. I wanted to live, mature, and learn. There's a hunger in me for knowledge, travel, and other lands. I needed time, but you insisted on marriage. I don't understand why you wanted it so soon when you cheated on me. You liked freedom, too."

"Stop delving. Get over yourself. Stuff happens. Admittedly, I saw a lot of girls while you were away, but I wanted to marry *you*. You might have slipped away from me in Dublin, and I always knew it had to be you. So let's leave it." She could have argued—*except for Carol*. He'd loved her. But that, too, could be compared to her feelings for Neil back in the city. Now, it was too late for - anything.

The two weeks drifted into a miasma of wandering in Tralee, not much there, and Killarney's posh hotels, lovely restaurants, and lakeside seats. They hired a boat, fed ducks, and swam in the cold sea. Driving around the Ring of Kerry's shard-like inlets and coastal wildness summoned images of shipwrecks and washed-up bodies. Della loved the sea, its storytelling, and life-planet mystery. Words from a favourite poet nudged:

> *One day, I wrote her name*
> *upon the strand,*
> *But came the waves and*
> *washed it away.*

Like the mighty foam that crashed onto the rocks of County Kerry, she could not flee from the juggernaut that threatened to destroy them.

Ed laughed at her screams when a guide held Della upside down to kiss the Blarney Stone in County Cork. In contrast, his performance amid the lofty turrets of the famous castle was stoic, athough Della detected a tremor on his face. Never one to show weakness, he gasped aloud as the burly attendant pulled him back upright. "Great view. Let's have a photograph together up here."

Posing for a bystander with Della's camera, they smiled in unison. Later, she would find shades of pretence in the image.

At night, they danced in the hotel and chatted with other honeymooners. Gradually, a companionable peace descended, almost dissipating Della's gloom. She did not refer again to his former 'girlfriend', for whom he had nearly left her, but the thought of the photographs in the car made her stomach turn.

A singular, powerful force, and it was down to that, might save their marriage. Their mutual desire and passion remained, firing afresh the attraction stimulated five years earlier. During those times, misgivings nebulised into a mist of hot air and floated far above their bodies.

But a honeymoon, in a genuine sense, it was not. Amid awkward silences, Della wondered if their future would morph into tangled wefts or wipe the past into a clean slate.

On the final Saturday, they set off for the four-hour journey toward the country's northern region. It had been a fortnight of mixed emotions, discovery, and, dare she admit it, ugliness.

On arrival at his home, hers now, a line of cars on the roadside cheered Della. She saw the cheerful smiles from both families. Normal. Welcoming. If she were to settle down with the in-laws, she might as well start on a sound footing. Cameras flashed. Carry her across the threshold, they shouted. Della felt foolish. A feeling of uncertainty washed over her. She did not want to cross the threshold but to sit in her father's car and drive away to Leam, the big farm, and her pink room. Smile, Della, they said. She did. None would learn of their turbulent time in Kerry. It would put Ed in a poor light, as well as herself, for not listening to her family, who tried to stop her from entering a marriage built on discord. But no one seeks vilification for fugacious love.

Monday morning. Ed got up at seven-thirty; no lazing about after the honeymoon. "Gotta get out and earn some money," he said, terse, sharp, businesslike. Would he leave her after just one night in his home?

"What will I do here all day?"

"Oh, unpack, hang up wedding pictures, do something, help my mother. Lay the table for breakfast."

But Molly Egan had done it all. Her son's bowl of porridge and mug of tea sat at his usual place. She gestured to Della to sit beside him. "Himself is milking the cow in the field. We get up early here, you see." Della did see. She wandered to the range, lifted the steaming teapot and poured herself a mug of tea. "Can I make toast?" she asked.

"If you want, we just have porridge, bread and butter in the morning."

Wrongfooting already, Della looked towards Ed for a snippet of support. But he seemed oblivious to his new wife's dilemma. Or for her to serve his breakfast? No one cared.

So this was it. With barely a 'goodbye', Ed went off to sell machinery. Della washed their mugs and dishes in the sink, then climbed the stairs and entered the big double room, which she soon learned the old pair had vacated for them. She unpacked their clothes and hung them in the one double wardrobe. She would spend her day with the old folk, not her husband. Ed had left her to adjust.

A blackbird's trill on the edge outside penetrated the morning noises; a lone voice raised to the heavens. She'd always liked blackbirds, especially the little one on her bedroom windowsill when she was four. Della gave him crumbs, and he'd stayed throughout the winter. Now her 'darkling thrush' had come again, a blackbird. Was he her symbol, a lone voice amid change? Hardy's bird had ushered in a new century, hers a new life. But right now, she had to find something to do.

In the kitchen, her mother-in-law suggested that Della try to cook to fill her time somehow.

"I'll make an apple pie later on."

The older woman bustled around the back kitchen, washing milk pails and creaming the crock in preparation for churning. I'm an unnecessary extra, Della pondered. Laura had mentioned that her mother-in-law was feeble; not so Molly.

"Fine, then you can find a place to hang all your photographs. I have to feed the hens and churn the milk. You know, we must make fresh butter every week." Della didn't. "And I don't have pie dishes, as I bake nothing but soda bread, so you'll have to buy them if you want to practise baking."

Practise. Della would ask her own mother, who made succulent pies and fruit cakes.

Hanging up the pretty dresses bought for the honeymoon, she realised a pair of jeans was enough with a casual top during the day. If she were to help in the house, it did not matter what she wore. She *would* keep busy, and Ed would be home later. In bed the previous night, he'd said,

"This is it, Della. No more dredging up old stuff." Yes, she'd agreed, muffling her voice, aware that across the corridor, two pensioners lay sleeping and might awaken to the sound of a creaking bed. Her father's warning came again: *You haven't thought beyond the honeymoon.*

As for love, it was but a conundrum. *No other pearl is found in the dark folds of life;* Hugo's depiction within a depth of misery seemed apt now, although Della's presence in Ed's life had to work, making him need no other.

Della wondered how to spend the rest of the day after a lunch of ham and tomatoes at the table, Himself at one end, Molly at the other. No friendly office banter would lighten the dull hours thudding by or excite her. Gone the hopes, the happy ever after dream. Through the narrow window, tall trees glowered darkly into the white house. Enmeshed in an image she'd tried to shun, Della wondered about her judgement or lack thereof. But didn't most women give up work for love? But not for an existence with two old people.

Across the countryside, couples lived with their parents, the son stayed, rarely a daughter, caring for the older people until they died. But the fact remained that her life on a small farm would differ from that on the O'Reilly estate in Leam, just as her father had said. And the blame lay entirely on her useless attempt to break free from a man in the name of love, a mere fantasy. She had to fight for a marriage to which she had acceded, albeit reluctantly. And on a practical plane, she must never let depression choke her brain again; it had almost destroyed her mind last year.

She might read a novel begun on the honeymoon. Where? In the kitchen, under the other woman's eyes? Be in the way and seem lazy? What else? Go for a walk, see the surrounding area, meet neighbours? She had never really liked the quiet countryside nor sought the peace city relatives yearned for. Two miles further on were the lakes she had glimpsed on that first visit to this house. But she did not drive, and it was too far to walk. She would have to get a little car and escape.

She sat on the only chair in the bedroom by the front window overlooking fields and bogs. She opened *Heart of Darkness,* bought in Dublin when the prospect of a literature course was possible. In the story, a white man shrunk from lording power over black people. Here, not one but three people ruled the domestic kingdom.

By five, Della felt a little excited. Ed would be home soon and tell her about his day. They'd chat upstairs in the bedroom before dinner.

She set the table while her mother-in-law stood over a pot of boiling bacon on the range. Now and then, the older woman poked a sharp knife into the flesh to test if it was ready. Near the end of the process, she shoved copious amounts of green cabbage around the bacon and placed a pan of potatoes on the hob. "Kerrs Pink, the best according to Himself, and he knows his spuds." Cabbage smells rose and circled the room, sour and oppressive.

Ed came in. Instead of shaving or changing, he sat down for dinner at once. Della sensed his new intensity as he discussed the business with his father. He did not include her, but when his mother cut in asking about the prices of lawnmowers, Ed responded. Della stood up and gathered the dishes to wash at the sink. They had not shared a single sentence. Maybe later. The feeling of superfluity clung, that she was a mere appendage with nothing to offer.

Three days on, same dinner, same routine. Unlike Bridie's tasty stews and mashed potatoes, the fare was simple beyond simple. Della's resentment festered. "Why didn't you warn me they were so old-fashioned?" she asked her new husband in the bedroom after he'd showered. "Set in their ways. It's awful."

"Get out my mother's bike and cycle up the road to visit Laura Linehan." A trite but wise suggestion.

"I will. It's claustrophobic here. This forty-acre farm would fit into my parents' ten times over."

"Don't talk rubbish, Della. It's a fair-sized holding. Make the most of your free time. You'll soon be pregnant, and that'll keep you quiet."

"Maybe." His reminder of the duty she must fulfil vexed her, even more repugnant, driven by his apparent intention to ground her.

"No maybe. You know how it happens." But the old pair's nearness at night made her cringe each time Ed came close, as did the memory of his confessions. An unspoken agreement not to dredge bad stuff up could not dim the harsh fact that he had been willing to drop her at will and return to the UK. Conversely, knowing she had left a young potential vet in Dublin was a sort of compensation.

The next day, Della asked Molly about Carol, with whom he'd cheated.

"Don't mention that lot. The mother came from a cottage down the road and went to England to have a babby, the hussy sniffing around here every year since she grew up.

She's always wanted Ed. But you're here now, so she can't bother him again." Bother him? The older woman's words did little to banish the uncertainty ignited in the Gap of Dunloe. Della related a little to what happened, but the need to unburden, more significant than the shame, soon led to the complete disclosure of their row in Kenmare and how it had almost destroyed them.

"Well, if he wanted that one, he'd not be welcome here. She'd never cross this doorstep." So she, Della O'Reilly, was a consolation prize?

"I'm going for a walk, Molly." Della needed air to breathe and to release the bete noir within.

"Right then, but see, you're back by five to set the table."

An inward scream died on her lips. Set the table and listen to everyday minutiae about cows, sheep, pigs, and machinery. Accept her place as a second-rate wife of a man who'd desired another woman. At the bridge, she threw pebbles into the trickling stream and watched each ripple forming bigger circles. Mother in the novitiate used to liken the pebbles to feathers, and once you plucked them, the effect was irretrievable. Gossip flew far and wide, destroying character in their path.

It was unbearably quiet. Unlike the bustling village where the O'Reillys lived in Leam, ten miles on the Roscommon side of Boyle, few travelled the quiet byways in this part of the county. An odd cyclist smiled and said hello. One man stopped on his way to trim the lawn on the estate. He told her it had belonged to the 'landed gentry', an Anglo-Irish family who gave employment to the cottage folk. Landed gentry. Hadn't her family purchased one such place from Protestants? As the day dulled to evening, she returned to the house amidst the glowering high leylandii.

Margie came on the dot of eight o'clock each night and took a chair beside Molly, facing the warm range in the middle of the floor. Della and Ed sat together near the Stanley range. Himself, reading a book, had a soft armchair on the far side. Chatter filled the kitchen, exchanging details of their biosphere, a tiny dot on Planet Earth.

Della tried to engage Ed about his day, the machinery he sold, and money taken, to shut out the rasping colloquial speech patterns: b*esht/best, sthop/stop, sthart/start, flure/floor, dure/door, lie/lead, toasht/toast,* but he seemed to enjoy the flow that continued until Margie left at ten-thirty.

"Why does Margie get up to go home at the same time every night?" Della asked anyone who might answer.

"She has to open the gate for Peter when he gets home from the pub," Molly replied.

"Open the gate? Can't he do it himself?"

"Well, he has a few pints in town and can't drive the car straight into the haggard unless Margie goes out with a flashlamp to guide him in."

"Why?"

"Get out and listen behind the hedge when he arrives home, and you'll know why. She'll get the rough end of his tongue if that gate isn't open wide for the car to pass through."

"Is she his servant or his sister? Why is she there anyway?" As if her question dropped into an abyss, it drew little besides tight lips from all three. Their recalcitrance was intriguing, and the secret even more mysterious. But she'd find out. What am I becoming, she wondered to the internal person within her body. Subsumed into local gossip and nothingness, I'm far from last year's cherished dreams.

In bed, she asked, "Ed, what's the problem next door? Why has Margie got to leave here at the same time each night to get to a house a hundred yards away, and open a gate for a man going into his haggard?"

"Hush, it's late." Then, blurring further questions, with a hard kiss, he turned out the light.

"Damn you, Ed."

In the morning, she probed further when Molly came in from the cow byre carrying two white pails laden with frothy milk: white pails, white milk, black secrets.

"Molly, what's so terrible about Margie that no one will tell me?"

"Now, girl, there are secrets, there's deceit, there are lies, and there's a disgrace. Margie's had it all."

"So, she did something bad, but her brother lets her stay there under his roof, although she can't live an independent life because she disgraced the family? Did she steal from someone?"

"Aye, but it wasn't stealing." Molly moved off, cans rattling, towards the scullery to pour the milk into a big urn.

Della determined to discover if more secrets or scandals abounded in the sleepy village. Here goings-on were as crucial as food on the table and money for the Friday shop. Della liked the little woman who came rambling, and she'd call on Margie - home alone each day with no company except for the old wireless on the dresser.

One month on, and the daily routine was crushing Della. Their union lacked spontaneity, with no privacy until bedtime, though Ed stayed in at night, and they were getting on. Neither mentioned the row in Kerry, with the potential to poison their present calm. And she did not wish to harbour distrust for the man who'd callously informed her of his pre-marriage activities. Della, she told herself, he's trying; let it be.

Every Sunday, they visited Leam for a roast dinner cooked as it ought to be. Ed chatted to Jim about the business and his hopes for expansion. Bridie advised Della to get to town and see people. Yes, Della agreed. She would call on Laura.

"Can I ride your bike to Laura Lenian's, Molly?" She asked on Monday.

"It has a low saddle."

Not only was the saddle low, but it moved under her. The spokes were rusty and horrible. Della's bottom slipped sideways as she pedalled the ascent to the Linehan house. When had she last ridden a bike? Years ago, during school holidays, to meet Mary Lally or Nan Hall, when they'd roam the roads looking for excitement. Oh, happy days before convents and complexities.

A smiling Laura opened the door. "You're here at last, Della. Come in and have a cuppa."

In the large kitchen, papers, boots, and shoes were piled high on an old cabinet, randomly peeping out from under the furniture. There was no sink, just a basin on a table by the window. A smell of fried onions clung, probably last night's dinner. Della averted her eyes and sat at the table. The other woman's boots, grey top, and tight trousers appeared soiled and shabby. Any wonder, considering her environment. Old Bea was on her afternoon nap upstairs.

Like a spring released inside her, Della described the honeymoon and her husband's caustic attitude when he discovered her minor aberration. "I tried to tell you Ed put himself about, but that's surely behind him, and he's staying in at night. It's a vast change for a man who lived his life to the fullest. Joe used to see him in the pub on weekends and said Ed went dancing everywhere: Ruskey, Moate, fifty miles away, even Bundoran and followed the Johnny Flynn and Clipper Carlton bands, I believe. They regarded him as one of their own."

More revelations about her husband.

"He's clever, only tells me what suits."

"Joe says that for Ed Egan to settle down is amazing and that he stays home at night more so. Della, be happy. Boring or not, you'll soon get pregnant and have a family."

That word again. "Seems you know more than I do. Anyway, enough about me. How are things here?"

"I've pressed Joe to build a bathroom. He argues that, as the house is on a hill, the water pipes could not reach the dwelling unless we paid the council higher rates than the neighbours. He won't, and we have to do without running water."

"Oh my God, Laura, that's primitive."

"I offered to raise money and go back into nursing. We'd soon have the price of running water and sanitary provision. But I'd need a cheap little car."

"What did he say?"

"I got an awful reaction. Joe's cheeks shook, and curses spurted from his mouth. On his way out to count the sheep, he banged the back door shut. He loves his sheep, all three hundred roaming the hills over the valley. I married a farmer, his mother, and his sheep. All of it, including me, comes in one mucky package."

CHAPTER 17

"Laura, there are no sheep on Ed's farm nor enough land to make a decent living. That's why he's out flogging machinery daily," Della said.

"From what I hear, Ed is a doer. In town, they say he'll make it big. Joe is a different type, however. He arrived home on market day, sozzled after a few pints, and said, 'You wanted a car, look outside'. My heart thumped; I was so excited; he was a good man. But there wasn't a car on the road or in the shed. Instead, a shiny bicycle stood propped against the wall. 'Go as far as that takes you, woman, and be done with this talk of nursing in another town,' he said. I wanted to hit him."

"Laura, that's awful. Why do you stay? You could earn a living, and be independent."

"Marriage vows are sacred, and with the baby, I need calm."

"Can he afford a car?" Della's eye roamed over the peeling paint on the walls; the rough stone floor, sparse and worn, unlike Egans' polished lino and easy armchairs.

"The farm would profit if he reared more cattle and had fewer sheep. Or he could sell off a parcel of land, but Joe likes the big farmer image, says money spent on the stock is sensible, not squandering it on cars and washing machines."

"That's my next goal, a machine." Della placed the mug of tea on the table. "And I will get one."

"You're lucky. Ed is a modern man. Joe won't budge."

Lucky. Only six weeks ago, Della had cried bitter tears of regret and hated her new husband. Since then, the tears had dried, but a trail of doubt still clung, eating into her self-belief. Like the bell for the Holy Office, warnings rang in her head before each new dawn. How long before he strayed?

As they sipped tea and ate Laura's scones and jam, the other woman's eyes wandered to the swaying branches against the back window, dense, untended. "My dreams of a happy life in the country away from the bright lights of London are dead. I just wanted a husband and a home of my own."

Della sighed. "I did not know how claustrophobic quiet country living in a small rural parish might be. I used to be bored doing repetitive office work in Dublin, but now I'd love to return there."

"Yes. Everyone knows your business in the countryside. I found it weird at first, after London, where you didn't talk to the person in the next flat. Here, gossip about nothing is an escape from hardship. Have you ever noticed how Council roadmen lean on their shovels, talking to each other instead of cutting back the hedges?"

"Yes, they do, but I love the friendly chat and how folk get down from their bikes and speak to me when I'm walking. But I wouldn't say I like the narrowness and the secrecy. Mentioning secrets, do you know anything about Margie Malone? I think she's a dogsbody for that brother and is afraid of him."

"I'll ask Bea. She'll know."

"If every family had a television, it would broaden their interests beyond local tittle-tattle. It's the sixties. Most homes have modern conveniences."

"Not here."

Della stood up to leave. Laura walked to the gate at the roadside and pointed to the cluster of trees further down the hill. "That's Coillte village, rooted in Celtic mythology. I looked it up in the library one day."

"Good for you, Laura. Go on."

"Under Anglo-Irish domination, the village spread into a huddle of smallholdings within a shelterbelt of trees. But today, the houses are still close enough for folk to earwig each other's barneys to feed their gossip later."

"Any young women like us down there? Someone else to befriend?"

"Yeah, quite a few. You'll get to know them soon. Nice, but insular. Most girls didn't go far to find a husband, a few miles at most. But they were glad to be wed, even if the 'ould wan' still sat in the rocking chair by the fire. You and I came from a good convent background. I grew up in a town with an educated family, and I've seen sights and sounds unfamiliar to the Coillte lot."

"Will we ever really settle here?"

Laura's laugh made Della gasp. "We already have, and the old sex is good. It renews the attraction that first drew me to him in the pub. Once you have kids, Della, you'll settle."

"Sex just gives me cystitis, which I never heard of before. Molly made me drink bread soda dissolved in water, which helped, but I went to Doctor Farrell in town, and she said it happens to new brides. She prescribed tablets. They worked. And it kept him quiet for a while." Their laughter echoed down the valley to the distant lake between the hills.

"Della, don't be shocked if I tell you I take Valium sometimes. It lightens depression." The word hung between them, in awkward contrast to the sex reference.

"And I, too, Laura, since I had that breakdown. Dulls the anger, too."

"Better than running back to an ageing mother with my problems."

Della waved goodbye to the woman standing in the shadow of a solid oak tree. Aged and glorious, its branches yearned upwards towards an azure void, its leaves shadowing the tufted grass underneath. Yet, like its owner, the tree stood solid, unassailable, and unchangeable.

"Great times, ye're havin' ladies, gossipin' away while we men work ourselves to the bone." The voice emerging from the side of the barn was that of the man himself, Joe Linehan.

"If you say so, Joe," Della replied. Then, she turned the bike towards the bog road and home. Glad of the air on her face and the pungent smells of blossoming brambles in the hedgerow, she pedalled downhill to the white house in the valley. The smile on her friend's face when Joe appeared, how she'd laughed at his joke, showed her desire to please him. Laura's life was tough; the man she'd married, a controlling overlord who allowed little freedom, expected her to run a house, milk cows, and fetch feeble lambs when the ewes dropped. But the older girl's yearning for a family and security transcended everything else, even deprivation. That Joe was boss, Della did not doubt.

Molly's wash day was a big event. "Awful hard to get the grime out of the shirts," she observed, lifting a black-laced collar. Della recoiled. "I never noticed how Mam did it. Why should I? And in the Convent, the laundry looked after all that sort of thing. I went there once with a bag of novice white veils and nearly choked. The air was suffocating, with white particles floating around in the steam."

"None of that here, just hard grind. Watch." The older woman filled the sink with boiling water. "First, souse the grease and sweat from the cloth, then scrub hard with a bar of carbolic soap before rinsing them three times in cold water."

She's teaching me how to do it. Surely I can rub a bit of soap on a shirt. Della bit back resentment.

"Besht, do it first thing on Monday. It has to be early for the neighbours to say Molly Egan's wash is as good as anyone else's. And if it's raining, wait until the sun comes out, or they won't dry."

'*Dear God, above*', Della breathed. Her mother's line on a grassy slope away from the house was far off the road. No one saw, cared or compared. But here, the Monday line was a matter of pride. Not three months in the house, it felt like she'd married Ed's parents, her days in their company, nights only with her husband.

"Let me help, Molly." Best offer before the order came.

"If it's work you want, wash Ed's shirts yourself. Mind you do it right. He likes them soaked first. And put a blue bag in the rinse for his whites. Then chase the hens from the back door. That'll give you something to pass the time." Molly smiled, induced tolerance ironing the lines on her crumpled skin, and, at that moment, Della glimpsed the woman's former beauty in the picture on the shelf. Now, the tousled hair and dirty glasses showed only her frail state. Molly's back, slanted forward like a banana by her condition, a prolapsed womb, appeared to cause her pain when she tried to straighten.

"Are you in pain, Molly?"

"Aye, but I put up with it. After seven births, what can ye expect?"

"But Ed has five sisters."

"One died at five months. When Himself was in the mood, there was no choice. A woman had no choice if her man wanted his rights. So I just offered it up for the souls in purgatory."

"Molly, that sounds more like rape. Do you know what that means?"

"No, 'twas me duty to lie with my man and fulfil the sacrament, but I hated it. Then, I got caught a month or two again after each birth. It was hard."

"It's old-fashioned control, like something from a Dickens' novel. The man rules the house and the woman. I won't ever be like you."

Molly's expression and half-laugh told Della that the older woman had little faith in her declaration and did not understand Dickens' reference. "You don't know my son very well then, Della."

"Well, yes, I do, and he can be difficult, but since we got married, he's trying." And she was trying to dissolve the distrust engendered during the honeymoon.

"Keep him out of that town, girl, or you'll see the other side of his character. Over the years, he's lost money at cards, and I've had to subsidise him. His father doesn't know it, or he'd run Ed."

"He lost money in Kerry." Once started, details of the honeymoon losses spilt out. The older woman's response came quick as a shot, opening up yet another sinkhole of worry in Della.

Molly Egan stopped scrubbing the last shirt in the sink and stared. "Girl, ye'll have nothing. Gambling is his downfall. He's never been a drinker but can't resist the horses, the dogs, and the cards. To think he gambled the present money on the honeymoon is mighty frightening. So I'm telling you, watch Ed."

Fear clawed into Della's guts as further revelations about her husband flowed from his mother's lips. "He's changed. All that's behind him now. He promised."

"Early days," came the reply, gloomy and prophetic.

"Ed never mentioned gambling before we got engaged. I didn't realise what he did when we were apart." The telling smile on the older woman's face annoyed Della. She might have to live with the woman, but the attitude of 'I know more than you' was somehow insulting.

"Anyhow, must get on with this quilt." Gathering a bundle of old skirts, trousers, and dresses, Molly cut swathes of material at the table into diagonal, square and diamond shapes. Over three hours, she sewed the patches together to form a neat, symmetrical pattern until one large piece of fabric covered the kitchen table. Every bed had a patchwork quilt made by her. Saved money, she said. But Della hated the coarse feel on the skin and its drab appearance. The sheets were rough, too, also sewn by her mother-in-law, a former seamstress in a large store.

How frugal her new mother-in-law was, like Himself. His warning, 'pay for what you get, no tick, mind', resounded around the kitchen whenever Molly took off for town on Fridays. She would buy thread and wool, stuff about which Himself knew little. The Egans were neither rich nor poor, but their shared fear of poverty was real. They'd married in the thirties during the economic war when most folks struggled and penny-pinched.

"See that dresser behind you, Della. I bought it with the turkey money one New Year, and only two years ago, those worktops around the walls, with the pig money." Grudging admiration made Della ashamed of her judgments on the countrified speech. They had come through it with nothing to spare, and a child every year.

Molly went on. "Sure 'twas hard to stretch food and clothing. But I never threw out leftovers and even softened bread crusts in tea for the cats. You see me boiling potatoes and turnip peelings on the range for hens and dogs alike."

"I hate the smell. It's nauseating." Della uttered without thinking and, seeing the frozen look on the woman's face, wished she hadn't.

"Himself is happy on his forty acres, and when work is slack, he'll stray through the farm, searching for fox tracks and peering into rabbit burrows. He'll kill anything that steals into his yard at night to eat precious fowl. And when the light outside fails, he comes inside and reads until suppertime."

Della understood. A man of habit, Himself ate Bridie's soda bread, baked daily, except on Sunday when they had fried eggs and some of their home-cured bacon. Old Mister Egan was proud of his skill in killing the pigs, his wife of the home built thirty years ago, the two-storey, tree-enfolded house. So Della had to respect their way of life, even if she hated the suffocating atmosphere, the continual squinting at passers-by with odd bits of shopping on the carriers, and the unmentionable secrets.

"Della, mind you scrub the collars well. Ed likes them perfect. Use the scrubbing brush." The command broke through her reverie. Regrets were pointless. But dear Lord, why did I not probe more nor wonder about my life after marriage? Too late. A voice, the one that talked to her frequently, came again. You have to go on. No going back. Pen-pushing in the Civil Service wasn't as bad as the mundane tasks here.

Immersing her arms up to the elbow into the pile of cloth in the sink, Della forced her fingers to work until deep red weals appeared from the carbolic soap. She'd show the woman.

How wonderful to hear the natter of wannabe women again, smell the Liffey outside a glass building, and share fun times with Sive and Eileen! As for Galway.

"Hang the shirts upside down, Della. You can't have peg marks on the shoulders. Ed hates that."

Another instruction, another order. I know what my son wants, and you don't.

Della hung the shirts as directed on the clothesline, but at the last one, a quirk took hold, a mischievous desire to flout the rules. She pegged a blue-striped shirt from the shoulders. Why not? She'd iron them flat until the marks came out flat and flawless. And that was how her mother did it, without a single complaint from Dad.

Half an hour later, Molly went to get eggs from the coop. Reading at the kitchen table, Della heard the door thrust open and the swish of a broom the older woman carried to root eggs from hedgerows. "What did I tell you about the shirts? Upside down, I said. Ed won't like it."

"So bloody what, Molly? I'll do what I want. It's my husband and not you who I'll please."

"Well, you won't last long if that's your attitude." The older woman fluffed around the kitchen, white hair bobbing, tone sharp and dictatorial. "You've put me off what I was going to do."

Ed must have known how life would pan out for his new wife in the house that belonged to his parents. Despite his modernity, he was part of the culture, soaked in its rusticity, and his life unchanged except that he had a woman in his bed at night. Instead of wandering the roads for excitement, he had it at home.

Della was not blameless. She had not listened to her parents or friends when they begged her not to give up Dublin, then Galway, or to delay marriage. She had to reset her targets now, learn to drive and get out more. Would God listen? Why should He? She'd left Him in Sligo. She was twenty-three, with a possible fifty years ahead. But there was hope; the oldies would die, and she and Ed would have the place to themselves and their virtual children.

Lying awake later in the darkness, she looked out at the millions of stars dotting the sky, tiny pinpricks of hope in the night, soothing in their steadiness, their completeness. In contrast, her insignificant life would barely register on such a canvas. But she *would* make it matter. Ed owed her. She'd given up so much for him.

Sunday. Della dressed carefully for a night out together. It might be a small town, but the golf crowd would be in the hotel and everyone who congregated in the Royal. In the main, she dressed for Ed so that he'd see again the young girl he fell for one enchanted evening at a dance.

In the first hour, he introduced her to Eamon Doran, who owned a haberdashery business in the town. Enormous brown eyes in a bronze visage, he stood beside Ed, equal in looks and physique. Were they all this good-looking in Boyle?

"I like your taste in women, Ed," he said with a quiet smile, holding Della's hand for a lingering moment. Easy to like this one. And he had brown eyes. Wasn't she a sucker for them? Oh, let that go...

"Thanks." The pride in her husband's voice was worth the effort of dressing. "What are you having, Eamon?"

"A brandy, please. Della, I think you might know my sister-in-law, Rose McQuillan. She's a nun in Sligo."

Della blushed; the convent was not a topic for discussion in a bar. "Vaguely," she said. "Older and fully professed, if I remember." End of convent talk.

The door opened, and the Linehans came in, Della having asked Laura after Mass in the morning. Ed bought them a vodka and a Guinness.

"You're downing shorts quickly, Ed," Della warned lightly. "The road was slippery after that rain last night. The sooner I learn to drive, the better. You're not fit to sit behind the wheel."

"Live a little, Della. You wanted this. Let it rip. Need the toilet." Shuffling away, he pushed the lounge door open and almost fell across the step into the lobby. Della felt her face flame as the awkward moment died. Why had he not stayed teetotal?

"Don't be ashamed, Della. But there's nothing worse than telling a man off when he's drunk. Wait until the morning when he has a sore head. I hate the effects of alcohol, too, but things won't get out of control when we're with them," Laura murmured.

"Out of control? Laura, I come from a non-drinking background. My parents are pioneers. They took the pin when they were young. Ed didn't drink until we got engaged, but I didn't see the harm. It seems now he's into it with a passion."

"In small towns, Della, alcohol is the main leisure outlet, a release from everyday problems. Perhaps when they build the Community Centre, it'll offer healthy activities and draw them away from the pub."

"Ed plays squash with Mark Keating midweek, which is fine, but sometimes they go for a quick one afterwards. I'm not sure Mark is a good influence."

"Didn't like him when we met after Olive's talk in the Centre. I often wonder how they're getting on since. Ed is his own man, Della. Keep him happy, and you won't have to worry."

"We shouldn't have worries, Laura. Do you miss your freedom? I wanted to stay in Dublin, but he wouldn't let me."

"When the wind whistles through the dales at night, I imagine the sound of the London traffic, the ambulance sirens. I see the slop pails in every can of milk I plank on the scullery floor. Joe's mother is incontinent, so in a way, I'm still nursing, unpaid, of course."

"Goodness me, I've not got anything as bad. Just fed up during the day, listening to lectures on how to keep my 'wild' husband under control."

"To a nurse, the work is nothing except for the endless washing, no machine, and no toilet. Listen to your mother-in-law, Della. After all, she knows him best; he has always been a one for the night. You're lucky he's changed since you married."

"I suppose. That's awful you've no machine. Keep pushing."

"Who'd dare push Joe Linehan? I'd never stayed there before we married nor noticed it on visits. He says the house is good enough for him, so it's good enough for me."

"Laura, what can I say?" Nothing, but they could share worries and stay close.

The bar emptied by degrees until two o'clock came, and no one remained except for the men drooling at the counter. Jim Linehan and Ed Egan sidled over to their wives, the heavy stench of alcohol wafting before them. Ed slurred, "Time for bed."

Della whispered, "I'll call soon, Laura. Have courage." She nodded a brief 'goodnight' in Joe's direction. She would store the other girl's worries in a quiet compartment of her mind. Enough, for now, Ed's driving. Going around turns, he veered across the road and almost hit the grass bank. Too afraid to shout, she murmured, "Careful, Ed. Let's get home safe."

Chapter 18

Morning vomits, lethargy. After a week, Molly said she ought to see the doctor. "You're pregnant, girl. That'll keep Ed in tow." In tow? Wasn't he doing fine? But when she told him it might happen, the delight on Ed's face was more than enough to compensate for the frightening change in her body. See the doctor at once, he said. The ride will do you good. Ride? Feeling sick? Why didn't he take time off and drive her there? No, too busy.

Early September, an Indian summer prevailed across the countryside, painting Nature in a golden glow, which did little to quell Della's trepidation. She struggled for breath on the hilly part, let the bicycle coast down the slopes, and arrived shattered at the doctor's residence. If it was indeed the big P, did she want it? Honestly, not yet.

She entered the doctor's waiting room, a mixture of dread and acceptance, each vying for dominance.

At the white sink in the corner of his surgery, Doctor Farrell held the vial of urine up to the light and then dipped a stick. A friendly soul, he cared for his patients to the point of delivering their children at home, if necessary.

"Are you ready for a baby, Della?"

"Yes, and no. It's what my husband wants. Maybe too soon for me."

"Ready or not, you've no choice." Choice. Della remembered whisperings among the girls in Dublin during canteen breaks. Pills, terminations. The courts had condemned a notorious Nurse Cadden to death for conducting back-street abortions in her flat. Instead, she died in a mental hospital in Dundrum. It was the city's scandal, and people crossed themselves when the infamous name came up in conversation. Della had not understood then nor cared much, except that the word abortion was anathema to Catholic thinking and a spore of the devil.

When she told Ed that evening, he smiled, took out a cigarette and pulled deeply, letting grey smoke float from his nostrils like a steam train. "Now you'll have plenty to do."

"You mean *we* will?"

"Well, not my scene. Babies are a woman's domain. Anyway, what else would you do here?"

"Bad enough feeling rotten, but worse still if I'm alone. Ed, face your responsibilities." A surge of bile in her stomach made the words spurt out sharper than intended.

"My parents can babysit. Not every couple has built-in minders." Was there a new tetchiness in his tone?

"But they're old and won't be able. No. It'll be down to me to rear the child. What if more come along?" She waited, watched his expression, and saw something akin to satisfaction flicker. In effect, the pregnancy would saddle her while he was free.

"One step at a time. It'll be fine." *Fine. For him?*

After two weeks, the sickness spread throughout the day, inducing a sense of loss, little zest for anything, or interest in her appearance. Listless and thin, Della just wanted sleep. Depressed and dull, she neglected her clothes; what was the point of bothering to chase hens or peg out the washing? Waiting for her husband to come home had lost its appeal. Dark thoughts assailed; pop one, but pills could harm. She'd always kept some.

There wasn't much to discuss except Ed's business in the evenings. She detected an unease in his attitude and behaviour, a giddiness. She was not much company. He'd go to town for a chat, he said.

"No, no, Ed, you'd drink. We have to get a TV." Della hated the pleading tone in her voice, which was more of a whine.

"Tell that to my old man." Oh yes. Let her do the groundwork and talk to a man she found remote and unapproachable.

During dinner, Della raised the topic. News on demand, exciting dramas; after all, he loved reading. Himself glowered, "Don't want noise in the kitchen, couldn't read with a rumpus in the background."

The boss had spoken, the Irishman, the master in the corner. But his son stood firm this time, "Well, we're getting one, or I don't stay in."

Della's heart missed a beat. If he were to go, her time would be entirely theirs.

Days came and went. Ed and Della did not exchange a single, meaningful conversation. Her reflection in the mirror of a thin, hard-faced woman made Della want to run away and hide back in the cloister, where it wouldn't matter. The appearance, of course, not the pregnancy! The cheekbones people said were her best feature now stood out gaunt on Della's face. "Handlebars," Ed commented behind her reflection in the room. He'd gone off her!

In O'Reilly's on Sunday, Eve's impatience spilt over. "Ed will go out without you, just as I foretold. Don't be a frump."

Bridie's face puckered into a frown. "I can't accept that just as you get pregnant - what he wanted - his attitude changed so quickly. Maybe your dad should talk to him?"

"It won't stop him. But his mother says he'll get caught up in the cards again."

Bridie stood up from the tea table, her country fruit cake and strawberry jam. "Jim, come with me a minute?" They went towards the bedroom along the corridor.

Della drummed her fingers on the table and gazed into the yard where Ed was chatting with one of the workmen. On this farm, the O'Reillys sowed potatoes and tilled the fields. Family life followed the seasons, rhythmically balancing arduous labour, time out, concerts in the local hall, and Jim's choral society. He loved the choir and participating in the musicals, but sometimes Bridie gave off steam when he got too involved, 'with corn rotting in the field'. But their innate contentment more than compensated, and she liked to tell her girls their daddy was 'a talented singer and performer.'

Jim returned and placed one hundred pounds into her hand. "Take this, Della, get your TV."

"Dad, I can't take your money after the expense of the wedding."

"Expense or not, your happiness is more important. I've five head of cattle to sell at the mart next week. So don't worry about us."

She could not suppress the tears that spilt from her eyes. Here he was, her kind father, always caring, never wanting to see her go without. Hugging him, Della put the money in her bag.

"Don't say a word to Ed until you're on the way home," Jim said. "Might embarrass him."

But she couldn't contain her excitement. Driving away from the house, she spurted out. "Dad's given me one hundred pounds for a new TV."

"Great." Just that, no spontaneous delight.

"You don't mind?"

"No, why should I? Saves me scraping the price together."

The very gall of the man, no qualms in accepting a handout from her father, generous to a fault at the wedding. Jim had also promised one thousand pounds as a dowry but said they would get it after the harvest. Maybe Ed expected it sooner? To think she had worried about his pride. What pride? It lay solely in his appearance.

"Right," she said. "Let's buy the TV this week."

"You can tell the old folks." Again, he would let her do the tricky bit, which was typical of him, always to the forefront unless it came to an awkward task. What the heck? He'd stay home in the evenings. Praise the Lord, and thank you, Dad.

Surprisingly, Himself said little when Della told them she and Ed were buying a TV. Molly must have warned him and let a hint drop about keeping things safe in the house and their son at home. A masked look that neither approved nor disapproved spread over the older man's face. Then he muttered something about electricity costs. Ed explained a TV would not use up many units at night.

Ed and Della went to Conlon's electrical shop on the Square on Saturday. After pricing and sizing mentally, she saw his eyes light on a sleek, slanted sides one, not too clunky nor big. It had few buttons and a twenty-inch screen. Big enough for our kitchen, Ed explained to the sales attendant. Despite her bilious tummy, Della felt a happy feeling engulf her. Ed had his wish; she was pregnant, and she had a TV that would keep him at home. Plus, the old pair would enjoy news and shows, which was better than feeding on backward and dull gossip. Satisfaction all round.

Unpacking the television on the units, Ed asked his father where he would like it. "On the higher end of the kitchen worktop, where everyone can see it." Della smiled - progress of a sort. Herein, lay new vistas for each night, seven days a week. Who needed anything else? She would not worry again.

Margie came early to ramble and pass on gossip to Molly. Seeing the shiny black box on the worktop, her mouth opened like a cavernous hole. "Bedad, ye got it, Molly."

"Not us, Margie. The young pair here bought it. Let's watch it now. Turn your chair towards the wall, and we'll see it better."

Together, they sat, legs spread apart under copious aprons, wide enough to reveal long, knicker legs stretching down to their knees. Instead of sharing 'besht news', they had genuine news and authentic entertainment tonight. Mouths agape, eyes dancing wide, they sat agog in wonder, comparing celebrities with locals.

"Isn't he the spit of Mickeen Shannon down the road, Margie?"

"Surely, aye, you're right, Molly." *Oh, dear me*, Della thought, nudging Ed. Even now, they could not break the habit of a lifetime; everything had to relate to familiar things. But, absorbed in the drama, Ed appeared content.

Molly and Margie, their bodies heated by the Stanley range, laughed and shouted at the antics of the *Black and White Minstrels*, *The Benny Hill Show*, and *Rowan and Martin's laugh-in* over the next two hours. Finally, at ten-thirty, Margie looked at the clock, jumped up and ran to the door. "Nearly forgot the time. Peter will be home. I'll be in trouble."

"Trouble? Why?" Della asked.

"Ah, sure, she has to toe the line when he's drunk."

Toe the line? Again, the secrecy and half-divulged information made Della want to scream. Was she a member of the family or not? No one explained. Ed, she blamed more than the other two.

As the back door closed behind Margie, Old Pat pulled out his rosary beads and dropped to the floor on his knees.

"Prayers," he announced; until now, Ed and Della not expected to share the night-time devotion, but the man's tone said he would not accept refusal. Perhaps the influence of an outside world in his sitting room had triggered his demand. Ed shook his head. Della said, "Yes," and they all knelt together—anything for peace in this household.

Almost without notice, December arrived, bringing dreaded night frosts. Himself complained of ice on the potato pits in the haggard and the bitter cold, too severe to pull the stiff tarpaulin off the heap.

"A mortal shame if those fine Records rot. I covered the mound in September but didn't expect the weather to turn yet. At this rate, there'll be nothing for dinner by March."

"The new spuds won't be ready until May," Molly said. Spuds, the word resounded around the country whenever a scarcity of the blessed vegetable loomed. For every Irishman and woman, it called out a hollow sound of famine, rotting bodies, and coffin ships.

"Make more soda bread, woman. Spare the praties." A simple demotic for a precious commodity. But Della had not yet learned how to make soda bread, although her mother said it was easy, and Molly liked to produce her sole baking item every two days.

"I reckon it'll be a bleak time selling machinery, with Christmas coming and people saving money," Ed said. Bleak was now the 'in' word in the house. Della felt bleak. The old people said things were bleak. They doubted Ed whenever he made a profit and asked about costs, over-heads, lighting, and income. Couldn't be doing well in a bleak time.

"Aren't you happy, Della?" Bridie queried in O'Reilly's on the usual Sunday visit. "Now that you're expecting, you'll have something more to do in the house, your responsibility."

"Well, I'm sort of happy but miserable at the same time. And I can't drink, so no socialising on a Sunday night."

"Rubbish. Go with him, drink a mineral. And look after your appearance, no matter how you feel. A maternity dress is fine, but put on makeup every day. Don't let yourself go." Again, a blatant inference - do something about yourself.

Listening in the background, Eve said, "Della, heed what Mam is saying."

"Why not get Ed to drive you to his sister's on Sunday nights? That'd keep him out of town." Bridie said. A wisp of doubt hung in the air. What were they trying to say?

One Friday night, after dinner, Ed said he had to collect money from a customer the best time to get the man at home. He would be back in a couple of hours. As the door closed, old Pat looked up from the paper and said, "He's gone."

Della, dragging her gaze away from Roger Moore in *The Saint* on TV, wondered what he meant. "He won't be late. Promised to get home by ten."

Molly looked at the empty chair. "That's it, Della. He's started, but you did well to keep him this long."

"Sure, there's nothing wrong with him going out on business. I don't mind." Della assumed an indifferent air, ignoring the knowing look between the two women and the inference that Margie knew more about Ed than she did.

"It's poker night." Molly attempted more information.

It was working if they wanted to sow seeds of negativity and doubt. Della said goodnight, got up from the chair, filled a glass of water at the sink, and went to bed. If they were right, which she suspected, she would deal with it later when Ed got home. But he'd promised.

Hours passed. She heard the boards creaking as the old pair made their way upstairs. Anxiety crisscrossed her guts. Where had he gone? Was he drinking, gambling, or both? Her mind raced. One-fifty a.m. She lay alert and shaking. *I'm not much company. I've let myself go, and he's bored with me.*

At two a.m., Ed staggered into the room, reeking of alcohol. The rattling noise of his keys on the dressing table showed his confusion. Removing his watch, he slowly and stupidly pulled his clothes off. They fell on the floor. He attempted to put them on the bedside chair and swore. "Feck it."

"Where the hell were you, Ed? I've not slept with worry."

"Worry, why? I met up with Noel Mahon about a machine he wants. Had a few beers." The slurring tone and the off-handedness made her lash out.

"Liar. Nobody gets that drunk in someone's house. You were gambling in the pub."

"Keep your voice down. Have you no respect for my mother and father?"

"You don't respect them or me and lied so you could go drinking. Until now, you seemed happy watching TV at night. Why do this now?"

"Think what you like. I've done my time sitting downstairs for three boring months. No more." Crawling between the sheets, he succumbed to sleep. Della buried her face in the pillow and cried, voices whispering in her head. Too late. A wave of weariness crept over her tired body, embalming her tortured being.

Ed did not talk the following morning but got up late and left without as much as a cup of tea. Reluctantly, Della passed on his excuse to her mother-in-law.

"Don't be soft, girl. He played cards in *that* town like before you married him. You have a job now, or you won't have a penny."

"I don't know how to deal with him."

"Didn't you realise you were marrying a pleasure-loving man? I'm surprised he lasted this long." Molly's unhelpful attitude indicated her impatience toward Della as if she were glad Ed had proved her predictions.

"How would I know? No one told me."

"After that Carol one tried to hook him, we were glad he married you and that you'd be an influence—out of the convent and all." A shadow of fear crossed the older woman's face. Della realised she must avoid igniting further anxiety in Ed's mother. Molly suffered from atrial fibrillation. Blast Ed.

Throughout the day, she prayed. Six o'clock came. Della sat on their bed and waited. He came in. She started, "Ed, please don't stay out so late again. I need my sleep. What about the baby and everything?"

"I'll do as I please. Your job is to have children, and that's that." Worse than a blow, his words hit her like a blunderbuss. This was not drunken talk but a man asserting his intention to do what he wanted. Nothing would deflect him, neither the streams of tears nor her pleading. Last night, he had tasted freedom again, and from now on, he would leave her with people she saw daily. Della should not have fallen pregnant. Everything had changed.

"I feel worthless to you and myself. It isn't good for the unborn child."

"You talk in riddles." There was no glance in her direction, only a thin lip line that showed he would not brook further discussion.

"So, my only choice is to put up with your ways?"

"Easier all round. You're sickly, no fun anymore."

"Fun! I'm bloody pregnant, which you wanted."

Had it been his plan all along? To bide his time until she got caught. Well, it had worked.

Two weeks later, Della went to visit Laura in the morning. She had not cycled the mile recently because of vomiting and tiredness. But now, she ached for a sympathetic ear and wanted to see the new baby. Laura's daughter, Siobhan had come quickly, and the Linehans had got to Sligo just in time. Ann, a neighbour, rushed Joe and Laura along the winding road to the regional hospital, waited for Joe, and brought him home again. Then, four days later, Ann drove the family back to the house on the hill, and the postman brought the news to everyone.

"Sit down, have a cup of tea. I made a soda cake this morning. You look worn. What's so bad?" Laura placed a mug of hot tea on the oilcloth and pushed a plate toward Della, who watched the butter melting on the warm bread.

"Not sleeping. Ed's changed, doesn't love me anymore; thinks I'm a frump."

Laura put two spoons of sugar in the cup. "Della, what led to this?"

"He's playing cards again and drinking. I lie awake crying, wondering when he'll get in. I'm miserable. Except for weekends when he takes me home, I don't see him much anymore, and we argue constantly."

"It's not hugely different here, and the nights can be lonely, but Joe only sings in the pubs on Fridays, so I daren't try to stop it, or he'd go mad. Gambling isn't an issue for us."

"Molly fills me with fear, says we won't have enough to live on and can't expect them to subsidise us. It's awful. I feel stupid that I didn't have a clue beforehand. His late start in the morning and his rebelliousness makes me ill, more than the pregnancy."

"Do what I do, Della. Say nothing at night. Let him get to bed in peace, and next evening, try to talk reasonably without pleading or fighting with him."

"I'll try, but I go mad with worry in the night. Who is he with, doing what? Before we married, girls used to ogle him at the dances."

"Don't blow things up because Ed was a wild one."

"He didn't drink then, Laura. It's brought out a dark selfishness, and he's vicious when I cross him. Almost hit me when I kept asking questions last night."

The look on Laura's face was serious. "Men like our husbands are mini lords in their kingdoms, Della. They care more about public opinion than relationships. However, you have no choice but to live in harmony with Ed. Do what I do, put up with it for a while and wait for a good time to talk rather than fight with him."

"Don't think I can take it. The sheer injustice and neglect are too much."

Della looked around Laura's kitchen and saw the ironing pile on a chair. Old Granny Linehan sat smiling in a corner as if the world were in harmony with her being. Laura seemed calm and bright in a home that was neither tidy nor attractive, regardless of her chores. *And I'm complaining. Her life isn't easy either.*

"How are you getting on, Laura?" Only right to inquire, after all, she had unloaded her troubles on the woman.

"We're just managing. I make do with the cost of the calf meal, the price of meat, and the baby food. Joe ambles along, doesn't care how I cope, nor does he bring in money like Ed."

"We have fresh troubles. I'm sorry for bothering you with mine."

"Della, we all need someone to listen. Although Joe doesn't go to town as often as Ed, he shouts at me to shut up if I cross him."

"He has a huge personality."

"Big man, big voice, little patience." The half-laugh did not conceal the note of bitterness in Laura's voice. There was more.

Della placed the mug back on the oilcloth between the remains of breakfast dishes piled in the centre. Molly Egan would have a fit if her kitchen table looked like that.

"Get through each day, Della, and aim for better things. Keep him onside and try to be positive. The birth will settle Ed."

Della let the sun warm her body on the return journey, right into where a flutter in her tummy signified new life. She'd fight the devil in her husband, give him a baby, and move forward. Her battle for change would continue, and she'd wish away the forces militating against her marriage. But Ed's socialising, the poker, and the temptations inherent in late-night drinking were powerful traditions for which Ireland was famous. Within six months of coming here, she was embroiled in a dual battle for health and spirit.

After dinner, she tried, "Ed, can we talk upstairs?"

Opening his mouth to object, he relented when Della touched his arm. "Please, just a chat."

Ed sat on the chair in the bedroom while she lay on the bed; good for the veins, the doctor said.

"It's unfair of you to expect me to sit in, night after night, while you're out enjoying yourself. So the only solution is for me to go out too." Words uttered, Della looked at her husband and saw his face change from almost pleasant to scowling.

"Maybe at weekends. But I must meet people, expand my business, and make contacts. Understand?"

"What business can you conduct at two o'clock in the morning?"

"Best time when we're drinking." Bland, ungiving.

"I'll go out on Sunday nights and drink a mineral."

"Suit yourself. We got married too soon." Had she heard right?

"For Christ's sake, you were the one that pursued me in Dublin and Galway. You didn't like it when I admitted to going out with Dermot."

"That was, then, a matter of pride. And I married a glamorous girl."

"I'm bloody pregnant, for goodness' sake. Don't you love me now? Want an exciting life, and I'm keeping you back?"

"You let yourself go." Grim expression, no effort to spare her feelings.

"I'll go back home. Is that what you want?" She let her voice rise to a shrill, desperate high.

"Keep your voice down, woman. No, what would people say? Just don't fight with me. I enjoy getting out after a hard day's work."

"So, a veneer of respectability is more important than our happiness? Doesn't it bother you that people see your actions? Laura said the Council girls hang around the bars in the evenings with men like you who buy them drinks."

"Damn the gossips." Ed turned away and stormed down the stairs. She heard him jingle the car keys on the hall-stand, bang the front door and leave.

Della pulled the dressing gown close around her shoulders and snuggled into its softness, its comfort. Of nature, Ed was a predator. The challenge lost its lustre once he'd captured the prey, and his commitment waned. His words, spoken in drunken mode - he was 'his own man' - were now opening fresh wounds.

Lying on her side, less discomfort that way, a veil of sadness enshrouded her person. She might be better off than Laura with a pleasant house, TV, and running water, but no great chasm existed. Laura Linehan had given up her identity by hitching herself to a hard-nosed man who would not let her have ordinary things. But unlike Della, her readiness for marriage had desensitised her to Joe's faults, making her more malleable and accepting of her husband's attitudes. Now, both women were suffering from mistakes they could not rectify. The families would not have it, and the Church would disapprove.

Later, when Ed stumbled into the room, she feigned sleep, held her breath and waited until he was quiet to go to the bathroom. Sleep, though elusive, finally came in the early hours. At eight a.m., Ed rumbled out of heavy slumber, "You slept well last night, Della. Didn't hear me come in."

Well, well. It had worked. Albeit against natural inclinations, she would, from now on, put up with a man she could not change and keep the questions to a minimum. It might not lead to inner tranquillity, but perhaps some semblance of peace. After all, had she not learnt the value of humility in the holy convent? And when the pregnancy ended, they would be an average couple again.

"See you this evening. It oughtn't be too late," Ed said, opening the back door to leave for the plant. "Fine," Della said. "See you then."

Molly was out milking cows, timing the job to avoid the morning arguments in the kitchen. Della placed her husband's white shirts in the water and soused them up and down vigorously until the bubbles lathered the entire sink.

She turned on the radio just as the dreamy lyrics of Unchained Melody floated into her space, transporting her beyond pedestrian chores and incipient loneliness. Raising her voice, she sang the 'Unchained Melody' lyrics in unison with the Righteous Brothers. Yes, time would go by slowly – and do so much.

CHAPTER 19

D ella planned to go out more, to breathe fresh air away
from the embryonic atmosphere and the cabbage
smells in the house—which added to the nauseating spirals
in her guts.

First stop, Malones. After a light knock, Margie's grey
head appeared through a sliver; few called after the postie
during the day.

"Margie, have you always lived here?" she tried after
peremptory hello's and chit-chat on her back pain - *'twill
be a boy then.* It was easier to probe away from Molly's disapproving little coughs and, perhaps at last, uncover 'the
secret'.

"Sure, I never got away, what with only the two of us here.
Peter'd be lost without me." Margie rushed to shun Della's
inquisitiveness.

"Well, he might have married if you'd left." So daring, but
what the heck?

The wrinkles on Margie's face deepened; her eyes blinked. *What have I done? Unearthed the death of her girlhood, stumbled into that secret?* But she had not stumbled.

"Sure, we live simple here, Della. Mind that man of yours and keep him at home. He's a wild one, our Ed." *So that's me in my place*, Della thought, no more to come. Better leave.

"Off to do the ironing, Margie. See you tonight." Yes, and sit in the same chair at the same time.

As the door closed behind her, Della figured Margie's smile, without its usual sparkle, hid a lifetime of suffering. And she had seen a trickle glisten in the older woman's eyes.

Back at the gate of the white house, Della stalled. Like an eagle, that powerful bird of prey, the building seemed to claw out and pull her into its realm. Gone the short-lived peace. And she did not know how to act; gone the feistiness and glamour. Undoubtedly the convent years had turned an extrovert, rock n roller, into a pliable minion satisfied with a modicum of harmony. She'd sacrificed it for love, attraction, or a primitive belief in predestination.

The pile of clothes stacked on the worktop's red shiny contours was ready and waiting when she arrived. Molly Egan sat dozing in a chair in the kitchen, her pride and joy, with its glossy units and white walls. Della wanted answers. Her curiosity blistered and burned like an itch. Molly rose to her feet, stirred the kettle on the hob, and filled the teapot with two scoops of loose tea.

"Molly, tell me why Margie never left home, why she's afraid of her brother and gets up from the chair at the same time every night to be back before him."

"Well, now, that'd be tellin'."

Della raised her voice. "Molly, I'll keep asking until you do, or I'll ask May Doorley. A right gossip, she is."

"May Doorley has a husband, and entitled to talk."

"What are you saying?"

"Margie is single."

"So, what's the difference? She's a human being." What was the older woman implying?

"It's like this; when I was expecting my first, Mary Jo, thirty-five years ago, we'd go to Mass in the trap. Folk used to wonder which of us was the biggest."

"So, Margie was fat. Well, she's sort of small and round now, right?"

"Not fat. She was in the same way as me."

"Pregnant, you mean? Why can't you say it, Molly? Margie was expecting a baby at the same time you were. That's it, the great secret. She was a single mother."

"Yes, but we can't talk about such things. 'Twas a disgrace, so it was, and she's not had a decent life since. Peter keeps her under his thumb, and when he's drunk, he reminds her of the scandal she brought to the family. That's why she does his bidding, and remember, she wouldn't have a home, only for him."

"Dear God above, the woman had a baby, so what?"

"'Twas a terrible thing to happen in a family and her an unmarried hussy."

"Hussy? Why? And who was the father? What happened to the baby?"

"The father, you know. That Johnny Cummins over the road, he did it. They live half a mile from each other, but he's never spoken to her since, and she, poor creature, never saw the child again. She had to give birth in the orphanage near Mullingar and afterwards return alone. No decent family would let an unmarried woman and baby into the house. So now you have the story and understand why we don't talk about it."

"Hypocritical Catholics, all of you. What did Christ say to Mary Magdalene? Go in peace; your sin is forgiven. Well, if He did, so should we? It could happen to anyone. What with the cuffufling in cars after dances and the drunken orgies at the back of halls, it's a wonder more girls don't get caught out. I'm surprised your son didn't get some poor girl into trouble before now." Gosh, a step too far and a barb too powerful for the older woman. Della stopped, seeing her mother-in-law's face pale.

"That's why those Homes are thriving. The girls have the babies, the nuns have them adopted by good families, and the mothers needn't take a boat to England. No one is the wiser. And Ed would never get a girl into trouble. He has the sense not to do that to us."

To them? Better tread safer ground.

"Poor Margie. She has nothing of her own, depending on her brother and his whims for her well-being." Della's tea had lost its taste; the butter congealed on the slice Molly passed on a plate.

"She had a roof over her head and didn't need to go."

"Wonderful. Holy Ireland, where its Christian people daren't discuss sex or its consequences. Ignorance, all of it. Margie probably didn't understand what she was doing."

"No point in going to Mass on Sundays, listening to the Word of God, then coming out and committing sin."

"But it's all right to ballyrag people. You're all the same. My mother is a charitable woman, but she used to tell us to avoid certain families in the parish and certain girls."

Poor Margie, under the control of her brother, Laura, under the control of Joe, and with me, it's Ed. Olive, we know little about yet, but Mark is one to watch...

That night, Della told Ed what she'd learned about Margie's downfall. He laughed, "Don't know why you're so obsessed with her. After all, such things happen all the time. Girls get pregnant and either leave it behind in an orphanage or take the boat."

"Why didn't you tell me before? It was the main reason I agreed to marry you so soon, to avoid sin and its consequences."

"Consequences? If that'd happened to us, we wouldn't be sitting here under this roof at night."

"Why not?"

"After disgracing my family?"

"You're as bad as the rest of the whited Pharisees." Then, seeing the sharp look on her husband's face, Della continued. "You're no angel, and I guess you wouldn't have stood by me if I'd got into trouble?"

"It didn't happen."

Being Monday, it was Ed's night in, the norm after a heavy weekend of alcohol consumption. Della foraged for a crumb of comfort to dull the hurt.

"Goodness, Ed, less than a year since I came to this place, and now we're living separate lives. You're out all day and most nights, me struggling towards the end of my pregnancy with little company except for your parents."

"I'm enjoying life with the lads. I wasn't ready for this."
So there. He'd finally articulated what she'd known all
along. Anger flamed and threatened to consume her. Any
attempt at logicism, or whatever one might call it, vanished
in a whirlwind of repugnance. The utter dishonesty of the
man! He had not been ready yet insisted on bringing their
marriage forward and not letting her pursue other interests.

"So, I should go back to Leam?" Her voice, shrill and high,
pierced the dense atmosphere in the room, now a virtual
battleground. Ed closed the door. It wouldn't do for the
parents to hear them.

"Maybe you should go there until the baby is born. Be
nearer the hospital. Right now, I'm going down to watch
TV." *Go away, let me alone.* Again, her attempt to touch his
heart failed. She followed him downstairs into the kitchen,
where two worried people looked and waited.

She scooped brown stew onto the plate with potatoes
and carrots and placed the meal before her husband. They
did not speak again for the rest of the evening. When, at
ten o'clock, the main news came on screen, Pat Egan gasped
in astonishment. Jack Lynch, Taoiseach of Ireland, was re-
questing emigrants not to return for Christmas for fear of
bringing the dreaded foot and mouth disease across the
water.

"Sure, 'tis awful sad seeing pigs, cattle, and sheep burnt
on farms over there. But the Taoiseach is right. It would
decimate our small farms."

"We'll miss the visitors at Mass and in the shops," Molly
said. "Linehans always have a houseful. Great to see the

church packed on Christmas morning." The fors and againsts parried over and back, obliterating all but the loudest ads on television. Tired and listless by 10 o'clock, Della said goodnight, poured a glass of water, and started up the stairs. Water the medium of the soul. Halfway up, she wobbled, grasped the rail, and stumbled, teetering downwards onto her side against the bannister. No carpet, only shiny lino the whole way up. The glass fell through the railings and shattered to the floor below. Pain shot into her hip. Terror gripped, merged with the shooting stabs in her bulging belly.

Ed dashed upstairs and pulled her into a sitting position. A mixture of annoyance and shock flashed across his face. "Be careful, Della. You might have lost the baby if you'd fallen to the bottom." His concern was welcome.

"Ed," she grimaced, the pain sharp between her ribs, "I'm hurt."

"Right, let's get you to bed." Linking, half-carrying her, Ed got Della up the remaining steps and onto the bed. She shuddered, the physical contact triggering something unexpected. Outside, darkness shrouded the house. He switched on the light and drew across the curtains fluttering in the draft. As he turned to leave, a half-smile morphed into unfamiliar anxiety. "Sleep now, and you'll be fine."

"Would it matter if I lost the baby, Ed? Life be freer for you?" No tears, just a hint of emotion in a shaky tone. "Better for me. I'd be the girl you married again."

"What an awful thing to say. Go to sleep, and don't be stupid."

"Stupid. Yeah, that's me. Stupid to have come here."

"Rest," Molly said, coming into the room, her features creased with concern. Old Pat's voice muttered from the doorway. "Rushing, always rushing." But Della had not been rushing.

By morning, Della felt drained, having turned and rolled during a sleepless night to ease the darts on her right side. Her leg ached where she'd hit the wooden bannisters.

"You okay now, Della?" Ed asked.

Tears came, uninvited. "Yes, but I'm sore."

"Better tell me mother. She'll know what to do."

She'd contained the condition slowing her life until now, but triggered by the concern in her husband's voice, physical pain merged with emotion and broke through her stoic resolve. She sobbed. Ed said softly, "Come on now, you'll be fine. Let me help you downstairs."

Waiting in the kitchen, Molly saw her distress and the rings under her eyes.

"Ed, take Della to the doctor now; there might be damage to the baby." Seeing the urgency in his mother, he put on a black leather jacket and nodded in agreement. Her disapproval of him, now blatant and intense, he could not ignore, despite being the glory of her life, the long-awaited, heaven-sent one.

In the car, he drove carefully, slowing on the bends. There was nothing to say.

Doctor Farrell said Della was lucky and could have brought on a miscarriage if she had tumbled to the bottom. Ed agreed to the advice that Della should rest until the baby came. *Make him stay in,* Della wanted to shout at the doctor. That's what he wants, me housebound, him free as a bird. But the doctor liked Ed, how he smiled at her; always the perfect gentleman, interacting, pleasing, and plausible. They thanked her and left.

By Sunday, Della was feeling better. Ed related how he'd rescued Della from a nasty accident on the stairs during dinner in Leam. Bridie nodded. "Good, you were in that night, Ed." *My, my*, Della thought. *Well done, Mam.*

"We might stop off at the Royal on the way home. OK, Della?" Again, the master attempted to whip up admiration in her family.

"Just for an hour then."

Her mother's nod made it easier to comply. After all, pleasantness was a scarce commodity she must grasp when it came her way. Ed was at his very best, charming and agreeable. Not once did Della divulge how tense life had become in the valley or how she longed for the pregnancy to end. But when Eve drew her to the drawing room, away from her parents' ears, on the pretext of seeing a new crochet cloth she'd woven for a marble tabletop, she related details of her loneliness in Cortober. Eve said they knew. "We hear stories about Ed's night activities in the town. Not long to go now, Della. See what happens after the birth? You can get out if he doesn't change."

What a comfort.

The group seemed larger than of yore in the hotel: more faces, more smiles. They'd been drinking a lot from the row of empties on the table, and the usual backchat was in full swing. Snippets uttered from alcohol-fuelled voices gossip about the school, the nuns, the weather, children, and the men. Laura pulled a soft chair into the group for Della.

"If I had a penny for every pound he's lost this year, I'd buy a new outfit," May Heslin said, putting down her vodka glass. Everyone knew the little woman with a pert face and piercing eyes liked to hold forth on such occasions. "The more it goes on, the stronger my belief we should stop the poker games and banish them from this small town."

"Agreed," Della joined in. "When I came to live with Ed's family, I was naïve, didn't heed his parents' warning about his losses."

"What about the winnings, girls? Do you pinch a few pounds when they're asleep?" May's voice rose to a high-pitched laugh. As one, they hushed her.

"Sure do," Della said. "He had a lucky strike last night. I took forty. Often pinch some when he's too bloody drunk to remember the next day."

"Alright for you, May," Laura said. "Your job in the nursing home on the Crescent brings in a wage. No money worries. If I had a car, I'd be with you."

"Go for it. I'll give you a lift."

"Have to ask Joe first. He might say no." Laura's expression changed to serious.

"Just do it, Laura," May insisted. "Show him." Getting up to go to the ladies, she wobbled, tripped, straightened, then strode through the door and out of the lounge.

"She can sure down the booze," Della said. "I never drank like that, even before I was pregnant. We only came in for one, but now you're all here, we'll stay on for a bit." Her single lemonade would neither abuse the bladder nor induce nausea.

"Isn't it good to be out, Della?" Laura said. "We don't do it often enough. Money and all that. We're a bunch of happily married couples out for a night. What a farce!"

"Depends on what you mean by happy," Della said. "For some, it's loving your husband. For others, it's ...." Her voice trailed off on the last syllable, and her glance trailed across the lounge to the figure of her husband, bending Ben's ear about god knows what. Laura squeezed Della's hand.

"Happy? Look around you, see those husbands of ours. At least four sit at the poker table every night, gambling our money." May was off again, face flushed to the roots of her ebony hair. She'd given birth to four children year after year. Her husband was an engineer with a good salary, but Ben was another committed pokerite. Then there was Ed, the loquacious, bold type building a successful business in the area, his strength of character and acumen renowned near and far.

Della surveyed the scene. "We're all pretending it's fine, but at home, we're a bunch of twenty-something-year-olds who have no choice but to tolerate the late nights. I dread the lack of money most, and if Ed loses at the table, we have to penny-pinch during the week afterwards."

"Well, at least they can't do much harm tonight." The words fell hastily from May's mouth.

"Why do you say that, May? Gamble, drink too much?"

"And more. Oh, ignore me. Too much vodka."

"It's Ed. You meant him." The woman knew something. Della needed to talk to Laura. Her friend would not lie.

The older, wiser woman, Nan, rushed to change the subject in a flash. "They're out earning a living daily while we're at home." Her amiable, likeable husband travelled for a seed company and was away during the week.

"I've let myself go. Sickness, inertia, apathy, call it what you like, might have crushed me," Della whined.

"Della, pregnancy takes it out of you. Don't criticise yourself. The worst is over now. But you took on a challenging man in Ed." Nan insisted.

"So he has strayed? I'll show him after I give birth."

"That's the spirit, Della," May said.

Straight-lipped during the exchange, Laura turned to Della and smiled in support. She, above all, knew how life was panning out in Egans.

"Laura, do you have anything to tell me?"

"No, Della, I have to mind my affairs."

"Sometimes, I tell myself off for not trying harder to keep Ed on track. But when he comes in late, I question him. Need to know where he's been or with whom he spent the hours between nine and three a.m. My tortured mind wants answers, even if they're not true. So I let him lie."

A line from her favourite play, Macbeth, sneaked into Della's mind; *And you all know, security is mortals' chiefest enemy.* But wasn't ignorance also vital for *her* sanity?

May patted Della's knee. "It's the hormones, dear. Plays hell with the imagination."

The lounge door opened. Mark and Olive arrived at the bar. He immediately settled onto a high stool beside Ed. To Della, he looked like a panther in a black jacket and trousers, lithe, fast, searching for prey. *Stop judging, she told herself.*

The covert admiration in her husband's voice showed his delight at the sight of the other man. "A brandy and ginger, Mark?"

Mark nodded. Ed wanted what Mark had: more money, an expanding business, and a bigger car; symbols of status and success. Disciple-like, he would follow the other man's example; not wrong, Della accepted, to desire more than fruitless toil on a forty-acre farm. But it was the pleasure-seeking side of him she distrusted. However, they were out together after months, and cloying doubts melted as time ticked towards midnight.

"No, just a beer. Aren't I driving? Unless she takes over." Gesturing towards Olive, Mark's voice rose in expectation. *She* ignored him and ordered a gin and tonic.

Della introduced Olive to the group. At once, Olive's gregarious, bowsy physicality manifested itself, her billowy top floating, wing-like when she waved her hands around. Her immediate commandeering of the centre seat gave her a vantage point from which to hold court. First off came her response to Mark's suggestion that she drive home.

"Do men bring their wives out to drive them home?" she thundered. "Never agree," she cautioned in a loud aside.

"I'd rather have a night out than fight with my husband," Nan offered. "And we women have a good time, too."

"No, you're soft. Men don't respect us for giving in to them. You mustn't let them rule your life." Her outburst drew immediate gasps from the group in the corner.

Nan, the epitome of happy domesticity, said there would be no money to enjoy a night out without men. They toiled on the land and worked as professionals or in business. Men were natural providers; women's role was to stay home and rear children.

Olive bristled. "Ladies, all that is changing in our modern Ireland. I think you should join the Women's movement. I'm starting a branch soon. I'll expect to see you there." Laura looked into her glass, May and Nan at each other, and only Della smiled a 'yes after the birth'.

Downing a gin, Olive's voice again rose above the babble in the lounge, drawing frequent looks of disapproval from her husband at the bar. Della detected blatant hostility between the pair; they were not happy. Despite being engrossed in conversation with Ed, Ben, and Joe, her abrasive manner clearly agitated Mark. But Della could not help envying the other woman's assertiveness. A little of her feistiness would sit nicely on herself.

"A gin, Mark," Olive's voice demanded, swallowing the last of her drink. Mark smiled around the circle of women as he placed the glass on a mat before his wife. How polite, Della thought, despite the provocation.

"Ladies, I'm sure you're having a great night. Don't let me hold you up." The long, black leather body turned and rejoined the men again. Della caught a scrap of a sentence from the counter where the four stood propped on elbows; 'keep the women happy,' followed by male laughter.

"He's philandering, and we're rowing," Olive lowered her tone. Silence fell, and the others strained to catch her comments. Wiser to discourage further unburdening, until now, their night out unspoiled and light-hearted, Della whispered to Laura. Ideally, she'd like to fold personalities into one cohesive whole. But Laura, fuelled by vodka, was visibly upset. "That must affect your kids, Olive."

Olive disclosing was Olive not hearing; but instead intent on pouring her troubles into patient ears. "I tell him their outbursts are his fault, and he says there's nothing wrong with them. They're just sickly, looking for attention."

"Children deserve stability, and when parents fight, it harms their well-being," Laura insisted. "None of us have perfect marriages, but we women are, by nature, peace-makers."

"I've got a responsible post out of the home, Laura. Mark has to do his share instead of gallivanting." Her face puck-ered into a grimace. Olive did not brook disagreement with her opinions. Laura shrunk back in her seat, squashed into passivity.

May attempted to speak, could not get the words out, and lay, head lolling sideways. Olive carried on. "I don't want more kids. But without the pill, how can we avoid it? Miracle how we managed in the back of cars, girls. Thrilling, though." Again, her raucous laughter drew a spectrum of attention in the lounge. "It's all or nothing with them now."

"There are ways," Laura attempted. "But you say Mark is not home much, so you've got natural contraception."

"Not what I want, either. Anyway, I'm thinking of going into politics, girls. That'll show him I'm my own person." A clever ploy, Della figured, Olive's dodging direct questions.

"Surely not, Olive. You're a busy woman. The family needs you, and your marriage needs you," Della gasped.

A broad smile spread across the woman's face. "Wait and see."

Two hours later. Until Olive arrived, it had been an enjoyable night; gone the lethargy, the listlessness. How good to be among nice girls, well, women, sharing gossip, hints on changing nappies, feeding babies, and avoiding another pregnancy too soon. May attempted to answer, drawing squeals from the group on how to dodge the sex when they got home. "I let him get to the bed first," she smirked. "By the time I'm finished in the bathroom, he's out of it."

"Fine, if your man doesn't cop your plan, like in our house," Laura added. "And yours too, Nan, with your brood of six." How drink loosened tongues.

Olive whispered in Della's ear. "But I want him to want me." Behind the feisty facade, her muffled revelation expressed more than any words uttered during the night, denoting hurt and loneliness. Olive loved Mark.

But Della's fears did not lessen throughout the night. Seeing men swaying at the bar did nothing to assuage her doubts about Ed's behaviour. His constant 'love' to the barmaid and his glances at girls who passed through the lounge spoke volumes. And he'd found his kind in Mark.

Between pints, Joe Linehan's voice rose above the smoke and the gaggle in the lounge. I like his voice, Della thought, clapping loudly when he sang *Green, Green Grass of Home*. A chorus joined in—Tom Jones, a great favourite with the Irish, a solid Celtic bond between the two countries. Anyone who enjoyed singing went down well in a bar. Surely, Joe and Laura shared good times at home if they both enjoyed music. Or was he just another Ed who sought attention outside the home?

Ben said if the Foot and Mouth disease spread to Ireland, few emigrants would put foot on the green grass of the Emerald Isle for a while. As the night died, vivid pictures of burning beasts, snow-caked streets, and empty boats floated.

Ed's expression, Della reckoned, was becoming twisted. Mark, with less alcohol intake, stood cool and detached. Ben's face, smiling benignly at everyone, reddened with every brandy.

At two o'clock, they bade goodnight and headed towards the cars. Della said she would drive home. Ed said no, he was fine. But he wasn't, and going around by the old jail, she sensed the car shaving grass margins. Fingers of fear gripped her stomach, but she said nothing. Better not rile him. Later in bed, he turned and put an arm around her waist. Not long now, Della, and we'll be back to normal, he muttered, then rolled onto his back in a comatose state. Normal? Assume relations in bed. Sex? Well, he was drunk. But it had been a good night out.

CHAPTER 20

One week later, Della burned to see Laura and probe for information. She would walk as the bicycle saddle hurt her bum.

At the house on the hill, Della brushed past Laura without looking at her. In the kitchen, she sat on a chair by the range. "Let's talk. Tell me what you know about Ed."

Then, a shard of sunlight on Laura's face showed an ugly mark under the right eye, a dark purple patch barely concealed by a trace of powder. "What's happened to your face?" Both eyes appeared puffy from copious crying. At once, her own needs vanished.

A tear slithered down the woman's face, dabbed by a sodden hanky. "Joe was drunk last night, and he hit me because I dared ask him for money. He'd sold two calves at the fair, and I needed shoes. Seemed a good time to ask." She had lain awake waiting to hear him fumbling with the key and promised herself there'd be no fight, just calm discussion. But hearing him banging his way upstairs, her anger had risen in sync with the heartbeats hammering in her chest. Finally, the doorknob turned, and he switched on the light with a flourish.

"Must've taken the price of a calf to get you into this state, more than enough for a pair of shoes, I'll wager," Laura said.

"New shoes? You women always want something."

"Joe, I'm only asking. After all, you've been singing at the pub festival all week, and I haven't complained."

"My business."

"What do you mean?"

"Take it any way you like," he retorted. "No woman will rule me."

Laura went on. "Della, I persisted, saying the sole was falling off my brown pair. Then he lashed out and hit me on the cheekbone. It hurt. I sobbed, but he ignored me and went to sleep. I stayed awake all night, wondering how to deal with him. But he was quiet in the morning, without the usual singing. During the day, he tried to talk, but I shunned him until dinner and gave in for peace's sake."

"Surely you tried to reason with him? Make him say sorry? Do you think he and Ed are going with other women?"

"Sorry means little to him. I'm not sure. It seems like it, but maybe not Joe. He prefers a pint and being the centre of attention."

"What are you saying, Laura? What are you not telling me? It's what I came to talk about."

"Never mind. You must focus on the birth. Anxiety communicates itself to the baby in the womb. Maybe they'll both settle with age."

"Settle, Laura? Are you a glutton for punishment, thinking life can go on as normal after a beating like that? As for Ed, he's far from settling down into happy parenting."

"Joe receives Communion on Sundays. I'll urge him to get Confession on Saturday before going to the altar. That'll make him think of his actions."

"Bloody hypocrites, keeping up a front!" Della snapped. A thought - Ed did not go the rails much nowadays.

The following Sunday, Jim took Ed to see the new tractor in the barn. Bridie said, "I wanted him out of the way, Della. Some men are not natural parents, and Ed is an example. No one can keep his type on a leash. He's a rover. Be as calm as you can manage, or you'll have a jittery, crying baby. And don't irritate him, especially when he's under the influence." Sensible advice, but wasn't it unfair that she be so compliant?

"I'm not alone. Laura has to put up with more than me."

"Bet they don't talk about you women at the bar," Eve said. Back from a gymkhana, her ponies had won no prizes. She was tired, her patience at a premium. "Unburdening your troubles on the parents again, Della?"

"Oh, shut up, Eve," Della said. "It's all right for you, with your freedom and money in your pocket. I didn't cost them a penny during my four years away."

"God, you'd think it was a prison. Well, sort of, I suppose. You're in another one now, and it's all your own doing."

Bridie's frown silenced her younger daughter as Jim entered the sitting room. Ed was in the toilet. Seeing his wife's tight lips, her father said, "Keep it cool, and be friendly."

"Dad, he wasn't ready to settle, but I just didn't see it."

"Just do your best. You mustn't let it break you."

"Della, if it gets too much, you can come home for a while, at least until after the birth," Bridie added. So it had come to that - separation, but somehow it was a pleasant alternative. When Ed entered, smiling as if the entire world were at his feet, she nodded in his direction, and they said goodbye.

As the car swept down the tree-lined avenue, the smiles vanished. "Happy for another week, Della?"

"Why can't we both be happy, Ed?"

"Because you'll find reasons to nag me." His expression once again showed intolerance. According to legend, Helen of Troy's face could launch a thousand ships. Ed was no Helen, but he could destroy her well-being with one look...

The O'Reillys settled down to tea, cold roast beef, tomatoes, onions, beetroot, and potato salad.

"We have to keep an eye on her, Bridie," Jim said.

"Yes, she's fragile. Eve, go down next week, take her shopping, and get her out. And be patient. She's a lot to deal with in that house."

By the end of April, Della was sinking, physically and mentally.

Unable to cycle, she asked Ed to drop her off at Laura's one evening. Would he pick her up at ten? Fine, he said.

"I'm exhausted, Laura. I must get away from him."

"You're due in a few weeks. Go back home. It's nearer the hospital. Drop me a line when you're there. I wish we had a phone." Egans and O'Reillys had one, but the Linehans did not—no washing machine and no phone. Laura said life was simple since the row, and she'd had the shoe's sole mended in McDermott's cobblers on the High Street. Joe said it was the best thing to do. Joe said.

Ed arrived on the dot of ten—he'd only drunk one pint. On the car radio, Engelbert Humperdinck was singing a song about release. How apt. Would he? Would she?

"Ed, take me to Leam tomorrow. I've had enough of your late nights and negligence. My mental state is at risk."

An expression, infuriating in relief, spread across her husband's features. "That's a point. No probes when I get in late. Sure, it's a great idea. Yeah, I'll take you."

"You're so cruel, implying I'm a burden on you."

"Your mental health was weak before you married me, so don't pile the blame on my shoulders."

"You are hateful." She'd said it. Hateful, an awful word that should not define their relationship. But it did.

Ed had barely stayed in since the night in the Royal, even on weeknights. The lateness, the smell of alcohol, and recent evidence on his shirt, blue eyeshadow, and perfume scent made Della miserable. On his return, they fought loud and sharp into the early hours. Frightened by the hatred stirring inside, Della only wanted to get away from her husband.

On Saturday at three a.m., it had come to a head when Molly knocked on the bedroom door and asked them to stop. Ed shouted blame, "Now see what you've done."

Della opened the door and explained to the older woman that her son had gone too far and was seeing other girls. But if she expected support or a reprimand to her son, it did not come. Instead, Molly said, "Ye rushed into this marriage. There'll be blood spilt in this house yet."

Della got back into bed. There was only one choice left to her.

Ed placed her bag in the boot the next day. "Women go through birth every day. It's no different from a cow calving. Don't know why you make such a fuss."

Quelling the urge to slap him, she said, "I'm going because I want peace before the birth, which I cannot get here." From the window, Molly waved goodbye, her crinkled skin white and sad. For long enough, the old lady had put up with the tantrums and the nightly rows. Both parents deserved a reprieve.

As they drove away, words from the Book of Daniel, long ingrained in her consciousness, came again. *"They shall drive you from among men, and thy dwelling shall be with the beast of the field."*

Not beasts, as in the holy book, but good people.

The car sped away from the valley, neither one willing to break the impasse of a void that might never heal. What they were doing, what Della had requested, summoned an ugly truth. The urge to solve their difficulties now lay smothered in the ashes of their marriage, which she had not wanted.

"I pledged obedience and honour only a year ago, but I can't uphold either, Ed. Unless you change your ways, we will nullify those vows. It's a shame there's no divorce in Ireland." The tear that welled in her eye fell unnoticed by him and dripped onto her coat. He pressed the accelerator to the floor. The white hawthorn whizzed by, and soon they reached the high road.

"Ed, do you think this coat suits me? The women said I looked good in it after Mass on Sunday." The last effort.

He sniffed, "It's alright, I suppose. Hides the fat."

"Can't you say one word to make me feel better?"

"Put up the window. It'll ruffle my hair."

"There's enough hair spray on it to glue a door."

"Shut up. Just do it. God, I can't wait to be rid of you."

His hair, sleeked to Grecian perfection, his arms, tanned and glistening on the wheel, his legs, long and graceful, depicted perfection, but she, contrarily, was fat, ugly, and puffed.

"Well, I didn't think it would turn out like this, Ed."

"I like the nightlife and the craic. You can't go out nowadays."

"Craic? You mean the girls fawning all over you and the booze that changes your personality?"

"Whatever."

"I'm not stupid. I have heard rumours. You're driving me away, making me hate you."

Silence. He was always the same when sober and never gave her enough ammunition for a balanced argument.

Laura had hinted about girls buzzing around the bars after work, but she'd always stopped short of specifics. Then, one night in the hotel, Della saw a dark-eyed, pretty girl blowing kisses at Ed; felt sure something was going on between them. But Ed wore denial like a suit of armour and was a master of the art; his lies glib and evasive, peculiarly easier to bear than the truth. However, she'd wanted peace to bring her child into the world without further aggravation or anxiety. She was allowing him to stray even more by leaving him, but tired and drawn, she wanted an exit.

The car pulled up on the shingle in a flurry of dust. Bridie came outside, and Della noted an uncharacteristic restraint and hesitancy in her mother's bearing. Bridie nodded towards her son-in-law. "Come in for a cuppa, Ed." A perennial peacemaker and symbol of motherhood, she would not give up on them.

"Thanks, Mam, but I've got to meet someone on the way back." Ed turned towards Della and said, "See you next Sunday." No kiss, no sign of affection. But he would come back. Brushing the spot with a flick of her hand, she did not wave goodbye. Weren't love and hate supposed to polarise people? Or merge them?

As she lay down to sleep in her old bed, it was February 1965 again when hope lighted the way ahead. Only moments ago, it seemed, had the room welcomed and enfolded her in its love. Della mimed a silent prayer, 'Direct O Lord all my actions', to the heavens. At another crossroads, a personal peripeteia, she doubted her present stance would lead to that longed-for nirvana. Instead, it might sever the bonds of marriage that she and Ed had made through a mixture of love and doubt. Moreover, an enormous responsibility loomed ahead in a potentially distressing situation: the expected birth of a child. Could she raise one alone?

But once again, like her heroine, Scarlett, Della would, for now, relegate the future to a realm beyond birth.

Here, life was normal and busy. People came to her father for advice and to help with form-filling. As a Justice of the Peace, the Gárdai sought his signature and stayed to chat and eat Bridie's gingerbread. The general thrust of each day was bustling and cheerful, creating in Della a new calm, not entirely devoid of anxiety but distanced in intensity. For now, it was enough to be still, to shed the restless waiting for the sound of an engine at night, and not lie face averted from the smell of alcohol floating across the bed.

On Wednesday, Eve drove Della to town for baby clothes, nappies, and more. They parked on the square, a short distance from the shops. Della kept close to the rails on the downward slope to the town centre. She dared not fall on the wet pavement, a recent shower drying out in the heat of the midday sun.

A voice shouted across the main street, "Hi, Della." It belonged to Olive Keating, resplendent in an undersized white skirt and top. Her blue eyes, agog with self-assurance, sparkled under flowing tresses, falling askance onto her broad shoulders. Olive kissed Della's cheek and smiled at Eve. Questions bubbled. Why were they in town? Had Della long to go? How was Ed? Della filled in the gaps in jerky sentences but struggled to stem the tears.

"Oh my. Come to the Royal for a chat." As before, when they had met Laura in happier times, Eve said she'd do her errands and left.

Olive chose a table in an alcove by the window, covered in an Irish linen tablecloth adorned with green shamrocks and harps. They might not be tourists, but Della appreciated the luxurious whiteness and classy Celtic theme. A waitress brought the menu. Olive chose a cream bun, a coffee, Della tea, and a soda bun. "I'm eating less and have put on too much weight during the pregnancy. Ed doesn't like it."

"Drat the man and his vanity. Anything bordering on overweight will probably annoy him, but you're expecting his child, Della." The northern twang held a comic element. Ironic, Della thought, that she still did not equal Olive's ample proportions. But now, it felt good to talk to the other woman, with whom a bond existed, born out of doubts about their men. Olive's cheery nature and overwhelming tenacity were her bastions against adversity. She also owned another powerful characteristic that Della envied and from which Laura would benefit. Assertiveness.

During the early days of friendship with the Keatings, Ed had once remarked Olive was 'a fine woman'. "Not your type, I imagine", Della joked. However, despite Mark's alleged behaviour, Olive's forceful personality was her mainstay. And she possessed that precious jewel: a career. If Joe allowed her, Laura could resume nursing, while Della depended on her husband's income. Neither woman was in Olive's league.

For an hour, they exchanged details, some funny, some worrying. "We have the right to fish for information. I know when Mark lies to me."

"Exactly, Olive. But worse than the lies, Ed's cruel comments were the last straw. I had to get away or be a nervous wreck by the birth."

"You know they meet once a week in the River Inn. I followed his car last Wednesday."

That clicked. Ed met Mark for squash on Wednesdays. But where was the River Inn?

"A few miles on from Leitrim village. Mark didn't see me trailing him one night as he drove fast along the road to Arigna, and there was little traffic on the road. That's a fair drive from us, Della, but I kept back and let the red taillights guide me."

"What were they doing there? It's miles from everywhere."

"Well, nothing. They chatted for an hour. I was only in the door when Mark arrived home."

"Mysterious."

"Well, maybe not. Mark's going to London to a machinery exhibition. Bet Ed will go too."

"Machinery? Ed sells nothing fancy. Why go to London?"

"Obvious, to have fun. Nightclubs, hostesses, you know."

Della didn't. "Hostesses? And you don't mind?" Yes, Della knew what such women did.

"I do, but try to accept what he tells me for peace of mind. He goes twice a year to see the latest models and buy extra equipment for the plant and the boat. He loves that boat, as I do, as it's where we spend time at weekends. So, Della, we'll get together later in the summer and sail along the river. You can bring the baby too." If the Egans were still together. If, if.

Olive and Mark had three children, one girl and two boys. "To give him credit, Mark does things with the boys and encourages them to swim, play football, and run. Running is a major part of school life, with kids chasing each other around fields for practice."

But Della wanted to hear more about London. "When is London happening?"

"He said it's an important exhibition in a few months."

"Ed hasn't said a word, but he tells me so little nowadays that's no surprise. I can't let it upset me. He can stray anywhere in my absence - London, Dublin - and it won't matter."

"Mark has to tell me a certain amount because I work, and we have to get one of his men to pick the kids up from school when he's away."

"Olive, a thought. If our husbands were to get the wildness out of their systems, and we looked the other way, didn't fight, and kept the peace, would it all stop? I've had time to think. I don't want to return with a baby and be miserable."

"Della, we lurch from row to row, from crisis to crisis, because I'm not prepared to let Mark shit on his doorstep. Well, mine, too. I have a public job and deserve respectability. But I want my marriage to last."

"For the children's sake, is it best to put up and shut up?"

"No woman should put up with it, Della. We must strive for change for all women in this church-controlled, male-dominated society. That's why I love my job and the opportunity to speak to groups. But I can't tell you what to do. I'd say this, though. If you still love Ed, as I do Mark, then fight for him, for a future. Before you go back, tell him it's a trial. That should settle him. No man wants to be disgraced by his wife in a place where everyone knows each other's business."

Della smiled. How good to hear similar views. Hope danced in the sunlight, pirouetted on the frilly tablecloth, beckoned through the darkness, and subsumed her in a least expected way. "Thing is, I don't have options. If I had a profession like you or Laura, I'd stay with my family, plenty of land there. Could build a house."

"Too final, Della. If you've even the slightest love for him, do what I say. Lay down the law. He won't want the alternative."

A week passed, two, then before she knew it, six weeks had gone since she left her husband's home.

"He'll be a different man when the baby goes home with you, Della," Bridie advised. "By leaving, you will have gained his respect, shown you're stronger than he thought. I see a difference in him when he calls. He wants you home."

"But I don't want to go back there, Mam," she heard her voice quiver, "back to his bullying." She had not passed on Olive's advice.

"The neighbours would gossip. Talk to him next time and tell him exactly how you feel. Easier here in our house than afterwards under his roof." Would neighbours gossip? Here, there? Did she care? They'd gossiped when she left the convent.

"You mean being respectable matters more than suffering? What if I didn't go back at all?"

"Not a good idea. You're twenty-five, with a long life ahead and no chance of getting another man as you're married."

"Don't care about that. I'd go back to Dublin and qualify for something."

"With a baby? No, best make it work." What her mother was suggesting was to do the honourable thing and go home to her husband. Honourable or respectable? Ireland demanded respectability in line with Church attendance, and *decent* people lived following the Gospel on the outside. However, furores rose and died inside, and walls alone retained evidence of blows, insults, and hurt.

Ed came on Sunday for an hour and ate a roast dinner and her mother's apple pie with custard. Everyone loved Bridie's pies, baked in the Stanley range slowly so that none of the juice ran around the oven. Molly baked nothing other than soda bread. Despite the non-confrontational atmosphere, Della found it difficult to warm to him, though he appeared chastened.

Afterwards, she drew him into the sitting room. "Ed, we need to clear up the situation between us."

"I know, and before you start, listen to me. My father says I'd better change when you come home, Della." So the boss had stepped in. Not his wife, nor his mother, but Himself. The male that ruled the roost.

"You'll change and become a loving husband, Ed Egan? Not so sure I trust you that far."

"I'll stay in more, but not altogether." A compromise of sorts. "The old man says he won't leave me the property if I don't reform."

Annoyance spurted; Della's heartbeat quickened. "Great. And what about when you don't? What then? How long will the 'good behaviour' last?"

"I'll try, Della." The last syllable of her name, uttered softly, conveyed an awareness of who she was. Ed had wanted her to marry him, had pursued her, and never expected her to leave him. Her actions must have affected him more than expected. God knows what he told people. However, in the final analysis, Pat Egan's threat weighed heavier than anything she might say. Still, she hesitated, an inner warning voice presaging possible further storms. He'd promise for now. But afterwards?

"I'm unsure if I'll ever be happy there, Ed."

"Get the birth over, and we'll take it from there," he said, kissing her lips, an arm encircling her wide waist. "I think something moved there, Della," he laughed.

"It's called a baby, Ed. Not that you've felt it before." She saw the flush on his face, worth more than gold.

Bridie had cautioned not to interrogate him. Instead, be a calmer, less hostile wife. It was challenging, but he came, talked, and left again. Bland and non-committal. She admitted to liking him a little more.

CHAPTER 21

O n Thursday night, June 8, at midnight, labour pains started, first niggling, then increasing to sharper darts. Eve pushed Della into the passenger seat and then set off along the dark road. They rounded bends in haste. Brigid said it was a good time to travel on such a journey. Della gasped as each pang surged in her belly, spurring Eve to drive like a hare along the nine miles to the hospital. At the entrance, Della cried. Bridie smiled and said all would be well. They helped her to the door and into Reception, where a sole porter smiled a weary face and let her in. She must seem like an unmarried woman whose man had deserted her. Absent by consent, Ed's shadow hung over Della as she bade goodbye.

Within hours came the dawning of new life: a son with a shock of black hair slithered out of Della's body.

"Black hair," Della gasped as the nurse held the child up for her to see. "Only my dad has black hair. That's where it comes from, not me with my blonde curls or Ed with his mousy brown thatch."

A son. Would Ed be proud?

She screamed as the nurse sewed stitches into her broken parts, then drifted into fractured sleep during which images floated - girls pouting red lipstick and blue eyeshadow. Wasn't there something common about blue? Consciousness came and went until the nurse handed her the bundle to feed at seven.

"Thank God he doesn't look like his father."

"Why is that?" the nurse asked.

Della shook her head. Enough, the pain was over.

At eleven, Ed came into the ward and pulled up a chair. "Eve rang the pub. I would have come sooner if you'd sent a message."

"Sad you weren't here, but they don't allow men into the labour ward. It doesn't matter now. Look at your son."

"Gosh, is that our baby? He looks old and withered." Peering over the cot, Ed did not lift the infant out. Della said the baby wouldn't break. Ed said no, it was too soon. The inept inability to bond spoke volumes in stark contrast to the other dads, cooing and smiling into cots.

"You'll be home in a few days, I expect. Ready for the bottles and the nappies?" Home. The word connoted warmth and love, elusive qualities in the Egan household.

"I'm sure you'll take your turn, Ed."

"My mother will help, I expect."

Here we go again. His scene, life, way, mother, everyone but him. Not once did he kiss her, the chasm wide and physical. He could be anyone visiting a relative. Ed left after half an hour.

Jim, Bridie, and Eve arrived. Bridie said, "Who wouldn't look after a fine boy like Ronan? So that is the name you want, Della? You told Ed, I imagine?"

"Yes. He's fine with it. But now, I have no excuse but to return to that claustrophobic atmosphere."

"It'll be better." Bridie's cautious attempt to assuage the doubts helped a little. "After all, it's a new start, and maybe you'll get it right this time."

Between feeds, she read Anne Frank's diary and cried. Whether it was her hormonal state or genuine empathy, she found the tears slipping onto the pages. In its evocation of hope, the poignance and acceptance of a young girl reached beyond the horrors and suffering of a Nazi hell to penetrate Della in a very different world. *I feel that everything will change for the better, that this cruelty will end, that peace will return once more*—a young girl's wisdom stirring a woman's hopes. But she mustn't let emotions rule. Think of Olive, she told herself. Be assertive. You have the right.

Days passed; visitors came and brought presents: blue this, that and other bits and bobs. Ed visited in the evenings, and an increased interest in their son was visible in his comments on hair colour and nose shape, like his own. God forbid, Della said, with your hook. It did not go down well. She didn't care. It was up to him if he wanted a family. Finally, on the fourth day, he smiled as Della put the infant in his arms, commenting on the similarity to his blue eyes. Perhaps fatherhood was a cure for waywardness.

Still, Della remained in the hospital. Others went. She said no, she didn't feel up to it.

Friday came, with no choice but to return to the house in the valley. Della placed all the presents into the travel bag and waited for her husband to arrive. She noticed his apparent good humour when he entered the ward at eleven o'clock. Ed picked up the carrycot and led the way along the hospital corridor to the main door while she gave gifts of chocolates and flowers to the nurses. Anna, one in whom Della had confided, understood her recalcitrance and whispered, "Chin up, Della." Outside, Ed placed the cot in the back seat and held the passenger door open for her. It was June, the air balmy, the sky part cloudy, part blue, summer, happy time.

Ed drove slowly towards the outskirts of the city. A light wind fluttering through the partially open window blew freshness for the precious bundle on the car's back seat. He lowered the shades. "Mustn't let the sun on his face." A good start. They headed south.

"I've not been along this road for weeks, Ed," she said.

"And probably won't for a while. It'll be enough for you at home now, Della."

"Is it necessary to remind me?" The notion of an existence she had avoided for almost two months wrapped around her tightly, like a hermit's belt. She repeated a mantra of positivity to herself. Maybe this new version of Ed was a positive sign, leaving behind his egotistical past.

As they approached the lakes, they swung east and descended into the valley. Ed talked about sales. The business was on the rise. In the countryside, during summer, farmers purchased machinery to cut meadows, prepare potato drills, and harvest corn. He omitted any mention of going to London with Mark. She kept counsel. Secrets had a way of outing themselves.

Della interpreted Pat Egan's initial reaction to his new grandchild in the wickerwork carrycot as reserved. He stood back in what she considered a staid manner.

"Congratulations," he said in a stilted tone. Perhaps the older man did not yet trust his son's recalcitrant attempts at reviving his marriage, or he might dread a return to nightly fights. Della understood. The house felt strange, with its white exterior and dark interior. Those damned trees, she swore inwardly. To knock them down would lift the gloom.

But, on the bright side, life had to be better with a new baby in the house. One man alone had the power to make or break the peace.

Before long, a pattern emerged. Ed held the baby while she prepared milk for evening feeds and boiled a saucepan on the range. But when the room filled with uncontrollable cries at night, he urged Della to change the diaper, as the noise prevented him from falling asleep. He had to work the next day. So, Della fed and settled her child at ten-thirty, two, and five a.m. before returning to a restless sleep. She said goodbye to her husband in the morning and continued the routine.

The days blurred with sleeplessness, quick naps, feeding, and changes. She hated the rough terry towelling that chafed soft baby skin. Molly suggested applying Vaseline on his bottom to prevent any wetness from penetrating.

One evening, Ed commented that very little substance was in the bottle to fill a child. "The boy is only two weeks old and is an awful crier. You can see he's not getting enough to keep him asleep."

"He can only have that until his stomach develops in three months. And you woke him coming in at twelve, Ed."

"So, broken nights until then. It's hard to focus on deals when I'm kept awake. Do something."

"Too bloody bad, Ed Egan," Della said, her wan and strained features staring back from the mirror on the wall beside the picture of the Sacred Heart with its red light burning in perpetual adoration. Molly withdrew to the scullery to bang basins of milk around. The older woman knew better than to offer further advice. Della didn't care either way. Before the birth, she'd been baggy and saggy; now, she was wan and listless. No one had prepared her for this. "I look terrible," she ventured.

"Come on, Della. Don't be ratty. You'll soon get out for a night," Ed said. Gosh! The man who rejected her before the birth when she was fat was now encouraging her. The older man's dictums at work, or the birth of his son, a Saul transformation? However, his effort to cover the hurt came as a pleasant surprise.

"Christening first, then we'll see. But I can't leave Ronan yet."

Ed said he'd go out on Saturday night and be back by twelve. Ok, she said, don't drink too much or wake the child. But, true to his word, he came in just as Della was feeding Ronan on the side of the bed. He'd only had five pints, he said and was sober. Sober?

When, a few days later, Ed started dropping hints that machinery exhibitions were the best place to see new models, her propensity to sniff an announcement sharpened. He would soon mention a trip to London, unaware she was expecting it. It had seemed to go away with the busyness of life, the baby, and daily minutiae.

During dinner one evening towards the end of the month, he said Mark was going to the annual machinery exhibition in London. This time, he'd asked three friends along, including Ed.

"We've not seen the Keatings since they visited me in the hospital. While you talked to Mark, Olive said he goes to the city every weekend, keeps a cool distance in the house and rarely wants group outings. When she tries to discuss their problems, he ignores her. So now you want to go away with him." She did not say that a chill gripped her insides at the thought of him and Mark together, two good-looking men in their late twenties. Here, tied to a baby, day and night, she could not look her best, and Ed, with his immaculate clothes sense, was attractive.

"It's an opportunity for me to see new inventions, different machines."

"Perhaps, but I don't like him. Olive's lost her exuberance and loudness and seemed almost timid."

"Mark says nothing about themselves."

"Didn't know you met that often, Ed." Draw him out, she thought.

"He drops into the garage for a chat and comes for a beer on Saturday nights." Again, a sparse disclosure. Della steeled herself for more.

"The excursion to London is in hand, tickets bought, and the car ferry booked. Mark's business partners, Ben Heslin and Roy Manning, are going too. It's an exhibition worth seeing. We'll never succeed by stagnating in our little corners."

"Are you Mark's parrot, Ed? What machines are you interested in? Those in the nightclubs?"

"Hush, woman, can't you accept anything I say? I'll tell you about it when we come back." Would he heck?

"You'll tell me a pack of lies with a little of the truth thrown in."

"I'm going with friends, nothing more. We're family men, all of us."

"Really? Mark, the family man, breaks free whenever the urge hits him. And you, the master liar." She bit her lip; must not resort to nastiness.

"Have faith. I'll ring you, and it's only three days." That he did not rise to her bait but appeared eager for approval was hopeful. However, his excitement at the prospect of a trip to London again summoned images of winking women and more.

All four men piled into Ben's cream Volvo on Monday morning, waiting in the square. May, Della and Olive watched their husbands load overnight bags bulging with their 'best clobber' - Ed's words - into the ample boot of the car. Then, hands waving from car windows, they zoomed out of town towards Dublin airport.

"Coffee and goss, ladies," Olive shrilled. "I'm not worrying. He's with your men."

"What do you mean?" May said. "Worry?"

"Well, Mark goes away regularly. We've lost direction, says I'm to blame for going out to meetings. The cheek."

"Now, don't fret," May hastened. "Surely he won't do anything foolish. They're off to see machinery, have a few drinks at night and enjoy the break."

Della smiled. Wasn't May naïve? Not that Ben was ever silly; his excitement lay in the opportunity to buy a classy machine for his plant, eat good meals, maybe go to a club, and not much else. She needn't worry. And neither Ed nor Mark would let themselves down in such a group. Strapping a sleeping Ronan into the car, Della drove home.

Two days later her imagination unleashed. Men were demons, women saints. Then, on Thursday, May had a call from Ben. She rang Della afterwards and said London was great: the weather, the exhibition, the food, and the fun.

"I bet it is."

"He sounded tired, sharing a room with Mark, who snores." No more information. Men closed ranks, while women couldn't keep their mouths zipped. Ed did not ring her, nor did Della try to contact him. Stay calm, she told herself, sleep between feeds, and doze until the shrill cry jogs her into wakefulness. And wasn't it nice, just her and the baby in the room?

On Saturday, Della, waiting in the Square's car park, saw the Volvo approaching along the street before the occupants noticed her. It seemed as if no one was talking. Odd, considering how much they wanted to go away together.

She watched all four men part company with a brief pat on the back before moving towards their wives and cars.

"Come on, Ed, tell all. The trip didn't go well, by the look of it. I couldn't get through to your room the other night. Late one? Talk."

"Nothing much. We walked, viewed impressive machines, and drank a little."

A little? His very stance, the tiredness, told a story she itched to uncover. But wait, a small voice whispered until he is under the influence and secrets slip. Don't badger him now.

In the house, Ed took his bag upstairs but came back down within minutes. The old pair were off visiting the daughter in Boyle, and the house was quiet. He handed a bag to Della, a smile crinkling the corners of his perfect lips. She opened the box on the shiny red worktop, carefully brushing the breakfast crumbs aside. Amid layers of white tissue lay a cream linen dress.

"Oh, my goodness, Ed, you bought this for me?" Della grasped the slim-fitting dress. Not since the early days of marriage had he given her anything—he hated shopping unless for himself. She occasionally wore the sapphire cluster ring he'd once purchased in Cork. Since then, nothing. Reaching up, she gave him a peck on the cheek. "Thank you."

"Done well this time, haven't I?" Bending down, his lips brushed hers. A forgotten sensation jolted her body. "You'll soon be that glamorous girl again."

"You sure have, Ed. I can't believe you went into a women's shop in London. Unbelievable." She stalled. "Spill, guilty conscience. What happened in London?"

"So I'm guilty of something because I brought you a present? Surely, Della, I'm not that shallow?" His look, akin to the wounded rabbit she'd seen in the field by the house yesterday, brought shame. Bloody and weak, it had limped towards a burrow for safety. Ed was not bloody, but he looked wounded and had attempted to please her. For months, suspicion had laced every deed, late night, and action, but since Ronan's birth, Ed was trying. Perhaps the upturn in his behaviour was real and would last. She hated herself for doubting.

Assuming his poker face, one who keeps cards close to his chest and secrets closer still, he said. "First, I'm not guilty of anything. Second, you looked after the business; third, there is something."

"Go on, Ed, tell."

"OK, but you cannot pass any of it to Olive. Understand, Della? Make tea, sit down and listen until I finish. Ronan is asleep."

Della put a tea bag into a mug, suffused it in hot water, and then transferred it to hers. There was no waste in the Egan household; she didn't like strong tea. Ed ladled four spoons of sugar into his, slowly, deliberately. Would he ever start? Until now, he'd never made a ceremony out of details, so what she was about to hear must be the truth, and, importantly, it wouldn't damn himself. He dragged on a Player, an indecipherable expression gracing his features.

CHAPTER 22

On arrival at the Exhibition Centre, Mark assumed a sense of purpose and strode ahead of Ben, Ed, and Roy, flagging at the rear. Ranged around the vast arena on Company-allocated stands were statuesque, colourful machines of all makes and purposes.

"There are three thousand listed in the catalogue," Ben said. "That's a lot of walking, boys."

"It's exciting," Mark answered, his face alight. "We'll learn how to compete at the top of the market and get rich."

"Not at those prices, mate," Ben responded.

Over four hours, they trudged around the vast, domed building adorned with balloons and company logos. Mark bought an earth-moving machine and would have it shipped over when the manufacturer completed the details. By two o'clock, all four were flagging. Ben said he'd seen enough machinery for a lifetime, Ron, that there was only one he could use back on the farm. Ed wished he had more capital to invest. Mark seemed pleased.

"Lunch, boys," Mark announced, leading the way to a table in the spacious rooftop canteen overlooking the arena. From here, they could command views of an expansive range of products on the floor below some - the sleekier types - graced with sinuous blonde bodies. "Wouldn't shove her out of bed," Ed laughed, pointing towards the girl atop a JCB.

"Worth a few bob," Ben said. "These shoes are killing me." His pointed dismissal of Ed's remark drew laughter.

"I meant the girl, Ben, not the machine."

More laughter. "I know what you meant, Ed, but don't spoil it now."

"You're daft, dressed in suits, ties, and hard shoes," Mark said.

"You didn't say," Ron complained, red veins bulging over a tight collar.

At five o'clock and satiation point, it was time to leave. It had been a long day at the exhibition, and their feet hurt except for Mark in comfortable loafers. "Now for some fun, boys," he said. "Dinner, then out on the town. We'll go on to a club afterwards."

"Fun? A few jars at the bar will do me," Ben, limping on one foot, strained a smile. "We came to see machines, didn't expect so much walking."

"London, bright lights, fun, sights. Come on. Soho is calling," Mark insisted. "Ed, you're up for a good time."

"Agreed. Drinking in the hotel would be foolish when we could sample London nightlife. I came down here a few times from Scotland in my single days. Had some brilliant nights dancing."

"Not in clubs, I expect," Mark said.

"No, but splendid ballrooms. I sometimes went to the Irish Club in Camden when the bands came over. I met the boys in the Clipper and Donie Collins bands. Their lead singer is Seán Dowd from near Carrick."

Seeing Ben's expression, he added, "In my single days, Ben."

Beside the taxi driver in the front seat, Mark asked him to recommend a club with music, drinks, and dancing. The Marquee Club. "Know it," Mark said. "I was there six months ago."

"Expensive booze, good music?" Ben queried.

"And more, just wait until you get in. You'll be like kids let loose in a sweet shop."

Mark whistled tunelessly on the brief journey to Piccadilly, his face alight with expectation. "Sights of the city, boys. What a change from good old Boyle."

At the club, a burly attendant led the four downstairs to a lower room from a side door on the street. Adjusting his eyes to the dim lights, Ed saw a row of sallow-faced women lolling by the crescent-shaped brass counter. Underfoot, a soft, deep carpet swallowed their footsteps as a doe-eyed hostess led them to a table in a corner. In the dim lighting, it was clear the club was only half-full. Ed scanned the scantily dressed girls, simpering by poles.

"Jeez, Mark, you come here?"

"Sure do. Great escape. How would I tolerate all the stuff at home otherwise? It's got everything."

Ron said, "I'm outa here. Not my scene."

"No, you don't, spoilsport," Ed said. "We're here now. Let's see how things pan out." Then, calling the waitress over, he ordered four brandies

"Nothing like brandy to get the blood stirring. How much love?"

"Fifty pounds, sir."

Ron jumped up. "Are you mad, Mark, bringing us here? Do you think I'll pay the price of a good heifer for alcohol?"

"Me neither. I didn't come to London to waste my money on booze when we can get it in the hotel," Ben exploded.

A short frilly apron distended over a basque top came and stood by the table. "You men not happy? We make you smile." Gesturing towards a dark-skinned girl at the bar, she spoke. "We're your hostesses for the night."

Ben spat, "I might be a chancer once in a while, but am bloody well not going that far."

"Not just for the drink," the oriental waitress said. "For everything, our attention all night."

"This," she opened her palm with the pound notes, "is your down payment on the rest. We're at your service." Her wink at Ben made him jump up, eyes popping, blonde curls bobbing.

"Get the feck out of here, boys," he shouted above the music.

Ed stood firm. "And leave that brandy behind?"

"Out, fools. Now." Ben said, racing to the exit, followed by Ron and a somewhat reluctant Ed, who pleaded, "Mark, don't spoil it. Come on."

Mark remained seated, motionless, indifferent, and not the popular animated character they liked. Ed tried again,

"Don't be stupid." No movement, nor a flicker of accedence. Lifting the glass to his mouth, he swallowed the golden liquid in one gulp.

As one, the three men bounded up the stairs, pursued by two burly bouncers. "Go for it, boys," Ed urged.

As they spilt out of the club onto the brightly lit pavement, Ben, at the head of the group, ran straight into a police officer. "Are you men all right? What's going on down there?"

"We're alright, but you should close that den," Ben shouted. "Hail a taxi," he urged the others, a foot on the road. One pulled over; they piled onto the back seat. Inside, he blurted, "Mark's a fool. He's lost it. I'm disgusted."

"He's not happy, Ben. It's not that I excuse him, but Olive is into many organisations, and he's lost interest. I'm no angel myself, and I've been where Mark is," Ed explained. More than the other two, he could identify with the man who wanted a 'good' night out in London, far from home and gossiping tongues.

Ron swore. Ben stayed silent.

A pall descended on the group as their night in London lay in ruins. They'd had fun: laughed, eaten well, and viewed some spectacular inventions at the exhibition, but now the trip had lost its lustre. Back in the hotel lounge, thoughts turned to home. Ron wondered how Kathy managed the one hundred cows; milking was a massive chunk of the farming day.

"She'll be fine, Roy, a sturdy woman like her. No trouble in your house," Ben said.

"No, thank God." A smile spread across the man's features of satisfaction and contentment.

That one word 'God' fell on three sets of ears -immediately affecting the men at the bar. Ben put his glass on the counter. "I'm for bed." If ever there was a happily married man, it was Ben, as was Ron.

Ed surmised that, given the opportunity, he would have stayed with Mark. But he'd had it all: the temptation, the excitement, the thrill, the lure. And he'd toed the line for a while now; no reason to return to his wild days. "I'm disappointed in Mark. I'm done for tonight. Off to bed."

Ron said, "Let's see if he gets back alright."

"His problem. I'm going up," Ben said.

"He'll wake you when he gets in," Ed added. Ben alone would know when Mark returned.

"I've travelled the world, seen amazing sights, worked in South America, did a stint on the oil rigs, but in all that time, no one ever let me down until now. So what is wrong with that man?" Ron said, letting the trousers fall in a heap on the carpet. "Three lovely kids, a wife who works, and a good business."

"Their relationship is complex, Ron. Olive can be difficult, loud, and brassy. Both have forceful personalities, and they clash," Ed tried.

"He's nearing the end of his thirties. Not exactly a young bloke."

Ed frowned. "Ron, let's keep this between us. No point in the women gossiping and making things worse."

Ron nodded. "I've enjoyed the break, though."

At breakfast, Ben was waiting at the table, face livid. "The bastard didn't come in all night. Eat up. Let's get to the airport without him."

As if on cue, features drawn and pale, Mark appeared in the dining room.

"No sleep then, Mark," Ron growled.

"Sleep, who'd sleep with that sort of attention? Had a great night." The malicious grin on his face showed he expected admiration. It did not come.

"Don't say a word," Ben said. "Get upstairs, pack your bag. We're out of here."

Della sat numb and still in the chair, the tea cold in her mug. Mark had 'dirtied his slate', and his behaviour angered and disgusted the others. She appreciated that Ed had told her about it. Sixteen months ago, on the honeymoon, they had shared damning disclosures that had almost stifled their union. Through the pregnancy, his errant actions had crushed her. She knew beyond doubt he would not have divulged any of it before Ronan was born. Had he, perhaps, witnessed a photo image of himself in Mark and was ashamed of his behaviour? And could she wholly believe the character change? Della heard a voice whispering, 'Accept the transformation' in her head. He'd brought her a lovely dress.

On impulse, she went to the table and kissed Ed. "Maybe, just maybe, we've turned a corner."

The smile on his face told her more than words could convey. And wasn't it easier to forgive and forget than to harbour?

But her thoughts turned to Olive. What might now evolve in Keatings' house? Della would not probe further. Ed was home, and all was well. However, she needed to see Laura, a level-headed woman, and discuss the Keatings. Ought they tell Olive about Mark? Interfere or help. Della had not visited the house on the hill for a while, what with the baby and little energy to go anywhere. So, on Sunday after Mass, she drew her friend aside from the group gossiping on the Church steps and offered a lift home to Breedogue in the afternoon. It would be good to catch up on the journey. Lovely, the other woman said.

At two p.m., Laura and her two children piled into Della's Mini-Minor, taking off from an exhaust of black smoke.

"Have to get a better car," Della said. "This was a good starter, but it's had its day."

"When old Bea dies, I'll find transport, somehow." If plans were afoot, life must be on the up in the Linehan household.

"Good on you, but Joe'll object, won't allow it."

"We'll see. I've learned to find ways of coaxing him to my viewpoint. But, like yourself, Della, I think the worst is over."

"I'm never sure. Ed is often on edge, especially after a night's drinking."

"Joe is nearly ten years older than Ed. They say the forties is a troublesome time of life for men. They crave attention from girls more than before marriage."

"But surely his singalongs in the pubs give him that?"

"Recently, his cousin Charlie offered him part-time work on the buildings, and he accepted. Said the extra cash would come in handy."

"Good old Joe won't let you earn but takes on more himself," Della said. "It's obvious he still controls you, Laura, with money to dole out as he likes."

"Yes, and a way of keeping me at home, but it's not just about money, Della. I want to practise what I trained for and be independent."

Independence, Della mused. That elusive denominator in women's lives manifested in diverse ways. "Some find satisfaction as housewives. Take Nan with her big brood of intelligent children, all doing well in school," Della said.

"Agreed, and May interviews candidates for the council in the library. Her job is like Olive's. I must tell you what happened in London." She unfolded the details of the London trip, including her husband's generous gift.

"My, your man is changing, Della. It's so unlike him to rat on a mate, though. He wants to ingratiate himself into your good books, I guess. Sounds good, but don't speak to Olive about it. And if she asks, pretend Ed hasn't told you anything. Mark might be ashamed of himself now, so telling her would cause a terrible rumpus."

"Of course not. We three women chose our paths, Laura, but poor Margie's path got mapped out for her because of a silly mistake."

Della wondered why the older woman came to mind at this point. The idea of independence probably conjured up the extreme conditions for many still in Ireland. And Margie was the worst example Della knew of.

"With no choice but to live her life according to that brother."

"She's cheerful and always has something to discuss, even if it's someone else's sorrows. But her visits are fewer nowadays, what with an arthritic knee and Peter's needs."

"Is he still mean to her?"

Della hesitated. Should she divulge the secrets that dogged the older woman's life and tell Laura she worried for Margie's safety when the brother came home drunk and took his frustrations out on her? Passing on Olive's story was maybe enough for one day. But no, she had to tell.

"He drives to town every night of the week, including Sunday. So last Saturday, when he got in, I almost intervened but couldn't, as it'd be worse afterwards if they knew I'd heard the uproar."

"Was it bad? Did he hit her?"

"I'll tell you. Everyone else was in bed but me. I hung around the kitchen, cleaned down the oilcloth on the table by the window, straightened the cushions on the soft chairs, dried the delph on the sink, and filled saucers with milk for the cats outside."

"You sure have energy, Della. I'm fit for nothing but the pillow at night."

"It was one of those clear nights, the darkness split by a wan moon, not the golden circle we usually see in September."

"And?"

"From farther up the road, a sound pierced the silence. I strained to hear and then recognised Peter Malone's voice. 'You stupid bitch, take that. Couldn't hold the bloody gate open for me to get into me own property.' I heard a smack, a loud, hard sound, and I shook. What was he going to do next?"

"Didn't you run to help?"

"No, no. I stood rooted to the spot. Margie sobbed, insisting she'd held it open the same as always, but he'd come in too close to the left. Not her fault. The sound of a fierce slap came again. 'Take that, hussy. You're just a slut that couldn't keep your pants up. And I have to put up with you—for life.' It was frightening."

"You should have gone to her."

"I opened our gate, slid between the car and the hedge, and peered along the road. I saw his car wedged between the open gate and the verge and poor Margie trying to direct him in."

"I can't believe you did nothing, Della."

"I was scared. Should I help her, beg Peter to stop? I remembered Mam's words, 'Never argue with a drunken man'. My parents employed men who slept in buildings on the property and spent their hard-earned few bob in the pub. Mam knew how to deal with them, leaving them sick and sorry for themselves the next day."

"So you went to bed? Della, I'd have gone down. Poor Margie."

"The thing is, Laura, we have to live close by them every day, and the embarrassment would have been worse if they knew I'd heard."

"Embarrassment or not, we can't stand by and let things happen to good people. Everyone in the area knew about our row and my black eye, but the neighbours were kind, their condemnation a shameful blow for him." Laura said, her comment bringing back old Pat Egan's opinion of Joe Lenihan.

"After the noise died and Peter's engine stopped revving, there was no more shouting. I went inside, glad of the warmth but upset by the distress in Margie's voice and her fear. It ate into me."

"Christians believe we're in a valley of tears, and Margie is an example," Laura said. Trust her to find a reason for suffering.

"I didn't go near them for a few days until Tuesday, when I called in for a chat. Margie was getting ready to go to the well for water. Just think, Laura, that old woman has to carry two heavy cans home most days."

"How was she?"

"Same as always, except for the dark patch on the cheek. She'd pulled the hair across, but it was there. Anyway, I said I'd go with her just for a walk. You won't believe what happened."

"Gosh, Della, you're making a big story out of it. As for not believing, I do."

"We walked the mile until we got to the well, where I helped her lower the rope into its depths and fill two buckets. It was good to be useful. Then, as we turned for home, a man came out of that old house in the trees, the only one. It's dark and dreary, with yellowed, sooty curtains on the windows."

"Whose is it?"

"Johnny Cummins, the man who got her in the family way forty-five years ago."

"Oh, my God, what happened?"

"He nodded towards me and ignored Margie. It was awful. I just nattered on about things that came into my head, the kids' football match, Ed's business, anything, and by the time we got to the end of the road, I could look at her again. Ronan was asleep in the pram all the while."

"That poor woman. We're tied to hard men who lord it over us, but she's worse. Also, we have children and a fair amount of happiness, but that brother is a nasty bugger."

"Think, Laura, of the girls who gave birth in places like the orphanage in Castlepollard, only to leave behind their babies, never to see them again. A lifelong sentence of misery and regret."

"Attitudes will change, Della, are changing. It's always been about conventions and respectability more than being good Christians. In small communities, everyone judges, and that's why we need orphanages. No family will tolerate disgrace. But I've heard terrible tales of graves of hundreds of babies born and buried in the grounds of such places."

"Maybe 'twas better they died, but what a terrible sentence for the poor girls who had to leave them behind. It's a blight on this country that disparages pregnant single women. Judge not, and you shall not be judged, Christ said."

"It's about keeping up appearances, and sex outside marriage is a sin, Della, but it doesn't mean you condemn the sinner. Forgiveness is mine, says the Lord."

"Not practised in our holy country, is it, Laura? Least of all by the clergy who forgive in the name of the Lord in Confession but who shun sinners outside of the Church."

CHAPTER 23

August 15, 1969. At two o'clock in the afternoon, Margie rushed into Egan's kitchen. What on earth? She never came in the daytime. "Did ye hear the news bulletin? The RUC shot a Catholic dead in Belfast last night."

"We did. Terrible, for sure, a man murdered for his religion. But the troubles are rumbling up there with those riots in Derry and Belfast," Molly said. "Hope it doesn't spread down here."

"Catholics must defend themselves when the police force their way into homes and drag Sinn Féin supporters out onto the street. Unfortunately, it'll get worse," Della said. "The soldiers killed seven people in Belfast during the recent riots and destroyed over one hundred homes. Sure, you saw it on the TV, Margie."

"But to kill someone because of their faith is evil. We're all Christians," Margie shrilled. The passion on her face bespoke a fresh fear. Her father, an Old IRA man, had served his country in the Civil War.

"Catholic Nationalists want civil rights and an end to discrimination," Molly added. "Seems to have started when the police beat up a man called Francis McCloskey, who died in jail."

Then, with a quick sign of Father, Son, and Holy Ghost on her forehead and deed accomplished, Margie scurried home to get Peter's dinner. Spuds took an hour to cook on the old range.

Della noticed Molly's face - anxiety weaving inroads on her lined features. A sister, Bridie, lived in the North with two sons in the priesthood. Would Protestant militia target them? That such upheavals should happen again on the island of Ireland was unsettling. But in a divided country, war was never far off. The predictions of Padraig Pearse, a revered Irish patriot shot by the English army after the 1916 rebellion, would forever resound across the nation. *Ireland will never be free until all thirty-six counties are under Irish rule.* Was this now to become a reality? By spilling blood?

Della wondered if, on the upside, such awful news might deflect the older women's insular preoccupation with local issues and gossiping about neighbours. Not that she wished such horrors on any part of the country, but the North, on the cusp of civil war, could spread beyond the province of Ulster into the Republic of Ireland. She and Ed intended to travel to Enniskillen soon to buy a typewriter. Could they, ought they? She needed affirmation. Until now, frequent coach trips to Ulster carried crowds of Southerners looking for bargains, cheaper bedding, cushions, and more.

"Ed and I drive to Enniskillen on Monday to buy a typewriter. Can you mind Ronan for about six hours, Molly?"

"Course I can if it's for the good of the business. But ye shouldn't be going up there with the guns and the killin' goin' on."

"Enniskillen is just across the border; the troubles are on the Bogside in Derry and the Shankill Road in Belfast. The two biggest cities. We'll be safe."

No troubles down here, only ordinary concerns, like improving their business output and presentation expertise. On a typewriter, they could create professional invoices and bills for customers. Della's typing skills were rusting, and her time eaten up entering income and expenditure by hand in the ledger. Also, Ed wanted to widen his client network with more professional customer invoices. In Enniskillen, they would see a broader range than in local towns and pay less for a machine.

As they set off on a late summer's day, a thrill coursed through Della. It felt good to share a purpose and vision. On days like this, her fears quieted to nothingness.

The journey towards County Leitrim took them through beautiful countryside—blue lakes and sloping purple hillsides that darkened on approach to the famous Arigna coalfields.

"I wish we could get closer, Ed. I've never been to a coal mine."

"Nothing nice about it. So few left, and the industry is dying out, hence the exodus of young people from this county searching for employment abroad. Leitrim is becoming an impoverished, desolate county. Zinc mining is more popular now. There's one in County Meath."

"I know little of my country, having been out of circulation for so long. But this part of Ireland is a sort of no-man's-land, far from Dublin's power hub and near enough to the Six Counties to shelter IRA men on the run. Olive told me about it. Drive carefully." Heeding her warning, Ed slowed down along the winding roads as if expecting something ominous around every corner. But there was nothing to fear except cattle gazing across hedges at passing cars, eyes bulging, tails flailing. No guns or bombs anywhere. Not that she was disappointed.

Crossing into Fermanagh, they entered the Six Counties, trepidation filling the atmosphere with each bend. What a sight met their eyes. From gardens and fields, huge Union Jack flags fluttered atop little Presbyterian halls and houses. Della lowered the window for a better look. The sound of 'God save our Queen' blared from gramophones into the car.

"No wonder there're clashes up here when the Proddies are blatantly provoking the Catholic population. See that one. 'King Billy forever'."

"Signs of defiance. We're here for a quick visit, no more." Ed's tone, terse and sharp, sounded unusually anxious.

Ten miles further on at the border, Ed got out and showed his papers at the checkpoint. From the car, Della saw an RUC officer point a gun through a lookout window, a stark reminder of the 'troubles'. Here, a part of their green and fertile land was under siege from both sides of the political and religious divide. What, she wondered, had religion to do with hatred? Whenever sectarianism reared its vicious head, that question spread throughout the population. And, as always, historically endowed academia laid the problem solely in greed, bigotry, and geopolitics. But soon, suppression of Catholics by the Ulster Orangemen might end - bloody or otherwise - if the fights continued. How long was soon?

Ed got back in the car, and they moved toward the town. "Let's buy the typewriter and get away fast." The process of entry had shaken him.

"Agreed."

He drove along the main street, parked the car outside the shop they had seen in the local Roscommon Herald, and went inside. On hearing their accents, a friendly owner behind the counter asked where they came from. Delighted to learn it was County Roscommon, not fifty miles away, he showed them a range of typewriters, his entire stock. Della whispered to Ed, "Much cheaper than Dublin."

The shopkeeper said he feared for the future of the province if clashes between the IRA and the UVF escalated. The recent riots in Derry and Belfast had decimated entire streets to rubble with the looting of goods and loss of stock. Business was 'flaky', with people shopping only for necessities.

Ed paid sixty pounds cash for a grey, shiny typewriter. Della nudged, 'out of here,' and they bade goodbye to the man trapped on the edge of time...

They did not stop again until the town of Ballinamore, County Leitrim and familiar territory. Then, over a steak dinner, they relaxed and reflected. The typewriter would improve their professionalism and, also, glue their partnership further. Deed done.

CHAPTER 24

By 1972, two more children had been born to the Lenihans, Tommy and Aoife. Della gave birth to Jimmy within three years after Ronan. It was not a competition, Laura laughed, just how things panned out, but it was important to show that men sometimes stayed home. Not funny, Della said. Men were always available for that sort of activity. She disliked how little the space in her life for socialising with the constant washing of terry-towelling nappies, making feeds, and guiding their young through various rites of passage. Essential, however, never again to lapse into the dowdy woman lost in a sea of vomit and self-denial. It had almost finished them. She'd commented the same to Olive. The other woman was emphatic.

"That attitude shows just how subservient you are. Please the man, or he'll stray. I say, get even, get independence, get a life."

Olive might veer towards politically correctness, but one must play the right cards.

But when Ed stayed out until the sky brightened in the East, she agonised, sleepless and anxious, counting the beads on her rosary until the familiar sound of the engine died on the avenue. She oscillated between tolerance and rejection, but could not risk turbulence with two children in the house. When traces of infidelity surfaced - a whiff of perfume on his shirt or blonde hair, always blonde, her spirits plunged. He'd brush aside her suspicions - a packed bar, women around him.

Like Mark and Joe, Ed did not intend to wreck the bastion of marriage, his safe place. Irishmen did what they wanted away from home but returned to domestic respectability without guilt, she observed in Lenihan's after one particularly rough patch.

"By putting up with them, turning a blind eye, we're providing stability, Laura. Is it a clever way of holding our families together, or perhaps, deceiving ourselves?"

"Both, Della. If I quiz Joe, he turns nasty, and the whole family suffers. So let it ride, I say. Time will change them. Women stay at home, and men play the field. If they still love us, it's for the best."

The best? Love? How far from reality was that? Her gut instinct told Della that making do, putting up a veneer of respectability, was no better than accepting cheating as inevitable. When Ed spiralled downwards under the influence of the demon drink, what ought one do? Fight at night and play calm during the day? Olive was right; independent women earned respect, but stay-at-home wives could not. It was better to assume perspicacity and remind her husband of how they appeared to the outside world. Yes, he'd agree. We're lucky we're not like the Keatings.

After Ronan's birth, Della had set out to re-ignite the spark between herself and Ed to get their relationship back on track. She dressed to suit her colouring and figure, applied makeup, and heeded her mother's advice to keep up appearances. Better still, when the old pair moved to a flat in town, a new beginning dawned in Egans'. Finally, they had space to talk and deal with life's detritus without whispering or arguing in the bedroom. And the world ticked along in harmony when they did things as a family: days on the river, trips to the city, football finals, and more.

Eve, a constant support, advised. "He's not the easiest man to manage. Be vigilant. You've coped since the children came along. Perhaps you could take a course now."

"I must wait until the kids are older. Ed still drinks too much and sometimes goes to the city with Mark. It isn't easy. I plan family outings, anything to keep him occupied. It works to a point. But his jaunts are farther away nowadays, to Dublin, the Navan races with his vet friend from Roscommon, and Seán in Castlerea."

"He enjoys being with the two boys, though."

"Yes and bought that boat to sail on the lake. So we fish, lie out on the deck and take a picnic. We live a normal life and are fine except for his deviations."

Normal. If they were part of an emerging scene wherein success stories abounded, then yes, they were on the right track. Men, always men, were making money, building, selling, developing, and employing. On the cusp of the seventies, Éire's economy was ascending. Soaring emigration during the peaky fifties and early sixties had condensed the South's population, but now ambitious young men like Ed, Mark, and Ben were climbing pinnacles, their businesses prospering, offices on sites and an accumulation of property. More money brought a better social life and holidays - Spain, Jersey, and Majorca.

Like flotsam, Della drifted along the turbulent waters of Ed's ambition but, often, strove to battle its effects. After one very tiresome night, she became alarmed at her husband's physical state. He could not get up. Midday came. She tried turning him, but he appeared semi-conscious; there was no response but a grunt from under the covers. He finally struggled out of bed at four.

"I drove the kids to school, Ed, then took five of your men to that meeting in Carrick. I slept less than you did, but I still had to get up early. You're a bloody disgrace."

She had not meant to unleash her fury thus. However, he was slipping into deeper alcoholism or a weekend one, as the doctor dubbed it when she sought advice and tablets to relax her at night; long gone her store of Valium from the convent days.

"If only you drank less, we could be happier. Under the influence, your personality changes from tolerable to ugly. I try to avoid arguments or to inflame your temper, but it isn't good. And you're worse off the next day with a sore head and sluggish manner."

"Lay off, will you? It's the same old thing with you."

It was, but how else might she arrest his self-destruct mode? They would plough through a week, regularly, until the whole circus started up again on the weekends. In their kind of marriage, she decided, one partner was a doormat. Doctor O'Farrell used the term and suggested Ed would be seriously ill when he aged.

After one awful night, she told Laura that no one should marry without understanding the partner's personality. "Ed didn't drink when I met him first, and I wish he never had. But I now must accept his powerful personality and coercive attitude toward our relationship."

"True, but some unions seem perfect, like May's and Ben's, and drink has little effect in their house. Others endure hell. But is anyone ever prepared to live with a man who drinks too much? Alcohol brings out ugly traits. In England, couples moved in together for a while but often broke up later. Good way of getting to know them."

"Agreed, but Ed wore me down too soon. Last night, he was so drunk he fell into the room. I wanted to push him back downstairs again."

"What did he say?"

Ought she tell everything or just a little? Drat it, Laura understood.

"He said he was following up on a lead, but it went on late. And as Mark said, they make more deals over a pint than in the garage."

"Do you care what Mark says? No wonder Olive is unhappy." Laura seemed uncharacteristically angered.

"There's more. Ed was nasty when I asked how Olive reacted when Mark came in late. He said 'that woman would push a man to drink. She's loud, talks a lot, and questions everything he says in front of us. Over the top'."

As if the vibes had winged their way to the house in Boyle, Olive rang at bedtime the next day, wondering if they might plan a trip to the city together. She would book a hotel for a long weekend.

"Not yet," Della replied. "Jimmy is too young to leave with my mother. Maybe later on."

The idea of being closeted for an extended period with two people who battled for dominance in their relationship was more than she could tolerate. Neither did the thought of excessive amounts of alcohol appeal.

Ed, upstairs, did not hear the conversation on the phone. He'd want to go with the Keatings. Della dallied. Let him get off to sleep - two children in a row and no contraception available in Ireland. Avoid the obvious. Laura had recommended she should keep him happy; 'he won't stray if you do'. All fine, but how did one fulfil such obligations?

On alternate Saturdays, after dinner, she took the children to her parents and picked them up on Sunday. Life was tolerable if you made things happen.

The postman arrived as usual around ten o'clock on Friday morning; Pat O'Neill was in no rush. On the last day of the week, there was plenty of time to chat and pass on scandal or gossip to willing ears. Parish folk welcomed the only face they'd see all day. Pat loved the 'curny cake' and liked to boast he'd eaten enough scones for six men in kitchens along the highways, down single-track boreens, and in tiny houses by the road.

Today, he shattered Della's peace, relegating Ed's intransigence to a lower plane. "Did ye hear that Laura Linehan went away? Left the bastard she did."

Margie, just arrived for a chat, burst out, "What are you sayin' man? She's not long after havin' a babby. There's plenty to do in that house, with three children and an old woman to look after."

A sickening feeling spread over Della. Why didn't she know that something awful had happened? It had only been two weeks since she talked to Laura.

"When, Pat?"

"Not sure, Sunday night, they say. I heard it in Mullens' today. Laura's brother came in his car and took her away, and the kids too."

When Ed got home, Della said, "I need you to stay in, Friday or no Friday. I've got to go to Breedogue to see Laura. She's left Joe."

"Sure. I'll have a few pints in the local while you're there."

"What about the kids?"

"Me mam'll mind them in the flat."

"Hardly able to mind herself, but I'll ask."

"Friday night. Won't matter if they're not in bed early."

Ed adjusted the wipers to fast as they sped through the night along the fourteen miles of wind-swept terrain. Rain, hard as hailstones, pelted the windscreen, making visibility difficult. The roads were empty except for the odd wagon returning from a cattle market in Sligo. Ed's foot lifted off the pedal. Della said nothing, her mouth dry, anxiety mounting with each mile. Finally, when the town lights flickered through the drops, she sighed.

"Don't pull up right outside the house, Ed. I can't let them see me coming. Laura might not want it."

"Don't be daft. Why not?.".

"Because I'd rather just knock."

A single light glowed from within the one-storey building at the end of a cul-de-sac, probably in the kitchen where most folks spent their time.

Ed killed the engine. "I'll be back in an hour."

"Wait until I speak to her first, Ed, and check if it's alright to visit." She opened the gate, mounted the steps, and knocked lightly. Mrs McMahon answered the door, her face drawn and anxious. Who would call at this hour?

"Come in. Laura's in the kitchen. I'll let ye talk and get off to bed." The old lady hobbled away towards a bedroom. Della waved dismissal to Ed outside. Laura rushed to clasp her friend while attempting to speak amid sobs and wiping a runny nose, the skin on her face stretched raw and red.

"Let's have a drink," Laura said. She poured a glass of whiskey and handed it to Della.

"I'm not one for spirits, Laura, but if it helps you talk, one won't hurt."

Broken down and unable to endure the rows, late nights, and suffering, Laura returned to her mother in the next town. "I found the courage to do it, Della. Seeing the three children crying and cowering in corners was unbearable. Lately, things have worsened. Night after night, Joe came home at three or four in the morning, often smeared with lipstick that he had not bothered to wipe off. It was awful on Saturday. When I begged him to tell me who he'd been with, he ordered me to shut up and said, I'll do what I like. I can get the best of them."

Despite her maxim to leave arguments until morning, Laura persisted, begging him to tell her the truth.

"Fuck off. Your place is on the manure heap!" The manure heap that stank outside the cowhouse by the road? Worse than a blow, his words cut her to the quick.

"Spent the night with a glamorous young thing who praised your singing, told you how wonderful you were?" she lashed, his cruelty unbearable now. The hurt, the insult, the horrible feeling that she was just a wife at home in wide trousers and a sloppy jumper tipped her into a zone beyond sense.

"Remember that infection you had three weeks back when you asked me what I thought, and I sent you to the doctor for a diagnosis? She gave you antibiotics and said I should see her, too. I got the result of the test yesterday. It turns out you had an STD, chlamydia, a sexually transmitted disease, passed on to me, and I now have salpingitis in the fallopian tubes. So no more children in this house, Joe Linehan, as I'll be infertile now."

"Shut up, woman. You're making it up."

"You vile bastard, not fit to be a father." Without thinking, she reached across and slapped the leering face hard, so sharp it echoed around the room like cracking glass. Then, as she turned to leave the room, the kick stunned her, its impact between her ribs sharper than previous thumps. Laura struggled to breathe, the pain in her lungs vicious. He knew how to hurt, over the kidneys, no evidence. His fist struck again. The taste of blood filled her mouth, spurted from between her teeth, loosened by the blow. In a daze, she staggered from the room, lights flashing, blinded by pain and fear.

"I sent Tommy next door for help, but they wouldn't get involved, said that they'd always got on with Joe. He was their neighbour, and I should try to be patient with him. Can you imagine being patient with a man who hit me and thumped Tommy when he begged him not to hurt his mammy? I cannot take anymore, Della. Pray for me."

"It was late to send the boy out, Laura."

"No, it was only ten o'clock. Joe had been in town all evening. I slept on Tommy's bed. The boys huddled up together, their sobbing unbearable. The next day, my face didn't look familiar: I had a swollen mouth and a split lip. I camouflaged the bruises and stayed inside for a day or two. Anne took the kids to school and picked them up in the evening."

Laura gritted her teeth and carried on. "Next morning, I cycled to the early Mass, went to the telephone kiosk on the square, and rang home, determined to leave my hell and never return."

"You did right. Joe Linehan's a smiling charmer in the public eye and a monster in his house."

"A drunkard whose vanity comes before me and the kids. He's a devil, and I can't fight him."

"But he'll be lost without you and won't manage old Bea."

"My heart bleeds for her, but my children are my priority now, and their welfare. I'm safe here."

"Would you go back if he asked or promised to change?"
What was she saying?

"No. Words are not enough. Let Joe suffer and put up with idle gossip when word spreads I've gone. That will hurt him more than anything."

"The thing is, Laura, such men can't bear shaming in a small parish like ours. Rumours spread and change with every telling. That's why poor old Margie lives under the ridicule of her brother. He controls her by fear and the need for a roof over her head."

"Another god in his own home. Isn't Ireland riddled with their sort? To think I left a job in London because of this. I could have stayed on and married there. Different society, less invasive."

"Like me. Back in Dublin, I went out with a considerate, intelligent veterinary student. Laura, I can't advise you. Your instincts will tell you what to do. I had no choice but to return home before Ronan was born because of Ed's behaviour. He's a wanderer, and drink leads him astray, but I've stood firm against him staying away during race festivals. He falls off the wagon occasionally but is concerned about his reputation. Ed needs me, and the children need us both."

As if on cue, the lights of Ed's car shone through the curtains, and Della stood up to leave. "Laura, if you return, I'll be there for you. We'll show him our solidarity."

"Thanks, Della. I don't know what lies ahead right now."

"Joe will want you back. He can't manage old Bea and the farm by himself. But don't give in. No one comes to protect women from beatings behind closed doors. And no one tells the Gárdai for fear of scandal. Respectability matters more than pain."

On the way home, Della imparted details to Ed, who did not defend the other man.

"I never really liked him. We played football on the town team as lads. He was powerful and would give a boot in the stomach when he saw an opening. So, I'm not surprised by any of this. Lenihan has a fierce temper." How gratifying that Ed did not defend the other man. His vanity and self-indulgence might lie at the heart of their domestic eruptions, but he would never hurt her.

At the flat, Molly stood, waiting. "Arrah, girl, why were you so long? The young one cried himself to sleep."

"He's not a baby, Molly, and you were here. Not too much to sit with him for a while, was it?"

"Reared me own six, not doing it again."

Della took the sleeping child to the car, covered him with a rug and hissed in disgust. What was it with everyone? Men who regarded themselves as lords in their tiny kingdoms and an older generation who defied harmony by refusing to help. It made little sense. The old pair had seen her pain before the birth and why she had left to survive.

"What a day. Laura is under siege in Breedogue, and your mother, stubborn and uncompromising."

Della dropped off the children at school on Monday morning, but instead of going straight home, she took the high road towards Linehans. As she approached the farm, there was no sign of activity around the dwelling or out-houses. It was early summer when most men were in the fields saving hay. Not that Joe Linehan had vast acres of meadow. Too lazy, the wags said, to do a stroke of decent work. He'd chat with foreigners in the hotel about the best fishing lakes.

Della mumbled to her inner self. "He's not at home. Why am I here? Eejit." And what could she say if he answered the bell? Broach the shameful topic of Laura's absence with this volatile man who could turn on a woman, man, or animal when his temper rose?

But as she was reversing the Mini into the haggard, the front door opened, and Joe raised a hand in her direction. Not bad, Della thought; a start. Oh, Holy Spirit, guide me to say the right thing and do this properly. He wouldn't hit her, would he?

"Della, can you help me get Laura home? Ed said you'd seen her. You're her best friend. Don't you want what's best for her, me, and the kids?" The long face and the melancholy in his bearing almost drew an unexpected pang of sympathy from Della. Almost. Why hadn't Ed told her he'd spoken to the man? See, she seethed, how men lacked the guts to confront each other with such stuff.

"That depends, Joe, on what is right for Laura and whether you're prepared to change, respect your wife, and give her the money she needs for essentials. She's unlikely to return until you promise never to raise your hand again. Laura can find work and earn a living away from you, some-thing you denied her since she came here."

"I never denied her; well, maybe when I was drunk, but no one heeds a man under the influence."

"Unless he uses his fist or kicks out. Get this, Joe Linehan. Laura doesn't deserve a life cowering in fear at night when you come in soused in alcohol. Bad enough wasting money your family need, but worse still is hitting a woman in front of her kids. I'm in two minds to report you."

"I'm sorry, Della. I am. Can you persuade her to return to me, my mother, and this house - her home?"

"I'll pass on the solemn promise you're about to pledge that the events of two weeks ago will never happen again."

"I promise. The empty house is unbearable; my old mother is pining for the kids. She's incontinent, and only Laura knows how to deal with such things. I had to ask Ann next door to help me. It's bad, but sure 'tis the loneliness that's worst, Della."

"Loneliness, Joe? Surely, you're never lonely, what with the singing and the craic in town? You heed this. I don't hold with Ed's or your twisted views on fidelity and a man's right to independence, which somehow precludes a family life. If I'd known that you and your kind would become such arrogant bullies - yes, I use that term - neither Laura, myself, Olive or the others would have married any of you. We did not take on a home, toil during the day, get up to the babies when they cry, while you lot squander money on drink, cards, and the rest. Change is coming, and divorce will be legal in Ireland one day. So again, I say, take heed."

Joe reddened. Had she overstepped the mark, gone too far? So what?

"We're only having a chat at night. It's enjoyable after a day's work."

"Stuff and nonsense. Do you think I was born yesterday?" Turning, Della almost ran along the path, away from the man with the downcast face and the beaten look. Good. Let him sweat.

After dinner on Sunday, the Egans set off to see the O'Reillys. Della planned to call on Laura in Breedogue first. Ed said don't delay. The kids will get restless. Della said she would take whatever time to help her friend. He must wait while she acted out her 'counsellor role'. Laura was expecting her.

On arrival, Della went in alone and hugged Laura, who looked better, brighter but still anxious. Her friend's glimmer depicted both hope and desperation for a crumb of comfort, of anything.

"I won't tell you what to do, Laura, but Joe is deeply sorry. He seems sad and not the coarse bully you left. But it's up to you, and I can't advise you to do something you might regret."

"Sad? Probably desperate because I'm not there to do the jobs. I want a decent life for the kids and me."

"And you deserve it. If you go back, state your conditions before you sleep one night in the house again, or he cajoles you with his charm. Joe Linehan is a clever, witty man who knows how to woo an audience."

"My mother said that if we stayed here, I could get the kids to school and find a job in the new nursing home on the far side of town, just a bus ride. But the disgrace would kill her, a strong Catholic who believes in sacred vows. And the house is too small for all of us. It's a mess. If I go back, he might be different. So I've got to try."

"I did it, but Ed's father had threatened to disown him if he didn't change. Now they've gone, it's our place, and Ed is more content. He didn't get on with the old man, two of a kind. He's not a saint, but there's no violence. Laura, we must confront one major issue here. It's the curse of drink that changes them into bullies and overlords. Over and over, you told me not to fight with Ed late at night, so I can imagine he pushed you to the limit when you slapped his face that night. We have to stop the drink binges."

"We never will, Della. That's a fact, with late-night bar extensions, festivals, sporting events, anything. Shame alone might sway them. They can't bear being the butt of gossip. Joe loves audience adulation and, like Ed, women fawning over him in bars. Neither can bear the shame of locals knowing their business. So I've decided to go back and try again, with stipulations. My brother will take me tomorrow, and you can tell Joe on your way home. Thanks, Della, for everything."

Della saw that despite her fears, Laura wanted her own home and to save the marriage. But she would have to dig deep and summon all conceivable courage to return to a place she had fled in fear. The following weeks would be crucial to prove her right or otherwise. And if Joe came in late and sloshed again, would he lapse into his former sinful ways? And would Laura, in fact, ever be safe?

Weirdly, her involvement in the situation empowered Della. No longer the meek, pliant wife who'd married into the valley years before, she felt emboldened by her stance on Laura's problems. She'd learned not to succumb to a bully herself, maybe not quite the Joe sort, but equally conceited. So, however ludicrous her negotiating deals with someone like Joe Linehan, who hurt his wife and terrified his kids, she had learned to stand firm against tyranny. Such men ought to be in jail.

A word whirled through her brain - misogynist. She looked it up and baulked at the explanation that leapt from the dictionary: *contempt of women, male privilege, belittling of women*. Well, well. And worse, one philosopher stated that '*women are by nature meant to obey*. But, she seethed, if Laura were to fall into the obedient little wife role on her return, she might expect nothing more than life as a subservient chattel to her lord and master. In addition, Laura's calm personality undoubtedly contributed to her servile state—until that fateful night.

Chapter 25

S tomach lurching with butterflies, Della approached the Linehans' front door. Determined and firm, she would face the man inside to ascertain if it was safe for the family to return.

When he opened the door, Joe's face looked drawn, lined, and older than his thirty-eight years.

"Come in," he said quietly, clearing shirts off a chair in the kitchen for her to sit on. Bea's rocking chair creaked back and forth by the range, but the old woman looked bewildered and, Della noted, dirty. Avoiding the mess on the floor and table, she listed Laura's stipulations. The edginess drained from Joe's face, and relief spread across his features.

"I promised Jim Kelly I'd call to sell the pony to him so I can give Laura money for the shoes she wants."

Della summoned courage. "That's a start, Joe. But be clear, Laura can leave again if you don't behave."

"Sure, I know that. Thanks for all you've done for us, and I'm sorry you had to get involved in our troubles. Goodbye,

Della." Gosh, how the mighty had fallen. He who always quipped a smart-alec riposte towards her when she'd called was now thanking her. That it boded well for the family's return must be down to Laura's prayers, belief in miracles, and, not least, her husband's present misery and mess.

It was nine o'clock, Della's brain a conundrum of exhilaration and exhaustion. Laura's battle had somehow also been hers.

In the car, Ed said, "You've done enough. She made her bed. Let her lie on it."

"Those old-fashioned sayings just prove how hypocritical you men are. You act like thinkers and leaders but rely on out-of-date attitudes to suit yourselves."

"Mind your own house, I say, and let everyone else mind theirs."

"What a classic, defensive attitude. You're just one of the boys, Ed." Della stopped; no reason to let Laura's marital crisis stir trouble between Ed and herself.

"Spare me, Della. We've got a business to run, and you've enough to deal with, so don't spread yourself thin."

"In your view, our bossy husbands will one day age and change! Sounds almost poetic. A wisp of hope to hold on to! Ironic, though."

"Ironic because we will be too old." The intended barb and its connotations stirred an uneasy ping in Della. When was too old? For what?

While she and Laura might support each other against their husbands' frivolous lifestyles, there were others for whom the suffering would go on. It was 1972, and change for women overdue. However, control varied in each house, depending on the couple, their situation, and their personalities. Mark Keating did not lift a finger to his wife but found more devious ways of ruling his roost while indulging in his passion for sport. According to Ed, Mark let it slip that 'a lot got crammed into a few hours on the squash court'. Or off it. And Mark's indifference towards his wife was, in her view, worse than a row.

Peter Malone could abuse his sister because she owned nothing. Joe Linehan was ruthless with the fist, and Ed Egan was a master of truth embellishment - powerful personalities within their domains. *I'm the king of the castle; you're the dirty rascal.*

Della would not call on the Linehans for a while but let them settle and avoid aggravating Joe with her presence. In brief chats at the school gate, Laura hinted at a new peace at home, nothing to stress about other than ordinary things. Joe was considerate, almost to the point of suffocation. But she just wanted normality. The money would always be scarce, and she'd find ways of getting around him for necessities. He prided himself in his children, especially the oldest, Siobhan, a brainy girl. If the child needed a coat or shoes, she would get them. Joe's pride was his Achilles heel, and he could not tolerate others disparaging his family. "Price of a bullock," he'd said when Laura coaxed him. But the children were cautious around him.

"You're a clever woman, Laura, and it's working," Della applauded.

"And you're a good friend, taking me home to my mother, giving the kids lifts to sports, dancing classes, and concerts. Thank you."

A month sped by. Della wanted to help more, but mere convention dictated how much or little one did without interfering. With money plentiful in the Egan household, she went shopping in Dublin and to city hairdressers with May. She stayed out late with Ed and the gang on Sunday nights. But despite their children playing after school, a chasm was yawning between the Linehans and Egans. Della tried to include Laura when possible, but the disparities grew with each new phase.

"It's a shame Laura doesn't come out, Ed," Della said one Sunday night on the way to the Royal. "Should we call and ask?"

"No. It might be her way of keeping him at home. What can you do? They can't afford to take holidays or do anything much."

"I don't want to humiliate Laura by embroiling her in our circle right now. I'm exhausted keeping up myself."

"You don't have to come with me."

"Oh? So when would we be together? And I like to keep tabs on you, boyo."

"Always suspicious, you."

Monday mornings bore down too quickly after dizzy weekends. Della struggled to retain equilibrium, get the kids to school, do the chores, and shop. Ronan and Jimmy spent more time in O'Reilly's on Saturdays so their parents could stay out into the small hours. As she picked them up one Sunday, Bridie cautioned. "We love seeing the boys, Della, but keep a steady grip on reality and don't neglect your genuine friends." Gosh: a veiled but obvious hint from her ever-sagacious mother.

"You recommended I take care of my appearance and get out with Ed. As for friends, you mean Laura. Yes, I see her, but they're not out much."

"I did not say to overdo it." Her mother used hints in a parsimonious manner, never confrontational.

It is peculiar how anniversaries throw up configurations of the nasty patches more often than contented ones. Ten years from the first day she'd set foot in Cortober, Della took stock. In her virtual diary—recording trials or other useless minutiae was loathsome—were tracts too bitter, too hurtful to sustain. Better, she opined, to nurture optimism and regard the 'cup as half-full' like her mother, who regarded forgiveness highly. So, as age came upon her, whenever doubts assailed, she zeroed them out by living hard. If all seemed well, then it was.

In effect, it would be ideal to have an alcohol-free man again. In the interim were oceans of regret, a husband she humoured when drunk and placated when difficult. Tears were of no avail, an outward veneer of respectability her only crown. Words from a favourite prayer came often:

> *God, grant me the serenity*
> *to accept the things I can-*
> *not change*
> *Courage to change the*
> *things I can*

*And wisdom to know the
difference.*

Or was she morphing into Laura?

Margie's journey through murky waters of obeisance nobody could alter; her life a daily plod eked out, year upon
year, in compliant acceptance. Of sterner stuff, Olive fed
on challenges of one-upmanship. All four, and women like
them, dealt with life as best they could. They assumed a
mantle of propriety before the outside world by keeping
trouble inside the house. Like the currachs moored on the
nearby lakes, steering a smooth path at first, but in strong
currents, tossed on perilous waters, they sought merely to
stay afloat.

Compensations came in abundance. Now ten and nine,
Ronan and Jimmy were doing well in school, though Jim-
my struggled with maths. "Takes that from you," Ed said.
"Maths is my strongest asset."

The boys lived for the family's annual summer holidays
abroad and during frequent breaks in Ireland. Despite their
father's fractiousness and their mother's vigilance, holidays in Spain, France, and Majorca were fun. For two weeks
every July, the children enjoyed taking turns with their dad
in pedalos while Della lounged on the beach with a book.

In July 1972, they stayed in the Hotel de la France in Jersey.
The sun glared down, too hot for Della's light skin. She

hired a table, beach chairs and brolly for them to sit safely in the midday heat.

"We should not be out," she warned. "See how the locals disappear for their siesta. It's the silly Irish and Brits who lie about getting sunstroke."

"Never mind, boys. Let's swim," Ed commanded, a true he-man who cared little for local customs. After all, a holiday was for fun in the sun.

Lathering thick layers of sun cream on their white bodies, Della let them off and opened a Harold Robbins novel. It was nice to be away together, like an average family. However, Ed would drink again by night, but she'd wisely avoid arguments. The holiday had to be perfect.

After dinner, they drifted into the ballroom where a singer shouted *Burning Love* by Elvis Presley, luring young and old from their chairs. Ronan took the centre floor, showing off Elvis's bendy moves and gyrations, immediately getting admiration from all sides.

"Good on ye, Ronan, following in your old fella's footsteps." Ed's pride brought even more bendy moves from the two boys, and soon, the floor resounded to music and pumping bodies.

"And mine," Della laughed. "Dancing is one thing we do well together." Hadn't it been the magnet that first attracted them? "Let's enter the rock' n' roll contest."

Ed said. "Daft. It's ages since we won anything."

"Never mind. Let's."

They stayed on the floor for two hours, and every second dance a jive with judges allocating marks from the side of the ballroom. At midnight, a drum rolled, and all competitors lined up for the result. Fun, Della whispered. It doesn't matter if we don't win.

"I'm knackered", Ed laughed. "But you know, Della, we haven't lost it."

Through a haze of disbelief and delight, she heard the result. First: Ed and Della Egan, 20 points. The lady judge smiled down, and the other couples shoved forward to congratulate them. Ed smiled and thanked the judge for the prize, a fifty-pound cheque.

"Not a bad night's work," he thrilled. "A quick drink to celebrate."

"No, you don't. I'm shattered. Kids to bed, now."

But when Della and the boys got up to leave, Ed strayed towards the dancefloor and joined the group of sweating bodies under the spotlights. Della stalled, half ready to join him, but the kids stood waiting at the lift in the corridor. She steeled herself and followed them. *Let him do as he pleases. Surely not risky.*

In their twin beds, the boys fell asleep instantly. Della, on the other side of the partition, tossed and turned. An hour passed. It was one a.m. She sipped water from the bedside locker. He would not be silly. A line from a favourite poet, Tennyson, stole into her head:

> *But I, my sons, and little*
> *daughter fled*
> *From bonds or death and*
> *dwelt among the woods*

Not death, in this case, just anxiety.

Ed came into the family room at three a.m. drunk and in high spirits. Della woke from an erratic sleep and had not realised she'd drifted off. He'd danced to great music with two other husbands whose wives had also gone to bed, he slurred, before dropping the shirt and trousers on the floor. Moving across the double bed, he pulled Della towards him, but the stench of drink was so powerful she pushed him back onto his side. Back off and sleep, she commanded. He immediately fell into a sluggish state, bringing relief, but she would engineer things differently again and see that he did *not* go off alone for alternative entertainment. Or else. She could not entertain the else. Better to book tickets for a family show in the hotel the following night.

On the beach, Ed slept in the deckchair. When he moved away to smoke and have a beer at one o'clock, the kids did not care. "Mammy, let him off. He's moody without a fag," Jimmy advised.

"All the more reason for you boys never to smoke. It's an addiction."

"But it keeps him from complaining."

On boarding the flight home on Friday, the boys fought for the window seat. It had been a mixed holiday with high-lights during the day, the beach, burning skin, and their dance triumph. Once back, he would, she hoped, stay in for a bit to recover from the effects of orgiastic immoderation. No poker, no drink; the two mutually entwined. She didn't mind the odd game in the corner of Brennan's pub and not on the former scale of big bets and heavy losses. But what she could not influence, however, was his racing. Ed never missed the local events, nor those he fancied in various parts of the country.

CHAPTER 26

August 1976. Roscommon, Tullamore, and Galway: Ed's favourite racecourses, featured events in the calendar. When Laura or the O'Reillys took the boys for a night, Della went along too. Spirits rose late into the night at the post-race dinner/dancing in rowdy ballrooms. She'd steer clear of alcohol during the evening, except for one little brandy and ginger early on, then sit behind the wheel while Ed lolled in the passenger seat on the home journey.

Win or lose during the day, it did not matter; the mood was always the same - could have, should have, maybe tomorrow. Ed's spirits soared when he won, and a stash of bookie cash bulged in his back pocket.

Then, one Sunday morning, he let something slip casually into the conversation., "I met Mark last night in the Royal. We're going to the Sligo races on Tuesday. Maybe stay overnight if we've too much drink."

She let it sink in. Danger signals flared in her head. "You want to go racing and not come back afterwards? Why?

Fewer familiar faces, no wagging tongues? Ed, you're letting Mark lure you into temptation again."

"Bloody dramatic as always, Della, jumping to conclusions. It's risky driving back after a booze-up in the Sligo Park."

Sinister tones tinkled. "I'm right to worry; first, about the money you'll lose at the track, but worse still, the late drinking, where it might lead, and with whom. I don't have to spell it out, Ed."

"It's arranged."

Ed's words, chilling in finality, took her back to dark, anxiety-filled nights alone in bed. But she might as well kick the table in a fury when he would not budge.

"I thought we'd moved on from your philandering. Are you bored playing the respectable husband, the dutiful father attending sports days and concerts?"

"You're exaggerating. I'm only taking time out with a mate."

"That expression, and your inscrutability, make it alright? Next, you'll tell me not to stress when I wake up in the small hours, and you're far away in a hotel with a race crowd. I've seen those used-to-be hangers-on zoning in on drunken slobs with anyone who'll have them."

Other than a slight tonal inflexion, Ed stayed cool. She wanted to scream, stop him from going, her fear of deceit again stalking her path. But Ed was Ed, and he craved adulation.

"Don't get involved with women, Ed. Promise." That she'd voiced her angst openly said more about her than about him or his weaknesses.

"Have sense. What do you take me for?"

"That's not a question I want to answer. You wouldn't like it."

The following day, he went to the garage for an hour, then returned, light in step and broad in smiles. She egged, "Happy, Ed, going off with your crony."

"Della, shut up. We're just going to the races." Brooking no further argument, he bounded up the stairs to let the shower run while shaving. In overdrive to god-knows-what, Ed was beyond reach. She did not follow him upstairs nor trust herself not to provoke a fight. Glimmers of suspicion would plague her mind in his absence, but there was simply nothing she could do about it.

Twenty minutes later, he twirled in patent shoes, a black silk shirt, and a white jacket. Della drew in her breath. He exuded confidence, self-worth, and achievement. Handsome and sexy, but not for her benefit.

"Mind you drive carefully and avoid whiskey. You know it affects your judgment," Della said. The last plea pitched towards normality came from somewhere within, and Laura's voice telling her to be pleasant.

"Probably be late tomorrow night," Ed shouted, almost running toward the Triumph 2000 outside, where he threw the overnight bag onto the back seat. His recent acquisition had cost more than Della liked. Still, he had parried her opposition astutely, insisting the sale of two machines would cover it. Then, with a wave, he zoomed away from the house.

She sat at the table, her zest for cleaning the blue Toyota Ed bought for her last birthday nebulised into ugly vapours.

Not for a while had negativity burrowed so deep. So why did she fear the worst and hear an inner voice telling her he was on the verge again? Her husband's excitement? How he looked? Going with Mark? All of it.

Images of girls with short skirts, laughing eyes, and tempting lips danced before her. An inner whisper suggested things she did not want to hear.

Ed did not come home on Tuesday night or the following night. Neither did he phone to say where he was. Della let her fears muzzle her brain, releasing darts of insecurity and doubt during fitful sleep before dawn and amnesiac drowsing. Nothing. Then, his car pulled up on the gravel driveway on Thursday afternoon. In the scullery, Della, filling the washing machine, heard the sound. She assumed an air of indifference when he opened the back door and slunk in. There was no other way to describe it: slunk, guilty, evasive. Despite her self-warnings to avoid confrontation, fury surged inside her.

"Where the bloody hell were you? I haven't slept a wink in two nights. Had to go to the plant, assure the men you'd be back. They laughed at me, and Des said, 'Ah sure, Della, he's off having a whale of a time'. A whale of a time."

Ed's expression - non-committal - showed he would not tell. Weariness clung to the fine lines on his cheekbones, making him appear gaunt. A blessing the children were in school.

"Where were you, and with whom? The hussy that worked in the bank here and moved to Sligo? Bet it was her."

Huddling close to the range, Ed did not want an inquisition.

"Don't push me, Della, not now. Too much booze, knack-ered."

Thumping her fist on the table, she said, "I'm going to town, and you'd better have an explanation when I get back."

An hour later, ready for a fight, she ran from the drive into the house. No, Ed, a mug in the sink was the sole evidence of his recent presence. She pounded up the stairs, anger pinnacling. How dare he dodge her questions?

Her husband's supine shape was barely perceptible in the bedroom under the duvet. The saliva in Della's mouth dried. Exhausted, he'd done God knows what since leaving home. She stooped over the bed, hand ready to shake his sleeping face. No, not this way. She *would* give him time to explain, even if it were lies. But she must not let her temper dominate their discussion; yes, she'd stay in control. Well, she'd try.

Hours passed, but still no Ed. During dinner, the boys asked questions. "Daddy's tired after a long drive home." She saw Ronan nudge Jimmy, who shook his head. They knew too much. Ronan, at eleven, and Jimmy, ten, were old enough to understand something was amiss. Ronan mut-tered about his father watching an important game that evening.

"Better let Dad sleep on, boys. He's been at the races for two days and got little sleep. You know how it is when men get together. Too much drink and silly talk."

"We do, especially our dad." Gosh, weren't they copping on to him? She'd let him lie on before extracting sense, lies, or anything. Either he had drunk so much, Ed was genuinely ill, or he had not slept at all, the latter too awful to counter.

The following morning, Della heard Ed in the bathroom at seven o'clock, a divergence from his usual yawning struggle at eight. "I'll take the kids to school and go on to the plant," he shouted, no reference to his absence. Blood throbbed in her temples. No, he wouldn't.

"You'll come back here and explain where you spent two nights away from home, or I'll go to the plant and confront you there. Which is it to be?"

"I'll drop back but have to get off quickly. Things to catch up on and people to see."

Della fumed. The half-hour would give her husband time to fabricate his story. After all, he was *the* master of deceit who personified pretence better than anyone.

When she got back, Ed was sitting at the table. Unable to look her straight in the face, the nervous movements of his hands on the table indicated he would lie. His long, slender fingers, she often told him, were of a potential pianist. No chance, he'd said. His sisters were artists: painting, macrame, satin bedspread maps, crochet, and cakes, while Ed's skills lay in perfecting his workplace, arranging tools, clothes in the wardrobe, and shoes in rows. His lawn-mowing in symmetrical lines drew admiration from passers-by. Now was his chance to give her a neat explanation that did not fray into looseness.

On cue, he poured water into the kettle and filled the pot with tea bags. "Like a cuppa, Della?"

"You'd like one, you mean, and what about some toast and marmalade or anything else you want, Ed dear?" Despite the anger, she quelled the urge to wipe the lop-sided smile from his face. Forcing him to look at her, she said. "Talk, Ed Egan."

"Yes, it was Triona. After the races, she and Rona were in the Sligo Park hotel, and we just got into a group, chatted, and drank until morning. Me and Mark got very drunk. Rona said we shouldn't drive but could stay on their couch for the night."

Della exploded. "You bastard. I knew it. That pair of hussies."

"Nothing happened. I wouldn't mention them if it had." The sound of his voice, husky and low, was almost convincing. But what a combination. Two attractive men, with two immoral predators latching onto big spenders and copious amounts of alcohol. A cocktail for disaster. And he said they slept on the couch! Mind, he wasn't much in bed after a skinful.

"And what about the second night? With them again?" There was more, and she had to know.

"Well, yes, they went to work, and we drank all day, but we couldn't set out on the journey home. The road from Sligo is dangerous across the hills, around hairpin bends."

"It didn't occur to you or your considerate 'girlfriends' to call me? We have a phone, Ed Egan."

"Sort of, but you'd only rollock me. And if one of them rang, you'd be even more suspicious. Anyway, I'm here now, so stop nagging."

Della squeezed her hand until the nails bit into her palm; that or clout him. In effect, they did not differ from the Linehans: Joe's control of the fist type, Ed's of the 'nothing happened, take it or leave it' type. His reluctant admission, Della had to accept. Either continue to fight, allow the boys to hear them, or attempt normality.

She could neither prove nor disprove his tale. Despite the doubts and the surfeit of images in her mind, Della was unsure if she wanted to know everything. It would hurt too much and take her back to the honeymoon revelations. Did she want that? *Let it go*, an inner voice said. Maybe conscience will click in, and he won't stray again. She got into the car and drove from the house along the forest road towards the lake.

At the jetty, Della sat on a wooden bench and watched the ripples on the surface forming little circles, ever nudging into bigger ones, growing, diminishing, dying. Drops fell on the water from the grey, mottled panoply above. She let it splash on her face and trickle down along her coat. Still, she sat, pensive, wondering, meditating. The drizzle became a downpour.

She moved to the car, took off her coat, sat in the driver's seat, and stayed thus for an hour. *He would not destroy her; she wouldn't let it happen nor live under the shadow of his escapades.* Then, letting a swell of reassurance engulf her, Della started the engine. She would divert her life onto greater planes.

This time, she would not cry on Laura's shoulder.

Olive called to Egans one day in April, bursting with news. "Guess what, you two, I've joined the Fine Gael Party.

Will you come to a meeting on Tuesday night to support me?"

"Support you for what? We're already members, so we go canvassing during the campaigns before elections."

"The Party is to nominate candidates for the local elections. So I might put myself forward."

Absorbing the shock announcement, Della gulped. Had she not nurtured similar hopes herself, a forum on which to speak out for women? But in one startling announcement, Olive had scuppered the notion.

"We'll be there. Ed enjoys the crossfire during meetings. Can get heated."

Unfazed, Olive went on, "Thanks, I need your support. Must dash." Almost running through the door, she hopped into the Volvo outside, revved the engine and drove off towards Carrick-on-Shannon.

"Well, I never. What will that woman get up to next?" Ed laughed.

"A council seat. Great. If elected, she'll make waves."

"You mean talk over everyone, drag on and on, and the papers will destroy her afterwards."

"To Olive, it's another cause; her job is one of care, and she's ready to take it further. But it might bring a further rocky episode in the Keating saga."

"Bet Mark will hate it and turn against her even more. She'll never be at home, and he'll find a means of escape. But we'll go. Can't miss the fun."

Della did not prod, nor ask if Mark mentioned his wife's ambitions during their time in Sligo. Too painful still for any reference to that episode. Whenever she tried to weaken his reserve, usually in bed after a skinful, he cleverly sidestepped her nudges as if an inbuilt mechanism flashed danger when she probed. *'I'm a sucker'*, she told herself after one effort. Ed controlled the elasticity of their lives, not just by his actions but by his subtlety. He would use nondescript responses. Therefore, it was better to jog on in standard mode as usual. Normal?

On Tuesday night, Olive met them in the function room of the Royal. "I need enough votes for selection. You each have one?"

"Good on ye, Olive," Ed said, his broad smile indicating his intention to take a rise out of the woman and have fun at her expense.

"It's demanding, Olive and your job is full-time. What about the kids and Mark?" Della asked.

"Oh, they're fine and can snack after school. Mark does his own thing so that I can devote my energies to the campaign."

What was she thinking? That Mark disapproved showed in the manner in which she cut off the query. Della wondered if their only genuine bond was the family they shared. However, as a couple, they could erode a social outing when tension flared. One word from Mark, pounced on by Olive, invariably led to an outburst. Della reckoned that given Olive's absorption in a new project, trouble would almost certainly evolve.

She watched the other woman work the room and gush at members, her loud voice resounding across the packed function room. A politician in the making, they shook your hand while winking at someone else. But Olive, not yet moulded into a true political persona, dallied with each one, showing interest in their comments.

"Will this topple their marriage, Ed? Do you know what Mark thinks about her latest project?"

"He seemed resigned. They'll see less of each other, freeing him to do as he pleases. But Della, why would Mark break up his home or ruin his family? It's an enormous world out there, lots of options."

"So, he'll continue with the sham? Is that how you see things, Ed? Keep up the veneer of respectability, but do as one pleases?"

"Don't jump ahead of yourself. Let them be." Once again, he had sidestepped the issue, not letting her into his mind. She might manage him better than Olive did her husband, but she could not control his aberrations. On the plus side, the chemistry they shared, despite his failings, was the glue that kept them afloat.

"Olive's doing this for all women wanting independence and also, I guess, to impress Mark."

"Now that is dramatic, even for you, Della."

"I can see it. Mark's indifference is harder to bear than the blows Laura gets from Joe or your made-up stories."

"Give over. Not on about Sligo again."

"I won't forget the lies, Ed." His half-smile implied she should let the past die. Let him off the nagging hook, more like.

As the night died, Olive said, "I'm hosting a secret meeting on Tuesday. Come on time. The key movers are John Carroll, Neil Cox, and Marcus Kane." A secret meeting. Gosh, Olive certainly did things in style.

Tuesday night. At eight o'clock, the Keatings' house was already straining at the seams when Ed and Della arrived outside the white dormer bungalow on the edge of Boyle. On chairs, sofas, and the ample lounge floor, faithful supporters sat together like broiler hens. Although autumn was making forays in the season and the birds tweeting late, Olive pulled the blinds down on all the high windows. Covert actions and optimum secrecy were necessary for the success of their plans.

Excitedly, she passed sandwiches around the group. "It's a privilege to be among men and women like these, whose loyalties stretch back to the Civil War."

"Lofty ideals, Olive. But is it right for you? What does Mark say?"

"He thinks I'm silly, not his thing." Olive seemed determined to ignore adverse comments, but her hesitancy indicated disappointment. Not once had she mentioned the Sligo races to Della. She, too, was protecting her emotions, preferring ignorance.

John Carroll was the first to address the group. "We plan to unseat Lyster and Cunningham in this election. They're doddering old men and it's time for them to go. But prepare to field accusations of destroying old allegiances."

"Agreed. Our Party needs fresh faces," Marcus added.

"Their stupid remarks in Council chambers make an embarrassing read in local papers," Neil Cox added. Despite his family's insistence on tending to his extensive farm, he, too, nurtured aspirations for a political career.

"People are tired of parish-pump mouthers. They're local wags, not politicians." John Carroll said. On a virtual podium, it seemed to Della that all three sought to turn members against the sitting candidates, but why did they hate them that much? And was it right to get excited about ruining another's career?

Neil Cox went on. "The situation in Northern Ireland is tenuous, with the hunger strikes gathering support throughout Ireland. As a result, Sinn Féin intends to add candidates in every constituency."

"So, there's a risk we may fuel the fire of patriotism further by adding extra names to the list," Marcus Kane seemed reluctant to join in the euphoric mood in the room.

"Bobby Sands and a group of Republicans are starving to death for the cause of a United Ireland, but the English Government's stance on terrorism remains trenchant; they won't give in to threats. Sinn Féin will push for seats in local and general elections in the South to gain publicity for their cause," Neil went on.

John Carroll stepped up the pressure. "Why should Sinn Féin get votes now? Their slogan, 'campaign with a ballot paper in one hand and an Armalite in the other', is vile. Fine Gael is a peace-loving Party rooted in the Treaty and attracts decent people to its ranks. Yes, sectarian strife is wreaking misery, suffering, and death in the North, and the blame lies at the feet of British MPs."

Marcus Kane interrupted. "Support for the strikers is running high from the old guard here, too, who fought for Independence and also from the new band of Republicans. Unfortunately, we'll lose seats in this election if Sinn Féin contests key seats at the County Council level."

"So, ought we to select a new candidate?" John Carroll queried

A ripple of unease gathered momentum across the room. Della saw Olive's cheeks burn. "Are they going to dump me?"

Della put a hand on her arm. "Hold on. It's just talk."

But the atmosphere, charged with outpourings of frustration and patriotic superlatives, was now warlike. Excited at the prospect of unseating shiny trousers from shiny council seats, Neil Cox said the election would relegate old faces to anonymity for the rest of their days. His battle cry at once drew a rallying response from the room. Della saw how words could stir even the lily-livered into action.

"Mob psychology," she muttered to Ed, sensing his delight. "You're enjoying this."

"Sure am. And they're right. Get rid of those two old fellas, I say."

"Tonight, if we achieve our aim and select Olive, we will take the seat, and if Sinn Féin does likewise, members may blame us afterwards. Are you prepared to face the flak?" Neil asked.

"Yes, and if those two seats fall to Sinn Féin and us, it's mission accomplished. We could lose support in the Party."

"Or deeply held loyalties." Brian Dunne spoke from the back. A quiet man, his voice pierced the euphoric haze eddying around the room. "After all, they're decent men who've worked hard for country folk in this area."

A hush descended, and then a rash of opinions fluttered. Neil stood again. "Two dunderheads. Come on, keep your minds fixed on the goal."

Olive came forward. "I'm the one you want to oppose these people. And I'm ready for the fight. So let's not back out now."

"Well said, Olive. You're a woman of courage."

Loud claps, as members enthused, forceful now. Ed whispered in Della's ear, "It's a mutiny. I'm in. Fair dues to her."

The innovators had won the night. Neil shouted, "The die is cast. Let's get rid of those two clowns." At once, his harshness dissonated to a weak clap from the group.

"Nobody will know how we voted at the Convention," Marcus said.

"They will," Sean Connor replied. "Someone here tonight will leak it. We're an island of gossipers, and small news gathers force in country places. They'll soon cop we're not on their side."

The night ended on a note of exuberance, hyper-tensed but ready for the fray.

CHAPTER 27

It was not until Della went home at the weekend that she faced opposition from the least expected person, her father. In his wisdom, Jim gave two reasons for disagreeing with the plans.

"I've worked with those men in the Party, mutually supporting one another on many issues. Now, you're engaged in a plot to destroy their careers. They have little to occupy themselves except to devote their energies to the locality. We might lose one seat and allow Sinn Fein to be the victors."

Jim also said that, as a Christian, Della ought to know better. They were preparing to ruin two men's enjoyment of public life. Despite struggling to defend the stance, Della refused to acknowledge her father's viewpoint.

"Dad, I can't agree with you. We aim to reform the Party. It's the first step," she argued.

"You've forgotten the human element. Irish people vote for individuals more than politics in a local election."

"Human, yes, but at the cost of professionalism." Della opened her mouth to protest but closed it again, seeing her mother's expression.

On the way home, the kids fell quiet, tired after football on the lawn. They loved the space at the big farmhouse in Leam. Della did not want to talk about her father's rebuff, and Ed was in good spirits. "I can't wait for the news to burst about the meeting at Olive's last week."

"It was a secret meeting."

He laughed. "Gossip is the life's blood of small communities. The cars lined up outside the Keatings, the men who told their wives at home, the tittle-tattle that circulates like a bushfire, means that those candidates already know about the meeting."

His unexpected grasp of the situation was a surprise. He would take a chance on a horse, a hound, or a game of cards, but this was different. "As your father said, there's an almighty battle ahead, but we can't aggravate customers, Della. Be wise."

"What about Ant, who supports Peter Mullin? He'll display the posters in the bar." A successful shopkeeper, Ant Brennan, allowed Party meetings in the pub. But as an open and honest man, everyone accepted his Fianna Fáil colours.

"Mullin is an established politician with support from all sides. But we're trying to sway voters away from Cunningham and Lyster."

As sure as night follows day, rumours of the caucus spread afar in the days leading up to the next constituency meeting. On Thursday night, tension hung heavy in the hotel function room, the tightly packed crowd strumming on adrenalin, expecting an uproar. Nothing in Ireland equalled a political gathering - bar a game of Gaelic football.

Liam Cunningham stood up to speak, his voluminous form shuddering in anger. Della saw the purple folds of his rubbery cheeks suffuse sweat droplets onto his collar. His voice shook with emotion.

"Skulduggery went on in her house," he hollered, looking directly toward Olive in the audience. "Her and her cohorts plan to get rid of me, to take my seat, but let me say this: she won't win."

Gathering herself up with a flourish, Olive ignored the barb. "Throughout long, wet evenings, members of this great Party tread the highways and the byways, asking the faithful for support. You venture into gloomy houses, where the light rarely shines across overgrown hedges. You poke your heads into small, thatched houses where pensioners eke out their days. Every vote counts."

"A brilliant woman," Paddy Kane whispered. "See how quickly he sat down and shut up."

"Yes, she has grit," Della said, looking around for Ed. At the bar with Mark, who had arrived late, he was drinking brandy and ginger ale. She'd have to drive home again.

Mark acknowledged her with an aloof nod. She barely nodded back. In him lay the devil, the one who could destroy her marriage simply by asking her man to accompany him.

Della drew her friend aside. "Are you sure about this? Mark doesn't seem happy. You'll need a thick skin to ignore criticism, even insults."

"I'm ready. And I don't give a damn what he thinks."

"Let's go home, get those two away from the bar," Della urged, glancing again at Mark. His tight lips and stern expression boded ill for his wife. Best to avoid an argument.

"Olive is a changed woman," Della said in the car. "She's merely regurgitating party rhetoric but doesn't quite understand it. Unfortunately, that's not her true self."

"Well, she's still outspoken and loud, and she'll spice up the campaign."

"It's about standards and intelligent representation."

"Della, you've got the right jargon. Don't you overdo it, mind? You're wanted at home by the kids, doing the accounts and the rest."

"But it's exciting, Ed. You enjoy the meetings. Admit it. And the kids can look after themselves while we're out together."

He did not miss the stress of her last word. After the Sligo episode, he'd cut down on drinking and was getting in at a reasonable time. "You mean I'm toeing the line, Della?" he said, voice muggy from alcohol. But, exasperating as he was, the mood was temperate.

"If Olive's successful, she'll push for funded childcare creches, immunisation free from cost, and additional provision for OAP's in their homes."

"A good prospect then. That woman has a gob on her big enough to floor any man, any Council." He said it as it was.

"She'll surely ruffle the old cronies in the chamber."

Paddy Kane picked Della up on Monday morning, their goal to canvass a remote townland within the electoral area. They skirted the lakes and followed a road that ascended a steep slope, a terrain grim in winter, aglow with purple heather in early summer. Here, sharp rock jutted from skin-thin grass gnawed bare by white and black hardy sheep. Della wondered who tended those animals, braved the heights or risked life and limb for a living. The answer was not far away. Paddy stopped the car before a lone house huddled under the scarp. From here, Boyle was a minuscule model of itself—Church spires spearing through spiralling smoke from early morning fires.

Cupped between the lakes, it looked perfect as an English postcard. Unfortunately, the Irish did not depict their attractions as the British did—little ash-tinted Cotswold villages, grey strings of Somerset stone, and Scottish battlemented bastions. Here, winter winds blew wild across the mountainside, and snow closed folk off for days.

Della knocked on the door of a man who lived alone. From the gloom, a grimy old pensioner peered out across the half-door. "The last time any of ye visited this hovel was before the election four years ago. Not a single councillor darkened my door since. So why should I bother voting for anyone?"

Della's spirits lurched. His words rang true; hypocritical politicians promised a new Gloriana if their Party got in, and this man was the human epitome of failed election promises.

"You're right, Bert. The proposed water scheme is still on the planning board back in the Council, awaiting approval. Fine Gael wants to elect strong candidates who'll do a proper job. So we'll send the car for you on May 7th and take you to the polling station. I'll come myself," Paddy said.

The man's face lightened into a smile. "And ye'll get the Council to widen the track to this house. It's treacherous when the storms wash the rubble down the hill."

Paddy nodded. Bert might not have long left in life, but his vote mattered, and he deserved something other than promises. Smiling goodbye, they moved on to the next house, a mile further on.

People liked Paddy with his wild, unruly hair, wind-reddened cheeks, and smiling eyes. Kind in spirit and nature, he could pass nobody on the road without offering them a lift and, of habit, usually arrived at the Friday market with a packed car. It felt good to share the vision of a better society with genuineness.

"Olive's inexperience is a drawback, Paddy, and she's vying for votes in the same part of the constituency as Peter Mullins, a powerful Fianna Fáil councillor. He's topped the poll in every election over the past twelve years. What are her chances, do you honestly think?"

"Pundits expect the Sinn Fein candidate to draw support from the same base as traditional republicans, the Fianna Fáil Party, so that may weaken their support, but Olive may not get in. She's too vocal about the Women's Lib movement, which is unimportant in an agricultural county like Roscommon."

"But she'll get the women's vote, surely?"

"No. By nature, everyone votes traditionally, the way their parents voted. Politics is next to religion in Ireland - sacred. But, with the troubles in the North peaking, our Party will almost certainly lose one seat to Sinn Féin, and it won't be Peter Mullins who'll crash out."

"It's the seventies, and voters more informed in making choices without pressure." If she were to concede to his viewpoint, Della might as well go home and do the ironing.

Throughout the day, they walked and talked. Della was glad to bid goodbye to the hilly boreens and isolated houses by six o'clock. How did people survive in such places?

With two weeks until election day, the faithful gathered at the Keatings' again on Saturday evening after the eight o'clock Mass. They had to find a solution to keep their two seats. Drinks spilt onto carpets, election posters, and flyers. Mark, hovering in the kitchen, called Olive into the kitchen. "To the bedroom, now."

Staining to hear the conversation, Della tip-toed along the soft carpet. She slipped unnoticed into the bathroom, where she held the door ajar. Mark's voice was vicious.

"You've drafted and redrafted speeches from Party policy documents and condensed them to bullet points. I've signed for posters delivered in vans, smeared in flashy slogans *'Fine Gael for Social Justice'*, but I tell you, your long discourses will not work. Mullins is a polished speaker, and you can't match him. Is it worth turning this house into a dirty pub, the children farmed out to different friends, no dinners cooked? I've had enough."

"After all this time and energy, I want that seat, Mark. You must understand."

"I'm running a business employing thirty men. You'll alienate people, perhaps insult a prospective customer. Where would that lead? Better off out of it."

"I never get into arguments. I was born into a family that suffered at the hands of an unsympathetic Party. How can I sit by and not redress it?"

"That's history. Leave it there."

"No, I won't. Let go of my arm. You're hurting me."

Della almost called out "Stop" but did not dare. Instead, she returned to the lounge where the faithful sat or slouched against walls. Through Mark's eyes, she viewed the scene: the scrapes on the cream surfaces, the black scuff marks on the polished floors. A proud man, he cared about his domain, and tonight was not his thing. Olive faced a two-fold battle: to fill a Council seat and to keep her family intact.

"Let's hear your speech for the last rally, Olive," Paddy Kane shouted as she entered the room.

Olive's face assumed a rebellious expression. What a woman; one minute reprimanded by an impatient and disgusted husband, the next transformed into a warrior. She stood, sheet in hand, and launched forth:

'*We must identify our fight for equality, like South African nationalists under Nelson Mandela. We live in a democracy and must adopt new thinking and ideas. Here, in Ireland, the freedom to vote is a reality. We are not living in Iraq, China, the*

Far East, or in places where newly established democracies deny human rights. But under the ruling Party in Ireland, similar practices abide.'

Della gasped and moved toward Mark against the arch between the kitchen and the lounge. His expression icy and impenetrable, his lips narrowed, he rasped, "Do you honestly think such stuff will influence voters? Folk couldn't give a toss about Africa or anywhere else. They want education, better Social Welfare, and jobs for their kids. Della, I'm sick of it all. She's lost her reason."

"Don't get worked up. But, yes, Olive ought to stick to local issues." It was important to calm the man despite her distrust of him.

"I'm out of here. It's not my home anymore but a bloody headquarters for a doomed Party." Mark turned towards the back door and vanished into the night. Somehow, Della had to warn Olive of the danger of losing a seat and a husband.

One a.m. Olive closed the door behind the Party faithful, drifting off to the cars lined along the road. John Carroll hung back.

"Olive, we chose you to contest the seat for one primary reason: to rid our party of the fuddy-duddies who represent Fine Gael in the chamber. If John Hearne takes a seat for Sinn Féin, that only leaves two for us in this area. We must get rid of at least one sitting councillor."

"I'm doing my best, John." Then, tired and devoid of energy, she closed the front door behind him.

It was nine o'clock before Olive woke the next day. Noise wafting from the kitchen told her the children were up. Was

Mark? She had not heard him come in, and he must have slept in the spare room. She pulled a dressing gown around her shoulders and fumbled along the corridor to the centre of the house. The smell of fried sausages wafted up her nose. "Oh nice, any for me?"

"Cook your own," Mark said. "I'm getting this lot to the school."

"In tonight, Mum?" Barry, the youngest, asked.

Olive rustled at the hob and made a noise in her throat. She sat, a cup of coffee in hand, and frowned at the toast crusts and spilt sugar on the table. Time was when she'd enjoyed seeing her brood off to school. On a whim, she rang John and said she needed a day off, a nasty headache.

Mark did not return to the house all day. Olive picked up the children from school and set them down for homework. An hour later, she gave them dinner. Still no Mark. She was not to see him again for two weeks.

CHAPTER 28

Late one evening, towards the end of the campaign, Della and John O'Brien canvassed the town again, one last sweep to mop up doubters who might swing under pressure.

"Let's finish in the pubs. Get the men before closing time," he said. Della was not in the mood. Her leg muscles ached, and her arms numbed from carrying bundles of election leaflets. But he was right. The wives would follow suit if they got men to vote for the candidate. Appalling.

Pulling herself up on a high stool in Brennans, she asked for a glass of orange and looked around the smoky interior where twenty men sat sipping pints, the last one for the road. None smiled in their direction. She sensed hostility.

"Let's have one and get off, John. Mostly Fianna Fáil and Sinn Féin supporters here. No votes for us."

"Those five playing cards could be floating voters, might sway the result. We'll stay for a bit."

John's loyalties lay in the Old IRA, the militant branch of a Party opposed to the 1922 treaty, and among this crowd tonight were men with long memories. Della felt uneasy.

To get the bar's attention, Mickey Gillen said, "Ah-ha, Johnny, you're wearing a different coat nowadays. I suppose you'll vote for John Hearne when the time comes." The leer and inference hit Della's companion like a slap. The allegation that he was out canvassing for one party but would vote for another was an outrageous insult.

Face turkey-cock red, John stepped down from the high stool, fist balled in response to leers across the smoke-drenched room. Della spluttered quickly. "And I expect you'll vote for us, Mickey, seeing you want the water scheme down your road?"

The return came sharp, defined. "Aye, if I thought your woman might get in! But *he* won't vote for her."

The barb hit home. Heading towards the sneering mouth, John shouted, "Shut the fuck up, Gillen, or I'll shut it for you."

Della tugged a black sleeve. "Let's get out of here, John. It's late, and we're tired."

The entire bar fell silent; banter one thing, goads another.

Gillen recoiled; John regained his composure. Della said goodnight. They left.

Families like John O'Brien's, with roots fixed in the State's birth pangs, yearned for a free Ireland and nurtured bitter memories of uncles, fathers, and relatives shot outside their houses by the Black and Tans, vicious mavericks sent over to control the Irish in the wake of the 1916 Rising. Yet, he was out each day asking for votes down byways, bog roads, up hills, and even to the foot of the local mountain - not quite a mountain, but high enough to claim such.

Ed was not amused when Della reported at home. "I told you it might harm us."

"I haven't made enemies. I smiled at everyone."

"Politics is a dangerous business. Best out of it. When it's over, Olive will not have a seat on the Council or a husband. I met Mark after the last meeting. He'd been to see family in Donegal. Needed to get away from her."

"Surely that's an exaggeration. Mark will be proud of his wife when all this is over."

"Della, can't you see the damage to their relationship?"

She let the comment float away with his cigarette smoke, spiralling upwards in the lounge. It was not the time to solve domestic problems; work to be done.

Days broke and merged into gatherings of the faithful as if by magic. Magic, yes, the magical quality of allegiance, fierce and proud. From Celtic myths, the spirit of ancient Chieftains, tribal and aggressive, was again resounding in the hearts of Irish people, only to die down when the battle ended.

On Saturday, six members came to paste posters in the Egans' spacious shed at the back of the house. Throughout the morning, Della plied them with sandwiches and beer, hoping Olive would appreciate their joint efforts in the campaign. A demanding task, they pasted and tied string through holes in sync with the strains of an old Fenian cry from a little transistor on the shelf:

We may have brave men,
but we'll never have better
Glory O, Glory O to the
bold Fenian men

The Fenians gave their lives. Instead, these would not have to die but sweat, nail, and talk for the cause. Some would neglect farms and shops. Ed said he did his bit by letting them use his equipment in the shed.

On the last Sunday before polling day, an unexpected element entered the fray, and one Della would describe as cathartic when the worst effects had passed. For her to address a throng of several hundred after Mass, Ed set up the microphone and waited for the congregation to emerge from the church. Paper in hand, speech reduced to key points, Della held her head high and gaze steady. With no other Party speaker around, she would have the full attention of the congregation.

Then Peter Mullins and the entourage drove up and took up positions beside Ed and herself. She turned on the microphone, looked at the expectant crowd, opened her mouth, and 'died', fustian flow melting into the blueness over the steeple. She mumbled something about social justice and halted.

The enormity of what she, a housewife, was doing hit home at that moment. On her right was a respected member of the Fianna Fáil party, whom most voters trusted. From behind her, Ed muttered, "What on earth, Della?"

Here she was, the voice of the Party, unable to speak. She opened her mouth again and stuttered in a Hades of her own making. Nothing came, not a single word of her rehearsed speech. Irrelevant now, her elevated position on a box! One man - she saw him through a haze of embarrassment - smirked provocatively. She faded back from the mic. Ed urged again. "Get on with it."

"Ladies and gentlemen, I'm asking you to vote for Olive Keating. Fine Gael will bring Social Justice for all, but..." As Della was about to criticise the Government's performance, she glanced at Peter, who was listening deferentially. Words froze on her tongue. She wished for nothing more than to run away from the laughing faces. Anywhere.

"Into the car, now." The urgency and embarrassment in Ed's voice pierced her fogged brain. She had disgraced herself, him and the Party. Quickly, Ed bundled the apparatus into the boot and spun around onto the main road. "Never humiliate me again like that. I wanted to fall into a pothole. Never been so embarrassed!"

"I lost my confidence at the idea of criticising Peter Mullins and the FF Party in his presence."

"A real politician has no time for sentiment." Right, of course, but from him, unique and surprising.

"Right. Drive to the nearest parish, and I'll do it."

He did, and she delivered a fluent, articulate speech. Life, she pondered, did mysterious things to one. Or was it just politics?

Ed was reading in the lounge.

"It's getting dirty. Listen. 'Alan Lyster publicly berated an opponent's dead father to a sniggering audience last night. The best way of getting votes was to tell voters about Paddy Connor up the road and how he hid under the bed when the Old IRA came for him to join the fight for Independence.' That is character assassination."

"Disgraceful. It proves us right, and the man should not be on the council if he can't fight fair. That gangly bastard should respect the dead and not use a mangled version of a Civil War tale to get votes."

"Muddying his opponent's character is twisted. Politics is a dirty game," Ed insisted.

"Yes, but ironically, it's not the opposition playing foul. It's our party. And it's not his opponent's father. It's one of Olive's supporters."

"Lyster cares little about truth or hard facts. His reference to a dead freedom fighter is disgusting and by defacing an old IRA man's memory, he will anger supporters. He'll damage himself more than her."

"Not so sure. I've picked up praise for Lyster in the campaign. He was well in with the doctors and council staff. Got several old folks into the Home. That's what matters."

The day of the count arrived, a weak sun in the sky unmatched by the enthusiasm of canvassers, counters, and supporters arriving at the courthouse. Olive looked buoyant, her bronze tresses tumbling in disarray about her excited face. Eyes lit up in expectation, she smiled and shook hands with Party members.

Della searched the crowd for Mark, but he was nowhere in sight. Surely, on this momentous day, he would support his wife. Olive said he had urgent business in the city, and they'd hardly spoken in the past week.

"Busy with canvassing right up to the end, Della. Busy, busy." But the glint in her eye told another story, and Della thought she saw tears glisten behind the long lashes laden with mascara. The so-and-so, he could at least have come along to show his wife support on this day, of all days.

Minutes flew by, all eyes straining towards the council staff, counting and re-counting ballot papers. It was easy to see which piles were growing fastest. Hush fell and gave way to babble as predictions flew across the chamber. Rumour was rife; Mullins was in, Sinn Féin was close behind, and Fine Gael indiscriminate. Too soon to judge, John Carroll whispered.

Neil stammered, "It'll depend on the transfers," which meant none of the FG candidate's piles was enough for election on the first count. Mumbles of 'splitting votes' came across the room from Cunningham's supporters. Olive shrank back into a seat, a teardrop oozing through her panstick cheeks.

Della whispered to Ed, "Where is that husband of hers?" He shook his head. Either did not know or wouldn't tell, the latter, she suspected as the truth.

Proportional Representation, an electoral system in Ireland that allowed candidates to gain seats in proportion to their votes, was fair. After the first count, the principal officer eliminated the candidate at the bottom and instructed the counters to add the second and third preferences to the names above them. Thus, every vote held a modicum of hope right to the end.

The total vote for three Party candidates was close. John Carroll demanded a re-count for Olive, Cunningham and Lyster. A disgrace, members rumbled loudly; all FG candidates were fighting for one last seat. Hard-line supporters looked over towards Olive and her group. Anger mounted with each dreary minute that passed.

Olive's pile of papers by nine o'clock was modest, Cunningham's slightly higher. Then, face twitching to stop tears, she muttered, "I'm done. Won't get in."

"Maybe next time, Olive," Della whispered.

"I'll neither have a seat nor a man," came the response, dull, devoid of emotion. No longer the loud, exuberant character of the campaign, Olive leaned towards Della for support.

"Hold up your head, Olive. You worked hard and proved your capabilities." Then, aside, she said to Ed, "The brat, he should be here to support her."

When Liam Cunningham stood up to make his final speech, Della wanted to slink into a corner. But, as her father had warned, the man appeared broken, and she had helped break him.

"I've lost my seat, and it's Olive Keating's fault and those who pushed her to contest it," he said, staring across the floor at the group. "In her house, they planned my downfall, and Alan's also, but they couldn't pull off both losses and fair dues to him for holding on. Underhand gerrymandering behind closed doors is to blame for losing a seat. Expel that lot at once, I say."

Della looked towards her elected father and saw his face, severe but understanding. He shook his head as if to say, "Do nothing. Show respect."

Lyster, the gangly one, stood up to speak. "I scraped in despite those schemers who wanted rid of me. But I almost bowed out because of their plotting. Instead, they've played into the hands of the opposition. They must now assess where they stand in Fine Gael today. Thanks to my faithful supporters for their courage in not succumbing to a wave of 'new thinkers' in our party. To your lot, I say this. Loyalty is what I have, but you couldn't garner."

"Let's leave," Olive begged. "I can't take it anymore."

Della whispered to Neil, standing stony-faced and disappointed, "What he said is not entirely true. The enormous impact of hunger strikes in the North swayed the old IRA faithful."

"Yes, but we chose the wrong time to do it."

On the Square, the church clock struck eleven-thirty. Olive, Della, John, Neil, and Paddy stood, quiet, together but vanquished.

John Carroll said, "The battle is over for now, but one day, we'll elect better candidates to continue the work we started. And Olive, you and Della will see the fruits of your efforts. So don't lose heart."

"I'll stay in the Party, but the future is uncertain, and right now, I have to repair losses in my house."

No one disagreed.

As the setting sun sank below the horizon, a panoply of stars began to twinkle and dot the universe above, and an orange moon turned pale.

Almost at once, life returned to routine. Della cleared the papers from the spare room, binned the candidates' smiling faces, washed the paste from the barn floor, and tidied her house. She stayed home for days except for shopping and avoided phoning Olive. The boys went to school, Ed took off for work daily, and life settled into ordinariness.

On the journey to O'Reilly's the following Sunday, the sheer extent of the damage left behind after the election was stark; sad, twisted caricatures dangling from poles across the countryside.

"You should stop and let me take them down, Ed. After all, we're responsible for some of them."

"No way. Let the wind blow them down. I wasted enough time pasting them. Not my job anymore."

"I learned from the experience about people and their needs, the lack of funding, difficulty getting benefits, grants, and government recognition of run-down areas. And now I want more, not just for women, but for everyone. We preached about social justice outside churches and in the towns. We can't let those aspirations die away as soon as the Dáil meets again.

"Della, get down from the pulpit, will you? Inspired as you were by electioneering, it must take a back seat now, with invoices on the desk and tax forms to fill.

"I'll do all that, but maybe more from now on." Yes, she would join the movement for equality and women's rights.

"I met Mark for a drink on Saturday night. He came to the Royal looking for me. I knew at once something was wrong. He was pale and depressed, not in his usual high spirits."

"Well, did he say where he'd been, why we'd not seen him for so long?"

"In his own words, he found the weeks before the election intolerable. He said it was a nightmare in the house. Floors were covered in paper, leaflets, phone numbers, streamers, the house a tip, and the children looking after themselves. He could not convince Olive that she was wasting her time and wouldn't get onto the Council. She flung a book at him one night when he pleaded with her to give in. It hurt, his cut bled, and he went to Casualty, where they put in four stitches."

"Oh, that's awful. Olive is loud but not violent. I guess she's been under a lot of stress."

"He left that night and didn't get home until the election ended."

"Mark didn't vote for his wife! So what did he do?"

"A lot. I'll explain if you promise not to tell her."

Della sensed another confession pending - of someone else's sins.

"Mark headed for Dublin in his Mercedes after their row."

"He loves that car more than Olive."

"Wouldn't I love it too, with its cream leather seats, pop-up wine glass, and fancy thingamajigs? He said 'to blazes with Olive, chucking away a good life, a thriving business, a stable bank account, and three fine children.' He'd go it alone after what she did to him. Dublin was a big city with ample distractions, and he'd find them. He needed space away from her voice: 'Answer the phone,' 'Mark, get the kids' breakfast', 'back late after canvassing', 'nearly there, 'I can smell success'. And so on. He did not want any part of it. And Dublin was the best place to get lost, away from prying eyes and gossip."

"Yes, I can see why he ran off to the city, which he knows well, with frequent trips to warehouses and sales. Mark is prosperous and wants the boys to follow him into the firm. I don't like him because he's not a good influence on you, and no, I'm not going on about Sligo again. But when Olive thrust herself into the political arena, he said she wanted fame, a platform to raise her image before the people. He was hostile from the start."

"Della, he realised their marriage was a sham when Olive said she loathed him and threw the book at his head, cutting it badly, so he packed a bag and left. But on the journey, he said he could still see her distorted features through the blobs of rain on the window screen, worn and tired. Well, she's older than him by a few years. He married a slim, bouncy girl with a huge personality, who soon spread her girth, and he did not like it. They drifted, in bed and out of it." Ed stopped, words dying out before Della's expression.

"Dear God, Ed Egan, I'm glad you're not describing me. That's awful."

"No. And you're none of those things, Della. Just listen. He drove to the Skylon Hotel, where he often stayed because of its convenience to the airport. Don't lose your temper. It's not me this is about. A young girl in a white apron caught his attention in Reception. He watched her delicate movements as she placed a salver of pastries on the coffee table in the lounge. She smiled at him. He saw his reflection in a mirror on the wall: tall, slim, with dark wavy hair and deep eyes. Not bad, nor insignificant by any means. Her look said she liked his appearance, swish in the leather jacket bought in Siena on a recent holiday.

In the room, he laid out his clothes on the bed and unfolded the white shirt and designer jacket, the same as Mick Jagger wore in a concert at the Westbury Hotel. The clothes that defined a pop culture idol would define him now.

Shaving, showering, and dressing, he planned to go to the National off Gardener St, where he'd often gone before, a brilliant spot for girls wanting a good time. But again, Olive's face wafted before him, wide and scowling. He didn't care. The opportunity to break free was his.

An hour later, and three brandies down, he needed the toilet. In the corridor, the girl was standing, tray in hand. Was she free? Yes.

In his room, the girl, Helena, stood on tiptoe to kiss him. Instead, he pulled her close and lifted her to the bed, head swimming.

It had been a while, but their writhing on the bed soon ignited him. He guessed Helena was not shy, nor was it her first time. A face flashed into his mind, quickly blanked.

Helena, a Polish immigrant with sufficient English to get by, was taking classes at Artane Tech. 'I'm sharing a room with two other girls from my country. It's enough until I get a qualification and earn a better wage.'

Her eyes exuded timidity, vulnerability and more, a passion for survival. Her skin smelled of cheap perfume, which would cling to his clothes. Drat it. He'd have to wash his underwear before getting home. Would Olive guess? Yes, she would. One thing about his wife - she was shrewd, intelligent, and super-suspicious. He'd wanted to deceive her, to make her pay for her self-centred behaviour, but not this way. If she were to discover his secret, his kingdom could collapse. She'd run him from the house, and he'd end up worse off. No, despite his longings, he had to take stock.

He saw again the girl's lure, not just her beauty but also her defencelessness, unlike Olive, whose strong and often too feisty character made him dislike her. He'd voiced the word in his head. Disliked. Not that he didn't care for her welfare. But Helena was the opposite".

Della sat, frozen in the chair, tea cooling in the mug. "I feel sick, Ed. How could he share all those intimate details? It seems you two do stuff I wouldn't want to know. Why are you telling me all this?"

"Because it's not about me, Della. You'll be glad to hear he felt like a cad afterwards, and the best thing to do was to go home, tell Olive that he'd been unfaithful, and break the union. However, the complications would affect his entire life, split up his home, and cause financial difficulties. He doesn't want to lose a chunk of his wealth, so best take his chances and kill his conscience."

"Ed, you told me what he did in London, and now this. What about all the nights you stayed away when I lay awake crazy with worry? You're no angel."

"But we love each other, Della. Aren't we still in love? See?" Ed pulled her into his arms and kissed her quietly. "Let's go upstairs," he whispered. *Lord, oh, Lord, what next? What a day.*

"I've beds to change, things to do. Love dies when suspicion destroys trust, Ed. How often have I listened to your fables about drinking late or some other lame excuse."

"Don't get riled at me. Maybe I shouldn't have told you what Mark did, but please don't dig up our stuff again."

"Surely you don't condone his actions. Next time you're off somewhere, I'll think of what he did."

"I don't condone them, but men don't stray easily, Della."

"They bloody do. You and Mark are good-looking guys who married in haste. And you find thrills in the excitement temptation brings. Not to mention Joe Lenihan, another one who yearns for attention."

"I *am* more settled nowadays. So, give me some credit."

"Ed, the Church has started courses called 'Marriage Encounter weekends' nationwide. I hear they're fantastic for renewing relationships. Maybe we'll go sometime?"

"You must be joking. Send the Keatings and Lenihans to it."

CHAPTER 29

D ella wondered if she ought to take Laura shopping somewhere nice. Suppose she offered a trip to Galway without the pressure to spend, just for the drive and to walk along the glorious Salthill promenade.

Outside the grey house, nothing was stirring except for a stray hen around the barn. No one home? Della knocked again, louder this time. Her ear picked up a rustling noise, and the door creaked open. Nothing could have prepared her for the sight of the other woman - straggling hair, thin jawline, and drawn features. Inside the door, Della stepped gingerly over discarded shoes, socks, and a few plastic bags along the hall. In the middle of the kitchen, a soiled oilskin cover on the table laden with breakfast things bore evidence of the breakfast meal. Stacked high on a sideboard by the wall were books, magazines, paper, string, and some children's clothes. A smell of dirty water and carbolic soap wafted in the air.

"Laura, what's happened? Sorry I couldn't get here before now."

Laura flushed and moved things from one heap to another—fruitless actions.

"Della, you have everything. Me, nothing."

"You've got three bright kids doing well in school. Sister Ligouri said as much this morning when I dropped my two off."

"Kids are fine, but Joe is seeing someone else. Last week, a letter with the postmark 'Horseleap' came from a girl he was with, according to her, the previous Saturday night. She knew he had a wife and children but loved him all the same. I'm afraid, Della. What can I do?"

"Love him? Someone he met in a bar. Some silly young one, I bet. Probably nothing to it, Laura."

"He goes twice a week, says he doesn't, but I check the mileage on the van and estimate the distance, roughly eighty miles round trip."

"For goodness' sake. Horseleap? Tullamore? That far? Did you give him the letter?"

"No, I hid it under the mattress. Joe's cousin, Larry, is doing block work on a new estate, and he asked him to help. I was glad of the extra money, but when they stayed away, it seemed odd."

"What was his excuse?"

"He had to guard equipment on the site and sleep in the caravan. But he's committing adultery, Della." Once again, Laura's perspective sprung from her deep Christian beliefs.

"Rubbish about guarding the stuff, but yes, it's adultery."

"The job is over, but he still returns in Larry's truck. What next, Della? I'm beside myself with worry. I might see Canon Kelly and ask him to speak to Joe. The Church is supposed to look after all its flock."

"I'm not so sure. Should you raise Joe's temper again? Remember last time? He won't want the priest to think less of him. As for adultery, listen to this."

As she skimmed over the more intimate details of Marks's escapade in the city, Laura's face crumpled with pity for Olive, a woman she rarely met. "Poor Olive, it'll break her. But Mark isn't physically abusive."

"No, his way is more subtle. But it shows that the sooner Irish women get the courage to leave terrible relationships, the better. In the election campaign, several inquired about introducing divorce. Meantime, I'll take you home to your mother."

"No, I'll see the Canon tomorrow. After years in England, I want a home, a husband, and peace, not divorce. It's wrong. Also, I'm older than you and glad to have a man. Joe will surely settle soon."

If that wasn't the epitome of suffering, then what was? Della stifled the urge to shake Laura out of her acquired submission and to get a grip on reality; forever bullied if she didn't stand up to the bully.

Della drove home by the swirling waters of the lake. When might women realise - as Nuala O' Faolain said in a Women's Liberation meeting - that men were helpful but sometimes useless? Laura's pursuit of happiness was brave and spiritual in her belief that suffering on this earth brought heaven in the next. Hadn't Della heard it all in the holy cloister?

With little space in her schedule the following week, she did not see Laura at home or by the school gate. The Linehan children arrived with a neighbour, but Della didn't think to ask questions. Neither did Laura come to the eleven o'clock Mass on Sunday, her usual. Were the children sick? Was she? Maybe the old lady, now failing quickly, was ill? Outside the building, she approached Duffy's car.

"Ann, what's the matter with Laura? Is she ill?"

Ann's voice lowered. "Best not talk about it, Della. Go when Joe is on the land, or he might run you off the property." Run her off the property? He was damn glad of her help last time. No, she was not afraid of Joe Lenihan.

Della drove out of town by the lakes, past the forest, and the pert gatehouse into the castle estate. The speedometer tipped seventy, then dropped to a funeral pace nearing Lenihan's farm. With the help of two barking dogs, Joe was urging sheep through a gap into the lush river grassland. He would be busy for an hour or more.

At the door, she banged the brass knocker hard. Time ticked by - an eternity on the doorstep. Not a sound within. Then she noticed the curtain twitch and a face peering through the lace folds. Della beckoned. The door cracked open, and Laura stood before her. Della stared, appalled, speechless, at the sight of the purple and black marks on the other woman's face.

"Oh my God, Laura, what's he done to you? Why?"

"After you left last time, I plucked up the courage and visited the Canon. He was sympathetic but hesitant about interfering. I pleaded, said I was desperate, our marriage in tatters. The priest then agreed to catch Joe on the street after Mass. I prayed while he was away that the PP would make him understand the cruelty of his behaviour and that he was destroying our family."

"So, he came home from Mass. What then?"

In broken sentences, Laura recounted the details of her ordeal. "He sent the kids out to Cunninghams' for the loan of a rope. Then, in front of his mother, Joe lashed out with his fist right into my face. I thought he'd knocked out my eye, the impact was so fierce. I cried and sobbed, but he kept hitting me everywhere on my body. And it was one o'clock on a Sunday, not in the middle of the night or when he was drunk."

"Oh, my goodness, Laura, you poor thing. What next? Did you run?"

"He shouted I was not to ballyrag him to a priest or anyone else. Joe Linehan was now a disgrace in the parish, a man folk respected for his voice and farming ability. I faced him and said I'd asked the Canon to help because he was seeing someone else. I took the letter from my pocket and handed it to him. 'Here's the proof of your shenanigans with a girl half your age'. That was the ultimate insult. He went mad and shouted that there wasn't much at home for him and that I was a frump. Frump that awful term again. He grabbed the letter and said it wasn't mine to open."

"Well, it wasn't, but what are you supposed to do, Laura, when your husband stays out all night, and an unexpected letter comes through the door?"

"He skimmed the page, stuck it in his back pocket, and said it was nothing, just someone he met at a dance.

'Nothing!' I yelled, 'a younger girl who says she loves you. Love? Sex? I'm not a mug, Joe'."

Sombre and incredulous, Della listened in despair to the harrowing account.

"All hell let loose as the monster launched into me. The children returned, screamed, and pleaded with their father not to touch their mammy. He was so fierce I just stood terrified. Then he hit me on the ear, left the house and went off in the van. He did not come home until six the next morning. The children asked why their daddy was so angry. What had I done? I couldn't tell them."

"After his promises, his desperation to get you back last time, Laura, he's done it again. Get out."

"I can't. Go, Della, before he sees you here."

"And leave you here to put up with that monster?"

"Go, I say." The urgency in her friend's voice moved Della towards the door as if she, too, would become a victim of a man whose temper knew no bounds. "See the doctor," she shouted from the gate towards the woman peeking from a barely open door, "and show evidence".

Days passed in mundane fashion, Della unwilling to call at Lenihan's for fear of igniting the beast on the hill. Then one day, she met Laura in the little shop near the castle, where folk bought random everyday goods for a few pounds. Inclining her head towards Della, Laura could not hear properly, still deaf after the punch. A thick layer of foundation did not entirely white out the blue, black marks. She described the doctor's response and shock:

"Get out, Laura, leave that man. He's a brute. I've heard about his behaviour on the football field and towards neighbours," Dr Farrell insisted.

"My mother-in-law is frail and needs me. She was distraught after the violent scene in the kitchen, and I can't have it on my conscience to let her die."

"Laura, your eardrum may have lasting damage. You ought to see a specialist."

"No, Joe'd go mad if someone else knew about him." She did not add that a man who kicked a faithful dog to death for driving a sheep through a hole in the hedge had no compunction for either human or beast. She couldn't risk further beatings.

"The children have seen and heard so much in their brief lives. It's heartbreaking. Tommy is the worst affected. He says he hates his father, wants to grow up and beat him."

"Violence in the home can destroy them for life, Laura."

"He's showing signs of alarming behaviour, sleepwalking, getting into scrapes at school, and being aggressive."

"A child psychologist is coming to the clinic next month. Would you like an appointment?"

"Yes, but if Joe finds out, we'll all suffer. Tommy is witless and might blab out the man's questions."

"Don't worry. I'll send you a letter saying the boy needs his knees examined. He plays football and has been complaining a while now."

"Thanks, Doctor. Tommy's conduct is a worry. The last batch of reports referred to him as a bully, is vicious and lashes out at other kids. Tommy says the bigger boys hit him first, but the teacher says he starts the rows."

Back home, Laura had kept counsel.

Tears stinging, Della trembled at the desperation in her friend's voice. Appalling how one man's behaviour could harm both young and old. She wanted to vilify Joe Linehan before the whole parish and report him to the Gárdaí.

"Laura, it's outrageous that you're cowering in your own home."

"Yes, but what choice do I have? Where there are men, there's power."

"A power rooted within the Church. Didn't we promise to love, honour, and obey in our wedding vows? But never mind the vows. Go to the barracks and report him to the guards."

"Never, Della. It would ruin our name in the village. No one would talk to us, and the disgrace would kill me even if he didn't."

While Joe Linehan ruled his kingdom, Laura's visit to the Canon proved how ineffectual priests were when confronted with marital issues. The Church preached God's love, but the State did nothing to support it.

"I'm powerless, Della. He didn't speak to me for a week, with no apology or attempt to make up to me. I slept in the girls' room, and sometimes Tommy came into the bed with us, and we all huddled together. Now Joe is distant towards me as if I were the guilty one."

Della reached for a hanky. Laura's suffering was unbearable. Why had seeking help from a priest driven Joe Lenihan madder than last time, and why hadn't he recognised his wife's desperation? Because self-assured, conceited, good-looking men cared little for anyone's opinion?

A couple of weeks ago, Della had campaigned for social justice in the country, for fairness and acceptance. Yet she was helpless in trying to help Laura escape the cruelty of a bullying bastard husband. Bastard. She wasn't ashamed to use the word. It felt good, her way of reviling him. *Thoughtcrime, George Orwell whispered.* Oh, drat his philosophical nonsense. Or perhaps not, in a society controlled by men as if a constant eye watched over women - a male eye?

"And now, Laura? Are you talking to each other?"

"I had to ask for grocery money." The shame and humiliation in Laura's voice made Della cringe.

"He attempted to offload his guilt by ranting about Tommy. He said 'That son of yours is turning bad, smoking and all sorts with the Fallons on the Council estate. And you've brainwashed him against me. No wonder he's in trouble.' I tried to explain that what children saw in the home affected their behaviour outside it."

"Leave, I say, and be safe."

"I can't take the kids out of school away from their friends. Yesterday I asked again for a small car. We could afford it with that extra money from the job, but like before, when I asked for money for shoes, it was the wrong moment. Also, he claimed I was a poor housekeeper."

"Laura, you're a doormat. But you have choice, with more qualifications than my religious knowledge. Worst of all are the beatings. You can't carry on in fear of being hurt. It'll destroy you and the children. Please say you'll leave."

"No, not yet. I'll play on Joe's pride. Despite his treatment of me, he wants the best for the kids." Laura's eyes roamed around the kitchen, Della avoiding likewise. "I've let things go, haven't I?"

"Well, Laura, ordinary things take a back seat when life is tough. But my anxieties die down a bit by keeping busy, and Ed is a stickler for tidiness."

But suggesting to an abused woman that she might be happier by cleaning was hardly reasonable. Laura would never leave. Neither would the woman down the road, the one in the village, the young wife on the council estate or the others....

CHAPTER 30

August '76 heralded in slow, sultry days. Golden barley, oats, and wheat drooped low in the fields. Sweet-smelling honeysuckle trailed over the grass along the hedges, and sloes grew fat and black. At the close of each day, crimson skies bade a lingering goodbye to the plenitude of summer. Like the corn in the field, sure and beneficent, Laura, Olive, and Della would mark time in little increments, waiting for their men to mellow. One day Ed would stop his 'benders', Mark rein in his wanderlust, and Joe quit his evil ways. A deus ex machina, something or other, would strike them where it hurt most. In the meantime, all three women had little choice but to live according to male whims.

Margie's journey through life, however, was unalterable. Della realised - again - she had not given enough time or care to her neighbour, just a few yards away. With the election campaign, the home, business and children, time sped by at an alarming pace, and Margie's nightly visits had decreased since the older Egans left. Margie went nowhere except to Sunday Mass with Peter and the spring well for water—her sole weekly outing. Sometimes, Ronan and Jimmy accompanied her, scuffing canvas trainers in the dust along the boreen. Jimmy said Margie paid more attention to their stories than their daddy, who came to life on hearing accounts of school fights - 'show them who's boss'.

Della likened Margie to the woman in Seamus Heaney's *A Drink of Water,* who gave the poet happiness and inspiration when he watched her and drank the water. Like two breaths of fresh air, Ronan and Jimmy shared football stories, delight in their dad's new car, and holiday tales. After Mass one Sunday, Margie bought two white plastic pails to carry water alongside hers. Not that they'd arrive back with a lot, their antics in the bushes resulting in less than a third of the precious water in the bucket. But it was fun.

On Monday, they trekked along the road by her side, proud of their contribution to Margie's water store. "Boys, you've saved me a second trip back to the well. Here are two lollipops I bought yesterday." Margie said, glossing over the small amount in each bucket.

"Gee, Margie, thanks," Ronan blurted. "You remind me of the donkeys in Spain with panniers on their backs."

"Off with you, scallywag," her mouth creased in smiles without a hint of annoyance.

Down at the house, Jimmy spurted, "Ronan called Margie a donkey."

"Oh my God, child, what have you done?"

"Nothing, I didn't" Ten minutes passed, Della shouted, Ronan cried and kicked his brother on the shins. The truth eventually untangled, and a grumpy silence fell. Della started tea, Jimmy disappeared to his room, and Ronan took out his toy gun.

"Ed, when Margie goes to the well, she's only yards from that man's house. I wonder if the proximity reminds her of her sinful state?" Della said at tea as the boys gloated about who'd brought back the most water. "I'm not saying she was sinful, but that's what her brother calls it."

"It's fifty years gone, Della, but I imagine it does. I've never heard her retort when he verbally abused her, not once. She just took it on the nose and got on with things."

"Country people never forget. Gossip passes down to off-spring, and stigmas stick. She's paid in full for her 'sin'. He does the shopping, and they eat a dinner of potatoes and a piece of meat, swimming in oxtail soup every evening. Simple fare."

"Margie knows no better and has never drunk tea in a cafe or a hotel. Della, you ought to take her out sometime."

"I suppose, but I don't want it to seem gratuitous."

Ed's affection for Margie, deep in his being, never altered. "It's all they both know, Della. I don't wonder at it, the same for as long as I can remember. Peter can be pleasant, but also ugly when he snarls at her. He's got a foul temper, and no one else can take the brunt of it."

"Margie accepts what she cannot change. He is her world."

"More or less. Don't fuss about it. He commands, and she obeys. We used to play cards in the house when I was a boy, and he'd remind her of the pity he'd shown her; a home, enough to eat, and so on. In return, she cooks, washes, and cleans for him."

"And waits to open the gate on his drunken return from the pub. But I've not heard her say a word against him. Of such stuff are saints made."

"Yes, Margie is a loyal sister. Some wives could do well to match her efforts." Ed buried his face in the Independent's racing page to avoid Della's scathing look. "Several races are coming soon; need to keep an eye on form."

Races - the word held dark connotations. Let it go, and it might, Della mulled.

One day, in mid-August, Margie came in, smiling and excited. "Della, can you drive me to Boyle? Martin Malone is getting married next month, and we're both invited. I've never been to a wedding before and don't know what to buy."

First cousins of Peter and Margie's, the other Malones lived a mile further toward the lakes. Margie had enough sense, Della surmised, to bypass the small draperies in town that stocked material, wool, shoes, socks, underwear, but few dresses or decent coats. Nothing smart enough for a wedding, and she might never go to another in her lifetime.

"Margie, I'll take you and we'll have lunch out." Della smiled, delighted to cheer the little woman and that Margie had asked *her*.

On Wednesday, she stopped the Triumph before the Malones' rectangular house. Once a tiny country thatched residence, Peter had, a year back, stripped away the straw and slated the roof himself. The building included two bedrooms, a small parlour where no one ever sat, and a large

kitchen with no running water or sanitary provision. Was
it Peter's cruel way of punishing his sister by denying her
a bathroom and toilet? The same conditions prevailed in
Linehan's, where another man stood firm. Like Laura, what
a difference it would make to Margie if she had a washing machine and a shower. Most days, her features oozed
grime, dust, and actual dirt. Della could only guess how she
might present a clean image for the wedding, with only a
basin in a corner and a rough towel on a hook.

But today, the sun's yellow light shone from a blue sky on
the way to Boyle, piercingly hot through the car windows.
Margie's eyes flitted left and right along the way, agog with
wonder at the sight of mature forestation on the King Estate
and the modern bungalows dotted along its margins in the
valley. Like the wind-up toy Ronan used to send across the
kitchen floor when he was little, she talked without stopping. Where did the money come from to build homes like
that? Good jobs, Della explained.

As they neared the town, the buildings became more
spectacular - the bigger, wealthier ones next to a golf
course, angled into towers, turrets, high walls, low fences,
trailing gardens, and decorative stones.

"Oh my, Della, you've got a nice house, but these are
posh."

"That's told me," Della thought, squashing new envy.

"Yes. That's Willy Ward's, the solicitor. Clever man,
beautiful wife. We sometimes meet them in the hotel at
functions." No need to add fuel to the fire of the older
woman's longing, her life aeons apart from such people.

They walked from the car park to Maura's Boutique in Boyle, just off the main square. Inside, Della asked to see the rail of wedding apparel, in which the shop excelled. She explained quietly that her companion was unsure of size and not au fait with fashion. Could she help? Of course, Maura said, pulling out a measuring tape.

"Now, Margie, let's dress you in style. First, your waist and length measurements."

"I'm five foot two. The doctor said so the last time I saw her."

"Let's see."

She was five foot one. Margie blushed, "Been a while since I saw Doctor O' Farrell."

"No matter, Margie. Most people lose height as they age." Age not the best word. But Margie did not care. Lifting her arms high, she fitted on dress after dress until Della picked a blue one.

"Yours for certain, Margie. It's been on that rack waiting for you." As Della would tell Ed later, the soft material wrapped around the tubby frame like a compliment and made the older woman look slimmer.

Margie handed over twenty-five pounds, took the bag, and walked out as if she had just won the Pools. Della added to the pile in Killalea's drapery nearby: Shoes, stockings, and underwear. Then, as Margie's cash store depleted, she stopped the spree.

"Time for a break and something nice. Tea, coffee, whatever you like." Della suggested

"I'd like a coffee. We never drink it. Peter only wants a mug of tea after dinner."

They chose scones, cream cakes, and coffee with cream at a table in Hanly's tea shop. "Cream makes a difference," Áine Hanly insisted.

"I feel like a queen, Della," Margie beamed.

"And you'll look like one at the wedding."

A wave of shame engulfed Della. Why hadn't she ever done this before? Perhaps she accepted the Malones as they were and had not thought to improve their lot without a specific reason. Now, as a guardian angel, she was conferring happiness. That such simple treats like a bun and a cup of coffee could mean so much was humbling.

An hour passed, and it was five o'clock, time to get back. "Milkin' soon, Della, the cows'll be waiting at the gate, but I've enjoyed today, thank you." Calm, wise and modest, the little lady sounded cheerful and trusting despite the burden of regret that overshadowed her existence.

"Margie, I don't know when I've had a day like this," Della said as they halted at Malone's. It was six o'clock, Peter's car in the haggard. Would he sound off because his sister was late? Sensing Della's fears, Margie said she'd put a plate of cold meat on the table covered in a cloth for her brother. After all, he'd want her to look smart for the wedding.

"I've *never* had a day like it in my life. Thank you, Della."

Tears tingling her eyes, Della slid the car down the road into the driveway. Ed was home and had picked up the boys as arranged. He'd also put a pot of potatoes on to boil on the electric cooker. How was the outing? Della filled in the details.

"That's something you should do more often, Della, better than traipsing around the roads begging for votes."

But barb aside, her husband's attitude towards the older woman was gratifying. Despite embarrassing him with babyhood tales, Margie's presence on the earth lay deep in his fabric. One story she liked to repeat - Molly's pride in dressing her son in pants soon after birth to prove she'd had a boy after six girls - brought blushes to his face. No wonder he's so vain, Della mused, growing up with a doting mother, an admiring neighbour, and six sisters cooing over the Wonder-boy.

"What's the word for doing good? Altruism, yes, that's it. You're practising it now."

"I'd prefer to think of it as shining a light into bleak lives."

"I hope they both enjoy the wedding. Except for funerals and the pub, Peter only goes to work."

All was quiet around the Malone house the following day. Ronan said a car picked up the brother and sister at eleven o'clock. With Mass on Sunday and the weekly visit to Leam, they would hear nothing until Margie came rambling.

"I'm dying to hear if Margie enjoyed the wedding. I hope he didn't drink too much or insult her." Della said on the way back from Reilly's.

"Wait until she tells you." Sensible advice, how well Ed knew the Malones and their ways.

Margie bounced in on Monday night. "We had a great day with an enormous beef, turkey, and stuffing dinner. Big helpings of vegetables too. And apple pie with custard afterwards. I even drank three sherries. I wish I could do it all again." Face aglow, the old lady's eyes sparkled under her bushy grey perm, her joy potent and natural.

"Well, Ronan's Confirmation is coming up in a few months, and we'll go to the hotel in town for a meal, Margie. Come too. You've seen a second generation of Egan kids grow up in this house."

"I'll look forward to it."

"You can wear the blue dress again and the straw hat." On impulse, she added, "Peter seems happier of late."

"Yes, I think so. He enjoyed the wedding and didn't have to drive. We don't do a lot, Della." Had he drunk much? Della itched to ask.

"Margie, you're a kind woman and have lived out your life in that house, working hard, both inside and on the land. However, you must rest more."

"I can't. Peter is slowing down. Age, I expect."

"Is he alright? I saw him coming out of the doctor's last week."

"Gets stomach pains. I tell him to quit the baccy. Rots the insides. Did it to our father." A fleeting flicker of anxiety crossed Margie's face. "I can't press him further."

September ushered in a new school term amidst a flurry of buying new shoes, trousers, and shirts. On May's recommendation, Della ordered a pack of name tabs from Gorvan's in Dublin's Camden Street, which her friend brought back on a trip to the city for art equipment. The Heslins lived on a rise against a backdrop of hills, and May liked to paint in her spare time and to exhibit at festivals and local events.

To the boys' embarrassment, Della sewed the tabs inside the collars. They argued that no one else had things on their shirts, but Della refused to listen. She had not paid good money for them to lose their stuff in the changing room and would also do their socks.

"Sports gear costs money, and you're both negligent. I've planned your badminton and basketball in the clubhouse, Ronan's football, and Jimmy's swimming lessons. I wish you liked the same ones to save me from dashing about in different directions."

"But they each get to compete in County championships, so it's worthwhile," Ed said.

"Yeah, but it's me driving everywhere."

"Can't be at work and home, so don't complain. I drive them to matches on Sundays." True, but Ed only did what he liked, albeit with evident pride in his sons.

"It's a lot of driving from a sports field on to a swimming club before an evening meal at home. And if you have a hangover after a late Saturday night, the chore falls on me."

"I bet you cheer the team like any man, Della." Clever.

Laura came on Saturday to watch the match, and together, they shouted aloud until their voices got hoarse. Sport, she said, was a powerful anodyne for many ills. It's the nurse in you talking, Della laughed. Anodyne. Painkiller. Well, she had a point.

"A chip off the old block is Tommy," the coach, Jim Shiels, encouraged from the side. Those with long memories saw in Tommy Linehan, a clever footballer with skills inherited from his father.

"Joe's might on the field, how he put the foot in when the urge took him, made him a feared opponent in football. I'll never forget his pegged boot kicked into my stomach and me vomiting into the hedge afterwards. A vicious player, he fouled when fury took hold, so I avoided him coming for me. So, never foul," Ed warned the boys.

As darkness fell each evening, night's canopy spread over the earth, allowing less time outside and more in bed on dark mornings. But with the onset of winter, that perfidious bogey, poker, emerged again in the town's hidden corners. Doubt, a close companion, was never far when Ed stayed out late, imbuing Della with niggling anxiety. Yet, in a queer way, the poker games provided a safety net; familiar, local, and among friends.

When Ed's chest began to wheeze and emit rasping coughs after long sessions in a smoky bar, Della tried to turn him on his side in bed, but, comatose and inert, his body would not budge, so she left him on his back gasping for air while she struggled to sleep. One night, she did not sleep in fear that his breathing might stop.

"You're smoking over twenty Players a day, Ed, and they're killing you. When you pushed the cases into the attic after the holiday, I saw you clutch your chest and lean against the steps. Your face went pale."

"Give over Della, cards, alcohol, now cigarettes. Do you ever hear yourself nagging?"

"One day, you'll have a stroke or worse, Ed, if you don't cut down on fags and booze."

"I'll never give up the fags until my last breath."

"Or they give you up. And please cut down on spirits. Those years in Scotland ruined you."

"Rubbish, Della. I never touched a drop..."

"Well, you've made up for it since." *Must have the last word, a triumph of sorts!*

"You're beginning to sound like your father, Della. Moralistic."

Was she? Jim O'Reilly's wisdom, Della respected, but sometimes newspaper reports on his outbursts proved embarrassing. Though well-intended, his 'sermons' came across as religious-heavy. A recent account in the paper made her cringe. 'This country is losing its Faith, Church attendance is falling, and left-wing journalists are coercing opinion. I quote from the Irish Press:

Why bind yourselves to a self-righteous Church? Ireland is part of the EEC and a bigger world where we can exert our independence from priests and bishops."

Della attempted to chasten his approach on her weekly visit. "Dad, that was preachy. You're a public figure, not a priest."

"Someone has to stand up for the Faith, considering Religious Orders built our schools and churches over the centuries. Without the Church that feeds the poor of our cities and towns, there'd be no education and much hunger. But we're sinking into depravity! Saw it in the States."

"Dad, you also railed against Saturday night dancing and late pub closing times but failed to change the law. People want more than a few dances on a night out. They want to socialise on licensed premises and to eat and drink."

"As long as I'm in office, I'll speak out against the decline."

"You alone won't stem the tide rolling across the green fields of Ireland," Della laughed. It was better to lighten the tone, or risk further pedantry.

"Prosperity is spewing up new ills. Hedonism. I call it."

"When I re-entered the world over ten years ago, the changes in morality shocked me, but I saw advances too. Most teenagers attend secondary school and have better job prospects. The Women's Movement will campaign for equal opportunities in the next election.

"That bunch of anti-religious fanatics. Next thing, you'll be supporting divorce."

"I certainly will. If divorce were legal in this country, fewer women would cower in wardrobes when husbands come in pissed. Sorry, Dad, no better word for it."

"To think you were once a nun."

"But look around you, see the good things, the advice you give people for housing and business grants." Lauding his utopian aspirations made her feel good, and apart from his over-effusiveness in public, her father strove to improve his patch. He pushed for schemes in out-of-the-way areas with little thatched houses along narrow boreens and for more amenities in local beauty spots in North Roscommon.

But Ed's suggestion that she was moralistic preyed on her mind for a while. Then, like a breath of air, she expelled self-doubts. His stance did not carry clout, considering his dreams of flashy cars, a thriving business, and a fine house. So, if Della wanted material things, she would have to deploy specific strategies, like boosting his ego with subtle propaganda.

"If we added an extension at the back, a larger scullery cum utility room for the white goods and the boys' sports gear, it would enhance the value of our property, Ed, and stretch it back further into the yard. Think of the advantages: no more dirty boots in the kitchen."

"It would cost a lot, Della. Not sure, what with expanding the works now."

"I'll ask my father to apply for a grant."

Easier than spice, it worked. The grant would come, but in the meantime, Ed could extend his loan in the bank. Excited, he said, "Johnny Caldwell will do the job. Best share work among neighbours."

Within a month, the room was at ceiling height. Ed warned the boys they'd have to keep it clean; he wasn't spending money for them to throw dirty boots across a white-tiled floor. His obsession with tidiness was pernicious; never a hair out of place or a sweater thrown on the floor, no matter how late going to bed. A shame the boys didn't follow suit, their mother said.

By November and longing for the last coat of paint to dry, Della set about organising the space to her liking. "We have room for the washing machine, dryer, and shoe racks."

"And my sports gear and the filing cabinets," Ed added.

"You mean the squash racket and trainers you rarely use?" Silly that. She liked it when he did something healthy.

But she wanted more than shiny surfaces and sleek cupboard units. On the pretext of buying new curtains for the extension, Della set off for Boyle to buy a dishwasher. There was no need to tell Ed, except that the curtains were in the sale and of good value. To the devil with recriminations afterwards.

Ed's voice drew her from the kitchen the next day when a white van backed into the avenue and pulled up at the front door. "What on earth are you doing?" he asked the driver as the man slid the machine down a ramp. "Nothing ordered from this house."

"Don't fuss," Della said. "It's our new dishwasher."

"You've two sinks, Della. Why a dishwasher? It'll drain the electricity." Ed gasped in disbelief.

"Your cost-cutting is a farce for a man who cares little about the price of brandy or Guinness. Think of the benefits, Ed. Instead of slaving in the sink, I'll have more time for the accounts. And that lump of winnings you brought home on Friday night will cover it." Wasn't she learning to parry objections? Or did constant confrontation create inner defence mechanisms? In addition, Ed lost steam when she drew grist from his winnings.

Battle over, he puffed to himself about money wastage and set about connecting the machine.

One learned, she told her mother on Sunday, to pre-empt protests. Bridie said it had taken her daughter a long time to learn. Years ago, in the mists of romanticism, Della's innocent self-believed marriage was a halcyon state of love and duality. Now, it entailed strategic skills and forethought.

"Sometimes," she confided to Laura, "I hate probing, subterfuge and deceit."

"It's being wily, clever, one step ahead. I know when Joe is lying."

"Agreed but love and hate are not so different. You'd have left Joe long ago if it weren't for that grain of love."

"Della, the attraction never dies."

Della reeled. It was incomprehensible that Laura still fancied the man who'd beaten her, left her unable to face the public, and threatened her children as they cowered in fear. An old saying came into her head; '*There's nothing as queer as folk*."

"Joe says he sees Ed in town most weekends and doesn't go far nowadays."

"Yeah, it's better since that episode in Sligo and the icy atmosphere afterwards. My weakness is that I can't keep up the animosity and always want things to be normal. But we must live as best we can. I'm a hypocrite for not delving more, but I'd rather accept his version of events than argue."

"Remember Olive saying that when we met in the Royal? We must get our kids through school, college or jobs and live in relative peace, even if that means tolerating faults. Only two weeks ago, Joe was looking for a lost sheep in the field as twilight fell. He heard grunting sounds behind a hedge, peered through a bush, and saw Lizzy Hunt and Mick Curley at it on the grass."

"What? They're both in their sixties."

"Yes, but apparently, he's been seeing her for years, and his wife knows, but she smiles in public."

"So you see, Della, there's nothing new about lust. It's always been here and will be as long as man is man and women are stupid enough to think they'll change them. All a sham, I say. Once the first gloss of true love fades, we sink into a state of acceptance."

What was love?

CHAPTER 31

One Friday night, Ed did not return from town. Two, then three, and four ticked by on the bedside clock. It couldn't be gambling; it rarely went on past two o'clock. Awake and alert, Della turned on the bedside lamp and prayed. He must be - she dared not let the thought in. She tried logic. Not again, after the Sligo debacle. Perhaps he'd crashed and was lying bloody and alone on the road somewhere. Torturous thoughts raced and chased through her brain. Distraught, she attempted calm. What? Where? Who? Oh, God. I can't bear this, she thought. But I can't go in search and leave the boys alone in the house. Her fear ran deep.

At five, she heard wheels crunching the gravel on the drive. Dim rays of sunlight pierced through the greyness in the bedroom. Dulled, tired, and tense, Della rushed to the front window overlooking the road. Below, Ed's precious white Triumph stood, dented and battered along the driver's side and bonnet. Pulling a cardigan over a frilly nightdress, she ran downstairs and outside.

"Oh, my goodness, what have you done?"

Pale and dishevelled, Ed elbowed open the door and eased himself out of the seat. Pain etched deep on his features as he tottered from the vehicle and grasped her outstretched arm. "Hit five bloody horses down the road. Didn't see them in the fog."

"You left here yesterday evening at eight. Where did you go, Ed?" Through the thinning fog, she saw a lump on his forehead. The questions could wait.

"You've bashed your head against the windscreen and might have got killed. The sooner they bring in seat belts, the better. And you probably have a concussion and need an X-ray. I'll take you to the hospital."

"I hit Cones' horses and slid into the bridge over the river. Must have passed out. At first, I didn't recognise where I was, so I sat for ages, and when it got brighter, I drove home slowly."

"You stupid idiot, so drunk you couldn't see animals on the road." Her initial concern was fast melting into anger.

"I'm in pain, Della. Drop the lecture."

Inside, she made tea and toast and gave him two painkillers. After that, he'd go to bed and sleep it off, and later, when the boys were in school, she would take him to Casualty. It was a blessing the accident happened near home.

At eleven, she found him awake. "Up. Time to go to the hospital, Ed."

"No need. I got looked over by the medic in Collooney."

"What are you saying? Collooney?"

"I hit a rock on the side of the Curlews on the way home."

"Curlews? On the way to Sligo? Why were you on Sligo road, Ed? Off to see those hussies again?"

"No. Remember, I had a call from a contractor in Collooney, so I went to see Gallogly, the group's boss."

"Why not tell me first, you idiot? I'd have gone with you and driven home. Laura could have had the boys."

"Only decided on an impulse to go. 'Twas quiet in town, no one in. After the bang, I sat in the car and couldn't remember where I was. I must have slept for hours. Finally, the guards arrived in a patrol car and took me to the post office on Boyle's side. The lady gave me tea, and I set off back."

"You'll be the death of me."

"Didn't mean it to happen. And I was almost home when the horses galloped out in front of the car. They came out of nowhere."

"Tosh. Nowhere. From a field, I expect. Cone shouldn't let those horses wander like that. As for you, it's home at night from now on, or we'll be back in the bad days again. You leave here to travel a mile for a drink but head off up the hills where you hit a rock, sleep in the car, get help from the guards and some woman, head home and crash into horses. Only you could concoct such a story, Ed. But it must be true, too far-fetched otherwise."

"Of course, it's true. Promise I won't be going far for a while. My head hurts."

Suspend disbelief, she told herself. Ed did daft things like no average person, as if an overriding thirst for trouble, or danger, call it what one might, drew him into murky areas beyond credence. And worse, he rationalised them. But this time, his story rang true.

November arrived without further turbulence in the Egan household. In Ronan's words, Ed's blue-black bruise flattened out, and he threatened to sue Tony Cone for damages to him and the car. First, Della said, he ought to approach the man and ask him outright for compensation. No, Cone was an arrogant type who would not budge. Ted Sweeney, the family solicitor, advised taking photographs of the car as evidence and sending a legal letter demanding payment or Court. He warned the process would go on. Ed said it didn't matter and he'd win. Sweeney would deal with it.

Soon, frost began to nibble on the garden shrubs and weave fancy patterns on the window panes. Darkness over the world allowed few glimpses of stars unless the air was cold and crisp. It was the month of the Holy Souls when, according to tradition, folk visited churches and graveyards to pray for the dead. On Sundays, Ronan and Jimmy delighted in watching the sombre-clad locals plodding along the path by the house. "Why are they going across our field to see tombstones? Where we play football?"

"Never kick the ball across the wall onto sacred ground, boys," Ed warned. "It's one of the oldest graveyards in the country. My grandparents and great-grandparents lie buried there. It's November, when we pray harder than ever for people in purgatory."

"What's purgatory?" Ronan demanded.

"A spiritual place most souls go to after death. Only those without a stain of sin go straight to heaven when they die. Purgatory is like a waiting room where souls get cleansed of all sins. Some stay a long time, others not so, but they all need our prayers."

"Well done, Ed," Della cut in. "Couldn't explain it better myself. But don't count me in for burial over there, mind. It's ancient and ought to be closed."

"Is that why the priests wear black at a funeral Mass?" Jimmy asked.

"Yes, but forget the gloomy talk of graves," Della foraged desperately to erase the darkness of death and black vestments. "Think of Christmas, boys. Write your lists."

Still, Ronan persisted. "So, if we go into the graveyard, we'll see souls there?" His wide-eyed expression said he wanted more. A thoughtful boy, any talk of the dead seemed to worry him. In sermons, priests talked about sin and not getting to heaven, which preyed on him afterwards. Della gave him leaflets on the saints and said he'd be one if he lived a good life, too.

"I don't want to fall asleep, Mammy," he probed at bedtime. "I'll see all those souls in that graveyard behind our house, and I'll imagine the ones that lived in this house coming here."

"They lived in the old ruin across the road in the orchard. This house is the new building your grandparents built. And if you're worried, pray for them. Anyway, only their bones are in the graveyard. The souls go straight into the next life after death."

Planting a kiss on her son's forehead, she added. "Think of Christmas and forget that stuff. We always pray for the Holy Souls, and you'll do it for us when your dad and I die. Now, don't go on about it."

Turning to Ed, she said, "I'll buy tickets for the Farmers' annual function. They'll sell out fast." A major attraction during the winter months, the event drew two hundred people together for a night of food, drink, glamour, and dancing.

"Sure. Go ahead. Great night, except for guest speakers droning on. They praise farmers for making headway and belittle the government for neglecting agriculture, the same old rant dished out, and we can't leave our seats to get a drink when they're spouting."

"Drink, drink, you poor thing. I don't care. It's part of the event and highlights our social life during the winter. We'll dance until dawn if you don't get too drunk."

"You can down a vodka as good as Olive," Ed laughed.

"But I don't nowadays. I learned my lesson by vomiting during the night when I overdid it. No point. But I'll talk to Laura and ask if she and Joe will come with us."

"Seems to be okay there again. I don't see him in town much."

"She's just ambling along, trying to make the home a better place for the kids, but in Linehan's they abide by that man's rule."

On Friday, no football, she piled the children into the car and drove towards Cortober.

"Is Tommy still seeing the psychologist?" Della asked.

"Once a month, but he won't open up enough. At home, he's irritable and senses my uneasiness when his father goes out at about seven in the evening, maybe not to return until the early hours. He begs me to sleep in their room."

"What about the girls?" Della tried.

"Both are nervous and withdrawn. Siobhan shrinks away when we fight."

"Yes, I've noticed her quietness."

"Aoife, the youngest, clings to me and has nightmares, afraid to close her eyes at night until the house is quiet."

"Time alone will reveal the total damage, Laura," Della said as a shiver slithered down her spine or an evil presence manifested itself. What childhood memories would those kids have?

"The school-day structure is normal, but Tommy is the most vulnerable. He listens at night until there's silence in the house. Only then can he let himself drift off."

"My kids, too, get anxious when I argue with Ed," Della said.

"You're the only one I tell, Della. But I can't risk him knowing."

"Rubbish, Laura, it's not your disgrace. It's his. I wouldn't be in that house if I'd suffered those beatings. But Laura, you seem intent on staying with Joe? I called to ask if you'd both like to come to the Farmers' dinner dance in December. I suppose that's out of the question now. I don't know how I'd tolerate the sight of the man."

"Thanks, Della; I'd love to go. Let's see in a few days. We're not talking at present. It's harder to move on. And I don't know if we can afford the tickets."

"I have them. It's an early Christmas present. You sound better, but surely you hate Joe? I don't know how you face him daily, clean and wash his mother and slave on without even the bare rudiments in the house."

And are still alive, she could have added. But that was the way, wasn't it, when drunks came home and battered their wives? Afterwards, life continued, and a veil of silence hung over their actions.

"Lizzie Nolan on the High Street hides in the wardrobe when Pat comes in drunk and only ventures out when he falls into a loud snore."

"Yes, we sometimes share our woes."

"You feed and clothe your family on a paltry income. Come on. You deserve a break."

"I wear clothes in fashion two years ago, stretch money to its limit, and scrimp so the children look clean. I ask myself about the love and the passion we shared at the start, Della. Doesn't it count for anything now?"

"We must keep it alive, Laura, and not let things slide at home. With housework and feeding animals, you're probably too tired to put on a face or change clothes. I try, and despite Ed's flings, a flame still burns between us two."

Had she gone too far? Even a friend should not hint. "Have you heard of Marriage Encounter? It's a Church funded weekend course for married couples who go to a quiet convent retreat and listen to talks on renewing married love."

"I bet they're bringing it in to stop divorce in Ireland." With that last comment, Laura turned away. For now, she would live in hope - without a marriage encounter week-end.

Two days later, Della picked Laura and the children up from school. She stopped the car on Carrick Road and let all five onto the hillside to play. Their childish laughter carried across the fields, down into the valley below, hollering loudly through the heather and gorse. Della pondered. How wonderful children could transition, on cue, from hardship and ugliness to being children.

She offered Laura a paper hanky from a box between the seats. It came in handy with sticky fingers in the back seat from the lollipops she bought in Greene's on the way home.

"I'd like to go to the dinner dance."

"You sure? Even after all that? You'll face the neighbours, the townspeople? Pretend you're a happy couple?"

"He regards me as a drudge at home in sloppy clothes, no makeup nor glamour. I want to show him I can be different."

"And you must buy a new dress."

"It's survival, Della. Last time, I wished someone would beat him up or even kill him, and my brothers might do just that if they knew how bad Joe could be. But this is my home, with no choice but to accept that Joe is volatile and bossy. We have children together, and their own house is the best place to rear them, not in their grandmother's while I go to work. I pray for the strength to be a good mother and a tolerant wife."

"A tolerant wife? You *are* serious, Laura. Violence in the home is worse than on the streets. Last night, we heard on the news that in the North, a young Catholic postman, Noel

McKay, was killed by the IRA on Finaghy Road in Belfast. Terrible things are happening in Ulster, and God knows how it'll end. But down here, we have men hurting their wives behind closed doors. Pure evil."

"It'll die down, Della, but I can't tell my mother anything. She's too old to carry my burdens."

"Yes, but I'll struggle to put up with him at the dance."

Tears dried, calm restored, they called the children back and set off for home. At the house on the hill, Laura smiled a watery smile and faced her body up the path again.

Driving homeward along the scenic road between the two towns, Della pondered. Of what mettle was the woman living with a potential wife-killer? Yes, she'd uttered the word in her mind. Killer. It could happen, happened and was covered up. But who did anything about it? No one in holy Ireland. A few months ago, a woman in Kerry met an unusual death in her home. The court heard she'd fallen off a chair, hanging clothes up to dry from the spikes in the ceiling. Really?

The idea of socialising with Joe Linehan made Della want to throw up.

But in an unexpected twist of blind justice, he received a warning from the law one evening when Guard Tom McGuinness knocked on the door and said his children had picked up rumours of Laura's black eyes and injuries. The guard warned of prosecution if trouble erupted again. Joe said drink made him evil, and he'd slow down.

But when the officer left, Joe hovered over her, trembling at the table, an unmistakable threat in his voice.

"Did you tell people about our business? Couldn't keep your mouth shut, woman?" In a menacing mode, he came close. She stood up and moved toward the door. "And as for the guards, I'll flatten the next one that comes to this door."

"So, the disgrace is worse than what you do to us, Joe Linehan? That your wonderful image is dirt in the parish. Do I care? No."

As if punched by a blow, he shrunk into a chair. "No, Laura, let's be calm. I'm sorry."

Sorry! Had Excalibur struck? Or something of that magnitude? The might of the Law more likely. "Sorry means change, Joe. I mean it."

Della heard about the apparent transformation outside the post office after Mass on Sunday. Laura spoke in a low voice, which, Della noted, sounded less whinging.

"See, Della. We'll be fine."

Fine. Was fine enough? The thought of sharing a life, let alone a bed, with such a man made Della want to storm Government buildings in Dublin, like a modern-day Lagertha leading Viking women-warriors, to demand divorce and women's rights. **Now**. But with an amalgem of men running the country and another the Church, both sets copper-fastened in the belief that Honour and Obey would remain the norm, what chance did 1970s women have?

The following Saturday, Ed busied himself counting cash. It was okay for Della to take the car. She picked up Laura and drove the hour-long journey to a new dress shop in the heart of Sligo. People came from miles away to this boutique; its owner, Josephine, a canny fashionista with an eye for the right dress to suit any shape or size.

"Joe gave me thirty pounds to spend on a dress." Laura, face aglow, opened her purse.

"Must be all the rosaries you say that softened him."

"And the Masses my mother gets offered in the Convent. Also, he doesn't want me to let him down in public."

Whatever it was, Della knew this outing was important and Laura longed for something unique.

The dance drew near. Della planned who would drive and what time to meet up for drinks. The possibility of a fun-filled night kept her going amid daily chores. Everyone would be there. "Ed, you'll sit beside Joe Linehan."

"Will do if you drive home. I'll take us all to the hotel. Makes sense, as you drink little."

"Sounds like you're preparing for a session. Just stay in control."

"Can't enjoy the night if I'm sober, can I?"

"This is when women dress up, so don't spoil it."

"Give over." Mood heightened at the prospect of a 'great night', he'd agree to anything.

Della took the boys to Leam to stay with Jim and Bridie O'Reilly in the afternoon. Ronan liked to watch the show jumping on TV with Bridie. She would point to pictures on the wall of long-dead grand-uncles on horseback in riding apparel, further whetting their interest. Afterwards, back home, the boys would nag Della and Ed to pay for riding lessons, but the only place that taught horse-riding skills was Cones, whose animals Ed had hit. Della surmised that there was bad blood between the two men but not between herself and the man. She would see.

The night was chilly, with frost in the air and warm winter coats wrapped tightly over filmy gowns. In a white, figure-hugging dress, Della glowed at the prospect of igniting old passions again to good music—nothing like songs to stir the embers of romance. Ed's appreciative smile before they left the house also brought a sense of immanence and expectancy. Later.

Inside the hotel, she appraised Laura, the other woman glowing and attractive in a velvet ankle-length maxi. Maybe she was right and Della wrong? Carpe diem. Why not seize hers if Lady Luck were to bestow beneficence?

Inside, Joe, Ed, Ben, and Tony rushed to the bar and ordered spirits, which, by tradition, they drank, standing while the women sat in the lounge chatting, glasses of vodka and orange in hand. Della sipped her only alcohol of the night, but the orange mix made her feel sick, and she did not need alcohol to fuel good spirits.

The meal, traditional roast beef and trimmings, dragged on for nearly two hours, prolonged by languorous speeches from officials in the Farmers Union. Della yearned to get up, dance, and jive to the sounds of her idol, Elvis, and to blank out all troubles, worries, and misdemeanours for a few hours. Besides, there was nothing like a slow waltz to recapture sleeping desire.

"After that enormous meal, they won't get too drunk," Laura sounded hopeful.

"I wouldn't be too sure. They swallowed a lot of red wine at the table," May said. "Let's sit down."

A half-hour passed, mingling and chatting as the hotel staff pushed back the long trestle tables and cleared the dancefloor. At the bar, the men ordered more drinks.

"Look at Joe, and his mouth stuck in a whiskey again," Laura said, her frown deepening into woeful ridges.

"We'll haul them out when the music starts," Della said.

Tonight, there must be no angst. At first, she'd barely responded to Joe when he tried to engage her in conversation across the table. But if she angered him, it might refract on Laura, transformed in green velvet, like a princess awakening from a long slumber. The woman who wore the same old trousers and loose jumper most days appeared radiant in a dress that complemented her pretty face and deep brown eyes. Della had insisted on eye makeup and blusher to contour latent beauty almost eroded by years of subjugation.

On impulse, Della urged Joe to take his wife onto the floor as the music struck up. Nodding, he led Laura into the first dance of the night. Few joined, but a panoply of black suits and coloured frocks swayed in admiration of Joe Linehan, a man famous for his old-time waltzes. The applause grew louder as their bodies and feet moved in perfect unison. Joe grinned; Laura blushed, embarrassed by the attention. Finally, a voice yelled, "Sing, Joe." Without hesitation, he mounted the bandstand and began, '*I was a wild rover for many a year*' to a chorus of voices.

Laura whispered, "We've turned a corner, Della."

"It'll take more than one night to rekindle the romance," Della almost bit her tongue. What had she blurted? But the pale trace of a black eye under stick makeup was a stark reminder of the troubles in that household and even more exasperating that the perpetrator was tonight, the centre of attention.

As Ed put his arm around her waist and murmured, "Della, you look gorgeous, come and dance," she let the Linehans flee from sight and '*Love me warm and tender*' swirl them along the floor in rapture.

Eamon Kenny's band played for three hours as the crowd sang, rocked, and waltzed. Partners changed on the floor, swinging, slowing, some falling in heaps. No one cared. Christmas was in the air. But when Joe's hand stretched in her direction, Della dodged it and grabbed Eamon Doran from the side of the ballroom. His touch would not make her stiffen in disgust.

By two a.m., Della, tired and the only sober one in the group, sat down to sip water and survey the scene in the room - a gaggle of forty-year-olds, and older, grotesquely plodding the floor in personal nirvanas, bald pates weeping, ties undone, shirttails out. Oh God, prevent me from falling into such 'seer' as Old Macbeth said. Women, pristine on arrival, sat nursing sore feet, bloody toes pierced by stilettos peeping from under hems. Yes, the annual dinner dance was a success.

Three o'clock came, the wives cajoling a bunch of drunkards to get home. They'd have to get up the following day despite the lateness.

"Ed, I'm tired. You'll doss in bed tomorrow while I go for the kids," Della urged.

"And that'll be a disaster, will it?" His laugh rose and died. Horrid, how alcohol brought out the old macho man in him? The smell of his breath on her face almost made her retch, but she could not lecture him after the smoochy dances and wild rocking earlier.

"It's time we all headed home," Joe said, winding a protective arm around his wife's shoulder. By the look on Laura's face, something good had happened between the couple throughout the evening.

"No drunken slobbering, Ed, and you're not having one for the road." Della urged. "He'll have a sore head, a sick stomach tomorrow, and eat goody for two days." A mixture of bread and milk always did the trick, not just for his stomach, but also for peace in the home. Then she saw a crimson stain creep across Ed's face. She had let out a terrible secret. A man that ate goody wasn't a man.

Ben laughed outright. Ed grabbed Della's hand. "Let's go."

"Serve him right," Laura nudged from behind as they stumbled to the car. The street was empty except for a few partygoers under pale streetlights. "He can't stop himself buying rounds, can he? I knew Joe had enough, but Ed and Ben can down a fair amount and get away with it."

Ed failed to get out of bed until late afternoon Sunday. After the third call on Monday, she gave up on him, got the kids to school, and headed for the depot. They owed it to his loyal men, who dealt with customers in his absence. It was their livelihood - and a good one at that; Ed's expertise was renowned in the area, and Della would not allow his weakness for the 'strong stuff' to destroy the firm he had created.

"All here," Don joked. "But we don't expect to see Ed for two days."

"You will if I have to drag him out."

Back home, she rang Laura on Lenihan's new phone, which was installed with money from the sale of butter saved over months creaming the crock. "Ed's still in bed, suffering from the effects of bad drink, he thinks. Too much drink, more likely!"

"Leave him there. He might want to head into town for 'the cure'. Joe took out a bottle of whiskey this morning and fixed himself a hot toddy with cloves and lemon juice. No poitín in the house, the quicker healer. He had to count the sheep and feed the calves, so there was no lolling in bed for him."

"You enjoyed the dance, didn't you, Laura?" Had there been, perhaps, a follow-up, a bitter-sweet confession-cum-resolution from Joe?

"Yes, to a point. But the amount of whiskey took its toll. He snored in a fixed position, and I couldn't sleep. At six, Tommy came into the room and asked if I was all right. I told him yes and that his dad would be nicer from now on."

"Presumptuous, Laura." But again, she ought not to have said that. *Her* doubts mustn't diminish Laura's aspirations. The Linehans were about to embark on the road to recovery, which might lead to that virtual pot of gold.

"He said he and Ed want to go to Lough Derg. And maybe Mark too."

"Oh, my God. Those three in Lough Derg. The Holy Ghost must have descended last night. Or was it another kind of spirit?"

Over the following weeks, Della looked out for the Linehan children emerging from school at three-thirty each afternoon. With the car window down, she picked up Tommy's voice across the schoolyard, loud and shrill, mimicking teachers to his friends. Siobhán stood silently and somewhat dispirited by the road, waiting for Ann to pick them up. Aoife, the youngest, was running rings on the verge. Their clean socks looked worn and thin, their shoes down at heel, but the girls' hair, swept into ponytails, was neat. Laura did her best.

Chapter 32

"I hate January," said Ed. "Scarcity of money, Christmas leftovers, socialising ground to a halt. A dull month. You get up in the dark, work with the light for a few hours, and settle into the night by five. The wind is bitter, and fog cobwebs spread across the bog."

"It's the power of winter, but I relish the quietness after all the money spent at Christmas and the parties. It would be best if you had time out, Ed." *Hadn't she learned to coax instead of nag?*

"It's bad for sales with no activity on the land, farmers reluctant to sink machinery into muddy fields, animals huddling close to stone walls for shelter, surplus cash in short supply."

Would he ever stop? Earth hurtled around in the same groove every year, bringing attendant colds, infections and sickness. But they'd get over it.

"Put up with it and stop whining like a petulant child."

"I'm off drink and cigarettes. Nothing to lighten the depression." Depression? The man didn't know the meaning of it.

"Think of the benefit to your health."

"I can go without alcohol, but not the fags."

"Agreed. Sometimes, I wish you'd have a puff - your temper's vile. Up before me every morning, prowling around, pulling out the filing cabinet to look at business projections for the year. Go on, smoke, burn out."

"Tax returns have to be in by the thirty-first. Ben came into the plant for a chat yesterday and reminded me."

"And?"

"He also said to keep sufficient merchandise in stock but cut back on further buying until spring. He and Mark travelled to Dublin last week for second-hand machines to offload cheaply. Better sell something than nothing. But they've both got secure businesses and rake in more than me."

How little it took for him to sink into a bad mood. In the past, before his intake of alcohol increased, Ed had always bounced back with new ideas. But now, his mood frequently plummeted, affecting the children and herself.

"Yes, but gadding about isn't how to run a firm. Mark should keep a tighter check on his employees, as Ben does. When the cat's away and all that."

"What you're saying is that Mark should monitor his place himself. I'm lucky to have Tony, Don, and Mike in charge. Good foremen."

"Yes, I'm saying exactly that. I saw an employee of his at home last week and spotted equipment stacked beside a wall."

"Temptation is hard to resist for low-income people, Ed. But paying employees decent wages is the solution."

"And itemising stock. We keep a tight ship."

"In the Civil Service, staff took paper, rubbers, stationery, etc. I'd heard our priest call it 'respectable stealing' at Mass and could never take the smallest thing."

"Shoplifting is rising, with big supermarkets spreading across the land. And you've seen me come home with a glass after an extension in the Royal. I went outside for a fag, sat in the car, and drove off. Not intentional."

"No, just drunken amnesia. However, I'll prepare the books. We're better off than the Linehans and many others. Laura only has the Children's Allowance for necessities."

"That's rubbish. Joe sells cattle and sheep."

"And keeps it in the bank for replacing stock. He's tight."

Since the dinner dance, the Linehans seemed happy. Della reckoned Laura's tolerance was that of a saint in waiting. Otherwise, how could she relegate to history the beatings, infidelity, and humiliation? Perhaps the solution lay in rescuing a man from himself. Laura was a wise woman, and Della ought, possibly, desist from pessimism.

Except for a card from the Keatings at Christmas, the couple had not heard from them. Della had duly returned greetings. *Wishing you all the best for Christmas and a happy New Year* - more optimistic than expectant. She worried for Olive and had picked up rumours in the town; Mark was here, there, everywhere he shouldn't be. She did not want to know. Well, she did, but in the present, relatively peaceful climate at home, she preferred to shun unwanted burdens.

By the end of January, Della was eager to share stories about the Christmas period, sales bargains, and other trivia. She dialled the Keatings' number, "Hi, Olive, all okay there? We're back to normal and wondered if you two fancied that trip to the city. The Gresham Hotel has an exclusive two-night offer, with breakfast, dinner, and dance?"

"It's good to hear your voice. I've wanted to talk but didn't like to bother you." Olive's tone sounded dull, unlike her usual self.

Della nudged. "Anything fresh?" A tiny probe and Olive would divulge.

"Mark isn't home much nowadays, barely has time for the boys, and it's down to me to take them to football, hurling, school, swimming, and just about everything. He comes in, dumps his clothes in the laundry bin, changes into fresh stuff, and leaves again. And he's been buying new underwear."

"Well, the sales were on, and I bought underwear for all of us. Great bargains in top designer stuff."

"No, Della. Not just designer stuff. Trendy, skimpy menswear. He's up to something."

How might she parry that? "Surely not. He's vain like Ed, two peas in a pod." Best make light of the underwear. "You both need some fun time. We'll do that weekend in the city."

"Maybe. I'll check with Mark when he gets back tonight and let you know. It might help to be with normal people again."

"How civilised," May remarked in the Gresham lounge before dinner. Ben, by her side, seemed uneasy. Ed sat sipping brandy in a black jacket, trousers, and white shirt. Mark, in black from top to toe, reminded Della of a vulture ready to swoop. Mindful of his performance in Galway and London, Della grudgingly offered him a seat on the banquette beside her. He must know she knew.

"I'm looking forward to shopping," Olive said from the opposite side of the coffee table. "We'll get to Grafton Street early and meet up with you men for lunch."

On the spot, Mark cut in, "I'm off to Ballsbridge, to the machinery exhibition. Coming lads?" Oddly, he had not told her his plans before she aired hers.

"Sure thing, better than dawdling around shops. Lots to see," Ben agreed. Olive relaxed. Men together were safe.

Della glanced at Ed - in his element with two of his best mates, Mark and Ben, whom he liked and respected.

"Let's have an early night, go shopping tomorrow, and be fresh for the dance later," Della said. "No late bar sessions."

"Agreed." Olive seemed relieved though jittery, her eyes following Mark when he went to the gents or wandered away from the group.

Dinner passed in a pleasant mood, with just two bottles of wine drunk. Afterwards, Mark suggested a nightcap at the bar, but no one agreed, and he had to give in.

"A lot of walking at the show tomorrow," Ben laughed. "Best be ready."

On Floor Five, they bade goodnight and headed to their rooms, keys jangling, light-hearted. "Too high for a jump off the balcony, boys, don't you think?" Olive joked.

"Stupid thing to say," Mark muttered.

"Perhaps we should have had another drink to soften his mood," Della said in the bedroom. "Did he say anything to you at the bar?"

"Nothing, though he seemed quieter than usual. Hey, you, get into bed; nothing like a hotel room for a bit of hanky-panky." Turning off the light five minutes later, she let the heat of his skin warm hers. January?

Saturday dawned bright and clear. Dublin on the eastern seaboard was notably dryer than the wild Atlantic west. At ten o'clock, the men took a bus outside the hotel for Ballsbridge. Meg said, "Let's walk to the shops. Exercise will do us good."

They crossed O'Connell Bridge over the Liffey, Dublin's natural divider between the more salubrious south regions: Rathgar, Ballsbridge, Mount Merrion, and the north side, where inner-city poverty sprawled upwards into high tenements and seedy backstreets of Mountjoy, and Cherry Orchard. A throbbing capital, Dublin had the best and the worst of urban dwelling.

"I have fond memories of Henry Street," Della said. "Couldn't afford much back then, but we often picked up a bargain. After work, I'd meet Sive and Eileen at the Pillar." No need to say Nelson's Pillar. Since the IRA exploded that blatant symbol of English domination in 1966, a proleptic fear of a Republican revival still lingered on Molly Malone's streets.

Della loved the city's history; her father, Jim, was born here, and across the street in Wynne's Hotel, her grandfather, a Wexford man, had, sixty years previously, been its manager. So yes, roots burrowed deep into this old Viking settlement.

"Stand for a minute, girls," she said, gazing down at the Liffey waters, oil-streaked and sluggish with city detritus rushing towards Dublin Bay. Memories flooded - of ambling home from the Department of Social Welfare towards the Grafton Street shops. A little sigh escaped. The famous General Post Office stood on the left, where Padraig Pearse and his men had died to free the Irish people. Born out of their sacrifice came the 1922 Free State Declaration, excluding the Ulster Six Counties. Yes, a great, noble city.

But they were not in Dublin to plough through historical events. "The sales are still on, and designer clothes down on Grafton Street," May said, sensible, despite money not lacking in the Heslins' beautiful home. Today, dressed in black, with a narrow velvet ribbon around her neck and long black suede boots that clung to her shapely legs, she epitomised natural style. Della, too, was ready for Grafton Street in a grey suede coat and fur collar. Olive in a white jacket with a smart fox stole seemed brighter in the morning light. Yes, they were all set for a shopping splurge.

From huge shop windows, massive sales signs beckoned to tempt and seduce the dense crowds milling through Dublin's fair city amid a cacophony of fiddles and wailing melodions. Cigarette smoke filled the air, mingling with perfume scent wafting out of Switzers and Brown Thomas. Here lay the very core of Dublin's 'fair city'.

"Let's do the shops first, have coffee, separate for a bit, and meet later," May suggested.

"Right," Della agreed. It would be nice to potter around by herself. The boys needed sportswear, and Ed wanted shirts. He'd given strict instructions on collar size and colours. And she'd surely find something glamorous for herself in her favourite haunts.

Three hours later, hobbling toward Bewley's, she cursed the kitten-heel shoes, making blisters rise on her toes. It was one o'clock, and the coffee shop jammed with eager shoppers.

"How my legs ache," May said. "Get a seat by the window."

"I love this place, a beating heart in the centre of Dublin. I resented leaving it for Galway."

"But you did what your man wanted, Della," May laughed. A happy girl, she viewed life in rosy hues.

"Not what *I* wanted, though." Images of the college dances and a dark-haired one drifted into her mind. Aborted too soon, thoughts of that inchoate love affair and possible absorption in literary enlightenment brought a sense of loss rather than shame.

"Here comes Olive. See what we can find out," she said. It was not curiosity, she told herself, but concern for the other woman.

Spreading a row of ostentatious, brand-name bags along the seat, Olive demanded service from a waitress. They ordered sandwiches, coffee, and cakes and relaxed. Then, without a prompt, she started, "I'm worried, girls. Mark is drifting away from me, living an alternate life, but don't say a word tonight, please." They waited. It came in staccato-like bursts, emotive scraps, and not her usual strident tone. Olive was lonely and feeling extraneous to her husband's needs.

"What do you mean, extraneous, Olive? Explain," May asked.

"I'm an unnecessary item to him. Mark doesn't need me in the business, which is fine. I have my job. I mean in other ways, you know, at night..." She stopped and blushed before two pairs of staring eyes.

May rushed to cover the moment. "After four kids, I often dodge going to bed simultaneously. Know what I mean, girls?" Her laugh, brittle and contrived, did not fool Olive.

"Late night secret phone calls finish when I walk into a room."

May cut in, "Busy men must stay connected with associates. I saw a fabulous mink in Switzers and must buy it. Down to eighteen hundred."

"Really," Della replied. "I always wanted one." An uncomfortable silence fell. Why had May stopped Olive?

"Right, we'll go together afterwards."

"Not me. I'm going to the Carmelite Church in Camden Street to light a candle," Olive said.

Two faces turned in her direction, and two mouths fell open. Olive was taking herself off to a church during a shopping spree.

"Meet you two back at the hotel later." The brief smile did not quite reach her wide blue eyes. Nor did the gold curls hide the dark rings visible in the midday sun.

"Why did you stop her, May?" Della queried when the other woman left.

"Because we can't get involved in their troubles, I want an enjoyable weekend, which she'll spoil if we let her. Olive is challenging at the best of times."

Harsh perhaps. Oh well, one had to accommodate everyone.

At 6.30, Della was dressing for dinner. A short sleep had left her feeling relaxed, and she was looking forward to the evening ahead. She brushed Ed's velvet dinner jacket and smiled into the mirror at the sight of her flushed cheeks, deftly applying mascara and eyeshadow. She'd go nowhere without it - eye makeup took years off one. But tonight was special: away from home, in a hotel, and later that big king-size waiting. Twirling her green silk skirt, she saw Ed's admiring look in the mirror. "You look handsome," she told him. "Not bad yourself, Della." Now, that was a compliment. Again came her mother's words - *keep up appearances.*

Although Mark seemed sullen, all three men were in good humour in the bar. Della willed a silent prayer. Don't let them ruin things.

"Here's to a good night, folks. Cheers," she said, raising her white wine. "We'll have dinner, then dance to great music. Nothing like a bit of romance."

"Good to feel young again," May laughed, dark hair brushed loosely around her oval face, her green eyes shining in expectation.

Olive's face reddened. "You three men are glowing like Christmas trees. Been tippling all day? A great start."

Della shot her a look that said, please don't. Olive's prayers must not have included patience for herself, but did she have to stir discontent so early in the evening?

"It was warm for January, and we were outside most of the time," Ben said. "Got the sun, too," he said, touching a red cheek.

In the dining room were four bottles of Black Tower in an ice bucket at their table. Mark filled his glass and swallowed the contents.

"Mark, it'll take a while to glean back the four thousand you spent on that machine," Ben said. No friction between men with similar goals. Tonight was social occasion away from their responsibilities.

"I've got a customer lined up already," Mark explained, filling his glass again. Was he drinking fast to quell inner tension or to nail his wife's probes?

"Better had," Olive said. "Early in the year for that kind of cash outlay, Mark."

Ignoring her, he refilled their glasses. "Slow down, Mark," May advised. "We can't drink as fast as you."

The first course arrived, and all three men were on prawn cocktails, the women pate, and anchovies. Calm descended, and over the next two hours, they consumed four delicious courses amid a low-key conversation about children, cars, houses, and businesses. Despite her ineffectual attempt to extract information from Mark, Olive shared jokes and tales from her varied life as a health advisor. She'd visited houses where people swallowed bread soda for bladder problems and took bottles of urine to a quack for skin rashes. Laughter rose as more anecdotes circulated.

By the cheese course, six bottles lay drained and empty, Mark and Ed more than tipsy.

"There's a dance in the lower function room," Mark suggested. "Let the party begin."

"We could move back into the lounge for coffee and a chat instead," Olive tried. "It's been a nice evening so far." The reluctance in tone, and her almost fearful anticipation made Della want to assure the other woman it would be alright. They were just six adults having a good time.

They sat at a corner table in the ballroom under soft, dim lights. Determined to enjoy the dance, Della said, "Let's dance, Ed."

"Not yet, stomach too full," he replied, but as if on cue, dreamy music wafted across the room from a quintet on the raised platform. Della took his hand. "No buts, Ed. Let's hit the floor. We came for this."

"Sure," he said, dancing their undying bond since that first heady encounter in August 1961. The lead singer droned, *Love me warm and tender* from the band: their music, their magic. But just as they glided onto the floor, a drink-fuelled husband zoomed by - spirits high, libido enlivened. Grabbing a pretty blonde girl from a partner, Mark twirled her around, then back to the man, and moved to another blonde. Well, he'd married a redhead.

"What did you do that for, you buffoon? You promised to behave," Olive shouted, her voice piercing through *Killing me softly with his Song* - of little relevance to the warring couple, well not the killing perhaps!

Della pulled Ed towards the table, where Ben and May attempted to calm Olive. "I'm dancing if you won't," Ed insisted. *No, not here,* when everything was good between them. If Ed were to follow Mark's example, Della could not counter the outcome, so she followed him back onto the floor on the spot, and they danced the number to the end. But the magic had gone.

Oblivious to his wife's high-pitched pleas, Mark continued his elective path to self-destruct. Eyes alight, he grabbed another woman from her partner and swung by Olive for the second time. Then, in one fell swoop, she leapt from her chair, lifted an empty bottle from the table, and hit her husband on the head full whack. He ducked, leered, and collapsed onto his chair. Olive's voice rose, all eyes on the scene in the ballroom. The music stopped. A woman gasped. Ben, May, Ed, and Della sat helplessly at the table.

"She's got a great swing." Ben laughed, his wit amid chaos, drawing a chortle from Ed. "A mighty woman."

"Olive's in bits. Stop him, Ben, Ed," May said. "How can you two laugh? This is a disaster."

Della cut in, "It is. But she won't control him. He's drunk, out of his natural mind, and Olive ought to know better than to cause a scene like this. We're watching a marriage die here in the Gresham tonight."

Silence fell as the band stopped playing. A burly man came from nowhere, took Mark by the sleeve, and spoke into his ear. Laughing, Mark grabbed Della by the elbow and leered, "How'd ye like to hang your knickers on my line tonight?"

"I heard that, you bastard," Olive screamed, hitting Mark another blow with her handbag.

He paused and stared at her through bleary eyes. "Shut up, woman."

Turning, she ran from the ballroom towards the lift. Through a blur of lights, Della felt the force of other dancers' attention. Embarrassed and furious, she shouted over the music to Mark, "How bloody dare you two ruin our night?"

Head lolling, he blubbed, "We're done. Me and Olive are done." Like a dark simian slumped at the table, his nostrils flared into battle mode.

"We've got to help them find her, make sure she's all right. Our weekend is in ruins," May cried, then grabbing her velvet stole from the back of the chair, she urged, "Come on, let's get out of here."

"Yes, but you know very well that tears and recriminations will follow," Della said. "I'm tired. We've drunk a lot, and I don't have the energy. You get to bed, May."

"How can I? Ben's taken Mark to our room, trying to sober him with black coffee. The waiter shoved them into the lift and offered to take it up."

Hours passed, as Mark recovered in Ben's room while May, Ed, and Della attempted to cajole Olive in the couple's suite.

"The drink went to his head. Never saw him down so much," Ed said.

"No, it wasn't just the alcohol. He wants to split us up," Olive sobbed, curls matted and damp around her tear-stained face.

"Olive, you can't behave like that in public," Ed insisted. "Mark would have calmed down after a bit."

"I agree," Ben said. "He's sleeping it off in ours."

"Oh, my God, and forgive me for using the name of the Lord in vain," May burst out. "Typical male, you are. She should control herself while he goes on a rampage! He drank at least two bottles of wine, careered onto the floor, grabbed girls he fancied and danced in front of her until Olive couldn't take the humiliation any longer."

"I heard him asking one for a phone number before Olive hit him. Give him credit. He's a slick operator," Ed whispered to Ben.

"I heard that. You admire him?" Della gasped. "Not your style, though, Ed Egan? More subtle, away from the glare, that's your way. But he destroyed the night for the rest of us. Would you blame her? I'd do the same myself."

"Let's hope you never have a reason." May's mild observation immediately brought order. Tired from excessive alcohol consumption, the arguments, and the time devoted to one couple who had ruined their lovely weekend in the city, they craved sleep.

"May, you've no worries on that score. Ben isn't flighty, but if it were a new machine, however..."

"Mark had the rest of a bottle of wine spilt over him," Ed said. "What a waste, and if it happened to my good suit, she wouldn't be around too long."

"Drink, lust, and jealousy are a dangerous combination," Della said as they finally got to bed in their room. Dawn beckoning through the hotel windows offered little hope of better spirits to follow. The night, begun with grand expectations, was now broken and desolate.

"Yes, but they're like fire and ice. Don't blend. Are we OK, Della?" Reaching across, he pulled her close.

Mark arrived in the dining room for breakfast as the clock tipped ten. He muttered something about a headache and said that he was sorry.

Where was Olive? They asked.

"In bed, we had two singles." Single. One word; loaded meaning.

Biting deep into a piece of toast, he clamped tight on further conversation. None argued; peace and distance the only viable commodity required to restore equilibrium in two, if not three, relationships. But Della could not erase the memory of Olive's features etched in despair at the inevitable outcome of a disastrous performance. The wire of fear on her face conveyed misery and deep sadness. Ed said Della ought to realise that some problems were not soluble.

"Agreed, but it's sad if only one partner sees it that way," she said.

"Della, the physical hopelessness of their relationship is draining both. Better to split. Let's get off."

Piling cases into car boots, they bade a quiet goodbye to Ben and May. No sign of the Keatings.

As they wound their weary way westwards, calm reigned until Ed broke the silence driving through Kinnegad.

"I can't imagine their journey home today."

"She'll accuse him, and he won't answer. They might resolve their differences if they talked it through."

"Funny what Mark said last night."

"What? Nothing funny about that man."

"That we should take up Joe Linehan's idea of going to Lough Derg in the summer. Scrub the pot clean."

"He can't be serious! A pilgrimage to Lough Derg to atone for his sins."

"Well, it's meant to. Staying up and praying all night, drinking tepid water, and having one daily meal of tea and toast. Penance enough for any man, I'd say." Della ignored Ed's laughter and his weak attempt to scrape off the scales of sin; a good idea, but not if they came back and started all over again. The critical element in the sacrament of Confession was the promise of amendment.

"Lough Derg is tough, but is it enough to repair that marriage? Does he want to?"

"Doubtful."

"Pilgrims tell sins to a priest who doesn't know them, go home, and revert to their bad habits again. However, that Mark wants to go shows he has a conscience. When you see him again, Ed, try reasoning for the sake of the kids and Olive. She's in an awful state."

"Their problem. I can't interfere. Marriages break down inside closed doors, but with few options and no divorce, couples put on a front, despite being unhappy."

"Oh, wise man, and why is that? Like Mark and yourself, men want it all: the home, outward respectability, and the freedom to escape at will. But is papering over the cracks enough?"

"I'm not in the mood for a lecture, Della. You should agree with me, considering Laura's position and what she endures."

"And also, what I've tolerated from you, Ed Egan. Your form of control was to flee when you felt like it. Take the Malones, where Margie's brother controls her life, and she, a single woman with no choice; but Joe Linehan's control is the worst. His sort - with the fist - is abusive and evil.

"Peter Malone was ashamed of his sister, and rightly so. My mam used to say that any girl who got into the family way outside marriage let her people down and disgraced them. Peter never forgave her."

"So, he punished her by treating her as a skivvy?"

"Better than being thrown out or taking the boat to England."

"Pious Catholic, Mass-going people dared to look down on someone who had sex when they were too young to know otherwise. Nowadays, men are clever enough to evade the results of sinning. If the Church has too much control, why, when Laura asked the priest for help, couldn't he interfere? They preach about sin, yet when confronted with abusive behaviour, are too weak to help."

"Hush. I've probably flirted with lots of girls, but no more, and my head is thundering from all that ranting last night, with another fifty miles to drive home." True, he'd never admitted to one-night stands when she'd lain awake waiting and wondering. In a queer way, the untruths were perhaps a protective layer.

CHAPTER 33

By the end of January, shiny tree trunks encircling the house shrank away from snow embedded in the ground for a week. In its place, mud and slush coated the paths, making it difficult to get to the car on the avenue. Della, wary on the road to school, slowed almost to a halt around bends along the narrow road.

Nights were cosy; the family cocooned in comforting confinement, coals bright in an open grid on the range. Outside, frozen branches sighed and moaned in the darkness as the last pangs of winter shrivelled the earth. Red-breasted robins hopped along the hedgerow, harbingers of springtime rebirth.

"Margie's afraid of breaking a leg on the slippery surface," Della remarked one evening. "I called today and asked if they wanted anything from the shops. She mentioned a few bits - far less than this household."

"Odd, they must need groceries, and Peter's car hasn't left the haggard in a long time. Worried about skidding, maybe, though he's a skilled driver."

"I didn't go in but glimpsed his leg by the fire. Margie said there wasn't much to do in this weather, but the look on her face said, don't ask, Peter can hear you. You never know with that man. Perhaps he won't allow her to call anymore? If so, why not? Is it my fault?"

"Only you can answer that, Della. Think back. Did you overstep the mark?"

"Of course not. But I'm calling again later with sugar and bread." Nothing came to mind, only that, again, she'd not been attentive to their nearest neighbours in the aftermath of Christmas, what with snow on the ground and minding themselves. At Malone's house, Peter's car was not in the haggard. Great; easier to talk in his absence. Margie answered the door to Della's light knocks.

"Della, sure it's yourself that's in it. Aren't I glad to see you?"

Shaking the wet scarf on the flag, she stepped across the threshold into the half-gloom of the kitchen. "Here's the few things you wanted, Margie but I see Peter's car is out. He's gone to the shops, I suppose."

At once, tears welled in the woman's eyes, spilling down her smoke-smeared face and into the surrounding fissures of her thin mouth. Margie ran to the fireplace, grabbed a rough towel from a hook on the hob and dried the wetness.

"Della. He's not well."

"Not well? There's a lot of sickness and flu around." The winter flu was a solid reason to stay home despite the terrible weather. But Margie's fear suggested something was amiss in the tiny house by the road. Composing herself, Della stared at the little woman's neck, stuck to her body, as the two boys, Ronan and Jimmy, often joked. Now Margie seemed genuinely concerned for her brother.

"Is it the flu that's hanging over him, Margie?" Della tried again. "They say it's harder to shift a bug in winter, with little sunshine and the wintry weather. Has he seen a doctor?"

Again, a flood of tears. "None of those things, Della. Peter's been complaining of pain in his side for a while now. Since he retired, it's worse. Weird after all the shovelling he did for the council on them roads over forty years."

"So, what did the doctor say?"

"Sent him for an X-ray to the hospital, and the result came a week ago. It's bad." A sob shook the little woman, moving Della to put an arm around her shoulder.

"Don't fret, Margie. Sure, they can do wonders for cancer, and I think you mean cancer."

"But he's been poorly for a long time and wouldn't see to himself, so it's spread." Della took the cup from Margie and poured a drop of milk from the bottle on the table. It tasted of scullery smells.

So the man who'd lorded it over his sister for forty years was now the source of her sorrow. Della pitied the older woman without modern conveniences, pulling cabbages, digging spuds, and piling turf into the shed. The only life she knew was her life experience, not notable in the eyes of an uncaring world. Now, she had no right to assume that Margie didn't care about her brother or had not forgiven him. She would be miserable without him.

Peter's car pulled into the haggard, and the noise made Della jump from the chair. How might she greet him?

"Wondered when you'd come, Della." Peter's voice sounded low, spiritless.

"I'm sorry, Peter, you're not well. If you need anything, Ed and I are close by."

"So, she's told you then? Couldn't keep a secret." A flash of annoyance crossed the man's gaunt face. "But thanks, we will need help. Maybe more so later."

When all is said, there was no more to be said. Della said goodbye.

Back in the house, Ed was furious. "You call on them more than me and should have seen the change. The odd chat on the roadside with Peter isn't enough for me to know his business. I've grown up with those people since I was a small boy, and I played cards with them, Ger Boland and me."

"Thought they scared the life out of you with their ghost stories?"

"Twas the same in all country houses. Nothing else to do at night.

"But you're sorry for him, for them?" Ed was good that way; old, innate loyalties rising to the surface when needed.

"Yes, and we'll do all we can. Della, you can never judge people."

"I've judged you often enough. Like Peter, you're not flawless. Far from it."

"But you always forgave me, and we've left the bad times behind. If Margie forgave Peter, we have no right to judge him either."

February arrived in a whirl of windy weather. A watery sun squinted from above, lighting new leaves, green and soft. In and out of the hospital, Peter lingered on, Ed driving him to Sligo for radiotherapy sessions or helping Margie with the cattle in the evenings. Two months later, Peter moved to a hospice in Ballisodare. During the following weeks, Della took Margie to visit the dying man every other day.

He slipped away one night and did not wake up in the morning. Della answered the phone call from the hospital and hurried to her neighbour.

"Margie, I'll take you there now."

"I've been expecting it, Della, and I'm glad Peter didn't linger on in pain. But I don't want to see him."

"It's your choice." Perhaps the sight of the man who had controlled and insulted her would only regenerate emotions she would prefer to hide? Or did she not want to see his body frozen in death?

In the following days, Ed helped Martin, the newly-wed cousin, make the funeral arrangements and procured gravediggers from the local houses. He opened gates on Egan land for the cortege to access the cemetery. He gave Ronan and Jimmy two pounds to pull weeds around the ancient burial ground entrance.

"I don't want to see dead people, Mammy," Jimmy said.

"You won't. It's only bones underneath the gravestones. The souls are in heaven." Would the boys ever let go of their fears?

At the funeral Mass, Father Beirne talked about the hard-working Peter Malone, who left behind a legacy of goodwill among friends and neighbours, hence the big attendance to pay respects. Midway in the pews, Della nudged Ed and whispered. "Pillar of the community. Huh." He shook his head.

Margie cut a lone figure at the graveside but did not cry. Martin moved close, and Ed stood behind with Della, a small bunch of mourners for a man who'd not made waves in the parish, only in his own house.

According to custom, neighbours and acquaintances congregated at The Royal for lunch following the wake, a long, drawn-out drinking session with Peter's former council mates. Offers of help to save hay in the summer, drive the stock to market once a month piled in. But Margie had plans.

"I'll sell off the cattle and keep one cow for milk. So why should I continue farming at my age? With the pension and Peter's savings, I'll be fine."

Della said she would take the older woman to town for the weekly shop and Sunday Mass. Margie's life was about to change; decisions to make, until now, sole responsibility for bills, her brother's domain. Not once did she utter a harsh word against her keeper for over half a century, but repeated, 'Peter did this' and 'Peter did that'. She would follow suit. It was their way.

Della wondered if some control was better than none, an anchor to which one adhered for security. Stories of captors bonding with their victims surfaced on TV now and again when police freed a snatched child. However, Margie's affection for a man who'd goaded her through life seemed inexplicable. At the peak of Ed's vileness, Della had hated him, a sentiment that, over the years, mutated into an acquired tolerance. Hurt, she surmised, remained deep in the gut, ready to rise like a snake from a pit.

Then there was Laura. Since the dinner dance, the other woman looked better, neater, and less frazzled. Once, at the school gate, she mentioned Joe was slowing down and on pills for heart disease, unusual in one of only fifty-eight. Though reluctant to 'do his father's work,' Tommy counted the sheep daily after school and helped spread hay bales across the field for hungry animals lowing at the gate.

Della marvelled at the woman's willingness to forget the hurt, the blows, the nastiness, for the sake of peace. What was it about Irish women that made them so pliable? It had to be their Christian beliefs and the example of Christ's suffering lighting the way towards an eternal reward.

Ed got the brunt of her frustration. "Why can't women understand that a nasty man is not better than no man and that children never get over the effects of beatings and bullying in the home?"

"Why can't *you* see that not everyone lives according to your standards, that people deal with their circumstances?"

"It doesn't make it right. Of course, I admire Margie and Laura, women who regarded misery as a path to heaven. I'm not disputing that, but it's still unfair. Olive fought hard for her marriage and lost."

"What's right for one isn't always right for another."

"I guess I'm proof of that myself. But if you had not toned down your wildness, Ed, I would not be here. Laura, Margie, and Helen in Carrick had no choice. So, they stayed and prayed."

"Told you, me, Mark, Joe, and Ben are going to Lough Derg to do penance for our sins. So, if you don't believe we've changed, I can't do more."

"Mark changed? Changing his wife for another model, more like. As for Joe, he won't be going anywhere."

"You just said that no one should stay in a terrible relationship. Maybe Mark is getting out of one? Shoe on the other foot, Della?"

They would never agree.

As Della waited for the two boys to appear through the secondary school gates one evening, she saw a grey Mini-Minor slide into place beside the Subaru, Laura Linehan at the wheel. Astonished, she jumped out and banged on the driver's window.

"Laura, you're driving a car!" A stupid observation. It must have been two weeks since Peter's funeral when they'd exchanged news.

"I didn't tell anyone until I passed the test."

"How did you persuade Joe to buy one?"

"Because he has hospital check-ups, cardiograms and the like, and it costs too much to hire a taxi."

"I'd have taken him, Laura, but this is better. You're finally independent."

"Yes, he gave in because it was necessary. No matter. It's heaven, Della. Finally, after fifteen years of begging, I have a car."

"Good on you, Laura. I'm delighted." Delight could barely cut it, but what mattered was that Joe Linehan had conceded a bittersweet victory to his patient wife. From an unexpected twist of fate in two women's lives, angels in the sky, men fearing eternity – whatever - had spewed incredible rewards. Did such a transformation as that of Joe Linehan and Peter Malone deserve forgiveness? The Bible says, *Forgive us our trespasses as we forgive those who trespass against us.* If the Lord could forgive, so ought we, like Laura and Margie.

After dinner, while clearing away the dishes, Della told Ed about the Linehans. "Here you are again, with no bubble to burst, no poor creature to rescue from an evil man. So, Della, the Christian teaching is right; turn the other cheek."

"You listen, Ed Egan. No woman should ever have to give in to a man, except by consent, either in the bed, the house, at work, or anywhere. And that's why I've finally joined the Feminists and will campaign for women's rights at the next election."

"You daft thing. We'll have every crank and drop-out hounding us from now on. Thought you'd given up on it."

"Only because there wasn't a branch down the country. The nearest office is in Athlone."

Ed looked up from the paper, opened his mouth, and closed it again. The racing page would not answer back.

Della placed the typewriter on the table by the window. When the ink thickened, it splodged the paper, and she'd have to start over again. Every person she might help, every bruise she might heal, every tear she dried might sap her enthusiasm, albeit sufficient reasons to join the movement.

"You can be a nuisance, Ed," she rasped. "And you irritate me."

"So will this. I'm going to the Galway races for a few days." His casual tone and bland announcement hit harder than a blow. Her skin tingled, and her heartbeat banged in her chest. Not again. She stood before him, but Ed, eyes fixed on the TV and paper on the coffee table, showed he would not respond.

It was weird that he should drop a clanger at such a time. In the depths of memory recall, Della had always sensed impending turbulence. It began when she started school as a shy four-year-old and struggled with the plosiveness of the Irish language. Later, with the onset of examinations in secondary school, the premonitory feelings increased, eventually rolling over into her convent life and its attendant suffering.

For days now, something unsavoury had crept into her wakefulness, which, from experience, suggested a downward spiral in Ed's conduct. Not that his announcement had great import for the wider world - no war or alien invasion coming Ireland's way, but his going off with Mark could again affect the fragility of trust Della desperately tried to establish in their partnership.

The Galway Races, the biggest sporting event in the country, drew thousands of avid punters, gamblers, moneylenders, gypsies, and, not least, socialites to the city. Aer Lingus even extended flights for ex-pats from the States and far-flung destinations.

"No way. Sligo all over again. We usually go for a day, Ed. Is there something else I should know?"

"Mark asked me to stay in the Seapoint Hotel for a few days."

"What?" Della rose from the chair, the book on her lap hitting the floor with a thud. Stifling an inner voice, she burst, "You don't have to stay overnight because Mark says so. Of all the men you could go with, why him?"

"He's a mate. What's the harm?"

"Think I'm soft, do you, that my brain has turned to jelly? I don't know what's planned. He'll lead you astray - again." Her emphasis on the word did not go amiss.

"Steady on, woman," Ed stood up, red veins on his temple bulging. "I'm going, Della. Understood? We're older, more sensible now." Strong and emphatic of his power, he would brook no argument. A moment later, she heard the door bang shut upstairs, followed by the impact of a boot dropping onto the bedroom floor and then silence.

Della lifted the phone and called May from the porch. "I'm worried, May. He'll drink too much, they'll dance late into the night, and the rest will follow. But nothing I say cuts ice with Ed when he wants to get his way."

"Don't worry. Everyone goes to Galway. It's a social occasion. They won't step out of line with so many friends there."

"Yeah, maybe, and many wives go, but he didn't ask me this time. Mark is a dangerous influence. I have no say, do I?"

"Mark, the tempter at work, luring and devious. But Della, Ed has calmed a lot. Try not to argue with him; he won't be silly."

Once again, not God's will but that of men would 'be done'.

The pending Galway trip hung over the household in the days that followed Ed's announcement, a legion of shadowy shapes and images impinging on Della's wakefulness. Ed's waywardness still infected their relationship. Back in the early years, she'd found addresses and phone numbers of various girls hidden in the glove compartment of the car, each one a knife in her heart. When, who, where, and how often?

Mabel, Ann, Cheryl, and Jackie - faceless names with massive implications - floated in spectral form towards her. Their unknown personas laughed, goaded, and pushed pins into her skin, threatening to orphan Della of all she cherished. Questions burned. Would Ed again destroy their reasonable stability? Her best mechanism now was to garner strength against possible hurt and the reopening of old wounds. Above all others: Bud, John Mac in Castlerea, or good old Tom Brennan - that man? Mark had asked *him*, but the delight on Ed's face told her he liked it.

One of Ireland's most important racing events, the Galway Festival, occurred in the last week of July. During seven days and nights, the great city opened its arms to all colours and creeds with a signal *céad mile fáilte*. Like New York, a city that never sleeps, gambling, drinking, singing, and dancing spilled onto the streets when the horses lay down for the day. Galwegians, proud of their unique Gaelic-ness, flaunted the mother tongue but embraced the strangers too. Win or lose on the racetrack, bonhomie flowed freely along the River Corrib towards Galway Bay.

But for the hardened gamblers, the racetrack wasn't the only place to lay big money. Deep into the early hours and fuelled with alcohol, players sat and stared at a handful of cards until they had no more cash left. 'Twas said that hardened card sharks dealt with the devil by night, only to stop for breakfast when the shebang started up again. Poker drew professional punters who lived off a duality of wits and wile.

On Monday morning, Della walked outside with her husband to the car, something she rarely did.

"Please do nothing foolish."

"I'm older and wiser, Della. Trust me."

"Trust you? Not long since you went to Sligo with him and didn't return for days."

"Did nothing wrong then either." Then, on a spur, he leaned forward and gave her a brief kiss, and for a moment, something abstract flashed across his face. He started the engine, lowered the window and shouted, "I'll tell you all when I get back. Keep an eye on the business, Love." Love? Smary or genuine?

"I'm sure you will, Ed Egan."

CHAPTER 34

K ids in school, Della planned to clean, read, and relax. She would not worry. He'd matured and was no
longer possessed by demons, leading him to terrible places.
And it would be nice to have a simple evening with the boys,
perhaps take them to the cinema for a treat. She was her
person now - not tied to Ed's will, nor bound by his moods.

Night fell, and after a brief hassle with devilish images,
she breathed out and floated into a world where only angels
dwelt.

Nine a.m. the following day, on her way home from the
school run, Della relaxed into a steady pace along the bog
road. She counted twenty cattle in the field by the river
before rounding the bend on the stretch to their house.
Ed's car was in the driveway. But he'd only been gone a
day. What on earth? Foot pressed on the accelerator, she

sped along the last half mile and pulled close behind his Triumph. She ran into the house.

Ed wasn't in the kitchen. Upstairs, she found him snoring on his back. Della shook his shoulder. "What happened? Why're you home? Lost all your money?"

"Don't ask. I'll tell you later. Must sleep." His green pallor and the black rings under his eyes showed complete exhaustion. Was this a repeat of the Sligo incident? No, a bundle of notes on the bedside table by the clock told another story - poker; tens, twenties, even fifties, two thousand pounds - typical gambler's stock. Lifting a twenty from the pile, she closed the bedroom door softly.

One o'clock came, but still no sign of Ed. Finally, he shuffled into the kitchen an hour later as she peeled potatoes for dinner. "Tea, please."

"Talk." Della dropped tea bags into two mugs and waited.

Ed's account uttered haltingly, was nothing less than cinematic. That, she would surmise when he finished.

The smell of newly mown grass, horseflesh, and perfume mingled and spread across the tightly packed enclosure at the racecourse. From a clear blue sky, a warm sun beamed down good luck on the hordes of racegoers milling across Lenabane racecourse.

Mark and Ed, careful gamblers who knew their sport, watched the odds change as the bookies roared their familiar tic-tac; five to one on the filly, evens on the bay, and placed their bets on the last shout. Then, running to the stand, they mingled with thousands of frenzied punters to watch the first race. By tradition, the field was large - up to fourteen horses. During the festival, some unfortunate animals would suffer broken legs and be put down, but the crowd would still roar and hope.

By five o'clock, Mark was three winners up, Ed four. "A great day, Ed, with a better night ahead. Let's get back to the hotel, have dinner, then hit the Great Southern for some action." The landmark hotel in the city centre was *the* place during race week.

"By action, Mark, you mean dancing, drinking, pretty girls luring us into God knows what."

"Sure, Ed. You up for it?"

Ed harboured no doubts. After all, he'd indulged in it more often than he wanted to recall. And he would *not* let himself fall back on errant ways. Della's words, 'If not for me, for the kids,' clung like a leech to his brain.

But as they finished the meal, an unforeseen peripeteia entered the fray. Francie Donlon, the hotelier who'd grown up in Ed's hometown, approached the table and whispered in Ed's ear. "Like a game of poker? There's a heavy one starting in the back. I heard you're a frequent Classics winner." The Classics were day-long poker games that raised large amounts of money for charity.

Should he? Maybe for a couple of hours. Nodding to Francie, he asked if Mark could come too.

"Not my scene, Ed, horses, yes, cards, no. Too much of a risk. I'm disappointed you're staying here. We'd have fun." Mark's crestfallen expression triggered unexpected guilt in

Ed as he turned to follow the oily-skinned proprietor along a shadowy corridor to a room at the back of the hotel.

A single, dim light dangled from the ceiling in a compact space for the group around a centre table. Narrowing his eyes, Ed adjusted to the dimness and the smoke filtering upwards from the bent forms of six people: one woman and five men. He judged all were card sharks, drinking brandy and whiskey, while dragging long pulls from ash-tipped fags. The woman, he guessed, was a hard-nosed, liquor-loving type used to big games. Not a pretty sight. Her witch-like long red talons glistened under the yellow light, and a false tan etched into the cracks on her face like putty on a windowsill. Could she drink? Boy, yes, downing a brandy in one gulp - of such that frequented casinos worldwide.

In Monte Carlo, on a week's holiday once, Della wouldn't let him gamble the holiday fund. Out of his league, she'd said. But he'd never since experienced anything like the atmosphere. As he sat in the empty chair, a wave of apprehension engulfed him - no lads here, alone among serious gamblers who cared little about big stakes or losses.

One man looked at Ed with a sneer on his face. Another swarthy guy he recognised from the local press was a well-known horse trainer. Ed breathed out. He was in deep - not Ant's place, after hours, with Bud on one side and Brian Mullins on the other, best friends, taking home a few twenties.

Dear God, should he go now? Della would go ballistic if he arrived home with nothing. He brushed the thought aside - he could always talk himself out of a corner. But this was the real McCoy! And he'd only had a pint or two - and with a clear head, must hold his own in the game. A wad of notes bulged from the woman's open handbag between her knees. Ed was among shady characters, unlike any table before now. An argument was in full swing.

"That bastard must've scarpered. Ten minutes since he went to the bar for drinks." The swarthy one glowered, his face flushed into deep purple swollen veins. Ed twisted the ring on his finger and swallowed. He gathered from the swearing that a guy had left the room with six hundred quid of their winnings. He'd stuffed the notes into his pocket and escaped. Hence the grim mood. Ed steeled himself and assumed a stony face. Like the lads back home, this lot would not fathom his intentions or hand of cards. Then, with a forced smile, he said, "I'm in."

The game opened at a tenner dealer and developed into an 'all in' within half an hour. This session would not finish before someone won high stakes - or lost. A trickle of sweat ran down his back. He couldn't afford to lose a sizeable sum. *They* could; the horsey, moneyed class, his turnover minimal to these people.

Time passed; his luck held. Two Aces and a Queen kicker as a decoy. He bought another pair of Queens for a Lady House. The betting started with one grim-faced guy laying fifty quid, then another doubling it. Ed checked the pot on the table and bet approximately five hundred. He must have the best hand at the table. Chest out, he threw in the decoy Queen. It worked, and he 'saw' his five hundred. Luckily, his Lady House won the game. He glanced at his watch. One a.m. Too late to leave. He must have well over two thousand but couldn't count it.

The group continued to down the brandy, their heads ever droopier and shoulders slouched. The drink was taking over, and the swarthy one was losing despite being a hardened gambler. Ed had to get out. These big-timers travelled across the country from one racecourse to the next.

A flash of light filled the room. A thunderous bang shook the building. Smoke filled the space. The light died. A strong, acrid smell shot up Ed's nostril - smothering, overpowering. He heard choking, gasping for air, and pinching his nose, grabbed the pile of notes from the table and slid through the door. Fumbling towards a back entrance, he reached the toilet and crawled through the tiny window. It was four a.m. He saw police cars, lights flashing.

"What happened?" Ed asked an officer. "I want to get to my car around the back."

"An incendiary bomb blew up in the front bar. Paramilitaries targeting the money bags, we suspect. Keep back. The bar was empty, and no one hurt."

The Triumph was intact. He turned on the ignition and drove towards the Salthill Hotel as if the devil were on his tail. He took the lift and entered the hotel room without stopping for breakfast, ready to sink into unconsciousness. But in the other twin bed, he saw two bodies, Mark's and a woman's. "Mark, who ees eet?" a voice asked in a foreign accent. Two heads rose from the pillow.

"Mark, who's this?"

"Helena, a girl I met in The Skylon last year. I'm leaving Olive, and we're setting up home together in Castlerea."

Shocked? Nothing could shock him after the night's film noir.

Succumbing to the freshness of the sheets, he said, "Please yourself, Mark." He would sleep for an hour and head home. The fun had died, and his respect for the other man evaporated. He would tell Della and clear his conscience.

"Ed, try to understand. It's been over for ages. We fight, and it's not good for the kids."

"But breaking up your marriage is? Mark, I've been tempted, left my tracks across Dublin in the past. But flings are not real. Think." That the female in the bed heard didn't matter. After the intensity of the night, nothing mattered.

"See you on Sunday night," Mark tried.

Ed left the room, overnight bag in hand, and closed the door behind him.

The poker players, piles of cash on the table, his winnings stuffed into a pocket, and his genuine fear passed before Della's eyes like scenes from a movie - a Wild West black and white horse opera with cards, smoke, booze, and rugged cowboys. His report, concise and honest, left no room for embellishments. Ed was telling it as it had happened. And, unlike past occasions when he'd tested her trust, the narrative fitted.

"You leave here, a quiet country town, and within a few hours, get into all sorts. That lot could have lynched you."

"Killed in the blast, more like." His tone and incredible pride in his achievements oozed delight in having both won at the card table and escaped danger. "But there's more. Mark is leaving Olive."

Della felt her face blanch. Like a mere addendum to a business letter, his last sentence cut through the euphoric atmosphere in the kitchen. But for once, he'd recounted something in its entirety.

"That's too much to take in right now. An IRA bomb, Mark's bombshell - which is worse? Or that life goes on uproariously in one part of the country when hunger strikes in the North wreak tragedy among its people?"

"It's the honourable thing for Mark. Don't ring Olive because she'll wonder why I'm at home and he's not. But, Della, promise you won't interfere."

"No. Not yet. God knows the poor woman will need support. But I will tell May. She and Ben should hear about it."

The situation was grave. What could any of them do to stop an errant husband from leaving his wife? Notwithstanding their flawed union, Olive would not expect Mark to walk out on his family. Men had affairs, formed liaisons, were hypocrites, and lived parallel lives within a changing Ireland. But they rarely left home or their marriage. It was easier to stay and have fun elsewhere. Women suspected but accepted, just as she and Laura had - to prevent family disintegration.

Della phoned May and described Mark's behaviour in Galway. Considering his performance in Dublin, the other woman said she was not surprised. "But it's not our place to ruin her life."

"Ask Ben to reason with Mark first. He'd do a better job than Ed. Say the cost of running two homes would be an enormous burden."

"Financially, he can afford it. So let's keep out of it for the present. Wait until Olive rings us." May's caution sounded sensible.

"We have to support her when he goes. With late boozing sessions in every town, wives at home with kids, and unattached women prowling for prey, it's no wonder men stray like wild animals. But their actions leave a trail of tragedy behind. I should know."

"Right, Della. But your stubbornness kept the marriage intact when Ed went off the rails. We all wondered how you did it."

"I couldn't give up on him. I'd left behind my dream of a career in Dublin, and of someone else to marry him, so I had to make the sacrifice pay. But feelings change, and they are never the same once they destroy that special part of you."

"I blame it on the declining influence of the Church. Nothing is sin anymore." Sin - that obscure word again. Della could have added 'and money'. Too much to squander made a difference.

The phone rang on Friday night. Olive sobbed. "Della, help. Mark's gone off with someone called Helena. Get Ed to talk to him. I can't let him leave us."

She had hyped herself up for this. "Do nothing now, Olive. Give him space. He hasn't been happy." She stopped - too much.

"So why didn't you warn me? Or tell me Ed came back from Galway on Tuesday?"

Gosh, how to answer that? "He'd been up all night playing cards and shattered, so he went straight to bed. Olive, we knew nothing until Mark told Ed in Galway." To divulge more would only make the suffering worse, but as the sobbing and choking sounds on the line continued, she said, "Hold tight, Olive. I'll come and see you."

Driving fast on the main Carrick, Boyle road gave her time to think and plan. What could she say? Mark had gone. Olive wouldn't get him back. Perhaps she should maintain his presence in the family for the children's sake. Daft idea, and on second thoughts, demeaning, but Della had to construe something.

She swerved around the circular frontage at the house and parked near the exit. Inside, Olive's tears had dried, her mood now enraged. Punching a cushion, she shouted, shrill and hysterical, "Why didn't you tell me Mark was leaving me?"

"Because I, we, did not know."

Olive blubbered, "He's setting up house with a woman he met in Dublin last year. I knew all those weekend trips when most premises were closed were suspicious. He'd give me excuses about getting into machinery depots early on Saturday. All rubbish, but he was plausible."

"Well, at least he's honest with you now." Trite, but useless.

"Honest? After sixteen years of marriage, I'd call it a betrayal. I introduced Mark to influential people who helped start his business in the early days. My father bought the first premises before we moved here."

"He's the children's father and must play his part. The site is only a mile away, and Mark will be there most days."

Tears spurted down Olive's distorted face. "But I still love him, Della." Despite their rows, Olive loved Mark, even if he no longer felt the same. "I'd be better off as a widow and more respectable."

"You don't mean that."

She did. "In mid-forties, I lose my husband, won't get another - don't want one. I would probably get a bastard. A shame they didn't go to Lough Derg after all. Telling his sins to a priest would have set him straight."

"Time ran out, but I'm not sure it would have made a difference. Let him see the new Olive, the woman he wants to keep in his life. You've had the sex, the passion, and, truthfully, was it that good? Or just a charade?"

"You do rub in the salt, Della Egan. Not sure if I want to hear your advice."

"In that case, I'll leave. When you have time, ring me."

Too outspoken you are, girl, Bridie O'Reilly used to say, and this was one of those times Della had said the wrong thing.

On the road to Carrick, she detoured towards Cortober. She'd call on Laura and tell her about Olive. In the past, Della had reneged on speaking about their socialising, weekends away, and interaction with other couples. But the Linehans were jogging on, in Ed's words, more settled, happier, and at peace. A regular act in Hanafin's bar, Joe drew numbers of ageing men and women who liked to sing along with his long-winded verses of old ballads. Joe Linehan was the star on Saturday nights. And Laura drove him back and forth - to the market in Boyle, where he continued to sell fine breeds of sheep, to the church on Sundays and the pub on Fridays. A man could never miss a Friday, or they'd say he was a goner.

But Joe's health was flagging - on medication for heart, lungs, and blood pressure. Only the previous week, Laura confided, "I'm grateful we got the two girls in uni, Della - now that Joe isn't able to do much in the fields."

"And both qualified for grants."

"My biggest relief is that Tommy stayed on the land, considering his resentment towards Joe."

"Tommy's a fine lad." If Laura knew folk considered Tommy Linehan a jack-the-lad like his father, she never said so.

"He's earning a decent income as a plumber and manages the farm on the side."

"How did you handle that?"

"Got Joe to sign over the property to his only son."

"There was a time, Laura, when it did not seem possible, or that Mark Keating would run off with a younger woman, while in Malone's, a cruel tyrant left the world to meet his Maker. In ours, an unspoken truce reigns."

"Men who indulge themselves destroy wives, children, in-laws, and even friendships. Vanity, excessive drinking, gambling, and sex are the devil's tools. I want a society where girls like Margie keep their babies and can hold up their heads."

"The fight for equality is just beginning. But I'm not sure Ireland will accept divorce or abortion."

"Don't mention that word, Della. I truly hope the Irish government will never legalise it. And I'm against divorce, too. I saw it in England - rushing into it without thought. Neither Joe nor Ed wanted to end their marriages or disgrace themselves."

"No, just to rule their roosts however they wanted. But surely you'd want divorce legalised, Laura? After all you've been through? Black eyes, swollen face, cracked ribs, tears and suffering in the house. Surely breaking up is better than that?"

"But who'd look after Joe if I'd left? He needs me, Della."

A flicker of pride and embarrassment briefly shadowed Laura's face. If tending to an ailing man constituted happiness, she, like Margie, was doing right by the man who had abused her. Biting her lip, Della let the sentence find its way inside herself. No amount of regret should erase the hurt, humiliation, black marks, stomach punches, or tears. Or, in her case, anxiety, sleepless nights waiting for the sound of *his* car...

Chapter 35

They buried Joe Linehan one bitter February day. He flagged, complained and deteriorated during the two final years on Earth. The mattress was hard, his leg hurt and the sheets were sticky. Despite his temper outbursts, Laura kept vigil, stayed up to tend to his needs, turned him around, and eased the pain with an extra pillow. She knew how to manage him - had the training - those who'd suffered verbal abuse from his mouth marvelled at the woman and her dignity. As the end approached and Joe's breathing laboured, Laura drew the family around the bed and prayed the rosary for the soul of her husband of fifty years.

In the graveyard, Della watched Laura dab tears from her eyes as they lowered the coffin into the ground. What was going through the widow's mind? Regret for marrying a bully who terrorised the family and rejected her? Or natural sadness for a once hopeful girl, fresh from London, who had survived the rawness of coercion to stand proud and erect amid her three children. Tommy's protective arm across his mother's shoulders conveyed his respect and care for her, the two girls a little less emotion. Laura's face - deathly pale during Mass, appeared swollen and crepe-like with grief. Parishioners and relatives clustered in true Irish fashion to press the flesh, kiss her damp cheeks, and to console.

"It's like watching a Shakespearean tragedy."

"What do you mean?" Ed queried - his knowledge of Shakespeare a pitiful zero.

"The good often die in his plays, the wicked survive, but in this case, the wicked died."

"Joe wasn't wicked. Keep your voice down."

"Typical man, you forget the beatings he gave her, the dog he kicked to death, the neighbours he cursed over mairns, and the boot in your face during football."

"And you should forget, Della. The Linehans did."

Vengeance is mine, says the Lord. Yes, according to the Old Testament, but not in the Gospels where Christ said, 'Forgive others as I have forgiven you'. And had she not closed her mind to her own husband's frailties? Not quite, but when resentment wormed deep into her guts, Della busied herself, hither and thither - anywhere to decompound the bitterness. Like Melanie Hamilton's in Gone with the Wind, Laura's piety never quite found a twin soul in Della Egan.

It's 1986. Ronan runs the business alongside his father, shares responsibility with his dad, buys machinery, and travels abroad to view new models. Jimmy is a civil servant in the city, working a stable job. Della did not encourage him initially, her memories of dull days in Records still strident. Ronan has a house in the town, a pleasant white two-storey, extended since settling down with his partner, Naomi. She does not see them at Mass but says little - their conscience, their souls.

Della meets friends between golf, swimming, and flower arranging. She still hopes to take a course in interior design but can't find a space in her life.

Regular as the clock on the wall, she calls to the O'Reilly's every week. Eve, who manages the farm and the quarry, now looks after the old pair, feebler now. She married Ned, and they have four children.

Wednesday, four-thirty. Della parks outside the white bungalow on the edge of Boyle. She *will* lift Olive's spirits. "Looking good today, Olive." The other woman brightens, allowing the lie to chase the haggard expression and soften the fine lines from her blue eyes.

"Lots to tell you, Della," Olive said. "Hope you're not in a hurry."

Together, they put out cups, saucers, and biscuits. "Mark came yesterday and took me shopping," she says, edging into a comfortable position at the table. "He still cares about me." That one word, *cares,* carries depth. He lives with someone else, but Mark *cares.*

"That's nice," Della replies in empty acceptance of a shaky situation.

They chat about everything and nothing. An hour passes. Della looks at the clock. Olive starts another conversation and doesn't want her to leave. They exchange tittle-tattle.

Della is careful not to compare lifestyles. Egans' golf functions, shopping trips, and jaunts are inappropriate topics for the sick woman to absorb. But Olive likes the gossip, especially the juicy bits about suspected affairs - ironic considering her present existence.

"A shame you don't join us, Olive, in the Royal on Sundays."

The remark falls away, ignored. "Mark's birthday is next month. I'm having a party here with the children. Can you two come along, Della?"

"Yes, we will."

How can they not come? Despite the farcical element, the occasion has enormous implications for Olive. And who could deny her a brief speck of happiness? Poor woman, holding a family celebration for the man who'd left her for a younger woman. Della and Ed had met Helena several times - difficult to avoid in their circle of friends but strange and uncomfortable. However, sharing a birthday party with him and his first and only wife is more awkward.

Mark's continued presence in Olive's life, if not in the marriage bed, seems enough for the once vibrant, voluble woman who fired up enthusiasm in eager audiences. Her condition - dependent on a plethora of pills, injections, and palliative care, is tolerable by the constancy of her children.

"Mark took me to the doctor last week." His name is again on her lips - and in the home built twenty years ago.

"What's the matter, Olive?"

"It's my back, deep sharp pain, and tablets don't work. I'm going for an X-ray next week."

"Sure we all get aches and pains with age, Olive." It's easier to say something bland than show excessive concern. A spasm halts the other woman, causing her to double over. The colour drains from her face. Della helps her back into the chair and says she must go. Settling Olive against comfortable cushions, she places her feet on a pouffe and whispers goodbye. On the pillow, Olive's eyes drift into sleep.

Back home, she said, "Ed, Olive is not well. I'm worried."

"Does Mark know?"

"Yes. By the sound of it, he visits often. Ring him."

"Do you want me to probe? Men don't."

"Do it."

He does. The conversation lasts a brief time. He comes into the sitting room and sits on the sofa. His expression is serious.

"It's cancer. She doesn't know, and we're not to tell her."

"Oh, my God, no. Brought on by stress, by him."

"You don't know that. It's on the increase. Peter died of it."

A week later, Della insists they both visit Olive. On the journey to Boyle, she warns there must be no mention of health. Let her tell only what she wants to reveal.

Della knocks on the door. It opens. At the sight of the woman inside, she stifles a gasp - so gaunt and pale the features before them - a terrible change in a short time. Gone the flashing eyes - now dull and empty. Olive brightens. "Come in, you two. Been longing to see you."

Words from *Noreen Bawn* steal into Della's mind - the ballad about a Donegal girl who returned from America to die from TB in her mother's house, enacting before their eyes.

Oh, my mother, don't you know me, sure I've only caught a cold but the telltale spots appearing on her cheeks, the story told.

It's not TB in this house, but an equally virulent killer. Della notices the cutlery drawer on the worktop, the mugs and plates, and everything to hand on the oak table.

"Mark puts things where I can get them," Olive says.

"That's good," Ed murmurs. He hates being here and cannot pretend.

Della rushes, "I've always loved this kitchen, Olive - bright pink, and those enormous windows that let in the sunlight." Oh God, above, why talk about the kitchen? But she had to say something.

Olive overlooks her trite effort. "Yes, he's good, sees to my needs, adapted the house to my physical state, and installed an accessible toilet with support rails."

They stay for an hour. Ed gets restless and throws entreating looks in her direction. Olive does not want them to go, but they have to.

"See you soon, Olive. Let's get to the shops in Sligo and have a day out." Her lie brings shame and a nauseous, creepy feeling.

"I'd love to, but ring a few days before, just in case I'm not feeling good."

Olive will never feel good again, and they won't see the shops together.

One day at the end of the month, Mark rings and says Olive is going down. They hurry to the house again. Inside, he sits by the bed, unstinting in devotion and care. Olive is content, gazing at him with a love that has never died. Della leans against the wall. Ed whispers he's going outside. He can't bear the scene.

Della watches the man stoop low to hear the woman's voice. Mark had never stopped caring, but Olive's efforts to control him had destroyed their union. Her powerful personality and her relentless lecturing had driven him away. Now, one constant remains intact - one small part of their marriage. Whether it be duty or care, to Olive, it's love.

An hour later, it's over. Della goes outside, where Ed is standing by the car. "We have to let them grieve."

In a puff, Olive's spirit returns to that wild, windy place she called home. But, like Noreen Bawn, she will never truly be at peace until they take her body there too.

> *There's a graveyard in Tír*
> *Connell, where the flowers*
> *wildly wave*
> *There's   a   grey-haired*
> *woman   weeping,   lonely,*
> *kneeling on a grave*
> *Oh, my darling, she is say-*

*ing, I am lonely since you're
gone.
'Twas the curse of emi-
gration, left you here, my
Noreen Bawn.*

Not emigration. Suffocation. Olive and Mark had suffo-
cated each other.

Margie had never met Olive, but Della tells her about the
other woman. After all, it's not long since Peter died, and
the older lady will understand. Alone but independent, she
takes the bus to town for shopping every week. Today, she
has news. Cheeks flushing into grimy wrinkles, Margie is
ecstatic. "I'm getting a lump of money from Peter's pension,
enough to build a toilet and bathroom."

Della's mind whirls, the other woman's joyous freedom
uplifting and contagious. In Peter's death lies Margie's ultimate escape from humiliation. She is creating something
better for the little house in her seventh decade. Is death,
therefore, the ultimate emancipator, not just for Margie but
for hapless marriages? Or will women, like moths, forever
be drawn to huge personalities and handsome faces?

"Ed, remember we talked about going on a Marriage Encounter weekend? I want to do it now. Olive's death made
me realise how easily life can slip away. But it shouldn't
leave behind terrible regret and emptiness, for hideous
mistakes never rectified."

"Not my thing, Della. I can't think of anything worse than sitting in a group and discussing our relationship."

"From what I know, you talk to each other in depth and come away with a deeper understanding that gets the marriage on track again."

"Holy smokes. We can do that at home. You want me to go?"

"Please."

Ed killed the ignition of his blue Volvo on the forefront of the long granite building. "Do you think I'm mad, Della? This looks more like a prison than a monastery. Three-storey high, small windows and no chance of jumping out. Let's go into the city for a good weekend instead."

"No, I've paid the deposit. It was a Redemptorist Head house but is now a Catholic counselling centre for marriages and other purposes." And for alcohol addiction, she could have added - better not, or he'd rev up and drive like a hare in heat back out through the iron gates.

Inside, six smiley couples roughly in their late thirties or forties shook hands and offered tea in a small dining room. Ed relaxed and, elicited by Ron, the apparent leader, described his business to the man who seemed to hang on every word as if it were his sole reason for being there. Ear cocked, Della chatted to Eileen about children, school and the town back home - a good start.

A memory intruded - of a similar holy house in 1961, where a God-fearing group of nineteen-year-olds waited in expectation. The difference - here, no starched coifs cupped severe faces into careful smiles or laid down rules on silence and decorum. She'd abandoned that vocation thirteen years ago for Ed, the man she loved but could never fully trust. So, hang in there, she urged an invisible psyche. First hurdle crossed, he'll be polite and listen. And we'll go home like a newlywed couple again, minus the sordid revelations. So much hinged on this weekend. Olive's passing, Laura's suffering, and Margie's blind acceptance were reasons enough to reflect. She'd got him here for that.

Six other couples entered, and the buzz of voices rose as introductions crisscrossed the group. Time for the first encounter, Ron announced, leading the group upstairs to a large conference room. From brown frames on the ascending wall, pictures of austere men glared down on the group of six 'wannabehappyeverafters' and the three presenting couples. In the room, the group sat in a circle.

"Can't think what I'm doing here, Della. You conned me into thinking it was just a weekend of talks," Ed whispered.

"Wait and see. I know no more than you."

It was Friday night, Ron said, and the two days ahead, would be led by him, Eileen, Jim, Anna, Alan and Rose. However, couples could exchange thoughts and worries as they never did in their long or short unions. They would delve deep into feelings - of anger, love, or distrust experienced on their life journey until now. It would be an encounter with Christ and each other, of renewing vows once taken in innocence and the first flush of love. Afterwards, they would go home enhanced by an awareness of the strengths still binding them, but in acceptance that sometimes dissension threatened to rift unions apart. Importantly, they would, again, bask in that first glow of love and passion ignited on a beach, in a bar, or on a dance floor. It did not matter where.

Della glanced sideways at Ed - on his face a familiar mask, his insignia - impenetrable and somewhat uneasy. Sensing her gaze, he muttered through pinched lips. "You brought me here to talk about us. Haven't we done nothing else over the years, Della?"

"Hush. We've argued more like."

Sheets passed around the circle headed 'daily dialogue'. She skimmed the items. *Honest feelings, no right or wrong. Exchange notebooks lovingly, without prejudice.* An uncontrollable urge to laugh aloud died in her throat.

Beside her, Ed shifted on the chair. "Dialogue," he hissed. "What the hell?"

Ten minutes of dialogue after each reading. Ask questions about feelings. Again, a hiss. *Don't use dialogue to get at your partner.*

"By Sunday evening, you will have gained a deeper understanding of crucial factors within your relationships," Eileen added, the look on her face akin to that of Mary Magdalene in the painting on the wall - saintly but knowing.

My reasons for wanting to go on living with you. What qualities still attract me to you? Do I accept you as you are? Do you accept me? What are my feelings about our sexual relations? What was the nicest thing you ever did for me? How did it make me feel?

"Now, lovely people, you will split up, the ladies going to room numbers on the top storey, while the men will go to the bedrooms. Apart from this, you will write letters to each other under different headings and express honest feelings about crucial aspects that affect you both."

Ed's beleaguered expression as he left the room almost made her clap. Caught.

Overlooking the grounds, Della read the questions. How might she honestly express the multitude of feelings quelled through the peaks and troughs of their colourful and stormy periods? She stemmed the bile. This was not how to approach it.

Dear Ed,

Insecurity and jealousy are elements in our marriage. Pride in your appearance, wanting to impress others, vanity, and awareness that you attract women have made me feel inferior to you, so I try to support others, like Margie and Laura, to offset the weakness between us to make up for a lack of communication.

Your drinking and late nights cause me worry and distress. You're a self-seeker, and it's affecting our family.

Della

Tears on the page made her stop writing. Perhaps this wasn't a great idea after all. Regurgitating bad stuff about Ed? Or an opportunity to make him see…?

Back in the room, Ed was sitting at a desk, pen in hand. His expression, she opined, was a mixture of shock and fear.

"Right, let's read each other's letters."

"I wrote very little. What a load of bullshit."

"Give."

Cold room, H block
Dear Della,
I feel sick. I want to go home. Yes, I wear several masks, one for inside and outside the home and the public. It's about pride in oneself. I'm good at most things, work, cards, making money, judging a good horse, and dealing with my employees.

We could be happier if you could stop constantly querying my movements - end of.

Ed.

"H Block? Where prisoners are dying on hunger strike in the North. Only you could say such stuff."

"Well, aren't I in prison? Can't go to the pub for a jar."

"We're not here for that."

Dinner, bed and the rest. She sensed a new quietness in him. Perhaps a change was coming after all. But it was just the start.

Day 2
Dear Ed,
There's too much tension in our home because of your lifestyle. You're making the boys nervous when you refuse to answer my questions after a late night away. We improved things after Ronan was born. I felt close to you then.

Dear Della,
Things can only change if you and I try more, as we did when we first married. I still love you.

Dear Ed,

I love you, too. In our 13 years, I haven't felt this close until now. But if you mean to change, spend less time in the pub and more on our marriage and children. Things are not just 'my problem' but both. We've made many mistakes and fought too much. I always felt like you never thought I was enough and that you never fully committed to us. You always wanted a better time somewhere, anywhere else. You respected me less when I pleaded, so I assumed a harder shell, and we grew apart.

Dear Della,
You show no signs of love and push me away. It's your fault, too. Let's return to how we were when we were first married."

"Ed, you only see things your way. I'm writing pages to you, which I read out as you can't wade through. You're missing the point of this encounter, which is to sort out problems that make us both unhappy. If you love me, you will take the time to do it."

"So I should be grateful to you for getting me to H Block? We could have gone to Majorca again."

"No. That would be the worst thing for our marriage. More of the same carry-on."

Day 3
Sent to bed at seven p.m.
Dear Della,
I want to continue living with you because I love you and our children. We still have much in common: travel, dancing, sightseeing, and socialising. Seeing our children grow up and succeed will fulfil my life. And above all, I still love you and only you. And you're as good-looking now as you always were and

never think otherwise. Thanks for bringing me here to consider. A fantastic three hours, don't you think!!

Dear Ed,
We have discovered each other again. From now on, we will respect opinions and share more. Let us go home and share our newfound couple love with all our friends. The greatest thing we've found this weekend is trust in each other. I love your comical way of phrasing things with your economic expressions. From now on, less criticism and more respect, please.

It was late evening when they got home. Ed went straight to the bathroom and then unpacked his things. Everything got hung up as if the clothes had never been off the hooks - the rest he dumped in the laundry bin by the dressing table. Della folded hers away. He lit a cigarette in the kitchen and took out a bottle of wine.

"More of this, Della. Right? As his arm slid around her shoulders, she smiled and said, "I'll get the kids tomorrow."

Della sinks into her pillow, afraid to sleep or drift into an indefinable state. Since Olive's death, the dream has come again. She's back in her cell, engulfed in a nightmare. She fights to escape, to find a way through the anguish - beyond the nightmare.

She seeks a safe place where they are - but always barriers rise - iron bars on the windows, high walls. Relentless the tone: tick tock, TICK TOCK, up to the strike - hour by hour, every sixty minutes until seven a.m. Between the sounds, she tries to go under - useless, so she gives up the fight for sleep and waits for the next chime. She's that sick girl again, shrouded in loneliness and fears. Sometimes, she is at a student dance, and a dark-haired man holds her close. On her pillow, her cheek is wet.

But birdsong trills in the brightness of day, and she emerges from the hazy mists of delusion—unchained and emboldened—no more.

Somnum exterreri

ACKNOWLEDGEMENTS

My sincere thanks to friends and family who have supported my journey into publishing, sometimes obstructed by my husband's decline and resultant inability to find time for writing. One group, Wild Women Writers, has nudged, suggested, observed and virtually 'held me' to this point, while the Cirencester-based Catchword group is my present bastion in completing a third novel. Our South-West Alliance of Self-Published Authors teaches me how to promote my books, find a niche, and successfully distribute them. I thank them all. I also thank Jason Conway of The Daydream Academy, who designed the cover and created my book.

About the Author

Mary Flood is a retired English teacher/examiner living in Cheltenham, Gloucestershire.

Her novels and short stories are set in the fifties, sixties, and seventies Ireland.

In 2012 Mary won the short story section in The Writers Workshop (Jericho Writers) Festival in York with *The Eviction*. In 2018, her short story *Baby Love* won the Stroud Literary Festival and was featured in their Stroud Short Stories anthology. In 2023, *The Journey* was short-listed in the Gloucestershire Writers' Network (GWN) competition for prose.

Since her part-teacher retirement, Mary has been re-shaping her writing with two edited novels, 'Waiting in the Wings'. Besides her passion for writing, Mary enjoys the theatre, cinema, travelling, being involved in clubs, and giving talks. She is presently caring for her husband.

Mary Flood's website: www.maryflood.co.uk

Printed in Great Britain
by Amazon

59567141R00273